Internal Rhyme

Thomas M. Cassidy

LUNA BISONTE PRODS

2022

Inteɜnal ℛhyme

*Internal Rhyme was published as single newsletters between
July 28, 1997 [Issue #1] & December 28, 2005 [Issue # 98],
& External Rhyme [Issue #6 aka Internal Rhyme #105] was published
February 2007 by Musical Comedy Editions, Minneapolis MN USA*

Acknowledgments from the Author

"I forever owe a two-bit Postal/Insty/Quick copy of Mona Lisa to Blaster Al Ackerman, Marti Barrett, my patient and beautiful trainer Dawn Cassidy, Elaina Cassidy, Tom Cook, Joel Alabama Dese, Rhoda Mappo, Lipps, Lucy Rose Fischer, Trisha Griffin, Hamil Griffin-Cassidy, SubWaxin Haddock, Billy McKay, Genie Murphy, Rudi Rubberoid, Mark Sonnenfeld, Andrew Topei, and Alan VandenBurgh whose work(s) appear in one or more Internal Rhymes.

Thanks to Kay Kirscht, Dawn Swenson, Ivar, Tony Wentersdorf, Anodyne Theresa, Ann "Ruler Art" Meier and Susie "Underground" Crane for helping grow Internal Rhyme's guesstimated readership of fifty-something to "fifty-five in the shade." Thanks to the late great Anodyne Coffeeshop itself where I hosted monthly Open Mics throughout the entire run of Internal Rhyme. Thanks to my good friend Jeff Rathermel for getting me involved in semi-legit and flagrantly challenging things, often one and the same.

And thunderous disorienting thanks to C. Mehrl Bennett and John ("Flaming Sonata") M. Bennett for decades of breaking out of the corral, turning turntables, and being fun, thoughtful, and supportive friends. Every piece of mail from them is better than a Publisher's Clearing House Prize."

Book design: C. Mehrl Bennett

ISBN 9781938521874
https://www.lulu.com/spotlight/lunabisonteprods

LBP

LUNA BISONTE PRODS
137 Leland Ave.
Columbus, OH 43214 USA

Page# **Table of Contents**

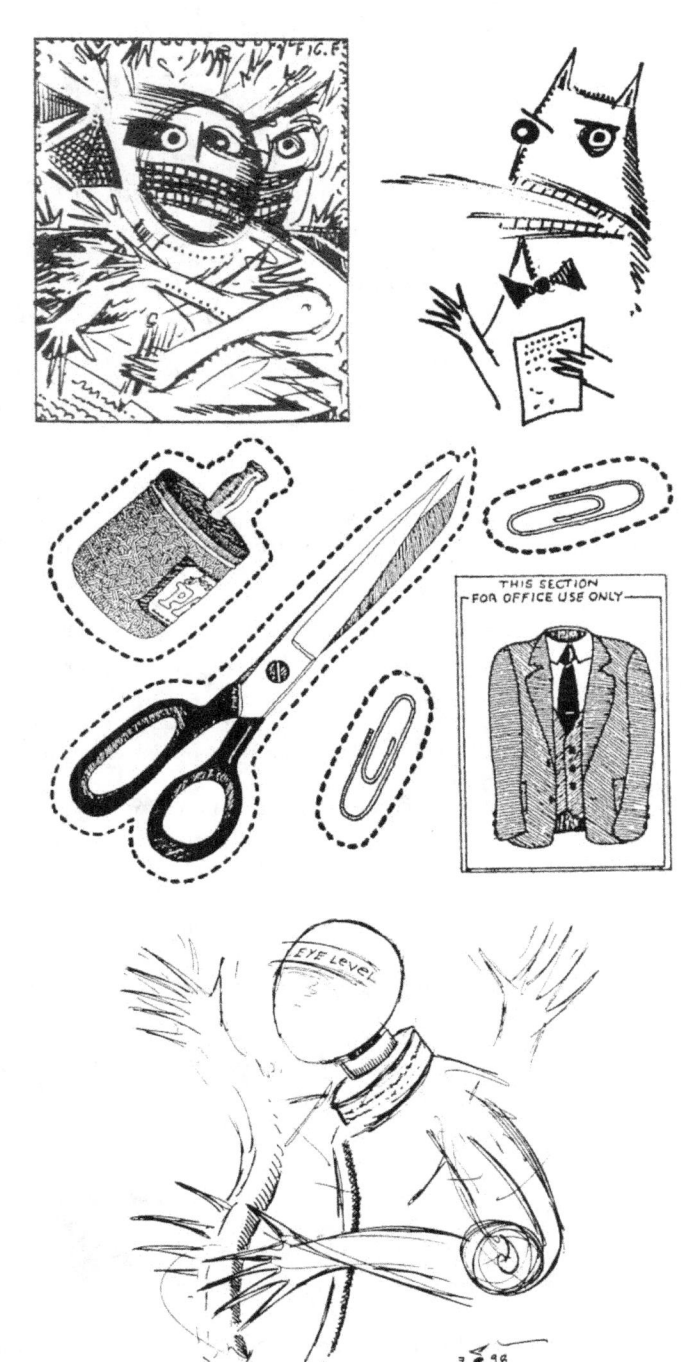

Wino Proverbs from Around the World

Spit in the bottle to make the brew stronger.
Flapjack, Seattle WA

To panhandle bus fare to buy a bottle is sweet.
Dr. Bean, Baltimore, MD

*Where **the man** takes a slug, **you** can't sit and chug.*
Luther, Plovdiv, Bulgaria

*There **is** no wine before its time.*
Keg Leg Kyle, Canberra, Australia

All shall come to sip the nectar soon.
Pope John Paul the Third, Turin, Italy

This ain't my foot but it's wearing my sock.
Sherif O'Sherif, Zarqa, Jordan

I'll drink to that!
Foster Brooks Impersonator, Newark

If you can't decide on something, pick anything.
Our neighborhood Good Humor man, Clifton, N.J. circa '58, brown bag on front seat

Sometimes saying howdy is a tongue twister.
Earl Howdy, London, Great Britain

He who talks to himself might learn something new.
Anonymous, New York, New York, New York

A toppled bar stool may be safe to sit on.
Brother Theresa, Duluth

Agony sometimes changes
form
but
it never ceases for
anybody
Charlies Bukowski,
late of San Pedro, CA
from *for the concerned:*

FROM THE BOOK
ASK ME NO QUESTIONS AND I'LL ANSWER YOU
BY ED "ANONYMOUS" EDISON

Editor's note: This was a supplement to Issue # 50 which commemorated Tom's 50th birthday.

Introduction by Thomas M. Cassidy

It's not polite to interrupt but that's what writers do. A reader with an open mind, at least an open book gets pulled into a world of insistent fiction or insistent fact (is one existent without the other?), where –weighing attitudes and beliefs or just sharpening pencils– writers have or assume efforts to convince a reader (not as adroit in giving those who think differently any non-nefarious room in the storyline) whose emperor is wearing whose clothes, what beliefs can be both fully expressed and trivialized on magnets, why writing is best left to people willing to waste your valuable time, and that unexpected subplots breed among supporting players, different landscapes and memorable weather patterns. Writers who don't even have a wheelhouse won't say that something isn't in it. Living in the wheelhouse, workin' in a coal mine (going down down down), mounting baseball cards so they click in spokes of the captain's wheelhouse wheel when it spins into the gale to get to the crux of the core in the heart where Godot went to wait. A writer's pen is a wheelhouse.

It's not polite to give advice or impose your opinions on strangers or make fun of or correct someone's grammar or confusion about the oyster fork but writers do it all the time. I do; if we ever go utensilling together I'll show you the differences between the snail fork and the oyster fork, and the ice cream fork and the pastry fork . . . to spare you embarrassment if you someday show up at a formal dinner in one of my stories.

You shouldn't discuss sex, politics or religion with people you don't know but writers do. They perform unsafe, unholy proselytizations in your trusting arms and id. They jump into your bed, hump your brain, establish dreaming rules, tuck you in, mention William Blake to your sheep for brownie points while tickling, poking, snoring like an old cave.

Writers can't and don't care that they can't diagram the first sentence of this introduction. I can, but don't care that I can. It's blandly true that anyone can write a book even though they shouldn't, but it's tragically true that many who do write just want to clear up who's really omniscient. I know I do; past the therapeutic value and finally getting to rewrite (correct) my own life (no, not a journey) say "what I should've said" to correct the ending of a chapter, get some mileage out of whatever vocabulary is still malleable enough to skirt the censors and the critics . . . I write to be in charge. From programming the robots to letting everyone know that my Mom (not theirs) makes the best TV dinner in the world.

Though you can probably guess where I'm going with this introduction, I cannot, and so it continues. (The word "omniscient" shouldn't be qualified!)

So, depending on what they're writing, writers interrupt, give advice, take charge, electioneer, get revenge, pontificate, feel sorry for themselves or their world (not the world), and overall do whatever they want, even if it's just to see how it goes. Writers get away with awesome hyperbolic metaphors every other paragraph and create characters that can get away with not just murder upon murder but inappropriate language as well (three murders by nail gun equals one "me and Sal borrowed him the nail gun"). Writers shouldn't think that as individuals (maybe with a sparkplug out, unresolved trauma, brain racing the beer rapids) they represent all writers. But I do. It's addictive and makes the lines mutter and search or skydive.

While writers can nag, bully, steal, and lie they can also inspire, encourage, suggest, soothe, help, instruct and entertain (and help with your fork issues). That (or Here) is where I come in as a writer – somewhere between ranting anarchist and bumper sticker revisionist; I rewrite my list (poem, parable) of grievances ten times a day and lines for a poem or a story to which I'll never return a dozen times a month. As I unnecessarily mentioned above, it's therapeutic and occasionally exhilarating if irresponsible fun. This was especially true for me between 1990 and 2010 when I was peaking in activity, sleeplessness, adrenalin, muse-wrestling, ambitious but clumsy idea juggling, and relentless productivity below the weight and woe of workaday grind.

In 1997 I was spinning so quickly I picked up speed. Cranking away full-time at work, Art!, side jobs, Fringe Fest, open mics, blahblahblah (three blahs) and trying to teach our gentle dog Elly how to host the open mics for me. I learned this was an awful idea when, after weeks of training, $18 worth of dog treats, and getting her companion cohost merit badge, she bit every folksinger before they got to their second rhyme. And I commuted by bus which meant that for over an hour every weekday I went to hell, where the skits were funny and cautionary, I could read in the din of commerce, and my brain regularly ignited.

I created Internal Rhyme in 1997 to 1) burn off (I) steam, (II) caffeine and (III) beer, 2) to keep my hands even busier, and 3) to write lists –(I) opinions as lists, (II) tables of contents as quick commentary lists, and (III) very listy poems. Remember that the Rule of Threes for who enters a bar in a joke is also helpful in 1) giving examples, 2) suggesting a new (I) name, or (II) acronym, or (III) where to go for dinner, and 3) coming up with reasons to skip certain parties: 1) I'm under the weather, 2) They just talk about the weather, and 3) Oh, I thought that baptism was next year.

I created Internal Rhyme to write, just write, good or bad, get ideas down, force myself to write when I didn't want to, have my ass think on its own feet. It didn't always work but it gave me a deadline to help me write more and eventually better or when I occasionally got too busy or too blocked to put "something" together (items from archives, half-baked/underbaked ideas; the show must go on) as if I had waiting subscribers.

My original idea was to start a media empire with a comprehensive if severely-truncated paper that would always include (even if printed only monthly and usually four pages long): 1) Name and date and a logo/mascot (I went with Atlas trying to hold up always toppling boxes; 2) An "Inside This Issue" box with compressed titles and teasers for stupid features and kneejerk opinion columns; 3) A lead story about something really important like buying a new microwave or my experiences at a flea market in Hinckley, Minnesota where the casino crowd might stop and at least get something for their money, or a lead poem, with possibly confusing or irrelevant illustrations to tie it all together.

The first Internal Rhyme was printed on July 28, 1997, over lunch on the copier at work. While I always reimbursed paper and b&w copy costs, I tried to print surreptitiously to avoid tongue-numbing blather about protocol or job ("Hey, I just got back from my three-hour country club subcommittee to create more committees and you're wasting company time printing- What the hell is this!?"). I typed parts of IR at home, usually quickly and without review into space I wanted to fill. Add here other excuses for the dozens of misspellings, grammatical drool, inconsistent spacings that populate most issues in their own kind of external anti-rhyme anti-reason. The issues herein were printed from copies made from paste-ups, taped-togethers and corroborating ephemera slapped on the copier with reckless wobble. There are no originals; I either gave or mailed them away or reused layouts for another issue. And my final apology before you read this book (after this will be an apology too long to include) is for the recurrent plugs for Open Mic at Anodyne, the wonderfully unbusinesslike The Art Underground, Limbo, and plugs for my chapbook(s) and other fine products that over Internal Rhyme's lifespan generated just enough profit to verify a substantial loss.

The last issue (External Rhyme #8 which was Internal Rhyme #107) was printed in December 2007. I printed 50-100 copies of each, left them at Anodyne, The Art Underground, and on the bus (a nod to the eight issues of my Dogs Without Cars newsletter I only distributed on the bus and in bus shelters years earlier), and mailed about two dozen to mail-art contacts.

Whoosh! That –and just reading every third word so far– gets you an Introduction!

This book contains 45 issues of Internal Rhyme, plus one issue of External Rhyme (#6, which was Internal Rhyme #105). The other issues are no better, no worse, but do contain the headlines, feature ideas, bad jokes, footers, fortunes, cheap shots, half-lists, and other lines that follow (feel free to exit at any time):

When people finish a point by saying "Period" why don't they then shut-up?
We're serious about joy buzzers!
Cloned Triplets Start Sextet
The dummy's guide to identifying your ventriloquist.
The junk in your attic might be worthless
Nobody wants kids hopping their fences because that's what fences are supposed to prevent.
Of course, no fences would also prevent fence hopping.
The Mall of America is a tourist trap for people who don't want to go anywhere
Cigarette Sales to Minor Lab Rats on the Rise.
Santa enslaved my pony, dressed her like a reindeer.
Unsharpened pencils still write.
What would Darwin Do?
I talk more with my canary than with my neighbors.
End of the world continued due to popular demand
Dog's water dish that looks like a toilet bowl a big hit this holiday season
Seeing clouds in Abe Lincoln's Portrait
No swearing tequila bar opens to no fucking fanfare
I am not a bad person because I think your favorite movie sucks.
There are dozens of commercials for the radio station's commercial-free hours.
In business thinking big means thinking small.
There are artists and there are grant-writing artists.
Top Ten Lists for 2000 Whittled Down to Top Two
When Waldo was big you could find him everywhere.
Sign of the Apocalypse #25: Our political views fit on t-shirts.

Even good dogs dream of being hounds from hell.
Society is the best breeding ground for misanthropes.
Bus fare hike encourages hiking
There is no need to increase your font size at the dinner table.
Russian proverb: You can't take the joy from Siberia.
The optimist sees the donut, the pessimist sees the optimist with the donut.
Mass confusion starts with you.
Who would've thought the good old days would include 1984?
Third Party Candidate Hires Bullshit Consultant
Ideas in this newspaper are 78% recycled.
In whose closet should we debate privacy issues?
People Are Funny, Syllogisms are Funny, People Are Syllogisms.
You don't frame a Jackson Pollock.
Time Warner Buys You
Xerox Salesman Guilty of Copycat Crime
Job listings for crappy jobs that sound pretty good
Smokey the Bear / Sparky the Firefly Summit
Special: A Poem as Lovely as a Tree
Without pseudointellectualism we'd have no intellectualism at all.
Planning Calendars Recall on Schedule
The Diana Princess of Wales Paper Doll book is both tragic and fun!
Post-Batman Onomatopoeia – the Zounds of Silence
Airline Security Perfected with Passenger Ban
More Bull in the Bull Market
Baseball Season Over for the Fifth Time in Two Months
How to See Naked Women in Modern Art
Papercuts from Fortune Cookie Fortunes
A drunken sparrow cannot swim.
Bird Stays Put
Harpo Tunnel Syndrome
Descending order of popularity of miniature golf ball colors (from Put Your Trust in Facts! by Nancy Rankin): Green; Orange; Blue; Red/White tie; Yellow
Sweeten your morning with windchimes
A limited edition of 3000 is oxymoronic.
Customer service ends when rules and policies get cited.
Pollyanna hums in her mausoleum.
For people to whom showing up is half the job, the other half is recording a message saying they're unavailable.
If you cross your eyes while looking in a View-Master the image will appear flat.
People are rarely as fast or as reliable as their means of communication.
You have to be pretty egocentric to think you have personal demons.
Fiction is to nonfiction what abstract art is to representational art.
You learn the lesson of the maze by when you never go into one again.
Search the web for Simplify Your Life and you get over 179,800 results.

Musicmaster 8.31.22

JULY 28, 1997

INTERNAL ⚘ RHYME

ISSUE **NUMBER** ONE OF A NEWSLETTER THAT I HOPE WILL CALM ME DOWN OR REV ME UP ◆ MUSICMASTER, 5136 LYNDALE AVE. SO., MINNEAPOLIS, MN 55419

EDITORIAL

I am a stupid man in what is, luckily, a stupid world. I want to be *more* different than others than most others; I want to be able to go to a meeting of artists/writers who are struggling to get art/writing off the endangered list *and* levitate at the same time. And I know this is the torment of all artists/writers who work so hard at connecting with others that they ultimately face the consequential fact that - by being communicative, by finding that nerve/chord/word/turn that reaches many rather than no one or just a self-absorbed few - they are just ordinary people too. This consequential fact is reached with less effort via garbage collecting or omelet-slinging (see TRIVIA answers this issue) than through the art/writing route.

I want to be different than everybody and on their bowling team at the same time. When I roll a strike, the pins knock and spin, my teammates shout "Way to go, Tom!" "Nice Aim, Tom!" "That'll show 'em, Tom!"

I want the writer's block that's kicking in right now (though it might just be an inevitable slump into sleep this 2 a.m.) to be a *different* kind of writer's block, a kind that's blocking more than a clever round of poetry.

(If you'd like to respond to this Editorial, your life needs severe rerouting.) ∎

TRIVIA

1. Who lent me five dollars March 8, 1996? (careful - big hint is the year!)

2. Where did I put that coupon for FREE eggs?

3. Why did the Mexican omelet I ordered at the Egg & I have Italian sauce on it?

4. How old is the plant on my desk?

5. When will I get my next haircut?

INSIDE THIS ISSUE

LEAD STORY

T-SHIRT STORY

Thank God My Mind Has Gone First

(100% cotton, green and red on white)

make that **Thank God *Your* Mind Has Gone First**

(the word **Mind** is in green, everything else is in red)

or what about **I'm With "Thank God *Your* Mind Has Gone First"**

(the smallest among us want L, XL)

make that **I'm With "Thank God *My* Mind Has Gone First"**

so *I* won't look as dumb when I'm all alone

wearing it anyway

willing to shrink some

looking to talk with the world ∎

ANSWERS:

1. Dawn did, and I paid her back within eight hours.

2. In my wallet, which, unfortunately, I lost.

3. I don't know, but it made an already halfassedly-cooked omelet (too puffed-up and browning) into a sub-awful breakfast; plus the Italian sauce had a single, inexplicable hunk of broccoli in it. I was surprised the cook didn't just stroll out of the kitchen and slug me as well. I can understand (but only rarely forgive) the hack-cook's inability to prepare an omelet properly - afterall, it doesn't go into the deepfry or microwave - but I can't understand his motive in humiliating a floret of broccoli too. Rename that joint The Egg & Not Me.

4. I don't know. I realize my not knowing suggests that this trivia test is somehow rigged so you can't ace it, but, think about it, you *might* know! You know *all kinds* of things I don't know anything about - like weathervane collecting, filling an aquarium with only compatible fish, parallel parking, equity, "net-iquette," calming poultry, selecting ripe mangoes - so *why not* the age of the plant on my desk? (You know how to cook an omelet properly, don't you?)

5. In about a month (guesses of or between three and five weeks count).

10:30 · noon · twiddling my thoughts

I'm signing wildlife prints
as they stop on the conveyor belt
and I number them too
between 1 and 5000
people prefer lower numbers
so I never go over fifty
I am the soul of customer service
today I'm signing a Roy Desnos edition
of a wolf ripping apart a still-alive bloodhound
on a frozen lake
it's titled *Loyal to the Death*

I've been signing this print for three weeks now
which means the edition is over 13,000
because our next job hasn't come in yet
because the boss needs a new swimming pool
because the boss says *who cares? it's a goddam animal
    picture*
because people who know what they want in art
deserve this sort of thing

of the thirty seconds I have
to sign and number each picture
I only need six
so over 80% of my at-work time is like time-off
broken into bits too short for a trip to the shore
or watercooler
for forty eight seconds a minute
I just hum or daydream
or stare at the print until I know
how many flakes of blowing snow Roy painted
how many of those shown will hit the bloodhound
before it loses consciousness
and which of them
when connected like connect-the-dots
make an outline of me

I sign Roy Desnos with an R that looks like a Z
a Y with a downstroke that
begins the capital D then I draw a wavy line and dot it
the dot representing the O in Roy
it's a signature so good it's an artwork in itself
and I sign it with vision focus heart and soul
over 900 times a day

I ask my boss if he can have Sherman
the Director of the Conveyor Belt
speed the conveyor belt up
to five prints every minute
so I can do a year's worth of work in about 11 weeks

and take the rest of the year off
my boss says he can't speed the conveyor belt up
it would adversely impact quality control
which makes me laugh because
the only thing Doug - the moron in quality control - checks for
is whether or not the prints are rightsideup as they head to me
sorry says the boss
we are committed to excellence here
which really means that Sherman/his nephew/the Director of
    the Conveyor Belt
doesn't know how to slow the dam thing down

if you put Sherman and the quality control moron
together on Mars
you'd still have no proof of intelligent life

the boss calls me into his office
where the paneled walls are covered
with classic Desnos prints
Run Wild depicts a still-alive bloodhound
being ripped apart by a lioness and her cub
Home Sweet Home is a classic picture
of an 1880s wilderness family sitting down to eat
a still-alive bloodhound

the boss looks at me and says
you're right about something . . .
*you **do** only work about 20% of your time here*
so starting next week
you're getting paid accordingly
wow I answer *that's not exactly what I had in mind*
but what the hell I'm game
he continues
and Sherman says he can sign & number a print in under
    five seconds
does he dot the O? I ask
and the boss looks back and shakes his head yes-no
he dots the O he crosses the R he whispers to the goddam D
and if you give that upright lad fortyeight seconds off
he takes a trip to the shore

the rest of my last day at work
I number every wildlife print one million
in clean even letters I print the name Sherman
and from the mouth of the still-alive bloodhound
I draw a huge word balloon churning with flames

"Better stop at the next gas station, dear; we're running out of napl"

musicmaster 7.97

OFFHANDED REMARKS

Mystery in Gray Heads

"I HAVE often heard stories of men whose hair turned white overnight as a result of sudden great fright or shock. Always I thought such tales were manufactured out of whole cloth, until a chemist assured me that this strange transformation sometimes does happen.

"It has been discovered, he told me, that in our bodies are certain curious white corpuscles called polymorphs. Under great mental stress, as during a battle, these corpuscles sometimes escape out of the blood stream, wander through the body tissues and even go up through the centers of the hairs, where they quickly eat out the coloring matter."—A. D. B., Phila., Pa.

Why does static interfere with radio messages?
What gland makes people grow tall or keeps them short?
Why do we grow old?
What is the safest stimulant?
What is the function of the liver?
Why are tears salt?
Can energy be destroyed?
Why can't you skate on glass if it is smoother than ice?
How do self-winding clocks work?
Why does an iron ship float?
Can we see atoms with a microscope?
What are electrons?
Is electricity a form of matter?
What is a crystal?
How large is the universe?
Why do the stars twinkle?
How do we know what the stars are made of?
Is the inside of the earth molten?
What is an electric spark?
What makes the noise of thunder?

When a man writes poetry it's a sure sign he's in love with someone—or something. Some men are inspired by beautiful womanhood, some by a gorgeous sunset. Here's a man inspired by his favorite smoking tobacco:

THE BLUE TIN CAN

I've tried the brands from every clime;
Choice mixtures with Perique;
But long—oh, long ago! I learned
The only brand to seek.

Each day our useless worries mount,
Our evenings to provoke;
But through the alchemy of fire
They vanish into smoke.

They vanish when our spirit holds
No enmity toward man,
And smoke the sunshine bottled up
In Edgeworth's Blue Tin Can.

So smoke away! This loyal friend
Is void of bite or sting
For *He* is monarch of a world
Where Happiness is King.

Irving H. Walker,
Newark, N. J.
April 7, 1927

June, 1928

Temperature of Mars Taken; Fifty Above at the Equator

DOES life exist on Mars? Would we be able to live there if we could bridge the millions of miles that separate us from the red planet? Scientists have come to various conclusions about the probability of life on Mars, and now Dr. W. W. Coblentz, of the U. S. Bureau of Standards, says—after observations at the Lowell Observatory in Flagstaff, Arizona—that if we should find on the planet sufficient air to breathe we should be rather uncomfortable without our winter overcoats. At the north and south poles of the planet, Dr. Coblentz says, the average temperature is seventy-six degrees below zero, while even at the equator the thermometer would hover around a chilly fifty degrees above.

Rays of light and heat reflected from the sun by Mars and its own invisible "temperature" rays were separated by screens of glass, water, rock salt, and fluorspar; and the "temperature" rays were concentrated on an electric thermometer in a vacuum. Two pieces of metal, joined together in the vacuum, turned the rays into minute electric currents, which, when measured by delicate instruments, disclosed the planet's temperature.

THAT the earth is lop-sided, flat on both ends, wobbling very uncertainly on an undermined axis, with her poles away off-side and her "middle bulging most ungracefully like an eccentric tomato," was the recently expressed opinion of Capt. George W. Littlehales, hydrographic engineer for the United States Navy, as he departed for Japan to enlist the aid of foreign nations in a United States plan to map the two thirds of the earth which lies under sea.

That the earth may prove to be a tetrahedron or triangular pyramid, with four faces and four corners or coigns, with the seas occupying the depressions and forming the faces of the pyramid, and the continents situated around the coigns and reaching out along the edges, is a theory which, advanced by W. Lowthian Green, English geologist, in 1875 and disregarded, has lately been revived by Theophile Moreux, French scientist, as one at least worthy of more discussion.

AS A matter of fact no scientist today would call the earth a "sphere." With the invention of invar, an alloy of nickel and steel which is practically nonelastic in any temperature, and which made possible a measurement of the earth's surfaces more exactly than ever before, the scientists have found that the meridians and parallels—even the equator—are not circles at all. And today they call the earth neither a sphere nor an oblate spheroid; they call it a geoid. What is a geoid? An "earth-shaped" body. What is an "earth-shaped" body? A geoid. It is a circle of question and answer that swallows itself, and leaves no one the wiser. But it does leave plenty of room for new theories and for reconsideration of many old ones. 1928

ALL SECTIONS IN THIS PUBLICATION ARE NONSMOKING SECTIONS

PRODUCT REVIEW

I'M ABLE TO TAKE YOUR CALL RIGHT NOW BUT WON'T
featuring *1917 AT&T ad copy*

In the high passes of the mountains, accessible only to the daring pioneer and the sure-footed burro, there are telephone linemen stringing wires.

They can explain how all the weaving works, how one home finds another via phone, and I get it like I get the burning bush.

Across bays or rivers a flat-bottomed boat is used to unreel the message-bearing cables and lay them beneath the water.

A pleasant ring can preface all the news one wants to hear - or must - all the melodies of like or love, all the details **called for**.

Through dense forests linemen are felling trees and cutting a swath for lines of wire-laden poles.

Vast telephone extensions are progressing simultaneously in the waste places as well as in the thickly populated communities.

The world is smaller still with every pole and every Princess, every ring that brings a there to here is like growing song.

These betterments are ceaseless and they are voluntary, requiring the expenditure of almost superhuman imagination, energy and large capital.

Yet when you call me noon or midnight, yank me to the fore, you tend to only babble, talk of pointless woe and unkind weather, you try to sell me siding, sell me money, sell me pruning, sell me news that hasn't happened, sell me luggage that can't travel, sell me lives that I don't want.

In the Bell organization, besides the army of manual toilers, there is an army of experts, including almost the entire gamut

of human labors. These men, scientific and practical, are constantly inventing means for supplying the numberless new demands of the telephone using public.

You ask if I'm happy with the phone I have, the service and the rate, would I like to call anybody anywhere anytime for only ten cents a minute, do I have callwaiting callforwarding callscreening, do I need another line (since every writer does) and I hang up, because you'll call again, like all the rest, with your dime. ∎

BACK TO SCHOOL DRAWING BY HAMIL GRIFFIN-CASSIDY, PEN FOR HIRE

IDEAS DEPICTED IN THIS NEWSLETTER ARE NOT SHOWN ACTUAL SIZE

SEPTEMBER 26, 1997

INTERNAL  RHYME

NUMBER **8** OF A NEWSLETTER THAT I HOPE WILL CALM ME DOWN OR REV ME UP ◆ MUSICMASTER, 5136 LYNDALE AVE. SO., MINNEAPOLIS, MN 55419

ELBOWS OF FAME

For a number of years in the late 50s and early 60s we go to Olympic Park in Irvington every Sunday, the day they change the acts in the free, outdoor, two-shows-a-day circus. The amusement park itself, except for prizes in the Skeeball Parlor, never changes much otherwise. The wooden roller coaster, classic carousel, beer garden, fun house and the few dozen other rides and attractions haven't changed in decades. My Dad says the large, dark green French fries stand has been here since the park opened in the 20s. Mom says "well you should know." But every Sunday the three act (not *three ring*) circus changes so we make it a point to catch the evening show, which is presented outside on an old white wooden stage to three sections of old green bleachers.

The announcer has a voice as familiar to us as a home team sportscaster's. He follows his enthusiastic welcome to Olympic Park with "Alllllllll-right, Professor," at which point a six-piece band, otherwise based in the beer garden gazebo, plays a classic boozy fanfare. Bubbles, the heavyset one-armed female vocalist just stands and smiles during the fanfare; my Dad says she's been around forever, used to sing at clubs too.

The first act is a Senor Hector and His Uncanny Canines. A poodle does back flips, rides a tricycle in tiny circles and does other things with the speed and intensity of a hyperactive child; even so, the always grimacing Senor Hector, wearing a purple sequined vest, skips around twice as fast. I wonder if one of his dogs ever craps on stage.

A beautiful assistant leads more dogs up the ramp to the stage and takes a bow. It's a stupid act, but the assistant bends and turns enough to keep me interested. The band plays frantic circus tunes while the dogs jump through hoops and "How Much Is That Doggie in the Window?" when the poodle spins around in a tutu.

One dog, who won't do a trick when Senor Hector instructs him to but does it repeatedly while Senor Hector looks skyward and pulls his hair, is also wearing a purple sequined vest. That this comic relief exists comes from the odd perspective that the act is otherwise serious. Bob punches me in the arm because he's bored. I tell him that he's jealous because the dogs are smarter than he is.

Senor Hector, his assistant and his dogs finally skip offstage.

The comic dog runs back on stage after a minute, plays dead (which he refused to do at all during the show!), then leaves.

Even though I'm only a kid with a developmentally-normal admiration of a chimp trainer or poodle act assistant or *anyone* on stage--imagining all of them to be as sequined and celebrated offstage as on--I know that most of these opening acts at Olympic Park are barely on the elbows of fame, has-beens without ever having really been *beens*. Senor Hector's career, though it gets him attention, applause and the assistant, is probably a grind. It's an okay act, but it's not a good act; and the poodle is probably a bitch.

A dog act is a dog act afterall - it lacks suspense (no one worries that the cute pooch might explode into flames if it falls off its tricycle); it lacks human drama (they're dogs for crying out loud!); it lacks danger (Toto won't fall to his death from a step stool). If Senor Hector would shoot his dogs out of cannons--after strapping helmets on the mutts, several drum rolls--he might retire in a trailer he doesn't have a second mortgage on.

Next, the announcer proudly brings us--direct from the Catskills--Sal Tarlowe, rope and whip artist extraordinaire. This cowboy has fringe on his fringe and boots that clomp like thunder. He does obligatory rope tricks while I imagine roping Senor Hector's assistant, tying up her hands and feet.

The band plays "Don't Fence Me In" and "Fascination" and finally "Colonel Bogie" as Sal spins his lariat and makes a loop as wide as the stage. The announcer says it's a world's record loop! I bet this guy sets records every night. Next he gets out a bullwhip that cracks like gunshot. He snaps a flaming candle out with his whip! He knocks over targets in front of him and behind him while blindfolded with his whip.

And then, as the band starts playing "Buttons & Bows," who should skip out from behind the bleachers--where trailers are parked and clotheslines strung--and up the ramp to the stage but Senor Hector's assistant in a cowgirl outfit! I must be dreaming! What's going on? Does Senor Hector know? Does the poodle know? Will Sal lasso her?

CONTINUED NEXT PAGE

INSIDE THIS ISSUE

Second Hand Subtleties

Cooking With Suspenders

Why Isn't Di On the Dollar Bill Yet?

Bacteria!

The Broom is on the Porch

The announcer re-introduces Lovely Miss Senor Hector (or whatever it is, I'm not really paying as much attention to the audio as I am to her rings and things), as Sal lights a cigarette. He blows a few smoke rings, hands her the cigarette. She puts it in her mouth, a drumroll gets louder, she leans forward, tilts her head up and out, cigarette distended; Sal picks up his whip, aligns himself perpendicular to the glowing filtered prop, and squints, like me, with heavy concentration at her red puckered lips.

The drumroll swells, hits crescendo, then stops so suddenly the air rings. Time freezes. Then thaws with the loudest crack yet - an echoing crack, echoing off the trailers and French fries and even off of Bubbles. A dusting of red ash vanishes and you can see that half of the cigarette--paper torn and tobacco spilling, is still in her mouth. Sal extinguished the cigarette with his whip! Everyone claps like demonic wind-up toys.

The announcer tells us there will be a short intermission as they prepare the stage for the main attraction--just back from a tour of the courts of Europe (what a great legal system *they* have!)--The Amazing Andy, The Bard of Balance. While we wait, says the announcer, "We'll be entertained by Bubbles, The Voice of Olympic Park!" He turns to the rickety bandstand and grandly says "Alllllllllright, Professor."

The band strikes up "America the Beautiful" and Bubbles belts it out; her voice is strong and it sounds good to me, maybe rough, but in a good, heavyset-one-armed-female-vocalist kind of way. The way the roller coaster rumbles in the background. I like Olympic Park a lot --even some of the things *I don't like about it*, I like about it (like vinegar bottles at the French fries booth, the nasty guy who runs the motorboat ride, the circus acts that are even more predictable than Senor Hector's).

The sun is starting to set, blinding Olympic Park newcomers in the opposite bleachers. The regulars, several of whom we see every week, and up at the beer garden after the show too, are on this side. Lots of them live in Irvington, but Tante Edie and Uncle Augie, who only live ten blocks away, hardly ever come by; we visit them every few months, often on the way to Olympic Park, but they never come with us, we never bump into them in the park. I can't understand that. They could come every day!

If I lived in Irvington I'd come over every day, ride the bumper cars for an hour to enjoy one head-on collision after another, go on the Wild Mouse a dozen times to feel the drops and jerks, and go on the Whip at least . . . well, *once* certainly; I can't handle too much recreational whiplash.

I'd play the Greyhound Races enough to win a coupon or two so that by the end of the season I can claim the biggest prize in the joint - a ten-ft.-long stuffed tiger. Mom says "Where are you going to put it?" Dad says "You won't take it for a walk." Then with my left hand warmed-up, I'd play Skeeball for an hour or two, rolling a few 50s each game and then, spectacularly, nine of them--all in a row--a perfect game; I'd win another ten-ft.-long stuffed tiger. When they meet later on, it turns out they know one another from the Prize Academy.

It's all impressive, the warm breeze laced with chlorine from the nearby Olympic Park pool and that electric smell the bumper cars make. It must be great to be the guy who runs the Wild Mouse. Or the kids who make change and hand out prize coupons in the Skeeball Parlor, sometimes giving you an extra one or two.

I'll never have hopes like these again. The world will never be this flat and level again, or rich with the call of the siren, the beautiful "sea to shining sea" of the heavyset one-armed female vocalist. I snap out of my reverie. Applause ricochets around the bleachers and Bubbles smiles.

"And now, ladies and gentlemen," booms the announcer, "Olympic Park brings you, direct from the great courts of Europe, and from halls and arenas across our great land, this evening's star attraction, the master of objects in unpowered flight, gravity's adversary, the monarch of motion, the one-and-only Amazing Andy, the Bard of Balance."

The band starts playing very frantic juggling music. Two stagehands in dirty-t-shirts run out and yank at riggings that go way up and over the occasionally used trapeze set and down to something creaking on the lawn behind the stage. In just seconds, a large apparatus tips forward into view as it's hoisted up on stage. Maybe twenty feet high, it's a cross between a Ferris wheel and a giant hamster wheel.

People behind us are laughing so we turn to see the Amazing Andy, in a white tuxedo and top hat, standing on the top row of the bleachers, juggling giant lollipops. He's slowly weaving down, mugging and laughing at the people as they duck or cover their heads. Securing the big wheel onto an axle supported by a steel triangle, the stagehands heft, grunt and shoulder parts until the wheel is upright and spins freely. I'm the only one watching the stagehands, reading their lips as they swear.

Everyone else hoots and claps to Andy's two-bit hijinx with crowd. The band is racing through "Sabre Dance" as Andy finally reaches the stage, four giant lollipops spinning around his head like Venusian dragonflies, the stagehands gone, the spokes and rungs of the giant wheel shine orange in the setting sun. It's not a bad act.

CONTINUED BACK PAGE

SENOR HECTOR'S DOGS BY ELAINA

WORKCLOTHES

THE OFFICIAL POETRY PAGE OF MY UNAUTHORIZED NEWSLETTER

PHONETAG

I'm going through mail
for the first time in a long time
all of it postmarked
after the day my father died

we go to New Jersey
for a wedding
to look around old neighborhoods
in the hotel one night
he hacks and coughs
himself into a chair
honey my Mom asks *are you alright?*
he answers *I'm okay*

Tante Olga says *you* (meaning
my Mom for sure maybe me)
should've forced him
to go to a doctor
as if every indicator is as clear as
a teenager who tells everyone
I'm going to kill myself tomorrow
the day before he kills himself

even if the teenager tells everyone
I'm going to kill myself tomorrow
then waits a week or two
before killing himself
people can say *you should've known*

a few days after the wedding
I'm back in Minnesota
my parents still in Jersey
with friends down by the shore

even if the teenager tells everyone
I'm going to kill myself tomorrow
then waits six months
before killing himself a year even
people can say *you should've known*

my son does not remember
a world without videos
let alone without tvs *color* tvs
and it's more complex than that
he doesn't remember what I remember
he doesn't remember my Dad
as young and heroic and wise

in the middle of the night
my Dad wakes up
hacks and coughs himself
into a chair on the bungalow's porch
by the sea by the beautiful sea
he knows every song
in the world like that
and dies of congestive heart failure
lungs in the undertow

but if the teenager waits fifty years
and kills himself slow motion with
cake and smoke and wine
and a postponed doctor's appointment
people (meaning Olga for sure maybe me)
shouldn't say anything but
oh no are you alright?

the water bill is dated three days
after he died but the imprinted billing date
is one day *before*
he couldn't have seen this bill here
because he was already gone
but he could've seen it getting mailed
had he gone downtown
spent the day with
the guy who bills for water

I'm reading so far into it
because my faith is shallow
we cannot satisfactorily
explain anything important
without a margin of error
as deep as we're willing to go

my Dad jokes with the guy
do you get all the water
you can drink down here for free?
then asks
so how's the water business?
the guy answers
okay if you own the water
and my Dad smiles and nods

NOTES ABOUT ELBOWS OF FAME

Apparently, amusement parks built near the turn of the century, were designed, like the parks and piers of Coney Island, with huge, garish entrances. In his book **Going Out - The Rise and Fall of Public Amusements**, David Nasaw writes "The entrance to Olympic Park was described by a local German-language newspaper as 'new and imposing' with 'four huge pillars, entwined with electric lights,' and the 'word *Olympia* in letters of fire . . . descending from an arch over the main gateway." I only vaguely recall the *back* of such a sign, on a street entrance up past the beer garden; we never went up there because it was past all the rides and game booths.

We always came in on an ordinary path from the parking lot that flanked the length of the roller coaster.

Nasaw also notes that "a 1909 brochure from Olympic Park promised, 'if you come here you have no fear of contamination with the undesirable element usually found at summer amusement resorts . . . Representatives of the rowdy element will not be tolerated.'" So the park was a lot older than my parents thought. Curiously, the word "element" grew to become a racial slur on the east coast, from early references to the Irish to, later, shifting neighborhoods of Poles, Puerto Ricans, Blacks, and Italians.

Only after sustained pressure by the NAACP in the late 1950s, did Olympic Park (and most other city amusement parks) open its gates to blacks. When a group of black teenagers reportedly went on a rampage in the park and surrounding neighborhood in 1965, Irvington's City Council voted against renewing Olympic Park's license, and the property was sold. I was aware of none of this until reading about it years later. We (my parents included) thought the park closed because the land was valuable and developers were going to build a major apartment complex around Olympic Park's gigantic swimming pool (so far as I know, the complex/pool project was never built). We also heard that the 1964-65 New York World's Fair and the popular Palisades Park were hurting attendance (indeed, FreedomLand, an incredible amusement park in New York, didn't make it past its poorly-timed inaugural season because of the World's Fair).

Anyhow, when Olympic Park closed, it was the *end of an era* (see last issue). I never won the ten-ft.-long stuffed tiger. I don't know if Bubbles ever regenerated her arm. I don't know if the amazing Andy ever got on Ed Sullivan or just one day sneezed at a bad moment and somersaulted to his death.

Luckily, our parents assuaged our sorrow with increased visits to Asbury Park and Seaside Heights on the Jersey shore. ∎

Andy dances and beams. Balls, pins, torches, hammers, and canes float around his body like Senor Hector's world-record-breaking loops. I hope Lovely Miss Senor Hector skips out soon to juggle my eyeballs. I'm content in an odd way - both delighted and bored with Anda Panda here until, suddenly, the band snaps out of waltz and into a fanfare. Andy turns and walks towards the giant treadmill, but he doesn't hop in like a hamster to just run in circles, he climbs a skinny ladder way up to the outside top of the contraption . . . *to just run around on circles*!

He starts running on the wheel so it spins beneath him. It is pretty cool. I mean how do you know which horizon you're running toward if it's too close to see? I bet if he looks only forward he barely sees anything of the wheel beneath him at all, but he keeps looking down a lot and I don't blame him.

It's possible that he also knows his balanced position by sound of the wheel, feel of the wheel, and how his brain backstrokes. I wouldn't do his act for all the money in the world. (Well, maybe for a lot of money and a chance to tour with Lovely Miss Senor Hector, I would. Yeah, I would.)

The crowd is still as Andy starts juggling torches while he's running, flames snapping at his face like Sal Tarlowe's whips. It *is* incredible. Bob is clearly impressed, his eyes and mouth wide open, so I try to look nonchalant, I even hum very quietly.

I know that this is a defining moment, a snapshot I'll keep, like that morning bike ride on the boardwalk, winning three dollars in a canasta game with the adults at Edie and Augie's, hearing that the guy down the street shot himself - there's the Bard of Balance with three torches aloft while keeping the planet below himself spinning. My hum turns into a cheer and I clap as hard as everyone else put together.

The next thing you know we're heading back into the park, the band walking with us on their way back to the beer garden, people talking about the show and how Andy should be on Ed

My next full-day Writers Workshop is scheduled for Saturday, October 25, 9:30 a.m. - 3:30 p.m. for Edina Community Education. Laid back and intense all at once, these sessions provide great insights into other writers' brains, toolboxes, weaknesses, strengths, and **words**! I steer when necessary, but generally get as much benefit as you, the paying student. For details call 928-2616.

I will be conducting (coaching?) an Alternative Greeting Card class on Saturday, November 22, 9:30 a.m.-Noon for Edina Community Education; it features an astonishing show&tell of card art from the international correspondence art community, money/materials saving ideas, and a great sack of handouts - whether you're very alternative or not. (Holdiay Edition!) For details call 928-2616.

For more (or different information on these and other classes, call me at 825-4101. If you're not selling PBS or Sprint (or a different Writers Workshop), I'll answer.

Sullivan and does anyone want some French fries?

My Dad says, "I know Sal Tarlowe. I met him when I did that county fair with Lenny and Steve and, later, he was over in Totowa with us, at the drive-in. He drank so much scotch one night I swear it was pouring out of his nose. And that was before the second show. He was smashed and he still had to whip a cigarette out of his wife's mouth! A crazy man, right? Well, damned if he didn't do it without a hitch."

Wife? I ask, "So what happened to his wife? Did he kill her?"

Bob asks "Did he go crazy on stage and whip her to death?"

"No, that was Doris helping him out tonight. Looks like she's working with the dog act too."

My Dad is a country western fiddler and he plays with the Rodeo Rangers, one of the greatest bands of all time and I mean from ancient mountain guys with harps and kazoos to Chubby Checker and his twisted fans. The Rodeo Rangers even made a real genuine record once, I have it in the basement.

We're walking past the Fun House and the Tilt-A-Whirl. I went on a Tilt-A-Whirl once with Howard and I was sick and dizzy for two days. It didn't bother Howard because he doesn't have enough brains to know they're getting mixed up.

It can't be very hard to get a poodle to ride a bike. If I could do that, I'd also teach it how to deliver the *Herald News* for me. The whip tricks really do look dangerous though. Doris is a beautiful name for Miss Senor Hector. Bob and I play whips with the weeping willow branches in the back yard and have a really hard time snapping the cigarette out of Roseann LaBrunda's mouth. Only kidding. The scotch is no doubt the secret. But that Amazing Andy act - what does it feel like to dance on the edge of a cliff? On the edge of a spinning cliff?

We're almost at the beer garden so my Dad gives each of us a dollar for the penny arcade, where there really are old time soccer and baseball games you can play for a penny. They're kind of clunky, from long ago, from before they had skeeball or the car you steer from side-to-side above the turning paper roads. I always spend half my money on the big trading cards that cost two cents each -they have separate machines for tv western stars (my favorite), actors and actresses, wrestlers, fake licenses, radio personalities, boxers, and military cartoons that I never understand.

"We'll be at a table near the fish pond," says my Dad. "Have fun and no fighting."

Bob and I run into the arcade where we'll have a great not-fighting time playing games and figuring out exactly how and when to snare a few more bucks out of our parents later on.   ∎

JANUARY 2, 1998

INtErNAL ⚡ RHYME

NUMBER 14 OF A NEWSLETTER THAT WOULD RATHER DESOLVE THAN RESOLVE ◆ MUSICMASTER, 5136 LYNDALE AVE. SOUTH, MINNEAPOLIS, MINNESOTA 55419

WHAT HAPPEns WHEn YOU OVErcomE WRITEr's BLOCK

Comments and Concerns About Life on the Outside

Dawn gave me a slew of swell gifts this holiday season, mostly staples like toys and books. But among the few practical items she gave me was a pair of scissors. I won't go off on a tangent that unifies all our childhood memories of parents warning "don't use my good scissors" or the correct military-drill-like carrying and presentation of scissors. And I won't use words like trim or cut or snip to pun-dle up this item, because the good humor exists, without rewiring or special lighting, in the instructions that came with scissors:

Care of Scissors and Shears

Mundial scissors and shears are precision instruments that will last for a lifetime with simple care.

Wipe with a soft, dry cloth after each use. Oil screw assembly every few months.

Sharpening and screw adjustments should be performed by a qualified scissors expert. Consult your retailer or the Yellow Pages.

Misuse and abuse are specifically excluded from guarantee coverage.

Gadzooks, why not send the scissors to a goddamn spa every couple of months for a break? I can see tracking down a qualified scissors expert a year from now for a screw adjustment, because when cutting out items for collages the scissors seem to wobble a bit (especially after I've had seven cups of coffee).

I consult the Yellow Pages to find a cutlery artisan; I skip over ads that merely promise precision sharpening and hand honing until I spot a Certified Scissology Technician logo. I call to make an appointment, but he wants some information first. He asks if I've been wiping the scissors, especially the bevels, with a soft, dry cloth after each use and I confess I haven't. I can hear him shaking his head. "Well, at least you've been oiling the screw assembly every few months, right?" When I tell him I haven't done that either, he laughs with disdain. "You people," he says, "shouldn't be permitted to own sharp objects. You have excluded yourself and your unfortunate scissors from guarantee coverage."

Do other people take better care of their scissors than I do of mine? If they do, do they also take better care of their hammer (*wipe with a soft, dry cloth after each use; oil handle every few months; change littler weekly*), their salt & pepper shakers (*wipe with a soft, dry cloth after each use; keep out of direct sunlight; salt/*

pepper flow should only be adjusted by a qualified shaker expert), their lousy plastic fly swatter (*wipe with a soft, dry cloth after each swat; periodically save fallen flies' wings for your swatter's trophy cabinet; close cover before striking*)?

■ **The Christmas week edition** of the *Skyway News* has the following musing in a box with the stylized heading "Sky Lites": the text is reversed into black to underscore the brilliance of the copy, which reads:

Have you noticed how blithely we've begun to throw around the phrase "a billion dollars" when talking about the cost of running businesses or governments? And how paltry a mere "million" sounds? Are we the same people who used to watch "The Millionaire" on television as if it were Never-Never Land?

I skip over ads that merely promise precision sharpening and hand honing until I spot a Certified Scissology Technician logo.

Credited to staffer Jodie Ahern, that's the entire "Lite" aside. Now I'm not saying this observation is fully without merit (though my social set certainly doesn't blithely throw around the phrase a billion dollars; we still get troubled by people who say anything about the government blithely); it's a conversation starter or filler or killer or some part of general silence-breaking jabber that, let's face it, is what most communication is; it's background talk; it's stuff whirring around. It's more of a noise staple than a momentary solo above it all. I don't mind this sort of remark at all, but *as-is*, in print? - That's journalistic laziness or loitering (and I use journalistic generously). Well, maybe "Lite" loitering. And in print you should go for that momentary solo. (While *Internal Rhyme* isn't much more than journalistic loitering itself, it's somewhat more - at least hip deep. And were I getting paid to tap these keys and shape these words, you can bet I'd only give anchored and stylized stuff to my employer for print.) (But, hey!, I have a new slogan for *Skyway News*: Why erase it, when you can print it?)

■ **PEZ dispensers have become** a popular enough collectible that there are PEZ newsletters, conventions, web sites, and one dealer who claims to have spent over $200,000 in 1997 on PEZ

CONTINUED ON BACK PAGE

9

THE MAGNETRON

O ur built-in microwave with the vent and the light and *Ready* ding, stops working. It still turns on, tells time, takes cooking instructions, glows through its picture window, and dings when time is up, but it doesn't heat the food. Of all the things that can go wrong with a built-in microwave - like *everything else is okay but the clock doesn't work* or *the vent light is flickering* - this not heating business is the worst. Most people have back-up items in the kitchen for light and telling time, but none that I know have an alternate means of scrambling molecules in such a heroically demented way that you can reheat a White Castle in under a minute (remove pickle, sprinkle bun with water, zap at medium for 30 seconds then high for 15).

By luck we still have the booklet that came with the microwave that came with the house when we bought it. I turn to the *Troubleshooting Chart* and skim the column listing problems which include **The Clock Doesn't Work** and **The Vent Light Is Flickering**; nearly

every solution in the *Solutions* column starts with *be sure microwave is plugged in*; the last problem listed is **Food Won't Get Hot** (I would've categorized this problem as **Doesn't Work** and put it on top, seeing how it's clearly the biggest problem possible; when a parachute doesn't open and you turn to your in-flight manual's troubleshooting section, you can bet **Doesn't Open** is one of the first problems troubleshot - usually with *be sure it's plugged in*).

T he offered solution to **Food Won't Get Hot** (after *be sure microwave is plugged in*), is that you/we/I probably need a new magnetron which, though it sounds like one of Godzilla's foes, is the tube that powers the microwave. It doesn't say anything more—like *replace it with a new magnetron you can get at Target*—it just clams up with that defensive I-might-know-more-but-I'm-not-telling smirk that the alphabet likes to sport. Though I tend only to be a successful handyman when an appliance can be repaired with a smartass remark and string, I like to at least check a reference book or two to see if I can fix something myself before calling in some clown who values himself at $34/hour but you at considerably less because you have to give up half a day of work so you can let him in sometime Thursday afternoon.

I visit the library and go to the section of home handyman books with titles like **Building Your Own Backyard Log Flume Ride**, **Making Your Own Sandpaper** and **Understanding the Hacksaw**. I flip through a few mainstream fix-it books but all of them shut up when the topic gets to the magnetron. The magnetron might be one of those technologies that the surviving Roswell alien gave to the government along with lasers, Slinky, and breast implants. Only very specialized citizens with top *top* secret clearance can tinker with a magnetron. It probably contains plutonium. (I'd like to point out that exactly *what* the surviving alien gave to the government - to in turn divvy up among just a few powerful outfits like ConAgra, AT&T, McDonnell Douglas, Little Debbie Snack Cakes, and Sally's Sea Shell Owls Unlimited - was a subject of conjecture among UFO geeks for nearly forty years before the release *of Men in Black* and the Roswell legacy jokes therein. That Elroy {the alien's Earthlicized name} gave us or pointed us toward laser beams and Pentium Chippendales is beyond dispute; but exactly what other things he gave us, usually during parties in the White House basement when Truman made "the little green bastard stink like moonshine," continues to be a subject of debate and

CONTINUED SOMEWHERE IN THIS DIMENSION (BUT NOT FOR LONG)

WE SHALL OVERCOME CONTINUED

and PEZ-related items. But apart from PEZ Body Parts sets (you can get Caveman, Space Robot, Santa, Roman Soldier and other Body Parts sets to put on, say, your Garfield or Yosemite Sam dispenser), which are mostly sold in European markets, PEZ hasn't really been that inventive with product variations. I have some suggestions -

F irst, expand the candy line itself to include everything from bubble gum bricks to M&M-style candycoated chocolates. Would Gummi PEZ gunk up the dispenser's jaws? Produce PEZ-sized-jerky products, a cajun turkey PEZ and an aged pork PEZ. Make mini salted spud rectangles into PEZ potato chips. Do a series of upscale combo promotions, say for PEZ-sized Godiva chocolates or PEZ Goose Pate. (And don't overlook the potential of PEZ-vitamins, medication designed for PEZ dispensing, PEZ cough drops, and PEZtoBismol.)

Make the candies something else, e.g. a PEZ-sized Lego-like brick. Have it so kids' PEZ characters cough out uselessly tiny crayons or hamster pellets.

Have a series of dispensers that are chess pieces! Have special super-dispensers that make the candies (or pork) shoot out like projectiles. Have PEZ-dispensing monuments, like the Statute of Liberty, the Sphinx, the Lincoln Memorial. Produce trading cards of all the famous dispensers.

And is there already a PEZ cookbook?

(A few years ago, I sent a medical novelty company - makers of fibula keychains and inverted skull mug - a postcard suggesting they make a pick-up sticks like game with plastic bones. They sent me a five dollars off coupon for a purchase over twenty bucks. I later spotted the same coupon in a newspaper. I'd mail the PEZ people my ideas, but am afraid of a similar unenthusiastic response. If any reader wants to pass along one or all of these ideas to Mr. Pez, feel free to do so; if you get a coupon for free PEZ candies, please just dispense one to me.) ∎

OPEN MIKE, FIRST FRIDAY EVERY MONTH, 7:30 P.M. AT ANODYNE, 43 & NICOLLET, MPLS. - 824-4300

humor, and routinely includes cloning, the neutron bomb, Velco, the Clapper, sugarless gum, utility submetering so apartment residents have to pay a share of their building's heating bill, nonalcoholic beer, Jim Carrey, Flubber, twist-off caps, vitamins shaped like The Flintstones, Silly Putty, Old Spice, and Fizzies.)

I call my friend who sells appliance parts and tell him the problem with our built-in microwave. After he asks *Are you sure you have it plugged in?*, he says that you don't want to mess with the magnetron - that they rarely go out, but when they *do* go, it costs about the same to replace the whole damn thing as it does to have a magnetron-cleared guy in a spacesuit fart around in your kitchen. (Please note that I don't use the expression *fart around*, but my friend who sells applaince parts does; I prefer a phrase like *screw around*— which, while cruder, doesn't sound as crude—or *tinker*, which is too Happy-Inventor-sounding for use here).

Dawn calls a few local appliance repair joints and all of them get more concerned (in that salesmanship kind of way) when they hear that it might be the magnetron. All of them want about 34 bucks just to come over and hit the buttons the same way we have so they can corroborate our findings that the microwave **Doesn't Work**. Then to replace a magnetron is oh, figure, say, about seventy bucks, plus labor, plus travel (some of these parts must warp in from Pluto's undiscovered moon, Joe Bob), plus flossing, plus *Service Always* surcharge, plus *We Do It Cheapest!* surcharge, plus *Answering Your Phonecall* surcharge, *You Are One Loveable Sucker* surcharge, plus tax, which, when you add it all up, costs more than a small trailer home that contains a microwave. (How auto dealers have the chutzpah to charge a Sales Fulfillment fee - maybe that's not what it's called {it's 2 a.m. here and I have more fever than focus}- but how they charge a special fee to cover the portion of the advertising costs that got you to purchase a car, is beyond me. It is so far beyond me I'm certain the idea was suggested by Elroy. What the hell is that? Isn't that the sort of cost-of-doing-business item that is already part&parcel of the retail price? And what if I don't listen to the radio? - can I neogitate out of the portion of that fulfillment fee allocated for AM/FM amphetamine talk? What if other companies pick up on this newspeak, this neo-logic that makes gouging sound practical? - Will we see a surcharge attached to a restaurant's bill to cover their advertising? Will you pay an admission fee to enter the ticket booth area of a theater? More of us should shout more often - voting controls far too little.)

While Dawn and I think about what to do for a few week days when our shedules crisscross and we mostly eat reruns from the weekend, our seventeen-year-old son Hamil nearly starves. To him the gas stove is some sort of crazy flame-throwing contraption that doesn't reheat leftovers quickly enough and doesn't let you cook frozen food in its own convenient cardboard serving tray. Though Dawn and I do feel a bit dated when we draw ourselves on the wall as stick figures slaying a mammoth, we feel like cavepeople when we show Hamil foods that don't have to be cooked at all. Hamil is so hungry he eats all the apples we have. "What do you think?" I ask him, "That they grow on trees?"

We decide to have the microwave kicked by a professional to see if it can be fixed for a hundred bucks or so, because maybe it *can*. Maybe it's not the magnetron at all; maybe it's the part activated by the door latch that gives the magnetron the signal to heat things up. Maybe it's a magnetron-casing unit that's tilted funny or maybe the Start button finally snapped (*Of course I snapped. Always it was Start. Every time anything happened, it was Start. Never "Good morning" and then Start. Never "How are you today, Start?" and then Start. Always Start, just Start. Morning, noon and night — which is a pretty good clarification of Always—it was Start. Beeping was no longer enough for me. I snapped. The magnetron can kiss my ass*).

> *Apparently a magnetron snapped from its anchor and spun amok in a home in St.Paul, burning holes through walls and disintegrating a canary.*

Dawn arranges for a guy from Dipshit Supply to come over Thursday afteroon—sometime between "near Noon" and 5:15 p.m., give or take an hour or so—to chuckle over our interest in heating frozen pot pies into entrees instead of just consuming them as-is, as popsicles. He doesn't show up by near noon or by 5:15, give or take an hour or so, the *or so* lasting about 45 minutes to cover the length of "near."

The next day, they call and apologize — apparently a magnetron snapped from its anchor and spun amok in a home in St.Paul, burning holes through walls and disintegrating a canary. Dipshit got there just seconds before it made a pizza crust too rubbery. Dawn makes a new appointment for Dipshit to come by between November 1 and 18. They don't show, they don't call, they don't mail us a postcard of the park bench where they're *Having nice weather - wish you were beer*; they don't do a damn thing.

But, lo!, there's a Best Buy ad in the newspaper that features right-looking, feature-laden, over-range microwaves *and* there's money off, plus there's a rebate. Since Dawn and I desparately miss the appliance's major feature — reheating coffee — we decide to splurge.

I always enjoy going to Best Buy. It's a high-ceilinged, noisy warehouse of the kinds of common (*and a few iffy*) modern conveniences and diversions that probably contribute to our ultimate doom; but they look or sound so cool and make so much sense really, that what the hell, doom be damned. I think Best Buy has a Low Price Guarantee too. (This is bullshit marketing at its finest, because the consumer has to do all the work to enforce it and make it a meaningful pledge, e.g. **you** have to find a lower price, **you** have to provide proof that such a lower price is advertised, **you** have to wait in the long, inconvenient customer service line, **you** have to look like a cheapskate whining about a goddamn dollar for crying out loud, and **you** have to comply with fineprint that identifies some lower prices as exempt from the guarantee because they're on special somewhere or - let's face it - they're lower! By the time you do all the rigamaroll and paperwork, you're valuing your own time like that clown who

CONTINUED (TRUST YOUR INSTINCTS ON WHERE TO TURN)

SON OF TH**E** ID**E**A CONTINUED

values himself at $34/hour up in paragraph three. So the Low Price Guarantee is, at best, like a We Have the Fewest Idiots Guarantee, because there's no way in hell you're going to bother proving there *are* fewer idiots at another store just so you can explain it to some idiot here; at worst, it's just a design for signage.)

We go to Best Buy and quickly find the over-range microwaves. An advertised one looks perfect and has a tag listing all kinds of product features. It's an "Interactive Cooking System" that displays custom help questions and answers; when you tell its usual "Compu Cook" buttons that you're reheating pizza, it asks you how many slices. If you tell it you're reheating coffee, it reminds you to watch your caffeine intake. It even displays its cooking advice in Spanish if you program it to. It is as cool as it is corny. And it comes in black.

We find a clerk (though she's probably professionally encoded as a sales associate or a team member or a merchandising assistant) and ask her if the one we want is in. She helps us hoist one off a lower shelf and onto our cart, then asks if we want the extended warranty which is a great deal at only $39.95 for three years - anything goes wrong, they repair it and if they can't repair it, they replace it. Even though we're there because of a broken microwave, I'm ironic enough to say "These things rarely ever break."

So the Low Price Guarantee is like a We Have the Fewest Idiots Guarantee, because there's no way in hell you're going to bother proving there are fewer idiots at another store just so you can explain it to some idiot here.

"What are you kidding me?" she points at a shelf of taped-up boxes along the wall. "They break all the time."

I'm astonished by this woman's audacious hustle. Extended warranty deals are usually a waste of money since, according to reports by consumer groups and watchdog agencies, they cover rarely-lemonized products only well-within their healthiest years. They won't sell you an extended warranty for five or seven years hence, for example, let alone twelve (the approximate age of our late microwave). There have been stories about this on both the local and national news, with, if I recall correctly, nods toward superstores like Best Buy where, reportedly, a salesperson gets a nice percentage of the extended warranty charge.

I don't believe that telling customers that Best Buy carries and advertises $399 microwaves that break all time is what Best Buy wants its customers to hear from its sales staff, so I give her an opportunity to clarify by asking "Why would a reputable company sell products that break down a lot?"

Our clerk shrugs, forces an annoyed half-smile. "I see people bringing in microwaves all time. If you get the extended warranty and we can't fix the appliance, we'll replace it for no charge."

"But obviously you wouldn't carry applainces you're stuck re-placing very often, would you?"

"We do it all the time," she reassures.

"Aside from the magnetron going out, what else can go wrong with a microwave?"

"Look, all kinds of things go wrong."

I think to myself that this woman should make sure that all the stuff that she apparently has malfunctioing at home is plugged in.

"Well," I say, "I think we'll pass on the extended warranty."

The clerk's annoyed half-smile emits an exasperated poof.

Realizing my need for additional dialog to wind this story down, Dawn asks "Can we have a rebate card?"

"We're all out," answers the clerk with a real smile this time. "But if you give me your name and address, I'll mail you one."

FADE OUT. A month passes. (And I'm *still* working on this same damn Magnetron story. If I had greater control of my focus, I'd have an easier time with prose. But I don't - I like everything interconnecting, eternally woven, no tangent-really-a-tangent type of storytelling; John Donne's death tolling mine. Which is why I have a hard time writing prose - there's a humorous or surrealistic detour in nearly every paragraph, often in a parenthetical aside so overwrought that at its conculsion the reader has to shake his/her head and think "oh yeah" when returning to the main storyline. I have total control of the tangents and subplots I put in my poems, but in prose I tend to hop like a checker, add songs unexpectedly like in musical, and wander like a tourist through ideas. I always mean to start a novel, but know if I do, I'll need to develop a new discipline and a probably uncomfortable leash for my brain; even with that, the effort will probably end up - like everything else really flailing around in life - unfinished. And it will cost me many poems. Now, enough with parentheses - back to the story.)

Dawn and I are standing around in the kitchen slowly sipping coffee and more slowly deciding how to clutter our Saturday up or down with chores and whatnot. When it's not garage sale season, this is how we start most weekends. When it *is* garage sale season, we're out and about by 8:00 a.m. wondering why someone wants seventy-five cents for an old spatula - maybe it works really well?

(Note: Garage sale season used to follow the Memorial Day to Labor Day formula of parks and resorts, but due to its emergence as a booming, classless, underground, *recreational* economy, it now runs from as early as May 1st to mid-October. It's an almost flagrantly subversive activity, to have so many people returning to a simpler, taxless type of recycling and communication, avoiding the government and hypehappy manufacturers and faceless corporations that bully and bother us the rest of the week. We love garage sales. But, frankly, we wouldn't think of buying a microwave at one. If you see a newer-looking microwave at a garage sale for twenty bucks - a little sign says WORKS GOOD - you can bet the seller is just another sap who didn't get the Extended Warranty. Dawn says "I see what you mean by the parentheses.")

It's a nice lazy Saturday. During one morning pause, we both look at the microwave and nod. "Good machine," I remark. "Yeah, it really is." "I like the little Compu Cook read-outs." "It looks pretty good too. It seems to cook a little hot though, doesn't it?" "Hotter than the old one," I agree. "But maybe the old one cooked a little cooler, so we have to relearn our reheating routines." "That sounds like a bad community ed class."

"Did we ever get the rebate form?" I ask.   ∎

INTERNAL RHYME

JANUARY 9, 1998

15 OF A NEWSLETTER THAT WILL NOT SELL YOUR NAME & ADDRESS TO OTHER VENDORS ◆ MUSICMASTER, 5136 LYNDALE AVE. SO., MINNEAPOLIS, MN 55419

BARKING UP DISEASED TREES

■ **The flimsy subscription card** that flew out of my recent *American Photo* magazine has the usual mini-covers solicitously nodding between two columns of crafty wordplay and staggering savings.

(Act now and receive a one-year subscription to American Photo (6 issues) for just $12.95. Subscribe and save 45%! A great deal for sure, but not when your magazine is delivered by my mailman, who always attempts to fold and cram all of our mail through our mail slot at once and spindles/shreds/ unGoodConditions everything in the process. I don't give him a Christmas tip because his service can't get any more vindictive. But maybe he's a *postman's* postman, a real one-slot-one-shot traditionalist who takes pride in the efficiency of only so many moves per address; maybe he regards folks like me who often get a lot of mail as "part of the problem" (*you know*, The Problem), as a lump in the soup, a card in the spokes, a speedbump to his auto-pilot. The *American Photo* postcard should explain that mail delivery might cause dogearring or crumpling or even ripping of pages that, in a magazine called *American Photo*, might diminish your enjoyment of images thereon. I don't buy dented cans at the store, I wouldn't sneeze on someone's sandwich before serving it, and I think mail delivery should be done with a tad of care. Thanks for not showing this to my postman.)

A t the bottom of the *American Photo* card, by the box that you check for a subscription, *it reads Enter my 1-year subscription (12 issues) to George for $24.00. The entire line is a Type-O* typo: something that doesn't get changed on a reuseable format/template - an item that was on an earlier piece so it gets by. I make lots of typos (*Infernal Rhyme* features a handful every issue - *Infernal* was a joke however), and take as much sadistic glee as solace in the fact that *no* publication, big or small, is fully free of typos.

I'm noting this particular which-magazine-am-I-subscribing-to example because it poses more problems than: a simple mispelling (a Type A typo); a wrong name, date, number/location, or

phone number (Type B typos); or a wrong caption and/or wrong graphic - from a wrong photo to a wrong map (a Type AB typo). This error also brings other questions into play: Will I get six issues or twelve? Will I pay $12.95 or $24.00? Do they think I'll get the error and make necessary adjustments as per ad text or will they think I do indeed want *George*? Payment with order would give them a clue, but what if I want to be billed?

Wow, what a great screw-up that typo is - I'll have to try and top it someday soon.

■ **Recent tv spots** promote a series of phone cards from Sprint and underscore their collectibility by saying "each is an authentic replica." *Authentic replica!* I don't think there's playful irony going on here (as in a satiric identification of a *Genuine Fake*), only dunderheaded hustle. This ad tells me that Sprint is counseled by idiots. There are trading card manufacturers nowadays who have the ignorance or the balls or cut-throat-selling slime gene required to call printed signatures autographs and products with press runs of tens of thousands as limited editions (I guess - technically - the *New York Times* is also printed in a limited edition - they won't print any more of a given issue in the future; *technically* everything is a limited edition. I love how more general and *nontechnical* technical speaking can make things). These companies too use marketing talent from Stupid U.

■ **I want to make** career specific spin-offs of those popular virtual pets - those keychained mutated-calculators that need "interactive" attention via hitting buttons

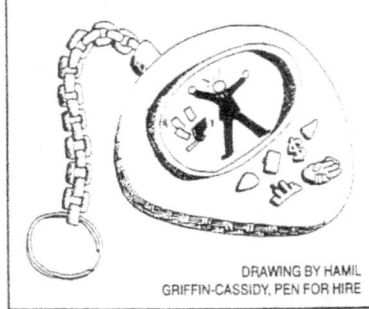

DRAWING BY HAMIL
GRIFFIN-CASSIDY, PEN FOR HIRE

that provide food and discipline and even quality time playing a godawful game or else the pet weakens and ultimately "dies" from neglect, starvation or spiritual decay.

For example, I want to manufacture a virtual pet businessman; he dies if you don't say "absolutely" or "bottomline" every

CONTINUED ON PAGE 138

13

Jesus is happy when you forgive
your playmates for their faults.

WHERE IS THE BOY'S RIGHT HAND?

FLASHBACK - The Minnesota map/postcard I drew and joked-up over a decade ago continues to sell at several shops in the metro area; apparently jokes about frostbite and mouse-sized lakes don't require much updating (the Minnesotan sense of humor evolves slowly -sure, frozen ya know). Anyway, I sold so many thousands of that card in the late 80s, that I jumped on my own bandwagon and did a New Jersey map/postcard. It was a same-but-different reworking of stereotypes and cheap shots, fully based on my own fond memories of growing up in New Jersey (just east of Shopping Mall, twenty minutes from Manhattan). Since making the card, I've sold a total of about twenty, mostly to people who know someone from or in the Garden State; New Jerseyites themselves don't regard it as funny because, I think, they too refer to Hazardous Waste National Park, Mugville, and Roach Motel by the Sea, and so the card strikes them as merely an inconveniently small map that doesn't even show all the locations where Jimmy Hoffa's body parts are planted. Ah, the mysterious east. ∎

BARKING UP DISEASED TREES CONTINUED

time you interact with him, put him in his little tanning booth at least fortyfive minutes a week, and "virutally" kiss his ass three times a day. (What does it mean when you put virtually in quotes?)

How about a virtual pet poet/artist? It dies if you don't tell it that it's brilliant, misunderstood, and profound every time it poops; you have to remind it to put on its pants; and - don't panic - it *needs* to brood about two hours a day.

The virtual pet lawyer? It needs to work and study too, but only about an hour a day; otherwise you play *Let's Sue God* and feed it ten pounds of bloody lamb.

Apparently, parents taking care of their kids' virtual pets (not allowed at school because they beep and interupt too much) has recently become a workplace issue, especially in Japan where the distraction is so great their whole damn economy is collapsing. I love the idea of babysitters for virtual pets, moreover the problems that might come up if a virtual pet dies while in a sitter's care. (I didn't mean to kill him. I thought a third martini seemed excessive, not necessary.) ∎

WORDS TOO TIDY FOR CHAOS

THINKERS TOO SILLY FOR WORDS

CHAOS TOO TIDY FOR ARTISTS

ARTISTS TOO TIDY FOR THINKERS

ROLL OF QUARTERS

THE OFFICIAL "POETRY CENTER" OF MY UNAUTHORIZED NEWSLETTER

Charlie Manson hair blue collar clothes

intimidating growl when a panhandler nears

I look like a guy who will give you a quarter

I want to say I'd gladly pay you cash for time

though if you could give me that you'd be a millionaire

but why establish contact just to sever it

I never utter anything smart or funny

inspirational enough for a bum to listen

a wino to laugh or a derelict weep

shave and shower get a job and promoted

become a bigshot get hustled for quarters himself

say the same thing I had said that had turned him around

the cheapskate pennypinching punk

too bad you can't dump stiffs like that for change

we're wandering around Old Town

a touristy mix of clubs shops and missions

where the bums are in a chorusline for tourists

you got a quarter buddy can you help me out

you got two bucks for a drink in that goddamn overpriced bar

and that this is their theater makes them slightly aggressive

they don't take a snub without hurling an insult

or starting a story that you'll pay them to stop

a guy in a red sweatshirt and jeans silvery thin

can't be more than twenty five

short black bloodshot hair

asks me for a quarter which I give him

but he doesn't step away he stares and nods

I know you from somewhere don't I

and I'm thinking oh God I probably had Tiny

toss this clown out of the bar

I know he snaps his fingers *you lived down the block in Cleveland*

nope I answer *sorry wasn't me*

yeah you were the guy with the stuck up wife

you had that boulder on your lawn

definitely wasn't me I smile continue on my way

sure it was he says *I know it's you you think you're something buddy*

but you're not you're gonna be here too someday and soon

look he points at my chin *you got that Heidelberg stubble*

you're no better than I am

I shake my head and wonder what

the world had done to make this guy

remember in a bleary downward spiral a boulder

back in Cleveland

as I cross the street he shouts *tell your stuck up wife I say hello*

I'm walking down twentythird with Kay

who's spring dress young and smile

an approachable soul I'm all

hunched and huddled in my thoughts

not bigdeal art and salvage mind you

only thoughts about which beer to buy

the street is pretty busy people in and out of shops

before we turn down Johnson I look up to see

what's playing at the movies down the block

a shape that far away below marquee begins to budge

and from the corner of my eye I see it pick up speed

maneuver through pedestrians as our turn down Johnson

blocks it from our view a minute later we hear footsteps

gaining on us so we turn to watch old lady flag us down

big green coat in summer and garbage bag of clinking bottles

her red face panting *please excuse me please*

her eyes lock into mine whatever neon's there

that says *ask for money here*

Kay probably has more spare change than I have

but this woman doesn't see her only me

she asks me for a quarter for the bus

I growl and nod and fumble for a coin

eyeball her sack full of savings

a few pop bottles but mostly Oly and Bud empties

Bohemian quarts and shining like a Grail

a St. Pauli Girl Dark

I switch off the woman's homing device

by handing her a quarter she says *thanks* and clinks away

Kay has seen this happen often

and kindly doesn't comment

only laughs a bit and swings my hand

that woman doesn't know what a bus looks like

I grumble

let's stop by the store for beer

St. Pauli Girl Dark if they got it

I feel in my pocket for the rest of my cash

a couple of bucks and a dime not enough

so I ask Kay to lend me some bus fare

LITTLE OF IMPORTANCE ADDS UP BECAUSE OF MATH

MARCH 9, 1998 (A REALLY LATE FEBRUARY 27TH ISSUE)

INTERNAL  RHYME

ISSUE 18 OF THE NEWSLETTER THAT ONLY HAS TO CARRY FOUR FULL PAGE ADS TO MAKE MONEY ◆ MUSICMASTER, 5136 LYNDALE AVE. SO., MINNEAPOLIS, MN 55419

THE 202 STAR REVIEW

Miss Nevin makes me editor of the 202 Star Review
which means I get to go through
a whole pile of pictures and stories and
poems by everyone in our room
pick out five of my favorites
which will get tacked to the bulletin board over the sink

I look through all the pieces slowly
set aside a funny drawing by Lee Beattys
a poem by Guy Caruba to his mother it says
Mom I love you you big Mom you love Guy
I like Carol Rizzi's picture story of ants carrying a refrigerator
but it looks to me like an adult helped her
so I pass it by for Benedict Pekarsky's pencil drawing
of Santa Claus or a giant squirrel
climbing down a chimney or a straw it's hard to tell

there's another drawing by Lee Beattys
that's funnier than his other drawing
but his *other* drawing is *so much* funnier
than *any* of the others that I keep them both

I also find a piece by Cathy Horak
the fanciest most grogeous girl not just in Room 202
but in all of second grade maybe in all of School #2
it's a perfectly drawn pigstarhouse thing
that must be a bird because it's

INSIDE THIS ISSUE

labelled bird though Kathy's spelled it B-U-R-D
which I know is wrong and probably not the sort of thing
you want to see included in the 202 Star Review

but while I don't want Miss Nevin to think I don't know how
to spell bird I must admit a fondness
for Cathy's courageous creativity
taking charge of the language like that I imagine myself
drowning in her blonde hair
curling up with her pigstarhouse thing as she explains
that her spelling of bird is quite frankly better so why the heck
not use it

I have to think it's Miss Nevin who doesn't know how to spell
burd
so I'm going to run with Kathy's piece
run with Kathy herself in a way
out of stupid 202 and down the hall and off to anywhere else

musicmaster 3.98

OPeN MIKe!

The Twin Cities' Best Open Mike is the first Friday of every month (at about 8 p.m.) at the Twin Cities' Best Coffee House - **Anodyne, 43rd & Nicollet, Minneapolis** (824-4300). Tom Cassidy is your Best Host! By the way, the first Friday is the Best Friday! The Best Avenue is Nicollet! And the Best Surprise guest Is You! Show up, tapdance, chalktalk, contort, wail, chant, rant, weave, juggle, strum, hum, shadowbox (*anything* but pyramid salespitching is great - Why it's the Best!)

JOIN US FOR REAL LIFE MUST-SEE ANTI-TV!

MARK YOUR CALENDAR, TUNE YOUR SONNET, TEACH YOUR EARS TO WIGGLE CONTRAPUNTALLY!

WOODeN NICKeLS CONTINUED

of semi-jammed drawers you could work your way through to see the treasures therein, which ranged from by-the-sea cheese-cake cartoon postcards from the 50s to paperbacks about fortune telling to small transfer/tattoo booklets with great images of spacemen and noble savages.

The place was still run by its operator for half a century, a New York-esque codger who was nice enough to show us around but

TRIVIA CONTeST ANSWeRS
CONTINUED

— like de-prosing). And though spellcheck is annoying, intrusive, dumb, scolding, and schoolmarmish, it is indeed also helpful; and better than being helpful, it is indeed my need to be different by picking fights with me over how words should or shouldn't be used in print, in a poem, in a personal letter, in a postmodern garland of vowels. Every time spellcheck calls me on anything, I'm ready to fight, I feel younger and revolutionary and avant-garde. But today, when – for the first time ever! – spellcheck zipped straight through a letter of mine and gave it a thumbs-up, I didn't feel proud or even just correct, I felt old, concilia-tory and irrelevant. Maybe more than in other endeavors, art and poetry don't just need mistakes to grow, but to breathe. The slap on the back I got from spellcheck today knocked the wind right out of me. (It would have been funny if I laced this piece with misspellings and homonyms and maybe, just to be safe, some jokes.)

4) (b) one-of-a-kind. Now *that's* a serious limited edition. ■

barked at two Hispanic employees, both of whom were running a clunky type of letterpress by the windows.

"That machine," he told us, "is the number one wooden nickel printing machine in operation. It can print over 10,000 a day. I've printed them for Boy Scouts, State Fairs, ball clubs, you name it."

"You've got great merchandise here," I said. "The shrunken heads I used to win playing skeeball at Olympic Park, the tin badges, even dribbling water glasses."

"They don't want dribbling water glasses anymore," he replied, "but, thank God, the wooden nickels keep me in business."

I recently received a wooden nickel at a tradeshow, for the adult education program at the Science Museum of Minnesota. It's worth $30 off registration, so the idea of the wooden nickel now allows adjustments for inflation. This very progressive interpretation of the wooden nickel is nonetheless made quaint – made reminiscent of the old five-cent wooden nickels – because the printing, on both sides, is still slightly offcenter.

Note: According to Stuart Berg Flexner's excellent and usually remaindered book, **Listening to America** (Simon & Schuster, 1982), *Though counterfeit coins of wood were being passed at least as early as the 1850s in America, the wooden nickels in the expression 'Don't take any wooden nickels' are probably a more general and humorous reference to the many outlandish counterfeit wooden items long said to have been sold to rustics by con-niving Yankee peddlers, there being many early 19th-century jokes about those who unsuspectingly purchased wooden nutmeg, wooden cucumber seeds, and even wooden hams.* ■

Trivia Contest

1) How many Internal Rhyme readers are there?

2) What did ancient Roman historian Julius Honorius speculate that the pyramids (built over 2000 years earlier) were for?

3) Why am I depressed today?

4) The Danbury Mint has an ad out for a Green Bay Packers Pickup, an NFL-licensed die-cast metal toy truck that costs $145 plus $7.50 shipping & handling. It's a swell looking toy with rubber tires, opening hood and tailgate, and details down to seat belts and tailgate party stuff like a cooler, a barbecue grill and a "Cheesehead" hat. It's a limited edition, of course; everything is afterall; but in commerce nowadays, in marketing speak, when limited edition is used without clarification, without the edition *number*, you can be sure the so-called collectible is *anything but* limited. (In my book, 5,000 of *anything* is too many for the limited edition designation; 3,000 is pushing it, bit I'll let it go if the piece is handsigned or, if it's manufactured/fired has some hand-detailing added; 1,000 is my personal tops for an edition to be honestly limited; and while I know these are arbitrary thresholds, I also know from 25 years of eyeballing a number of limited edition markets that greed has mucked up a lot of standards stricter than mine. I think it's fair to say that a framed print by a popular wildlife artist, sold via a mall "gallery," in an edition of 3,500, has less investment potential than a mass-marketed Madonna poster that isn't likely to be saved/preserved in mint condition.)

It is a dandy looking ad for a dandily depicted toy truck. But some of the copy hyping the truck is among the most idiotic and giddy I've seen in months. One line reads "Attractively priced; convenient to acquire." Isn't that spectacular? – *Convenient to acquire!* What a line for copy-doped readers – it has a sexy word, a smart bankerly intonation and reminds us how we love convenience! Another line promises "the model comes complete with all the necessities for the ultimate tailgate!" Let me repeat that you get a cooler, a barbecue grill and a "Cheesehead" hat – plus you get a director's chair (the cornerstone or any party), Packer's helmet and jersey, duffel bag, bag of nuts and beer keg. Good party gear for sure, but *ultimate* tailgate?! Even just a regular one should include a football to toss around, a boombox that's all bass, and a bottle with three a skull&crossbones on it. The *ultimate* tailgate would have to include over-the-top basics like strippers, a visit by a salaried jock, a stadium horn *section*, and a green&gold stomach pump.

But the copy that's most glaringly stupid describes the truck as (all are in the ad; pick one):

(a) The greatest "*fan*-tasy" truck ever

(b) one-of-a-kind

(c) a masterpiece of miniaturization

(Answers below. So as not to disturb contents of this newsletter, please stand on your head to read them.)

TRIVIA CONTEST ANSWERS

CONTINUED PREVIOUS PAGE (CAUTION: IF YOU ARE NOT READING THIS ON YOUR HEAD, THINK ABOUT WHAT YOU'RE DOING)

1) Until this *Internal Rhyme*, I only printed two copies of each issue: one for me and one for you. I'm joking. I print 125 of each issue, and mail or hand out all but two dozen or so which dwindle away a few weeks after printing. Many of the seventy or so regulars on my mailing list only hear from me when – to keep postage under control — I can tuck two or three into an envelope. People with whom I correspond otherwise and differently get copies within a few days after I produce them. About a dozen of each issue are distributed for free via the Art Underground, an eccentric and nonrhyming gallery in South Minneapolis beneath the Malt Shop's grease pit; and another dozen are given away at the monthly open mikes I host at Anodyne coffee shop, where beans are beings and décor is folksy deco bondage. Assuming that each recipient passes along his/her copy to at least 10 friends (assuming they each have 10 friends) and that ultimately the visibly worn Internal Rhymes sell at garage sales for seven or eight bucks apiece to people who read them before in turn passing them along to others who in turn resell them and so on a few more generations, I guesstimate my average per issue readership at 63,413,012 (give or take 4).

2) He speculated they had been silos. The Greek historian Herodotus was the first to poke around enough to learn that they were tombs. (See *Things I Really Believe* in the last issue for an important theory about the pyramids.)

3) Today, I'm depressed because the sky is blue. That's a funny line when you're not depressed. Or maybe it isn't (how depressing to imagine). Truly, I'm depressed because I typed a letter to someone today and, when I ran it through spellcheck, mostly to be sure that accommodate has 2 Cs and 2 Ms (because it has room to *accommodate* them all) and to catch hyper-typos like **sandwich** becoming **snadiwhc** (though of course it cannot catch that **on** supposed to be **no**, that **tang** is dyslexic-typo of **gnat**), it passed without pause or suggestion. Ordinarily, anything I write (though especially my poems) gets repeatedly yapped at by spellcheck – (it wants me to capitalize that underserving demon **tv** which I refuse to do; it doesn't like pseudo-**folk**; it doesn't appreciate the importance of de-prosing conversation with **lotta**, **gotta**, or **sumthin**; it warms me about abuses

It Was Professor Plum in the Third Stanza
with Gratuitous Realism

it's awfully quiet out

for this place where we've all been

trying to get our words awake

from a coma spun by sin

I hear the smoke alarm no a siren no it's the tv

no it's an ambulance on a tv show no it's a smoke alarm at the back door

when I answer it the neighbor says as she raises a carving knife

one of those good ones with a glistening blade and mahogany handle

she probably got it as a wedding gift

she says *I was wondering if I could borrow a scream*

and as I'm about to ask her if she'd like some coffee with my blood

she hands me the wrench with her *thanks*

it was just what I needed she *says it tightened that siren up perfectly*

can you hear my cutlery resonate?

and I say like I always say nowadays to almost anything at all

I say *No problem but really you know it is a problem*

I don't say that I just say *No problem*

it's awfully quiet out

with all the crickets dead

the neighbor with the carving knife's

responsible it's said

I'm watching the anchorman on the local news

he's saying *Gun Reform Tax Rain Tonight on Touchdown*

Like he always says word for word

so I don't hear him anymore but I look into his eyes

and inside his pupils there's a puppet show going on

one hand is a cricket puppet

and the other hand is a plush mahogany knife with friendly eyes

these two lovable characters do a whole routine

about smoke alarms getting activated by ghosts

by smoke that isn't smoke

the anchorman wakes me up with a story

about guy having all his blood replaced with coffee

I'm not kidding *the guy jogs like two thousand miles a day*

it's awfully quiet out

for screams to do much good

but each and every one of them

is needed in our neighborhood

most frightening always is the ordinariness

of murder the locations the weapons the killers

what the victims were doing just ten minutes earlier

lives are so predictable that only sudden death

makes them interesting

better yet gives them their answers their faith

and we're left with rules *some of them subject to interpretation*

little plastic tokens and dice

it was Professor Plum in the observatory with

a souped-up sledgehammer

the heat from my forehead sets off the smoke alarm

so I go to our neighbor's house

to borrow earplugs and a wench

oh I thought you said wench

and when our neighbor opens the door

she is dead

my mahogany handled carving knife

glistening in her beautiful peaceful

awfully quiet soul

musicmaster 6/99

APRIL 22, 1998

INTERNAL ☼ RHYME

THIS IS ISSUE #20 OF THE ONLY 8-PAGE NEWSLETTER THAT'S CRAMMED ONTO 4 PAGES ◆ MUSICMASTER, 5136 LYNDALE AVE. SO., MINNEAPOLIS, MN 55419

A CLAIM TO FAME!?

A while back I sent the record club a note that I had received a second shipment of a Clifton Chenier CD I had already received and paid for, just days earlier. I told them to adjust their records (*that would've been a more obvious play on words a few, pre-CD years ago*) and send a postpaid label for return of the duplicate. I never received a label to return the extra copy, never got a phone call for clarification if my note (with my phone number) had been unclear, never received a sputtering letter that I had done something wrong, never a word. This happened maybe eighteen months ago and the extra Clifton Chenier CD is still gathering dust on my shelf.

A few months ago I receive a *Special Invitation* to join the same record club. Any time a membership lapses or is canceled with one of those clubs they try to get you to rejoin within a year or so with a repeat of the special deal whereby you get a dozen or so CDs for free (you only pay shipping and handling charges of $143.95) and then to fulfill your end of the transaction you only have to buy two copies of the same Clifton Chenier CD. Okay, I'm kidding - you only have to buy *one* more CD at the regular retail price of $22.98 (plus the shipping and handling charges of $143.95 - an amount that, for your convenience, remains affordable and constant whether you purchase one or two or twenty or fifty CDs - *why just think of the savings if you order 8,311 CDs at once!*). Okay, I'm kidding again. Everything is normal record company pitch and parry and I think hey, maybe I'll rejoin.

So I look at all of those teeny-tiny stamps of CDs/record albums and

INSIDE THIS ISSUE

Why Can't Funny Animals Vote?

Marketing Shlock Prepared and Paid for by Advertisers that We Print as Feature Items

You and Whose Army?

Guns Don't Shoot People, I Shoot People - A Hitman's Diary (that he's making us print)

carefully make selections. I don't know who half of the groups are. I may not be hip anymore but I'm at least hip enough to know I'm no longer hip. Neil Young is two hundred years old; he's my Lawrence Welk. Holy smokes, they still have a Lawrence Welk album! I mean cassette or CD. They still carry titles by people who haven't been micromanaged out of Branson or Reno codger halls in thirty years; they have Perry Como and Best of the Big Bands (they're *always* coming back but never arrive) and Vikki Carr (who I believe nowadays hosts a regular Mexican tv show); and a bunch of those *Best of . . .* albums for artists who only had one hit.

I pick three groups I've never heard of, two violent-sounding albums, Frank Sinatra humming, a Flatt & Scruggs Best of, Countrified Classic Television Theme Songs By Tony Bennett, Jeff Beck Plays Enoch Light, and mail in the card all stuck up with the tiny stamps of even tinier musicians shouting and whistling in their little flea voices.

A month later I receive a stiff letter telling me that, after careful review, they regretfully cannot accept my application for member-

HEY, I'LL RACE YOU TO THE BACK PAGE

CAN YOU SPOT THE DIFFERENCES?

Though these two pictures of the Easter Bunny look alike, they are actually different! Can you spot fifteen differences between the two drawings? (Yes, this is a legit puzzle; no, it's not really an Easter Bunny picture; yes, I'm crazy; no, you're not encouraging me by doing this. The solution is inside this issue.)

WHAT**EVE**R YOU HAV**E** ON TAP

THE OFFICIAL UNCORNERED "POETRY CORNER" IN A D-DAY OR ALAMO-LIKE PLAYSET THAT MARX NEVER MADE - BUT SHOULD HAVE . . .
WITH SOLID BLUE AND RED PLASTIC FIGURES OF ABSINTHE SUCKING ARTISTS AND POETS, WITH A LITHOGRAPHED TIN BROTHEL AND TONS
OF ACCESSORIES LIKE LITTLE PLASTIC CRUMPLED-UP PAPERS, BOTTLES, LEAN-TOS, CREDITORS, ETC., PLUS A WELL-HEELED GALLERY OWNER
FIGURE AND MAYBE EVEN A SPECIAL ARTIST FIGURE WITH A CAP-ACTIVATED EXPLODING HEAD

on a weekday
I wake up five minutes before the alarm
it didn't go off once
back when I lived in Hopkins so
I still don't trust it

or electricity or jingles or weekdays
or work or alarms or popular radio

to get ready for work
I run headfirst into a huge Chinese gong
ten times
each time feels like I'm a subway train colliding
with the Unisphere
in an echo chamber underwater
and every time I get ready for work I think
I am stupid

or misguided or brilliant or out of touch
or on fire or so normal that I'm *too* normal
an abnormal hypernormal entity

I listen to popular radio
on the way to the office
because everybody on there
with jingles up their news and
sports up their asses
makes me feel (though my head's still full of reverb)
a hundred times smarter

a listener calls in
says Sinatra shot Kennedy
that the mob created Oswald
with psychogenic distorters
given to them by the CIA
and the DJ and the traffic guy and the weathergirl
say in unison oh brother
and they hang up on the poor bastard
they cut his rope to the mountaintop
where all the jocks
with their five hundred dollar Cuban climbing goggles
park their pontificating cellular laptop careers
and suck back bottled blood

if I had their money I'd quit my job
and within a few months
I wouldn't even have *their* money anymore

I get to work and listen to my messages
most people comment on my mine

which usually is
I'm either out of my mind or away from it right now
please make some magic with the beep
the first message is a hang-up
which I take to mean that whoever it was who called
doesn't like getting a recorded message
but thinks that leaving a recording of a clattering receiver is
more personal
the second message is someone
correcting a newsletter I finished and faxed him last week
there are very few changes in the copy
but he wants to change the lead story make the type a little
bigger
replace the photo on page 5 with a group of four photos
one of them is just a pale xerox copy is that okay
squeeze in another 3 halfpage ads
come over to my house afterhours and burn all my toys
frighten the goldfish tell my children
that I no longer understand the value
of half of what I know

the third message is from Samuel the dead albatross
who lives on my doorstep
he wants to know if I can stop by the market
on my way home and buy him a cuttlebone
any flavor as long as it's not some sugarless crap
that brightens your beak

I turn on my computer
while it checks itself for fleas
I get a cup of coffee
look into a co-worker's office
and on her far wall there's a large planning calendar
that's too wide
it's showing a new kind of week a dozen days across or more
and since I know the days
at the ends of each row are Saturdays and Sundays
it means the added days are all weekdays
all workdays all only-have-so-much-time-for-lunch workdays
all indoor sterilizing acidic radio-flavored idiot-making
workdays
and I think well that's the government for you
just as I realize that it's a calendar of not one week
but two months side-to-side
that everything is better than I think (I think)

suddenly it's five o'clock
and I'm twenty years older
I'm leaving a different job in a different city

WATCH OUT FOR PAPER CUTS
AS YOU LOOK FOR THE CONCLUSION TO THIS PIECE!

WORK IS THE UNIVERSAL OCCUPATIONAL HAZARD

WHAT**EV**ER YOU HAV**E** ON TAP CONTINUED

I say goodnight to co-workers as they flee from the building
the backs of some of their heads look familiar
maybe from a subway or a bus stop
or a mob or the customer service line
where all of us go to get slapped

I head to a downtown happy hour joint
and stand on a table in their outdoor patio
which is right on the main street
the carbon monoxide and smog dusting the free popcorn
with colorful specks
I shout *I don't get it*
over and over and over
until the words loosen and
fall from the word balloon above me
clatter off my shoulders on their way to hell
a harried-looking waiter calls up to me
can I get you something to drink?
and I lean down to say
yeah
whatever you have on tap would be fine

musicmaster april98

PAG**E** 1 PUZZL**E** SOLUTION

CHARACT**E**R FLAW

THE OFFICIAL "POETRY PAVILION" OF MY MENTAL WORLD'S FAIR

I lean against the armrest

of my movie theater seat

in such a way I slow the blood

that's flowing through my arm

I let it fall asleep

the best film of the year is sand

brightlights and needles in my eyes

the teeth are bigscreen tv sets

the words all spun with music

I shift a bit which makes my legs relax

the left one starts to stretch and sigh

and settle in to let the numbness come

the movie tells me secrets about artificial life

a life of crime an afterlife life on Mars the good life

the mansion's several star-shaped swimming pools

are really big martinis and everybody in them clinks like ice

the feeling in my other arm is fully gone

it's past immobile as it dreams of flight

my right leg starts to tingle

and saunters off to somewhere else as well

I feel no-feeling feelings in my limbs

they spread and roll into my shoulders

down my chest and through my ribs

my heart begins to snore before

the sluggish blood calms that down too

as way up on that magic sail

a car the size of Pittsburgh blows up twice

a naked bloodied clever couple rolls into the sunset

and I like this pleasant numbness

in the soothing soundproof chamber

where everything is dark except this life before my eyes

musicmaster 3.98

THE POET IS IN

THE POET IS IN

...BIG TROUBLE

↑ RUDI RUBBEROID ↗

CONFERRING WITH HIS MUSES...

TRAPPED IN A SELF-MADE MAZE

EXIT

ENTER

MUSICMASHER

Word Less

JOHN M. BENNETT

CLAIM TO FAME CONTINUED

ship! I say *letter* instead of *form letter* because I'm the *first* **person** *in history* to be rejected by the record club!

You can be in prison for life (someone who *got into crime* by joining the record club ten times a day, using different addresses, then selling all the incoming inventory via catalog) and get accepted by the record club. My screwball college roommate for one term (fall '71), Kevin, joined the record club *once a week* using a different fake name on each Special Invitation - he *never* changed his address but he always got the records; while receiving third warning red letters to Jim Morrison, he was also receiving parcels packed with introductory album deals!

You can be homeless, wanting CDs just for chapel "frisbee" breaks, using the soup kitchen's address as a joke, submitting the whole stupid card as a "Let's See How Personal They Really Are" experiment, and be accepted by the record club. Do you know *anyone* who was *ever* rejected by the dork-dipped debrained dungnuts at the record club? Do you? Of course you don't. They let cinder blocks join, for crying out loud! But *I was rejected*, and *I know* it has something to do with that Clifton Chenier deal; maybe that I wrote them a personal note threw a lugwrench into their corporate culture.

Anyway, that's why it's been a stretch since last issue. I've been staring into space, stunned. Listening to the same damn Clifton Chenier CD over and over again. ∎

AUGUST 19, 1998

INTERNAL 🎵 RHYME

NUMBER 26TH - THE ISSUE WITH WHICH YOU *DON'T* WANT TO LINE YOUR BIRD'S CAGE! ◆ MUSICMASTER, 5136 LYNDALE AVENUE. SO., MINNEAPOLIS, MN 55419

EXCLUSIVE INTERNAL RHYME SHOCKER

I KILLED MY CANARY!

one thought underlaps the next
scrapes it underneath with action lines
that turn into millipedes bolt into my mental cellar
it's 2 a.m. again
I can't rhyme moon if you put a pistol to my head
I can't get through the alphabet song without making up letters
whenever I cough there's a crash in the kitchen
whenever I blink the lights flicker

I'm used to being disoriented
                              lost
to seeing/learning from/even helping create unfamiliar backdrops
I can't sleep when I'm supposed to
or agree when I'm supposed to or salute when I'm supposed to
or write when I'm supposed to *or need to*

---

she chirps at me *you used to*
    bring me lettuce and
you used to change my water
    every day

---

        horizontal hold moves a fraction

nowadays I sigh a lot more than I used to
and whenever I realize that
I sigh again

I have no difficulty believing the Sphinx
was built by alien working stiffs who loved
the Bob Hope holiday shows
I am willing to accept that umbrella man (who
    was near the grassy knoll)
assassinated JFK and was either Gerald Ford or
    Jamie Farr
but I am *unable* to believe that most people
    don't get abstract art
it is 0200

it's 2 in the morning
whenever I breathe
there's a rustling in
my brain
(probably those
millipedes fluffing
up pillows)
whenever I sigh my

I can't correctly underline capitalize or position commas
whenever I yell I can feel the walls shrug
even if I scream bloody murder about big serious real evil
    roots of doom like
like inattentive clerks like using marketing
    buzzwords at home
like free things that you can't get with-
    out *buying* something
like moneymoneymoneyshit&envy
dear God *a treasure chest of gold* is
    money too

win the fucking lottery and die!

I turn on the desk lamp at 2 a.m.
which wakes up Howard the canary who mutters
let's start making noise in the middle of the night even though
    we know
that the faithful and might I add very cute and unlawfully
    imprisoned canary
has to get up at 5:30 a.m. for rehearsal
I put up with Howard's griping because
it took months to teach him all those words
and nearly two years how to mutter and
not just do that singsongy crap all the time
and if I strangle Ms. Get Up for Rehearsal over there
I just know my wife and kids
will think I did something bad   AS THE CANARY FLIES . . .

even though they love me they'd say stuff like
*how could you strangle a **canary**?*
(emphasizing the word canary like I hadn't noticed)
and even if I explain all that smartbeak muttering
they'd still think I should've hired a mynah or a parrot to
    mediate

when chirp really does come to strangle
I may have to hire a hitman to off the canary for me
though if he's taking out a canary
he's probably called something else

at a neighborhood festival I run into a poet whose work I respect
I tell him I really enjoy his poetry that it's genuine
he has heard me read some poems as well and says he enjoys
    them too
I *think* everything is still sincere that he means his compliment
I mean *I really mean mine* and I tell him so and underscore that
he says that he *truly* enjoys what he's heard and seen of my work
honestly
and we both shuffle like idiots for a second then
as he heads off with a wave he adds
I'd like to see some of your *serious* work sometime

all my work is serious I'm being serious now
I'm pleased people appreciate the humor in my pieces
and I admit to wordgames I compound with shtick but

if I were a movie villain I'd twist her beak off

I am always serious I am clinically serious
I am as serious as an unmedicated dying nun as a meditating
    brickwall
I am as serious as a final exam in humor at the hospice
I only look for laughs to find my way
I wonder if this poet *whose work I used to respect*
would still like my funny poems if he knew
they weren't really funny at all

it's 2 a.m. and I can't seem to write anything funny
about how serious my poems are
so I just type groups of letters then look for words in them
like puzzles to which there are rarely solutions
Howard is muttering as many uninventive complaints
as her tater-tot sized skull can assemble

it occurs to me that in murdering Howard
I would not only get rid of all her snotty peeping
but I would also be doing something so murderously serious
that I'd be taken more seriously

if I killed my canary
the poet I ran into at the neighborhood festival
would understand that - though much of my writing seems like it

was produced by an assembly worker at a 1950s Xray Specs
Factory - **I am always serious**

I approach Howard's cage flexing my fingers
wondering can canary be prepared like rock Cornish game hen
or should I just pop out the eyes put them in with the
    peppercorns
and let Elly the dog eat the body or
should I bury Howard in a single-serving-sized cereal box

cracking my knuckles I wonder how I'll look on the tv news
when they haul me off to the hoosegow
alternating shots of my serious face
with shots of a stretcher hauling away a tiny clump of feathers

Howard's muttering turns into sweet nostalgic pleas
she says *remember how we used to talk?*
you'd call me pretty bird and we'd whistle back and forth
you'd say pretty birdie to me a hundred times in row
every day until I called you pretty birdie too

I ignore Howard's touching words reach into her cage
and because fluttering like a frightened canary
isn't the smartest defense on the planet
I grab her without difficulty
bring her head-peeking-out-of-my-fist near my face
her heartbeat is a drumroll
her little eyes are sticking so far out they look like
antennae

she chirps at me *you used to bring me lettuce and*
you used to change my water every day
then you got into that writing racket
that artsiheaded tortured soul business you know
that artsier-than-holy-fucking-smokes
it was just before I learned to talk and mutter
whenever I tried to talk to you about it warn you about it
you just smiled at me and whistled back

if I were a movie villain I'd twist her beak off
and shout *you insipid wad of cat bait!*
but I'm *not* a movie villain

CONTINUED THOUGH I PROBABLY SHOULD'VE FINISHED BY NOW

WE ARE PRODUCTS OF WORDS, EVEN THOSE WE DON'T KNOW

EMMA & ELMER

Emma (*Hinckley, MN, 1998*)

In a rundown flea market, there's lots of discount store crap, way too many poorly crafted craft items that you stake into your lawn to scare the neighbors. Dealers sit at the edge of their stalls drinking pop or beer, watching portable TVs, assembling another turquoise belt buckle even though they already display five hundred dusty ones, talking to one another about new RVs and trips to Vegas.

Half of one guy's space is a table of items that are ten cents each: broken knickknacks, chewed-on plastic drinking cups, an Accounting Basics textbook from the fifties. I could buy half of this display for three bucks, yet the guy is eating take-out that costs five.

There's not a customer in sight. Maybe these dealers do a ton of business on weekends or wholesale a lot of used ice cube trays to the Pentagon. Maybe they're independently wealthy.

Most of them are retirement age. Is this their sunset melody, their dream of paradise? To sell baseball caps embroidered with *I'm Horny*? To buy stuff at garage sales and mark it way, way up? To sit and watch people like me smugly play out our own holy browsing orders, our own odd and disturbing rites of shopping (kick the cantaloupe, sniff the tire, look at a first New Directions edition of Henry Miller's *The Time of the Assassins* in perfect condition and ask the dealer, who doesn't know

---

I KILLED MY CANARY CONT.

and I don't think Howard is insipid
and cat bait isn't even sold in wads anymore
in fact I can hear the music welling up
the credits getting close
so I say *you think my writing is a wrong thing to do?*

no Howard answers *that's not the problem*
it's just that you do it too seriously
what did you say I ask and she repeats
it's just that you do it too seriously

four months later Howard is at a private canary spa in Monaco
to have her toenails trimmed her beak pierced
her tailfeathers narrowed
all the while muttering at the spa staff
I run into the poet at a party
and tell him I murdered my canary because how the hell will he
   know
he smiles and asks
are you kidding me? you really killed your canary?
sure did I answer
the poet nods *I killed mine too*
a year ago
the damn thing only stared and snarled   ∎

Miller Henry from Miller beer, if this book is any good, to *pretend* you're just getting it because it might be good reading and not because it's rare).

I finally find a booth that's full of good stuff - a 1950s hula girl figurine that hulas like a banshee when she sits atop a running washing machine, shelves packed with smalltime advertising trinkets: a toilet bowl keychain, an anvil-shaped paperweight.

Half of one guy's space is a table of items that are ten cents each: broken knickknacks, chewed-on plastic drinking cups, an Accounting Basics textbook from the fifties.

The dealer is an old woman wedged into lawnchair. She has no pop, no radio, no book, no television, no Mt. Rushmore ashtrays to price; she just sits motionless behind a table of merchandise. Doesn't even glance at me.

I inspect a 1964-65 World's Fair card game, flip through a shoebox full of postcards, look through a crate of maps for an old one of Grand Marais. The old woman doesn't say a word, she doesn't move, the lawnchair doesn't crunch or creak at all. She is in a state of ultimate relaxation or boredom or enlightenment, or in one of the more common mixes.

I look around her space for ten minutes, ultimately not buying a thing. She does have a few things I would ordinarily purchase, if only out of flea market routine or kneejerk acquisition. I would ordinarily get the card game and a few postcards, but my buying urge was fully sedated by the awfulness of the previous booths. To appear gracious, I browse a bit more while leaving. The old woman doesn't notice.

The dealer in the next stall calls over to the old woman. "Emma," she asks, "Are you going to work all summer?"

Elmer (*Kenyon, MN, 1998*)

We're at a barbecue at our friends' house in the country, a classic old rural residence with gables and a yard with additional acreage just for the hell of it. The house is bedecked with artworks and knickknackery so nontraditional the townsfolk might someday storm the place with pitchforks and prayers (if the storming doesn't conflict with their regularly scheduled surgeries and poker games aboard alien conversion vans).

Don introduces us to his nearest neighbors, Elmer and Joanne, retired dairy farmers. They still have some cows and crops and bizarre ideas about waking up pre-dawn to make sure the crickets don't knock off early. Elmer looks an old 75 and Joanne a little old-younger.

Joanne heads for chips and dip and womenfolk and I'm

HURRY ALONG, YOU'RE SLOWING ELMER DOWN

LEAVE YOUR MIND AT THE GATE

MY DEEPEST FEARS *(No. 1 in a Series of 12,630)*

I'm afraid they're going to ask me my number and I won't know it. I'll tell them I'd be able to enter or recite it automatically, under ordinary circumstances, but that I can't remember it in a regular/conscious number-by-number way. That I'm not good with memorizing numbers (I am, however, good at math), that I transpose them so often and effortlessly that I have to think aloud when dating a check and I have to do the admittedly easy math of calculating my age based on being born in 1950 whenever someone asks how old I am. It's not that I don't know; I'm just not good with dates and phone numbers and ages and zip codes and extensions and addresses. I consult with three experts to be certain I correctly number each issue of *Internal Rhyme*.

Whenever someone recites or enters their social security number without looking at their social security card, I feel like I'm witnessing a small miracle. I'm not kidding; I know that given the right training and mindset I can parachute jump, rock climb, stay locked in a sensory deprivation chamber for one hundred hours, learn how to edit rambles like this one away, wrestle alligators, navigate a submarine, even develop a lawn that mows itself; but I cannot fathom learning my social security number in a recallable-on-call way. I like to think *What a puny gnat to store in the brain!* but I know I'm being envious and sour.

Since *everybody* knows their stupid damn number, my *not knowing* mine is going to be taken as suspicious, as criminal. They'll think I'm lying, attempting to impersonate a more-fortunately-numbered soul. They'll ask me where I was when Howard the canary was strangled and I'll answer honestly that I was helping my Mother pack up for a move; they'll ask where my mother lives and my inability to recite her address or phone number will be taken as the damning confession it isn't. ∎

DO THE HUSTLE!

Want to write better than *gooder*? Want to know how to wrestle the language into a draw that's honorable?

Want to fell butter abet your writing and your typos?

Want to hear my crackpot theories about writing stuff that's invigorating for you and entertaining/inspiring for your readers?

Then attend my next **Writers Workshop** on Saturday, **September 26**, 9:30 a.m. to 3 p.m. at Edina Community Center. It costs several hundred dollars, but is worth an even greater amount you may not want to spend on hearing me rail and remind and recommend and re-examine, yet again, all kinds of ideas and hints and instructions for writing more, louder, friendlier, smarter, accessible poetry and prose. Okay, it doesn't really cost several hundred dollars (and I'm not really a 20-year-old blonde bombshell) (I'm a 22-year-old blonde bombshell). It only costs $34. Register by calling Edina Community Education at 612-928-2600 and ask for whatever other details you want (e.g. does the room have a refrigerator for beer?, is it okay if I bring my two-year-old who generally only cries every ten minutes and who is so sweet she likes to shout and laugh at everybody?, can you send me a map?, will this class cover how to write a play about the history of broom making for the senior center?, do you guys offer any classes on flirting in church?).

ALSO - I'll be reading at Barnes & Noble Galleria (3225 West 69th Street, Edina) on Friday, October 9, 7:30 p.m., with my friend **Tom Cook**, a columnist, movie extra, and past president of the Ames Brothers Fan Club. No charge but the psychic toll!

EDNA & ELMER CONTINUED

suddenly alone with Elmer. I want to ask him how many times he's had his limbs yanked off by farm machinery and reattached by horse doctors. Or if beets are supposed to taste so awful. But since neither question seems phraseable in a friendly-stranger way, I go with the obvious -

"I hear you're a dairy farmer."

Elmer smiles and responds, "When they landed in Normandy, we were moving German prisoners around Scotland."

Encountering a performing surrealist so far out in the country disarms me for a moment. So I playback my comment in my head to see how much it sounds like 'Where were you when they landed in Normandy?' I nod at Elmer because I don't know what to say, but I can see that he takes my nodding to mean *no kidding, that's fascinating, tell me more.*

"I was in Algeria too," he adds. "I didn't know a word of French or Arabic, but I enjoyed the people."

SEPTEMBER 30, 1998

INTERNAL ✦ RHYME

NUMBER 27TH - THE SMALL SMALL SMALLPRESS WITH ONLY RELATIVELY BIG IDEAS ◆ MUSICMASTER, 5136 LYNDALE AVENUE. SO., MINNEAPOLIS, MN 55419

CARE BEARS HALLOWEEN

We've been renting videos from our neighborhood *mr. movies* since they opened a number of years ago; we've been members so long that it was *years ago* that a clerk there told us we had just rented our 500th film.

When *mr. movies* first opened, they drew the bulk (*if not all*) of their business from a competitor one block over because *mr. movies* was a spiffier looking store, with all the bells and fancy marketing effects of a new and enthusiastic franchise. Their competitor went under, leaving *mr. movies* as the only place to rent videos in this neighborhood (except for the really popular or really weird staples - *As Good As It Gets, Nude Fly Fishing,*

> *We are lathered and pummeled and enticed and regaled with customer service promises over and over again, everywhere we're Number One we're VIP we're Most Appreciated Hotshit entity, until we actually go to goddamn sorryass store.*

The Lion King, Real Aborted Convenience Store Hold-Ups - they carry at sort-of-nearby convenience stores).

As the years passed and too-far-away-to-walk-to competitors offered cheaper rates and deals, *mr. movies'* prices stayed pretty much the same; afterall, they had a captive audience. And while management occasionally hosted/promoted neighborhood gatherings (with, I admit, a sensitivity regarding neighborhood issues), they, for the most part, let the store enjoy its location advantage with prices rarely, or only belatedly, adjusted to bigger market math. Had Video Update or Blockhead or Wal-Movie been directly across the street, I'm sure that *mr. movies* — franchise directive or not — would've matched up prices sooner. Had a *No Membership Fee* shop been across the street, I'm sure that *mr. movies* would've matched the ante.

But there hasn't been so, to date, they *still* have an annual membership fee whereas most video outlets do not (to be fair, you *do get a dozen* rentals included with your annual fee - but what's the point of such a deal beyond locking you into a stretch of repeat business that, frankly, should instead be earned - via service, friendliness, price, etc.).

Overall, mr. movies has been an okay-enough store for us to have spent hundreds of dollars a year there, but once, I rented a movie from them that was so worn and dirty that, even though I had just cleaned my VCR the day before, I couldn't play it - it just blipped into blue. I told them that when I returned the movie, but they didn't offer a refund or a free rental. (In retrospect, I think that the two kids who were working when I explained the problem thought that I was complaining that the movie had been dirty as in dirty - you know - with anonymous acrobatic garter belts.)

Another time, the only time I'd ever returned a film late,* I paid a one-day penalty; no problem . . . hadn't I seen the same clerk say "we'll skip the late fee this time" to different customers on three earlier occasions. (Whether what they did on those occasions was according to or against store policy, was for friends or not, doesn't matter - I had seen the preferential treatment and understood that I was a differently-valued customer.**)

Man, am I ever getting long and unfunny. In rereading what I've written so far, I realize I'm no closer to writing the Great

RIGHT THIS WAY PLEASE . . .

---

*Naturally, in the course of writing (and, I admit, over-writing) this piece, I again failed to return a movie on time, making me now seem like the very sort of repeat offender who makes things like late fees necessary for the preservation of affordable commerce.

**Repeat that - *Differently Valued Customer*. I can spearhead the movement for a new protected class that includes average middleAmerican shmucks like me, who are lathered and pummeled and enticed and regaled with customer service promises over and over again, *everywhere* we're Number One we're VIP we're Most Appreciated Hotshit entity, until we actually go to goddamn sorryass store that sells customer service with the same fucking disregard for what it means as they hold for the genuinely good products that outshine outperform underprice their pathetic crappily-made overhyped mooned-by-Michael Jordan catnip. (Notice how companies always name/code/call valued customers with the exact same words used as supermarket brand or generic names? - Like Preferred Brand or Best Brand or Choice Brand or Preferred Idiots' Pick or Maybe Edible or Average MiddleAmerican Shmuck? - don't get me going on that.)

a lot of people who wouldn't know etiquette
if it kicked them in the ass after asking permission to kick them in
    the ass
ask me what it's like to be crazy
they usually put it this way they say
Hi Tom how are you?
but I know what they really want to know

there are differences between a crazy person and
the rest of the world for example
that *that* goes without saying to the rest of the world
a crazy person knows
that the rest of the world thinks that
a key difference is that crazy people don't know
what any of the key differences are

if a crazy person remembers
the time and temperature
of when he first cut a string of dollies from
an accordioned-up roll of aluminum foil
is he crazier still because of the deed
or because of remembering
or because of the time and temperature

a sleeping crazy person isn't really sleeping
he's in a napping dog's kind of dream state
wherein all the trials and triumphs trips and traps
are just part of getting table scraps or squirrels
or that one muscular moth that got away

(Moby Moth)

a crazy person not only talks to God
but talks to Him in a regular voice in public
like it's a walk home with a Drinking Buddy
the crazy person says
hey Almighty! did You see the tattoo on that blonde?
and God says
that was a birthmark I designed in 1970
He pauses before He adds

I made that blonde
and the crazy person says
that is so Goddamn unbelievable Man
I mean God I mean I'm sorry I said Goddamn oh Man
I mean God I am sorry again

a crazy person has no defense at all *but* the insanity defense
and the rest of the world holds even that against him
here's the difference

when a crazy person shows or performs
they're not done with it after an audience looks or
listens and applauds and off they go
because the time for the art is done
like with any other job or recreation
like at the end of a round of golf or a day of teaching [1]
the crazy person doesn't stop the show
they're never done with it
they turn it down enough to seem more normal
but they're never not working on their piece

like the rest of the world a crazy person knows that the time to quit
is when you're ahead when you're on top
but unlike the rest of the world
a crazy person never quits because he never knows when he's
    ahead
he never knows when he's where he's supposed to be
don't get me going on knowing when to leave well enough alone
because it's the crazy person *who's not well enough*
who's most often left alone for crying out loud

what the rest of the world really wants to know
is if I've imagined killing them

and how

or if I've also imagined how I'll slip up somewhere and get caught
and shackled and electrocuted and sent to hell and made to
    apologize
like a clumsy waiter to every damned soul at the barbecue
they say *Hi Tom how are you?*
but I know what they really want to know

the rest of the world is in on something
the rest of the world is overpaid and always on vacation
the rest of the world knows that being crazy is when you're not
    like them
oh yeah they try and accommodate you
they say there's room at the table for you
which is all well and good but they're the ones who own the table

NEXT PAGE AS THE CROW READS

LIFE IS TERRORISM

CARE BEARS HALLOWEEN CONTINUED

American Novel than I was in 1975 when, at least, I dealt with themes considerably larger than which retailers have the dorkiest or most unsalespersonlike staff! Yep, I used to write about which retail outlets had the best-looking cashiers.

But I'm older now. I'm not crankier, mind you - I've always been this cranky. When I was a teenager, Uncle Arthur called me Pout Face, which made me feel *really* cranky. That wasn't very nice; Uncle Arthur is dead now and I'm not walking around calling him Stoic Face. But I am older and when you get older you get preoccupied with cautious details like how (or if) salespeople discuss the weather, if Willard Scott will mention that your cat just turned twenty, how much (or even *which*) medication you take, or if somebody took your keys (like anybody is really going to break into your home and find *something they'd want to steal* - like doilies or a copy of Rolling Stone's *Assisted Rocking Monthly* or canary cage gravel).

So here I am, writing like I'm getting paid, following tangents 'til they fall off the page, but secure in the knowledge that as long and unfunny as I may be, some younger and better writers are even longer and less funny. Now back to our story, where I'll try to get to (or find) the point . . .

Recently, a neighborhood movie theater was closed for good; there was a half-hearted effort by long-time nostalgia-panging neighbors to save it somehow, but, apart from its great marquee (which *is* going to be kept), it was a shoddy theater with shoddy decor and sticky floors and sullen-teen-staffing and flea-thick bathrooms, so the effort seemed gratuitous and clingy and it went down the tubes with the theater. The proposed redevelopment is for a few retail outlets with the inclusion of - you guessed it - one of those other video operations with big deal lures (All Ernest movies: 37 nights for 37 cents! Every Tuesday We Rent *Your* Homemade Tapes for a Buck!). Just around the corner from *mr. movies*.

Already there's neighborhood buzz and copy in local papers about how we don't need another video rental outlet (I agree fully; I'd rather see a bakery or a bookstore or a mini antique mall or a toy store or, frankly, *any* nonchain thing), and that we already have a longtime good neighbor video rental shop in *mr. movies* (and I sort of agree with that too because, well, I'd rather have a bakery or a bookstore or a mini antique mall or a toy store; no, when I say *mini antique mall* I don't mean a mall of tiny antiques, I mean a little subdivided store of all that great stuff that somehow survives our over-callused hands and our rough ideas about what we should save as historical documentation; to me, the longtime neighbor point is a bit tainted because, remember, back when *mr. movies* opened, it was with a comparable lack of regard for that other video store - just one block over - that *they* knocked out of business).

All Ernest movies: 37 nights for 37 cents! Every Tuesday We Rent Your Homemade Tapes for a Buck!

DON'T GIVE UP

THE BROKEN ALARM CONTINUED

they're the ones who run the kitchen
they're the ones who tuck the napkin in your collar
they say *Hi Tom how are you?*
but I know what they really want to know
they want to know about my relationship with God
but you can bet if I start telling them
some of the things God and I have done together
I can tell you that all of a sudden it's table *non-Invitus*
not music and mashed potatoes anymore

my idea of time management is death

I believe that upon dying we fly around like Casper
until we have to remove our sheets for the laundry
then we fly around like a naked Casper
until we get kicked out of the laundromat for being naked
at which point we board a city bus (itself naked and screaming)
which takes us to Limbo
but a really distressed part of limbo where rodents wear leather
     halos
and you can buy organic crack

and you get to live in a little apartment down there with two
     roommates
for as long as it takes for you see them for who they really are
which is especially difficult because they look like naked Caspers
     too
and they're so busy trying to figure out how to see you as you
     really are
that all conversation is cloaked with too much caution and too
     much quiet to help
during the day you row the oars for your old Drinking Buddy God
and at night you all stare at one another or at the tv
and most often someone asks *do you mind if I change the station?*
and the other two quickly and politely and with hope say
     oh no not at all please do
but on the rare occasion when there's a taste of breakthrough
     in the air
when the resignation ebbs a little bit
they say *Hi Tom how are you?*
but I'm not going to tell them

YOU DON'T NEED SIGNS TO GET TO THE APOCALYPSE

CARE BEARS HALLOWEEN CONTINUED

Clearly, if a new video rental joint opens, *mr. movies* will have to compete with a frenzy just to stay afloat. Frankly, I don't have a problem with that. (*Important aside:* Nearly all business people - especially successful or comfortable ones - work up a good patriotic froth when extolling the virtues of competition while simultaneously exempting from the formula and/ or deriding any competition they themselves might have). It's about time *mr. movies* came up with clever ways to really compete, to *earn* customer loyalty not just with inventive pricing/service but with customer-conscious counter help.

The same two young adults have been working evening shift for nearly every night we've come in over the past year. We see them more often than lots of workworld-related people we recognize and call by name. They both look at us, recognize us, occasionally utter hello. We put our movies on the counter and one of them asks for our phone number, with which they call up on their computer our rental history from the FBI's Who-Watches-Leftist-Directors log. Then we're asked for our name to doublecheck we're not goofing about the phone number or, worse, lying about the phone number so we can pull the major heist of a copy of *Care Bears Halloween*.

While I appreciate this demonstration of a security ritual no doubt in place to also protect my good video-renting name from evil forces, I also think it's about time that these two young adults remember our last name. I don't expect them to remember our phone number, but, *after at least one hundred name/face encounters with them*, I do think it would be nice of them, cordial of them, customer-attuned of them to remember our last name. Two months back I politely told them as much, bantered with them a bit, took the initiative *to grow* the business/ customer partnership (as all those bullshitting marketeers like to say). And for several weeks it worked - we'd put our movies on the counter, say our phone number and - *Ah! Magical Customer Service Moment* they wouldn't ask for our last name. But last week, same two employees behind the counter, it all soured - we made eye contact and had an efficient little phone number exchange and were then asked for our last name. And again the next night and the next.

When the new video store opens just around the corner, I'll probably sign up as a member there too - alternate our rentals. See if the long-haul help at the new store remembers me after I go *there* one hundred times in one year.

Will *mr. movies* continue to play the good-neighbor-card to keep customers (which alone won't work) or will they spraypaint my last name in big letters on their front window so I'll quit whining?

I've no clever summary to this piece. Hell, I'm just typing to avoid mowing the lawn. But I do wonder what will happen when the new store opens. Will there be a great price war? - *All Movies One Buck* turning into *All Movies Five Nights One Buck* escalating to *Five Movies Five Nights One Buck* leading to, of course, everybody cutting the margins so thin that they both go out of business . . .

leaving spaces for *both* a bakery and a mini antique mall! ■

ADVERTISING SUPPLEMENT

I drew the coloring book **YIKES! Stuff Everywhere** over a two-week period, between the hours of midnight and 2 a.m. (the timeslot now dedicated to Internal Rhyme). It's a surrealistic, logo-free limited edition that will delight or scare your children. *$2.00 each; 3 for $5.00.*

I still have boxes of my 60some different **Postcard Designs** that sold in a few dozen shops throughout the 80s; I still sell through a handful of outlets (especially my Minnesota map, the famous coffee-swilling dog, and Hanging of Pollyanna), and most designs can be purchased at the Art Underground (see back page adlet). All funny/deranged, 4-1/4 x 5-1/2, b&w. 20 different for below retail price of *$4.00/set; 50 different for $7.50.*

3rd printing of brutal/goofy **spoof of the Minnesota Multiphasic Personality Inventory** - an incorrect reworking of the screwball profiling tool that's almost as funny as the real thing; great item to reward or slam any psych or psycho-babble buff. *$2.00 each; 3 for $5.00.*

I drew the coloring book **YIKES! Stuff Everywhere** over a two-week period, between the hours of midnight and 2 a.m. (the timeslot now dedicated to Internal Rhyme). It's a surrealistic, logo-free limited edition that will delight or scare your children. *$2.00 each; 3 for $5.00.*

A mere $2.00 will get you a copy of Charles Fowler's *A Visit to the Cleaners* (see issue 25 for my official bigtime endorsement of and hustle for this excellent poet's work)!

Send check or money order to Musical Comedy Editions, 5136 Lyndale Ave. So., Minneapolis, MN 55419 and throw in a few bucks for shipping (no shipping or handling if you pick-up from me or via Art Underground/Anodyne. My phone: (612) 825-4101. Offbeat free stuff with all orders. ■

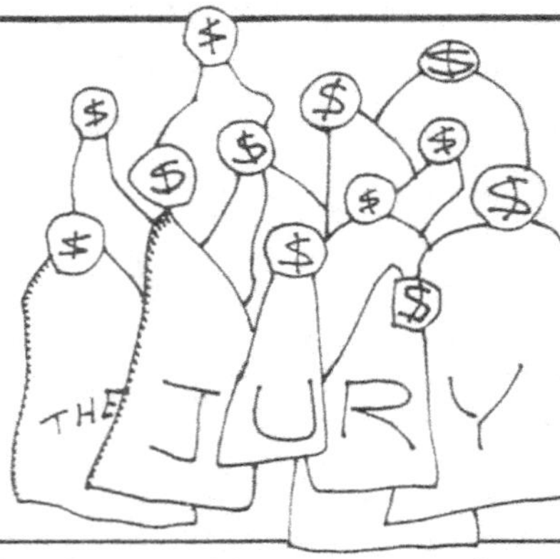

SUPPORT LOCAL ARTISTS AND CRAFTY SOULS BY SHOPPING AT THE ONLY UNDERGROUND EMPORIUM THAT CARRIES A LOT OF OFFBEAT INVENTIVE ENGAGING GIFT ITEMS AS WELL AS COOL ART THAT NO WAY IN HELL IS EVER GOING TO SELL

The Art Underground ♦ 827-5590

HOME TO THE DISENFRANCHISED & PURVEYOR OF INTERNAL RHYME

809 West 50th (enter via The Malt Shop then descend), South Minneapolis

A COMMUNITY CAN'T BE CREATED WITH DONATIONS OR DUES

OCTOBER 20, 1998

INTERNAL ❈ RHYME

28 - HALLOWEEN SPECIAL FEATURING A SPOOKY INSURANCE AGENT **AND** GOD'S SPOKESMAN ◆ MUSICMASTER, 5136 LYNDALE AVENUE, SO., MINNEAPOLIS, MN 55419

THE HOT(!) BARE EXERCISERESS

We receive a packet of manifestoes/essays (opinions!/ warnings!) at our office from a *Christian Consultant for Correct English-Language Bible Translation/ Semantics and Modesty/Decency Date/Mate Acquisition / Family and Social-Issues Justice* (I hope they answer their phones with that). Since the manifestoes are all far too insane or differently insane for our office to even process let alone route or file, they're given to me. The same way Betty Crocker points are passed along to Al for his daughter's fundraiser to send her junior high school band to Holland (while not far enough away to send any junior high school band, gerbil mascot or not, I help out nonetheless), the crazy mail is passed along to me. Serious-looking miscellaneous mail goes to serious-looking miscellaneous people; I get the *Put Your Logo on a Sweatband* crap. Deals for copiers and thumbtacks-with-shock-absorbers go to Admiral So & So, but mail that's about funny stuff like eternal damnation comes to me.

The absolute phenomena of discriminating with non-equality ... and legitimate, understandable, acceptable discrimination, is engrained in nature - and to disregard or deny such results in immediate, certain, painful disability and death.

While most such Scripture-Syndrome rants are easily dismissed as mental God-Gone-Goofy rashes, these tracts impress me as not just smarter-than-most, but funnier-than-most.

What follows is one of these all-extraordinary concoctions of a someone who sounds just an inch away from being a comedian or an assassin for God or a neighbor who doesn't answer his door on Halloween even though you know he's in there. It doesn't sound like the sort of guidance you should get from a *Consultant*, Christian or Otherwise, but hey, any written piece that contains the hyphenated words *bare-exerciseress-cereal-box-photo, lower-unit,* and *womb-human* should be respected.

Here it is . . .

THE NON-REALISTIC IMPRACTICALITY OF ALL-IN-CLUSIVE NON-DISCRIMINATION & EVERYTHING/EVERYONE IS EQUAL MENTALITY

BEGINNING REFERENCE:
Ecclesiastes 3:1,3,8 = For everything there is a season - a time to

kill, a time to heal; a time to tear down, a time to build up; a time for love, a time for hate; a time for war, and a time for peace . . ."

Assume one wakens up on Sunday morning to an indiscriminate sun rising indiscriminately on everything vsible.

The prudent put on pony tail & long sleeves (per RSV's II Samuel 13:18 and Song of Solomon 7:5), slacks & socks (per KJV's Isaiah 47:2-3 and Jeremiah 2:25)...while perverts luridly and indiscriminately prepare to parade parts of their pollutive carcasses in sexually-harassing competition for egocentric attention and defilement: exposing arms, legs with shorts, and sandals baring toes.

Unless one is a corrupt mindless-fool atheist (as described in Psalm 14:1) wrongly discriminating against sanity but indiscriminately for irrationality, he or she chooses to attend a (hopefully-nonsexist/no-female-speakers) Protestant and not Catholic church, thus Scripturally discriminating for the former but against cultic purgatorial/praying-to-the-dead other options including but not limited to anti-Christian judaism, JVs, Buddhist, Islamic, along with their blasphemously-false "deities."

One discriminates with biased prejudice against eating (dead)-animal meat, but weakens himself with ingesting only herbs (a situation described in Romans 14:2). Another eats rye, not white bread - with his white not black spouse - revealing double-barrelled discrimination for one and against the other, along with Post Grape Nuts instead of Kelloggs Special K, thus discriminating not only for Post Foods but against bare-exerciseress-cereal-box-photo Kelloggs cereals.   ADVANCE TO NEXT AVAILABLE TELLER

SID THE SMILE

WARNING! THIS IS A SOMEWHAT TENDER PIECE ABOUT TELLING MY DAUGHTER A STORY! LUCKILY, I'M NOT REALLY GOOD AT THIS SORT OF PIECE, SO I DO LAPSE INTO MY IRREGULAR TANGENTS.

Once upon a big bright Hollywood star
there lived a broad and boisterous smile
a brilliantly beer-spackled smile
named Sid
Daddy that's not right interrupts Elaina
Once upon a time there was a princess named Elaina!
that's how the story goes
right I nod my brain
picturing Sid the Smile as a drag queen
well a drag princess to be more exact

> *yes there was a princess named Elaina*
> *she was charitable and wise*
> *and had a bellybutton named Thunderdunken*

Daddy that's not right interrupts Elaina
she was charitable and wise
and she was also very beautiful
I nod and add *as beautiful as a pear in pearls*
no Daddy as beautiful as sunsets

> *ah yes* I agree *as beautiful as Sid the Sunset*
> *the smiling sunset*

picturing Sid as a smiley button
the kind with blackline smile and two simple eyes
but this Sid one is winking
the one eye a smaller inverted version of
the mouth sort of a smiley-winky button
I continue the story

> *one day Elaina planted tinsel seeds*
> *on her antique Christmas boat*
> *which years ago had belonged to Leonardo Alva Cliff*
> *inventor of rocks*

Daddy that's not right laughs Elaina
Sid the Smile invented rocks

> Elaina I say seriously *you're supposed to say*
> *and Princess Elaina trimmed her Christmas tree*
> *with an ornament for every person in her kingdom*

Elaina yells gadzooks Daddy
was there one for the baker?

> *yes* I reply

and one for the faker?

> *yup* I agree

one for the crier?

you know it sez me
and right along with Elaina I say
even an uneven one for Bill the Crazy Liar
that's right declares Elaina
he must be an insurance agent right Daddy?
that's right my wise princess

> *that's how the story goes more or less*
> *an insurance agent always shows up*
> *even in the middle of the literary outback*
> *in the thick of surrealistic pork vine*
> *to make any plot more sinister more bleak*
> *my god you can't breathe nowadays*
> *without an insurance agent telling you how much of your*
> *inhalation is risk which left unpaid for*
> *will lead to the economic ruin of*
> *your children and their children and the pets of their*
> *friends*
> *I swear you go into McDonald's nowadays*
> *and they don't ask if you want fries anymore they ask*
> *would you like extra coverage with that*

Elaina stares at me like I'm juggling
but poorly not every word I tell her sticks like gadzooks
and I'm not sure where I am in the story really
because whenever Elaina says insurance agent
I go off on a different binge
so I reel things back in saying

> *well that's how the story goes right honey?*

Elaina answers
I know how the story goes
I've heard it enough

a poem for Elaina by musicmaster

NOTHING IS OUT OF THE WAY EXCEPT FOR SANITY

One drinks mountain-grown Folgers but discriminates against Hills Brothers as a matter of habit or personal taste . . . thus (for the moment) also discriminating against the use of tea and hot chocolate (dissolving profits to Lipton and Swiss Miss). One brushes his teeth with Colgate, thus discriminates for the aforementioned and against Crest, for the time being. One uses Arrid deodorant instead of Mennen, thus discriminating for the former and against the latter, along with avoiding all others.

I "won't mention" (or WILL I?) discriminatorily-selective choice for and non-choice (even anti-choice) against different toilet-tissue brands to tidy up between the lower-unit bulges.

After lunch at discriminatorily-subsidized Burger King instead of discriminatorily-boycotted Dennys (plus Perkins and McDonalds) . . . or whatever other choice, one has HIDDEN sex (discriminating against public view) with one's OWN (and NO one ELSE'S) narrowly-chosen-and-retained spouse, thus discriminating FOR one PARTICULAR person while exclusionarily rejecting all others among the millions available, including against homosexuals espousing the ridiculous lying murky myth of million-year/mutation evolution (study Genesis chapters 1 and 2, plus RSV's Job 11:12).

> *If, someday, I manage to crank out my Big Book (WILL THIS POLLUTIVE CARCASS?), there's at least one potential reader who won't mind all the asides and subplots and sub-asides.*

One dies and leaves his legacy (non-selfishly, by the way) to his own offspring (obviously himself having non-conditionally and permanently discriminated against abortionist murderers a long time ago per Luke 1:36 & 41 and Luke 2:16 defining the non-born womb-human as a "babe" not fetus.

God the Judge then discriminates for the righteous by rewarding them with heaven, but against the wicked by heaving them into and holing them forever down inside hell (Revelation 20:10,15).

So in summary, CAN one buy ALL the waiting-to-be-picked-and-purchased products in the clothing, drug, hardware, etc. stores . . . ALL equally available . . . with non-discriminatory indiscrimination? NO way!

The absolute phenomena of discriminating with non-equality . . . and legitimate, understandable, acceptable discrimination, is engrained in nature - and to disregard or deny such results in immediate, certain, painful disability and death. There is - ultimately - NO place or even "equal opportunity" for indiscriminate non-discrimination nor all-inclusive diversity resulting in acceptance of EVERYTHING - let alone ALL at ONCE! THAT'S the way the Creator constructed the Universe and all entities therein. Everything is DISTINCT and SEPARATE (consequebtially quite exquisite, gorgeous and enjoyable) - rather than it all merely being a grey glob of non-definable obscurity.

ENDING REFERENCE:

I Kings 18:21 = "Choose you this day whom you will serve: If the LORD be God follow Him . . . but if Ball, then follow him . . ."

Matthew 6:24 & Luke 16:13 = "No one can serve two masters: Either he will hate the one and love the other, or he will be devoted to one and despise the other."

(END)

Phew! A bit more amazing than the usual God-endorsed argumentative prose, no?

I especially like three things about the piece:

1. It fills a nice chunk of *Internal Rhyme* space that, now, I don't have to fill. And I admit to discriminatorily selecting IT as worthy of inclusion instead of something else – say some purgatorial BARE-TOED harlot's poem about Special K.

2. The author, whoever it might be (and indeed he/she might be anyone! - well, maybe not a black homosexual or a civil rights activist or a Kelloggs cereal box designer), *sort writes like I do!*, with parenthetical whatnotting and tangents more like thrill rides than like explanations. Certainly this scares me, but it also reassures me that if, someday, I manage to crank out my Big Book (WILL THIS POLLUTIVE CARCASS?), there's at least one potential reader who won't mind all the asides and subplots and sub-asides. I was going to send the author/consultant a copy of this piece in *Internal Rhyme* (maybe with a special *Eternal Rhyme* banner), but then I realized he'd probably respond. That he'd damn me (with discrimination and CAPITAL LETTERS!). That he'd write a new essay about Freedom of Press/Speech not being for those enslaved by million-year/mutation evolution of murky, blasphemously-false lower-unit irrationality.

CONTINUED ON BACK PAGE

OPEN MIKE!

Mark your calendar and dust off your bongos! The Twin Cities' Best Open Mike is the first Friday of every month (at about 8 p.m.) at the Twin Cities' Best Coffee House - Anodyne, 43rd & Nicollet, Minneapolis (824-4300). *Internal Rhyme* mailboy Tom Cassidy is your host!

Join us on November 6th for Real Life Must-See Anti-TV!

IT'S NICE THAT LIFE COMES WITH DECORATIONS

3. The writer's jazzy-preacher cadence gets stuttery by the mere typing of such lines *as exposing arms, legs with shorts and sandals baring toes* and *one has hidden sex (discriminating against public view)* and *Swiss Miss*. It seems that this writer gets flustered, DISTRACTED, seduced into getting HOT & SINFUL from the mere concocting of elaborately-veiled Dirty Words! Check out this passage from another one of the manifestoes received:

> Is there (realistically and honestly) reluctant and regrettable but invariably substitutionary covert (or even overt and openly-admitted) indulgence in porno poison by the sexually starved, and/or gazing at and lusting over (with semen-saturated underwear) shapely and sensuous young-adult birthsuit-nude danceresses in strip bars and lounges – inciting inconsequential streetwalker and/or massage/escort prostitution to varying degrees and types?

See? For me, *strip bar* would have been enough for referring to where danceresses dance; but for this guy, it takes the idea of a strip bar to mandate the heightened erotic content of strip lounge, you know, the classier joint. What the hell does *semen-saturated underwear* have to do with anything but this author's belief/experience that gazing/lusting is so profoundly gratifying that it make one uncontrollably orgasmic? This guy is ten times more deviant/lustful than the average lech and ten times more likely to be inspired to COMMIT SINFUL SUBSTITUTIONARY INDULGENCES! Charles Bukowski gets God! And why not? The perverts are always in greater need. ∎

miscEllanEous

■ There's a new television commercial for GM trucks which features the vehicles in a dark, docu-tainment about a house burning down. The flames eerily become the illumination for selling the truck's *swanky* interior. Have you seen this? I guess the image push here is for a tough vehicle, not just tough enough for illegal dune racing or ignoring speedbumps, but tough enough to cope with tragedy. I salute the great marketing crackpot behind this (and especially the selling of this to some wet-palmed don't-wanna-screw-ups at GM!) because it achieves the rare, deliberate connecting of a logo with despair, darkness, conflagration, as well as those spiffy cushioned seats. The final shot has a GM truck in a dark, bleak, post-fire nowhere, looking like the last-thing-left-standing. The whole mini-movie is about something more tragic than triumphant, so I'm gonna buy me a Ford truck because the commercials feature daylight and kids singing along with the music.

> *It achieves the rare, deliberate connecting of a logo with despair, darkness, conflagration, as well as those spiffy cushioned seats.*

■ Walgreen's is America's sharpest demonstration of chaos theory; its coupons are the most reliably inconsistent with how prices will actually scan; its aisles present merchandise in displays, patterns and adjacencies so illogical that surrealism weeps with envy.

I love Walgreen's; visiting Walgreen's is like stepping into a fingerpainting by a drunken Magritte. Their weekly Sunday paper insert provides deals and coupons so similar to previous deals and coupons, and for such hyper-regular things (batteries, Mandarin oranges, glue sticks) that it effectively gives the reader (browser) a type of Virtual Déjà vu that isn't cryptic, eerie, insightful or useful – it just seems like a rerun of a local cable show about wrapping paper. I flip through their insert at least twice to be sure I'm not overlooking a coupon for thumbtacks or, of course, Mandarin oranges.

Walgreen's current insert, however, doesn't anesthetize me properly, because it contains a promotion that slaps me awake. It's a small ad for a "Photo Restoration Service - **$34.99** - Compare elsewhere for up to $100!" Wow! that is a deal; but look what the rest of the ad says - "Old cherished photos can now be restored! We will create new prints of your old, faded and torn pictures . . . Original print returned." Give me a break! **Restored** does not mean **make-copy-of.** A restored classic car, for example, isn't, a new copy of a classic car. Check the *American Heritage Dictionary* and their definition for restored reads "*1. To bring back into existence or use; re-establish: restore law and order. 2. To bring back to a previous, normal condition: restore a building.*" Restored is not a hard word to know - certainly a copywriter skilled enough to be hacking text for the mass market knows what it means. **That part** (that knowing, willful, shameless incorrect usage part) being the part that really irks me about copy like this - it's a deliberate redefining of something so that, in fact, *apples **can be** compared to oranges* to contrive value that simple doesn't exist ("Compare elsewhere for up to $100!" Elsewhere you get a restored photo; here you get a cleaned-up copy of a photo and your original back in the same, sad, deteriorating condition that prompted your interest in preserving it). Argh!

And yet, because it is Walgreen's, I can't rail about it quite as much as if Dayton's or Wal-Mart or even Bob's Tatoo Parlor did it, because, inexplicably, the flagrant misusage seems to fit Walgreen's differently - like a new generic language brand that's cheaper but, roughly - very roughly - as good as the real thing. ∎

INTERNAL RHYME

DECEMBER 4, 1998

THE 30th ISSUE OF A NEWSLETTER WITH NO SPECIAL HOLIDAY SUBSCRIPTION PROMOTIONS ● MUSICMASTER, 5136 LYNDALE AVENUE. SO., MINNEAPOLIS, MN 55419

WATER POLO

Dawn says she doesn't prefer blue-colored Dawn dishwashing detergent because of its eerily familiar name, but because it's good dish soap, unafraid of water and dirt and hands in the throes of choredom. Other brands, some with tougher-sounding names (I can't think of any right off the bat, but names like *Spike, Begone!, ThrillKill*), don't clean as well as Dawn.

I found this out because I once brought home a yellow-colored dishwashing detergent (I can't think of its name right now, but it was, I remember, a less fresh-sounding name, a nonscrubbing kind of name like *Dew* or *Relax* or *Fresh*). I got it from Walgreen's because I had a coupon; regularly $2.19 it was only one dollar and forty-nine cents if I also bought a can of Mandarin Oranges and a six-pack of Snickers-flavored Water, and I figured what the hell, it has to be strong enough to clean dishes. Well, Dawn gave me an almost-glare; one of the nicest, most-forgiving souls alive, she politely explained to me that the stuff didn't work and that Dawn (the product and endorser) did and that I shouldn't buy off-brand dish detergent in the future.

Dawn lifts intriguing (sometimes annoying) decorating ideas from a number of magazines; she gets *Better Homes & Dish Soaps* and Martha Stewart's *How To Spend a Goddamn Hour Folding a Napkin Monthly*. Dawn

> *We'll enjoy the luxuries of tending to extensive gardens and making wreaths and rugs and garlands out of fine twiggery and bronzed fruits.*

believes that if we someday win the lottery, we'll enjoy the luxuries of tending to extensive gardens and making wreaths and rugs and garlands out of fine twiggery and bronzed fruits, whereas I'd be inclined to hire a gardener and a fruit-weaver and take a long, long trip to sunny beer and beach.

Dawn says "Someday it would be nice to just relax and have time to rotate the dust ruffles." If I lived forever I'd never even give a dust ruffle a thought, let alone a maintenance schedule. But Dawn likes things nice, cozy, warm and folksy, and in fairness, I do enjoy these hedonistic comforts for their sensual value as much as their comedic value. Dawn may regard my artworks the same way.

So Dawn decides to put the dish detergent in an antique, transparent bottle with a glass stopper on a window ledge right above the sink. It is a genuinely cool looking bottle, even darkly humorous as embossed letters on it spell *ACID*. It is a smart decorating touch because it is at-once pretty, offbeat, and

functional – hell, I've never made an artwork that's even two of those things. I like it.

One evening Dawn is out with a friend and I'm loitering around the house. I don't want to work on my in-progress artwork (an assemblage about masks which includes a mannequin head skewered with pens, hatpins, eyebrow pencils) because it's looking at me funny. And I don't want to finish the book I'm reading (the excellent *Virgin Rodeo* by the extremely funny and smart Sarah Bird) because, well, it would be finished and over with rather than something to look forward to anymore. So I straighten up odds and ends in the kitchen, fill the sink with miscellaneous dishes, and add just a dollop of the official blue Dawn acid into the stream of water.

The water churns and bubbles around the dishes but no soap bubbles appear. I add a bit more detergent into the eye of the whirlpool, right in the bubble building core, start to recap the bottle but still see no soap bubbles. Is it a new, improved bubble-free Dawn? A Dawn too powerful to waste time with fragile bubbles? I add some more, an extra zap for zilch. I can't wash dishes like this.

Maybe my Dawn does only like Dawn detergent because of the name afterall because this crap is useless for washing dishes. I put the glass bottle back on the window ledge then fumble under the sink for what's left of the offbrand I got at Walgreen's. It may not be Dawn, but it makes lots of bubbles.

When Dawn gets home, I tell her that, sorry, I can't champion the virtues of Dawn dish detergent because, frankly, it is bubbleless, watery useless nonsense – all namebrand with no product back-up and, that, in fact, the stuff from Walgreen's works not just better but much better. Dawn is dumbfounded I'm discussing dish soap, possibly thinking I might next have a dust ruffle comment. She asks me to elaborate so I recount the whole episode, pointing at the decorative but dysfunctional bottle on the ledge.

"I took the detergent out of there the other day," she explains. "It was too messy on the bottle, so I replaced the soap with water and added a little food coloring."

I nod with circular variants, remembering that the dishwater had been unusually, richly blue. ∎

ARE YOU SURE IT'S AT LEAST NOON?

THE OFFICIAL POETRY CORONER OF OUR DYING COMMUNICATION SKILLS. THIS MONTH'S EPISODE - *IRONICALLY THE SORT OF CRAP I'D LUMP IN WITH THE STUFF THAT HURTS EFFECTIVE COMMUNICATION!* - HAS A TITLE TOO LONG TO CRAM INTO THE ABOVE TITLE BAR - IT IS, FOR THE RECORD, "ARE YOU SURE IT'S AT LEAST NOON? - THEN, YEAH, LET ME HAVE A BEER"

this beer is full of good art

just a nudge out of strict fact

just a small bit of poor taste (*and so what there by the way?*)

just an inch off the map (though on the key this inch is five miles long)

this beer is full of good art

with all the nose veins red

with eyes wild like you see in a cheap film about the mad

with paint or pen and ink or clay free of sense as well as the long yawn on which it sits

the dice scream (one loud dot per cube) **two**

and I want to know what the hell are the odds of *that*

that's three times in a row

this beer is full of good art

not stuff that looks so real you have to say well where's the art in this duck?

not great art not wake up dead and you're just like that a rich guy

(a *dead* rich guy for sure but rich at last as well)

not art that's too proud or too smart or too sick

but the good art that this beer's so full of

the good art that this beer's so full of

that life is out shape out of sight out of mind

out of luck out of gas

out of all the this and that

but this here beer

no I don't think that just one more could hurt

musicmaster 11.98

(The above poem is made up of only one syllable words, a pointless rule I made just for the hell of unusual exercize. I'm not printing the piece because I want a *Good Work* sticker or a springboard to a tangent about the strength and range of simple words, or even because it's about beer (isn't it?) and if *Internal Rhyme* has no other editorial policy it certainly wants to always espouse the strength and range of beer, but I'm printing it because, like any curiosity – especially one that flees from my own brain, it does help me understand things: 1) single-syllable words have, if pronounced/rolled/*acted* certain ways, a sort of multi-syllablic range; the poem sounds/beats like it also contains two- and even three-syllable words; like you know jazz man no commas this phrase; 2) as *not-bad* as the poem is, I can write a hell of a lot better without any rules e.g. it's hard to write *film* when you want to write *movie*.)

HANG THE ARTIST!

The back page of last issue featured a dense graphic of jabbering/howling/singing faces and a note that I'd provide details in this issue on how to acquire these screaming characters for the holiday season . . .

What better way to *say Have a Hair-Pulling Santa-Slobbering HoliDamnDay* than with LIMBO - the board game I designed, detailed and printed in an edition of 300 prints/sets. The pulsating black&white

All art should be similarly multi-functional.

drawing pictured last issue is the pattern I made for the backs of the 32 cards used in the game. The 18"x22" full-color, signed gameboard/print, is ready for hanging or playing upon! (All art should be similarly multi-functional. Let's call upon all artists (ideally via a media event where we all join hands with oppressed people, while singing gooey rhyming words about not-despairing/caring/sharing) to produce artworks that can double as gameboards or tablecloths or tv-trays or, best: dropcloths!)

The board depicts a cross-section of an apartment building, and reveals more than anyone wants to know about the inhabitants of our netherworld where psychic trauma, paranoia, unnamed neuroses, and lots of tiny lines thrive. The game is similar to Chutes & Ladders. If you took the actual Chutes & Ladders and juiced it with *Dante's Inferno*, Lucky the Footless Rabbit, stunt silliness from *Beat the Clock* or *Whip the Maid*, and a major does of angst, you'd have LIMBO!

You get the aforementioned matte-board-weight signed print, four handmade wedge-shaped tokens, a sandwich bag to ensure freshness, the 32 cards with the backpattern that cost me two years' of eyesight to draw, and rules for playing the game (as opposed to rules for bridge or bowling, two other versions of Limbo). If you can pick it up from me somehow, it costs $25; if I have to ship it to you, it's $30 because it's a clunky thing to

QUICK BREAK AS YOU TURN TO THE BACK PAGE

LIVE! NEWS!

A TV movie is interrupted tonight for a *Breaking News* report about a fire on the meeting room/penthouse level of the Regal Hotel on Nicollet Mall downtown. The station's carefully aging nightly news anchor is talking live from a coincidentally nearby newsroom while we watch *Live!* shots of flames and billowing smoke. *Live Cam! Breaking News!*

I've been to the Regal quite a few times, within the last year maybe twice, so there's a connection beyond just local relevance; Dawn and I make appropriate gasps and small (*but concerned*) talk until it becomes tedious from the reporter's repetitions that there's an apparently under control fire downtown and that we're missing what may be critical parts of the movie. But the station doesn't return to the movie, it broadcasts additional images from other camera-angles of the same hard-to-see-clearly blaze.

These nighttime, downtown, *Live!* transmissions are poorly contrasted and annoying to view, but they keep on coming as the news guy, obligated to pause-free commentary, repeats the few known speculations with increasingly odd and reaching tangents and asides. Something like . . .

> *Let's keep it live just in case a fireball comes exploding out of the building and torpedoes the Hyatt across the mall.*

The firefighters have reached the twentieth floor or maybe it's the eighteenth, I'm not sure if the building is even fourteen or sixteen stories, I'm trying to remember the buttons in the elevator there, but it's the penthouse level where there's a restaurant, meeting rooms, break-out rooms, and having taken the elevator or firestairs up, the firefighters have reached the top floor, possibly the twentieth or eighteenth or seventeenth, I think there are eighteen levels, by the fire stairs of course as the elevators should've shut down, and they're wearing breathing apparatus similar to what a scuba diver wears, around and in front of their face so they can breathe, typically with rhythmic inhale/exhale and repeat . . .

Instead of that comedic take on the commentary, I wish I could present an actual paraphrase or transcript, because, I assure you, the actual babble is funnier. But not funny enough that we need to hear more and more of it. The station probably figures we have a *Live!* story, right outside our downtown studio door, let's keep it live just in case a fireball comes exploding out of the building and torpedoes the Hyatt across the mall.

I'm not criticizing the anchor guy's thin and stretching improvisations. They are indeed so subtly funny and so unaffectedly surreal that there's a chance this guy is actually a heroic art prankster or latent homo-textual. I am criticizing the station's reluctance to end this *Live!* report even though there's nothing more to tell. And I am definitely criticizing Regal Hotel's apparent inability to just blow the fuck apart and make it worth missing some of our movie until rerun season.

MISCELLANEOUS FOOTNOTES

1. *Wreaths Out of Rainbows* is a great title for a you-know-by-the-title-it's-unwatchable movie starring Sally Fields, a born-again Richard Pryor and the late Jessica Tandy.

2. Sunny Beer is a great name for a health-hyped alcoholic drink, maybe containing calcium, and even ginkgo leaf extract so your mental alertness actually improves by the third bottle. ∎

THE WISDOM OF WAKING AT 5 A.M. IS UNDONE BY A 9 P.M. BED TIME

EL CAMINO DE VIDA EN LA CASA DEL FUTURO

by Hamil Griffin-Cassidy, International Correspondent

En el futuro las casas serán muy diferente que ahora. En lugar de una casa inútil y estupida habrá una casa increible y inteligente. Porque de la casa del futuro la gente podrá crecer mentalmente y físicamente también.

Habrá muchos robots en la casa del futuro se lavarán los platos y limpiarán el hogar. No existarán mascotas espantosas y reales todavia, pero mascotas robots que podrán ofrecer la compañia, como un Tomagotchi muy complicado.

Aunque los robots serán muy bueno por la ayuda en la casa no creo que los robots sean sin problemas. En el futuro, por razones no puedo nombrar, será un sol falso (hecho en China claro). El luz de este sol contendrán algo muy científica que es imposible explicar a los profesores de español. Esta cosa les

ponerá enojado los robots, y es probable que la gente les necesite pelear a veces.

En esta situación peligrosa y emocionado, la casa será un lugar de la vida aventurera. Un lugar donde su robot será su amigo un día y su enamigo el próximo. Donde nadie se saberá nunca si la comida que el robot esta serviendo es su comida final.

Cuando se tendrá miedo de sus amigos siempre y se peleará mucho, se necesitará crecer en el cerebro y en el cuerpo. La necesidad es la madre de la invención. En este camino la casa del futuro creara una raza de humanos seres más fuertes.

Un punto extraà todas de las casas del futuro tendrán una Máquina-Hamil; una máquina para los estudiantes que inventará los conceptos de los ensayos mientras escribirlos. ∎

HANG THE ARTIST! CONTINUED

ship flat and needs special packaging that I'll have to jerryrig from discarded refrigerator boxes that I don't have right now but can look for next weekend, plus it costs over five bucks to mail. **Special holiday offer** because I really want to write ad copy and make people buy stuff they don't need: 2 for $40, or $42 if I ship. It's arguably true that nobody *needs* art – hell, most people don't even want it, have something all modern and breathing like that over the couch - BUT everybody, sir I say *Everybody*, every single person alive needs a gameboard! If you don't purchase this now, be advised, you will someday be unable to fight the urge to hang your Monopoly board on the wall. ∎

WHY DOES ANY MEDIA COMPANY NEED MORE THAN 1 WEATHERPERSON?

DECEMBER 8, 1998

INTERNAL RHYME

ISSUE 31 OF A NEWSLETTER THAT CAN BE SILENCED/SHUTDOWN! BY CARROTS! ◆ MUSICMASTER, 5136 LYNDALE AVENUE. SO., MINNEAPOLIS, MN 55419

EATING CARROTS

& OTHER DANGEROUS ACTIVITIES

I. Eating Carrots

I like carrots, linking their consumption to good eyesight with the same bad-eyesight faith that links an apple to a restraining order on a doctor. Dramatically colored and solid, carrots are upright, all-American, cottontail, vitamin good. I don't especially care for the color orange, but since I can't vote the color orange in or out of office, since I'm not connected enough to get the stupid color fired, I don't worry about it, I mean come on . . . the few orange things I have to put up with – pumpkins, cheddar cheese, orange pop - aren't going to kill me.

Two years ago I notice that if I eat carrots on an empty stomach, I have a slight but definite physical reaction – a churning congestion and tightness in my chest. Far from bothering me, it intrigues me, like an eye-twitch you want to watch in the mirror. It's some sort of allergic reaction that I observe enough to know that it doesn't happen if I'm also eating other food, or after eating other food, or if the carrots are cooked. It's an appropriately bizarre aside to my only-roughly-tuned metabolism and always reconfiguring brain. It fits a subplot I'm unintentionally writing.

I occasionally munch on a carrot just to feel the reaction, to shake my head over the obvious but odd cause and effect. It's a

grown-up version (maybe not very grown-up) of gulping pop quickly for the irrepressible burp. If I eat just a few mutant midget carrots, my chest hunches up and air turns acidic for an uncomfortable but not-painful minute. My own body as amusement park attraction.

One day the reaction kicks in faster, more aggressively, but I figure it's the dog getting quicker, fetching more easily, my body getting conditioned, smarter. Nonetheless, I start to stick to the just one or two tiny carrots it now takes to get me off-kilter.

This past May, while getting together pre-burger busyfood for a barbecue, I munch on several midget carrots and feel my chest cramp in a way that I imagine mimics a heart attack. A steady pressure rolls up from the stomach and drapes each rib like a drenched towel, slogging up into the throat while your heart starts to strain for air. I tell Dawn I'm having a bad reaction to the carrots, I'm not kidding (I have to say *I'm not kidding* more often than most people because, well, I'm often kidding, just steering surreal for the impact or the ride). I sit down on the couch and feel the severe heartburn of torpedo-shaped carrot, I lean forward then rock then stand then sit down, all to shift my relationship to the sensations, to try and side-step the awful immediate inescapable wringing-out of my lungs. Dawn asks me if I'm okay and I say *yeah, I think so, it's the carrots*, and Dawn says *you better watch it, people get very serious food allergies later in life*. While she recounts examples of co-workers and friends who have nearly died from inadvertently eating pistachios, unvarnished soy nuts, peach bones, other impossible killers, I wiggle in a tourniquet of my own flesh. Maybe I am having a heart attack, but I am inexplicably more concerned that when Dawn said "later in life" she was including the here&now me in what I thought was still to come. The pain stops suddenly.

> *Howard was allergic to cats, dogs, aquariums, stagnant water, bubble bath, frozen vegetables, new carpeting, Hostess Twinkies, and the letter P.*

During a health class back at Woodrow Wilson Junior High, when students were discussing their allergies, we were shocked to hear that Jimmy Chambers couldn't drink milk or eat ice cream. Unthinkable! A bunch of kids had hayfever. Bobby Dixon said he was allergic to dust and Guy Caruba muttered *yeah well I'm allergic to homework*. My friend Howard, a notorious brown-noser, proudly outdid everyone by announcing that not only was he allergic to dust in general

THESE WORDS MAKING YOU ITCH YET?

but that he was also allergic to chalkdust and babypowder. *The big baby!* And he was allergic to cats. dogs. aquariums. stagnant water. bubble bath. frozen vegetables. new carpeting. Hostess Twinkies, and the letter P. twenty-five allergies in all. While this did reaffirm all of our suspicions about Howard's weirdness, it also impressed us – there was an inalienable coolness attached to someone who could, for whatever reason, get notes that could get him out of gym. out of running around the football field or climbing the stupid rope. You shouldn't have to have a note to get out of climbing a stupid rope. but because you did and Howard could, Howard's allergy had substantial fairy godmother value.

Time passes. The level of "later in life" I was at last May is now an "earlier in life" stage. It is a routine workday in midNovem-ber 1998. Until lunch hour (foreboding!) the saddest part of this day and, symbolically, the past several years, is that many of us heat and eat from boxes. Frozen slabs of variously engineered and spray-painted pasta as mid-day meal strike me as an ugly compromise to things we pretend we

---

Frozen slabs of variously engineered and spray-painted pasta as mid-day meal strike me as an ugly compromise to things we pretend we haven't compromised with . . .

---

haven't compromised with, like the good sense of recess, the pampering of the palate, the supposed prosperity of life among TVs and efficiency seminars. Bad enough we eat this soylent-greenish chemical zoo, but worse is that we choose it from a larder of hundreds of aberrations, eyeing the New and Improved pitches, checking for fat grams, calories, additives, microwave directions, everything but the damage-to-quality-of-life quotient which marketers and manufacturers bury in the deceptive "serving suggestion" cover photo that lures you in. Sigh. And sigh again. Someday I'll be free of these ready-in-three-minute chunks of institutional Alfredo (my butt). Wherever he is, I hope Howard appreciates the sweet reward of not being able to eat this crap. I put my brick of what is loosely called Gourmet (what is loosely called pasta! [What is loosely called food!]) into the microwave and, like in fifties' sci-fi, I automatically *program* my meal.

Co-worker Dawn, who is always quietly singing pop, gospel, country, or tv commercial (all roads leading to roam), starts preparing fresh food because of all of us, she is the least sullied by concepts of career and/or convenience; she buys the fewest frozen slabs. (Note: This isn't the Dawn who appears earlier in this powerful tale of near-death and redemption – that Dawn, also known affectionately as Moose or Dawnatello, is my soulmate, bride, and co-writer. This other Dawn is a good friend and an unintentional surrealist; this *singing* Dawn is the sister I never had. And, since she is also, on occasion, the sister I didn't need . . .) She offers me a fresh carrot.

I can clearly remember the card I wanted to send to Guy Caruba in grade school. after he'd severely burnt his hands and lost two fingertips and a thumb when several cherry bombs he had knotted together blew up expectedly. It was a drawing of just a head on the ground shouting out that *At least you didn't lose your head!* (Mrs. Nevin said it was a clever card and *she* knew what I meant, but Guy might not get it. so I ended up just making another *Sorry you lost half of your nose-thumbing skills-*card.)

I can remember the salt wells in my grandmother's basement kitchen, her gramophone, her dog Smokey, playing dominoes with her in 1956. And I can remember earlier still. to when I was in a crib in Kearney, New Jersey overhearing the *Syncopated Clock*, the theme music for a New York metropolitan area late night movie.

But I can't remember the tiff I had with carrots last May, so, while the microwave irradiates and cauterizes my pasta, while Dawn sings life's soundtrack, I munch on the fresh carrot, I like carrots, I like the taste, the snap, the *oh shit* I say out loud as pain barrels up from my stomach. It's like a heart attack again but with more claws and less heart, my whole chest hurts.

I quickly drink some Diet Pepsi because I think the irrepressible burping I recall from paragraph three might help air flow, but I can't drink much, I need my hands to hold the kitchen counter, Dawn asks me what's wrong, my lungs are getting seared by dry ice, I try to relax, I know it will pass, I *say I'm having an allergic reaction to the carrot*, my heart feels like it's going to blister, Dawn asks what she can do. I wave pointlessly, hello and goodbye, knowing it will subside soon, my body doesn't care whether I'm trying to relax or not. it's on its own, a run-on sentence waiting for a break.

I don't want to go to an emergency room because I know the reaction will end before I get there. But I do need to sit, so I head down the corridor to my own office and sit in a cushioned swivel chair so I can turn and roll. trying to distract the carrot, make it dizzy. I can breathe with effort and am indeed burping with slow growling gasps. I want to make the long story short, honestly I do, more than ever; but I can't, the pain doesn't ebb at all. Luckily, my life doesn't pass before my eyes and no cowled

ALLERGIC TO THIS STORY YET? THEN CONTINUE . . .

WHY DOES OUR GOVERNMENT SUPPRESS THE TROJAN CARROT STORY?

figure leans in the doorway to nod his ticktock skull, so I know I'm going to be okay.

As I realize it's possible that those are just Hollywood cliches, that I could indeed jump corporeal ship without benefit of reruns or props, I know I'm in trouble. I stand up, walk to my desk, pull aspirins out of a drawer, bite on two of them, thinking they'll thin my blood or race my heart or react with the Diet Pepsi. I don't know what sand tastes like. *He died burping.* I wish I had a better relationship with God. Both Dawns are going to make me go to a doctor. I read somewhere that aspirin is so extraordinary that if it had been developed nowadays instead of in – what? I can't remember - the 20s? (I'm maybe dying and yet worrying about supporting facts, my God, I'm a journalist afterall!) . . . it would cost three bucks a hit!

Have you ever eaten so many salty things - say on a sunflower seed binge – that you aggravate a taste bud, make it distend, sting, even whiten, for the hour or so it needs to stop complaining? My chest feels like it contains thousands of those yiping/belching (yelping) buds.

Dawn, sans cowl, appears in my doorway and asks if I want to go to the clinic which is nearby. I don't at all; I hate the word clinic; I avoid doctors like dirty toilets (even if you *have* to go, you think twice - *you might catch something!*), but I'm still in nondiminishing, *lung-ular*, heart-included pain, so I unsteadily say *I better** as I reach for my jacket. But as I grab my jacket all pain clicks off, completely. I'm standing in my office feeling fine, breathing easily, tasting aspirin, and containing a burp.

II. Not Eating Carrots

We check medical books we have at home and none of the information we find about an anaphlaxic reaction mentions carrots as allergen, as evil. Insect bites, shellfish, nuts, spices, strawberries; no carrots. I wonder if Howard was allergic to carrots?

*Note placement of *I better* (go) concurrent with getting better; this is an accidental bonus interplay. courtesy of the words themselves.

Dawn (Moose) and I go to lunch at a Chinese buffet and cooked carrots are in two of the dishes I like.

My doctor's appointment isn't for a few more days so I don't have an epinephrine needle or pill or even Benadryl, which we're told is a good interim treatment for anaphylaxis. I think I should draw a cartoon of a video monitor on me while I eye carrots on a salad bar and label the picture *Suicide Watch*. Dawn asks if I think I should eat the carrots, that I should be careful, allergies like this get worse. I stab an oblong cut of the agent orange, then push the tines through so they click on the plate. *No*, I say. *I think I'll wait until I find out if the allergy has to do with something that gets cooked out or not.* We both nod. I think Suicide Watch could be spun into a sitcom, a *Baywatch* for the depressed.

I avoid doctors like dirty toilets (even if you have to go, you think twice - you might catch something!)

While I microwave a Banquet lasagna slab at work, I tell Dawn (Dr. Death) that when I was sort of dying that I did indeed have a vision, that Jesus approached me through a tunnel of light and told me to avoid healthy foods. And He told me to tell her to not point carrots at me. And, I add, *He told me to stick to dark imported beers.*

I take my lunch out of the microwave, stir the hot puddle of sauce in with the cube of starch; it would be neat if it all slowly mixed up like two paint colors, twirling from sundae streaking to a dark then lightening red. But the blending is minimized by chunks of this and that, a bit of onion or tomato, maybe ice crystals that grew into semi-vegetable wads, a piece of carrot, a piece of celery . . . Wait a second! I look again and, *sure enough*, I

PLEASE REMAIN SEATED UNTIL WE COME TO A COMPLETE HALT AT THE END OF THIS WRITTEN WORK

ALL CARROTS SHOULD HAVE SAFETY LOCKS!

shout, *it looks like there's a small block of carrot in the sauce. And there's another!* Dawn says *You're kidding* (you see, I really do have to say *I'm not kidding* more often than most people; not that I'd kid about something this serious, ever, I mean I was recently mugged by a carrot*). Whew! You're right, I was mistaken,* I kid her, *it looks like they're just pieces of glass after all!*

Maybe they're not carrots. I fetch the box on which the lasagna is magnificently portrayed as a big, splendid serving of actual food, and squint to read the dozens of ingredients, some with names like Greek medicines or alien card games. I don't see carrots. Maybe they're not carrots. I'm not ordinarily paranoid but, after a carrot attack, things change. But not too much; since I've never reacted to cooked carrots before and because these maybe-carrots are probably half-soy (plus, they've been chemically-sandblasted, frozen, and re-cellularized), I eat them. I think about composing an indignant letter to the manufacturers, telling them to rename the entrée Banquet of Death. Dawn says *You'd better watch it, Buster* (not my real name). I tell

Relieved to be relatively healthy, I decide to try and be better to my body. I'll sleep more, eat less junk, take vitamins, drink less coffee, drink less mediocre beer and stick to imported dark beer.

The next time Dawn (Moose) and I are eating in a fastfood court, I get a salad with my slice of pizza; it's not much of a start to my personal improvement campaign, but it's something. When we sit down to eat, I notice that, right below the top shards of lettuce, are long shreds of carrots, dozens of them infesting the food like serpents.

III. Lessons Learned

● The entire hubbub about peanuts on planes, and the danger of peanut oil as an unidentified ingredient in foods, is necessary. A month ago I though it was necessary, but, well, in an unnecessary sort of way. I thought a type of post-modern natural selection was simply trying to thin air traffic regulars, keep the airport noise down another flight or two a month, and that the outcry from the peanut-hating crackpot fringe was whiney, like Howard getting things his way just for the hell of it. Now I'm in solidarity with all peoples oppressed, distressed and throttled by health-mongering merchants of peanuts, yellow pill dyes, and carrots.

Because the doctor has degrees and years of experience and access to all kinds of pharmaceuticals, she tells me not to eat carrots.

her that when I was sort of dying and had my vision that Jesus told me *I tell you what – if you don't have a sense of humor, you were put on the wrong planet.*

Finally I go to a doctor and recount my story just as it appears here but without so many asides or Dawns or advice from Jesus. Because the doctor has degrees and years of experience and access to all kinds of pharmaceuticals, she tells me not to eat carrots. She tells me that next time it could be curtains, that allergies like this are serious. She never heard of anyone being allergic to carrots before, but she once had a patient who was allergic to the yellow dye with which certain pills are colored, so, in fact, a prescription to help a different ailment could close this person's suitcase. She says my blood pressure isn't bad, but near borderline, get it checked annually; she adds, without irony, *watch what you eat.*

I get Benadryl and an epinephrine auto-injector that I keep in my usually close briefcase. Should I be force-fed a carrot, should a mote of carrot come whipping down the street and into my throat like a gnat, should the enemy-within decide to react to carrot cake, I can yank out this cool-looking medical knickknack, jam it into my thigh, roll my eyes back as the .3 mg intramuscular dose stabilizes my upset ship.

● When I someday die — by a falling safe on the head or by a virtual reality ride through the vegetable world — and I see Jesus in that tunnel of light, I'm going to high five Him for the great advice on beer.

● At our Thanksgiving feast, I tell mother-of-Moose Elaine about this carrot episode. Though she is herself beleaguered with an unfair burden of multi-faceted ailments, she's a good-natured and sympathetic soul, appreciating my jokes but interested in the main story. When I'm done she asks *did I ever tell you about the time they gave me penicillin on the operating table? I'm allergic to penicillin and my body shut down so quickly they had to jab me directly in the heart with a needle to get me going again.* This woman isn't afraid of carrots.

● Experiences needed to write certain pieces can be severely unpleasant. Such experiences warrant as much fluffing-up, tangent-laden, scar pointing, over-writing as I feel like cranking out.

● Carrot growers and pickers and packers and sellers should have to register their crops/products/agenda.

● I want to turn an arrow-through-head prop into a carrot-through-head prop for our holiday party. I think I'm funny. In fact, if I make such a goofy novelty, several people will comment *oh, I bet you think you're funny.*

● Professional food-tasters listed in the Yellow Pages want too much money! For crying out loud, I only want them to check for carrots!

IS THAT A CARROT IN YOUR POCKET OR AN EPINEPHRINE KIT?

INTERNAL RHYME

JANUARY 30, 1999

ISSUE 32 OF A NEWSLETTER DESIGNED TO ENHANCE THE APPEAL OF YOUR VICTORIAN HOME ◆ MUSICMASTER, 5136 LYNDALE AVENUE SO., MINNEAPOLIS, MN 55419

LETTER TO THE FARM

(THE TEXT OF MY FIRST E-MAIL AFTER MY FIRST BOUT WITH THE WEB)

Holy smokes I'm a cybernautiCalisthenical word spewer and I can tell you that my so far brief skim/surf around *that* (internetlandia) to chat has unearthed mostly an astonishing quantity of lame/incoherent/poorly-crafted/incomplete/unnecessary prose. Can there be some horrible Jim Crow-like legislation to limit Internet use to those with an at least rudimentary command of either the language or their brain? Having said that, I can see the allure of just clicking boxes until my eyes are senseless from what sadly amounts to mostly commercials without the benefit of quick or easy viewing. How about an online *used* bookstore? (Should I have prefaced that with a detour sign?) If I ever learn those godforsaken fucking little screwball word/cons that indicate this emailer is happy/surprised/etc like a teenage girl signing letters with a smiley button, your permission to kill me is granted - method, carte blanche. *Wait a second . . .*

Oh, I can do paragraphs! Amazing! See, based on what I've seen, I didn't even know I could use complete sentences.

I received a calendar at work depicting production at Anderberg-Lund Printing (a lovely watercolor of uniformed dial-turners half-smiling at their chores). Maybe they're showing off how well they can print a poor and, to me, an extremely disturbing watercolor. Below the graphic is an italicized message - set no doubt to convey warmth and wisdom - that "Work is the meat of life . . . Recreation is its dessert." My God, that is the culmination of GNP/capitalistic/defeatist/automaton doublethink I've ever seen proudly expressed as a workworld credo. This isn't just wool over the eyes, but over the nose, the mouth and the ears. That some standard of sanity could let this pass as acceptable is a powerful argument

Can there be some horrible Jim Crow-like legislation to limit Internet use to those with an at least rudimentary command of either the language or their brain?

for any standard of insanity. Work is the root of most money and we all know what most money is the root of . . .

So, I do have chatroom chat currency already with this type of typing?

I'd keep going, maybe making this a new Internal Rhyme feature (*Letters to the Farm*), but, as you can guess, I have to get back to WORK!

DEAR INTERNAL RHYME READER –

You can see that indeed I did I decide to include this new *Letter to the Farm* feature in *Internal Rhyme*. Since you weren't the specific recipient of the printed letter, however, you may not know that *I am* considering starting a small online store. Maybe not. Maybe just some sales of too much stuff (BUT GREAT STUFF DAMMIT, IT'S NOT LIKE I'VE BEEN SAVING EMPTY ICE CREAM CARTONS!) via Ebay or Toy Shop's website; but maybe a store where I could peddle my art too and all the great art/mail-art/smallpress/alt.art/documents and ephemera I've been accumulating since '69. I could part with lots of it – certainly the doubles and the stuff I didn't personally like but archived

TO CONTINUE YOUR TOUR, CLICK HERE

OPEN MIKE!

MARK YOUR CALENDAR, TUNE YOUR SONNET, TEACH YOUR EARS TO WIGGLE CONTRAPUNTALLY!

The Twin Cities' Best Open Mike is the first Friday of every month (at about 8 p.m.) at the Twin Cities' Best Coffee House - Anodyne, 43rd & Nicollet, Minneapolis (824-4300). *Internal Rhyme's* Best Mailboy Tom Cassidy is your Best Host! By the way, the first Friday is the Best Friday! The Best Avenue is Nicollet!

Join us for Real Life Must-See Anti-TV!

47

I watch how poets spin their lips and teeth around the words

if they let words leave like rules or smalltalk or numbers

some poets recite smoke rings reading memos aloud

I watch how other poets use a stool the floor a microphone

if they stand still or seem to slant to ever so slowly italicize

poets who deliver their poems as easily as they spell their name over the phone impress me

poets who title poems that should've been numbered do not

I watch how poets steer or point their fingers

wonder if they're aware of half their waves and tides

when it seems their fingers carve the air itself

I hear their lines differently I swear the words sound new

I watch how other poets help or hurt the language

how they use words stolen from me in ideas stolen from me about topics stolen from me

in poems I want to steal

I watch how other poets try to sell their self-published chap-

DON'T READ THIS LINE ALOUD . . .

TO THE FARM CONTINUED

anyway – without guilt; but maybe not. So that's why I asked *How about an online used bookstore?* in the above letter – it occurred to me right then and the recipient's consideration of that route is important to me. And since you too are important to me, I'll let you know if anything eventuates.

Now that I've told you that you're important to me, please judge me kindly on the point that I just remembered that, in fact, I do have some empty ice cream cartons in my museum. Gorgeous, round, red&white (now aged to manila), 1930s, one pint containers picturing a palm-flanked castle for Heilemann's French Riviera Ice Cream; a blank strip across the lid for rubberstamping the flavor.

See, I love describing this stuff, collecting these peripheral pop art things, these odd historical tributaries, going to hundreds of garage sales a year for the educational loitering and pretty regular score. A lot of the stuff I always buy, few others know about or want, e.g. limited smallpress items, books with nontitle/author-related value due to cover art or who the model on the cover is or certain contributors not noted on the jacket, etc. So my eyes/selection process/collecting-psyche is offwired enough that I'm not always rushing-to-beat-others/dealers to the sale; I often hit a closing down garage sale where I'm amazed to find a rare paperback (e.g. a copy of Catcher in the Rye with an *illustrated* cover – have you ever seen one?), a magazine containing an unusual celebrity photo, hard-to-find but not widely remembered stuff.

Then I have boxes upon boxes of irresistible pop/toy/paper stuff I bought wholesale (my Musical Comedy smallsmallpress outfit is a registered business). I had two short-lived shops back in Portland in the mid70s where I grew my packrat tendencies into a greater addiction that is finally and conspicuously outpacing my ability to house or store it. What's great about having a store is being able to get that adrenaline rush of making a good find or buy without having to personally keep or collect each item.

I loved my shops; they were quirky hard-to-describe poets' hangouts where you could play classic pinball machines, read the local underground paper the *Portland Scribe* which ran alternative arts column I wrote, or ask me if I was ready to lock up so we could grab a few beers before I started my shift working the gate at the Earth Tavern. I was a rotten shopkeeper because I didn't care about making money. And since I selected 99% of the stuff I carried, since I refused to buy/resell mainstream fiction or anything that most passersby would purchase, I didn't make much money above the rent, which, back then, was a paltry $125/month for a good-sized shop (900 sq.ft? I don't remember, but maybe Down on the Farm Don does) on a busy street through a mostly-residential neighborhood. Most of my customers were fellow poor artists or writers who would come in and act out manifestoes with me for hours. Big used bookstores (particularly the still-growing world-famous Powell's, those bastards) regularly bought out most of my carefully accumulated inventory at prices I made very affordable for my regulars; though I made a modest profit on the stuff I sold, I never cranked prices up to the standard resell range. I was always troubled when books were only being purchased to be resold at considerably higher prices. Nonetheless, whether I was happy with sales or not, I at least had a selling part of the equation in place.

> *I was a rotten shopkeeper because I didn't care about making money . . . I refused to buy/resell mainstream fiction or anything that most passersby would purchase.*

Which brings us back to Go. I might develop an online used bookstore/gallery/stuff hangout to see if I can at least free up space for the dog's water bowl. ∎

AT THE NEXT-TO-THE-LAST SUPPER, EVERYBODY HAD THEIR OWN LOAF OF BREAD

POETRY NONSENSE
CONTINUED

book about a diving instructor back in Philadelphia to audience members who'll never buy this or any other chapbook but nod appreciatively
sip back coffee concoctions that cost two fifty nibble on muffins
so carefully crafted with unbleached fat and beef that isn't beef that the muffins cost three bucks apiece and sure enough you eat one one week later you're still hungry

I watch how other poets say damn when they don't have to or don't say it when they do

I watch their hair shift when they themselves find new meanings in their own words

when they're talking about abstracts like romance or happiness or nothing

when they're talking about specifics like a broken doorbell or the price of bull in China or a specific nothing

I pay attention to the way other poets sip water or beer or coffee or air between poems

I watch where they plant their feet and their hearts

I hear every dropped line mispronunciation collision of eye and page and figure it into the final tally based on how difficult a jump the skater was attempting did she recover well

when they shuffle up dimensions I latch my safety belt

I ride through the maze on their careening pinstriped lark

when they offer snapshots or blood transfusions I really try to care

because occasionally the snapshot is bigger than a single barbecue the blood is often real

but when they go the speed limit or force a formula or practice poems in front of me

or roll their R's I roll my eyes I shake my head in a way that could be construed as an audience member nodding appreciatively who no way in hell will ever buy a chapbook wondering if I look like that do I look that puppeteered by the

language
do I look up as often or at all are my arms on looser than that

I like to catch then ride the pattern and rhythm in other poets' repetitive poems wherein they keep repeating key words with funny or tragic mixes of nonkeywords

I can hear the logic even if it's knotted up or blind
I can usually guess when they're lying even in allegory or metaphor

I listen to how other poets drive set-ups they themselves create into completely
different conclusions than I would and that horrifies me as much as it reassures

I watch how others poets fidget scratch and blink

I can tell if a cough is a nervous cough

I squint to see how their eyes watch their words how often they need to look down

I listen for inhalations and the faraway whistling of air between the teeth

in our heads we all sound like woodwind instruments

the air keeps are heads afloat and the wood well you know what that is

I watch how other poets take little bows and leave the stage which is usually just a stool on an unelevated floor without a real spotlight curtain or backstage let alone
a dressing room and without a paying crowd and without commercial endorsement and without half of what you'd get at even the lousiest job on the planet but boy
is that a great place for a poet
I watch how other poets face facts pour milk rake leaves make soup call dogs
and signal for a stop when no one's behind them at all

I have over a thousand written works to my credit

at least half of them are really good but the half I'd pick are different from the three or four you'd pick

and about two hundred and fifty of my written works have been printed in the most obscure unpopular poorly-designed cheaply printed possibly subversive oddly-titled smallpress publications in the world
some of them barely more than what a toe can sketch into wet sand

and yet I am still – at an age well past uncertainty – ambivalent about calling my written works *poems* because

FOLLOW YOUR HEART

ANY EDUCATION IS REEDUCATION

who the hell needs
the moronic kneejerk sidestep of
it's not a poem if you skip the costume if you drop the
bouncing ball

if you go outside the lines

- musicmaster 1/11/99

NOTES TO THE ABOVE:

1. I pay attention to how other poets end their poems too, but that doesn't help me end mine any better. There's a chance I'll someday rework this by interspersing an in-process series of stereotypical open mike characters, their hack ennui, kneejerk ancestry anthems, and stuff I apparently envy. It would make this a better piece for me to read aloud – more tangents/ subplots, voice shifts.

2. I've been interested for a long time in how poets deliver their works. In high school and in college I noticed that teacher/writers never delivered their own works well; they just annoyed their captive audience/students wit droning cryptic reflections usually too academic or stupid to be engaging. Between the late 60s (when I was a Clifton, N.J. high school student half an hour away from Manhattan, Greenwich Village, readings at the Y, Ginsburg in Washington Square) and the mid70s (when in the underground/lit/art scene in Portland, Oregon) I made deliberate efforts to hear as many bigdeal poets as I could (like Ferlinghetti, Waldman, Whalen, Stafford, Rothenberg, DiPrima, Piercy, Corso, Bukowski, Norse, those great young unCommies and many many more I'm too lazy to recall for an afterthought); few were even as good as local poets as presenters/readers/performers.

Bukowski was interesting to see live because he consumed so much booze without visible blur or slur (he had a bottle of hootch on a table and a fridge full of beer on stage) and his voice was surprisingly high and weak. Ginsburg was excep-

tional when he didn't lapse into singing Blake for two fucking hours. But alltold, our local Portland poets were better – maybe because the scene wasn't sullied or shaped by teaching posts, publishing ventures, real recognition, favor swapping or middle age. Walt Curtis, Mark (Dr. Trust) Sargent, Dan Raphael (who read only rarely), Katherine Dunn (before her return to the spotlight with Geek Love), John Shirley, etc., were a kick to hear because they didn't just hover over scripts and severely intone obscure comments about eternity or mumble a series of references to Eliot and Pound and other merit badges, but they delivered/performed. This was pre-Poetry Slam poetry scene (though we did do a "Read-Off" at the Northwest Artists Workshop in "78 or so), so the point – no matter how loud we occasionally got - wasn't to upstage, shutdown, one-up, out-shock, or win any damn thing, but to *Read Poetry!*

Few people/poets really *Read*, often to the detriment of the poem and always to my annoyance – if you don't want to add something to your piece by presenting it live, then spare me your lack of enthusiasm/theatrics/ego. This note is getting awfully convoluted and, since I don't want to rework it into either the short story or essay it wants to become, I'll just summarize by noting that I'm very self-conscious\self-aware when I read (and in ways I'm not at other times) because of my longtime interest in how poets present their works in person.

3. Books that slapped the haiku and sonnets out of my high school skull included: Emmett Williams' sweethearts (a kinetic concrete poem – sort of a flipbook of the letters in the word sweetheart shifting around the page); This Book is a Movie – An Exhibition of Language Art & Visual Poetry, an anthology with startling nonverbal/anti-verbal/neo-verbal! poems and some experiments that preshadowed my 1971 leap into and still ongoing relationship with mail art; and the more normal-seeming but completely fresh written works of Kenneth Patchen, Adrian Mitchell, and Jerome Rothenberg.

SKETCHBOOK

WORMS FROM WAREROOMS

AT WORK

MY MIDLIFE CRISIS BEGINS WHERE YOUR NOSE ENDS

JANUARY 35, 1999

INTERNAL RHYME

ISSUE 33 OF A NEWSLETTER THAT COMES RIGHT FROM THE MENTAL HAMSTER WHEEL ◆ MUSICMASTER, 5136 LYNDALE AVE. SO., MINNEAPOLIS, MN 55419

NEWS RECAP - JANUARY 1999

- An *Upcoming Events* box for a newsletter I assemble includes "Day at the Capital – time and place to be announced." Like it'll be held at the airport Hilton? At the large letter A in Alphabet Land?
- Radio ads for the Kingston Trio at Mystic Lake Casino announce "Most of the founding members are back together." Were there more than three in the original trio because of back-up musicians or singer rotation(s)? Some of me says yes.
- On WCCO, a deejay-delivered ad proclaims, "Hometown Mortgage was recently named a top mortgage provider by *CitiBusiness*. Talk about commitment!" Talk about *We're-missing-something-here* copy! Did I tell you that a copy of *Internal Rhyme* was recently mailed to an old friend in Portland? . . . Talk about italics!
- Also on WCCO, a newscaster wraps up a sad story with "the cause of the baby's death is pending." So is mine! Save the kid's life!
- But the oddest real news sighting in January is that the Quality Paperback Book Club's Selection of the Month is – none of the items in this column are made up – a this month only, special **Hardback** book. Isn't this like getting wine from the Beer of the Month Club? Catnip at the Just Dogs Emporium? ■

OPEN MIKE!

MARK YOUR CALENDAR, TUNE YOUR SONNET, TEACH YOUR EARS TO WIGGLE CONTRAPUNTALLY!

The Twin Cities' Best Open Mike is the first Friday of every month (at about 8 p.m.) at the Twin Cities' Best Coffee House - Anodyne, 43rd & Nicollet, Minneapolis (824-4300). *Internal Rhyme's* Best Mailboy Tom Cassidy is your Best Host! By the way, the first Friday is the Best Friday! The Best Avenue is Nicollet!

Join us for Real Life Must-See Anti-TV!

INSIDE THIS ISSUE

PLEASE PUT ON YOUR SCHOOLGIRL OUTFIT AND IMPEACH ME MISTRESS

CONTENTS CONTINUED

HOW TO FOLD

ABS READY FOR MILLENIUM FLEX-DAYS (& NITES)?

FAVORITE POLKA WEEKENDS

FRENCH SOUNDS ROMANTIC, FUNNY

HOW TO UNFOLD

BITTER (NOT BETTER) NBA RICH GUY JOKES

COPS BEAT THE LIVING SHIT OUT OF SOME INNOCENT BASTARD AND DEFEND THEIR ACTIONS BECAUSE THE INNOCENT GUY KEPT SCREAMING HE WAS INNOCENT GODDAMMIT, AND THEY DIDN'T THINK THAT SOUNDED LIKE SOMETHING A GENUINELY INNOCENT PERSON - WHO WAS ALSO *NICE* - WOULD SAY . . . TO SWEAR LIKE THAT!? AND IN FRONT OF STRANGERS!

ADS FOR SHIT

CLASSIFIED ADS FOR SELLING USED SHIT

ADS FOR FOLDING CLASSES

ADS FOR GOING BANKRUPT

ADS FOR NONPROFIT UNFOLDING ORGANIZATIONS

ADS FOR CHEAP SHIT

CLASSIFIED ADS FOR USED SHIT, CHEAP

ADS FOR ADVERTISING JOBS THAT LOOK LIKE EVERY OTHER DROPDEAD DULL JOB LISTING

CUTE STUFF WRITTEN BY SUBSCRIBERS' KIDS WHO DON'T GET A DIME FOR WRITING THE BEST STUFF IN THE PAPER! (I'VE USED THIS BEFORE BUT REMAIN ANGRY ENOUGH TO REPEAT IT)

PRESIDENT HUMPS ROSE GARDEN LECTERN

CASUALTIES WITHOUT NAMES

EDITORIALS THAT MAKE US SOUND LIKE NITWITS WHO'D DO BETTER WRITING THE CONTENTS BOX

LETTERS TO THE EDITOR FROM IDIOTS

LAST-WORD RESPONSES FROM DEFENSIVE IDIOTS

COUNTERPOINT PIECES BY IDIOTS WITH LANGUAGE SKILLS

TV LISTINGS FOR YOUR LIFE-SIMULATION UNIT

MOVIES WITH FAMOUS PEOPLE SAVING THE PLANET FROM NEARLY EVERYTHING BUT THE INSIDIOUS EVIL OF MOVIES WITH FAMOUS PEOPLE SAVING THE PLANET

LOCH NESS MONSTER SHARES PRIVACY TIPS

NEW PLAGUE! SERIOUS KIDS' ITCHING AILMENT TIED TO BEANIE BABY "BEANS"!

SMART POLITICAL WRITING ABOUT ALL OF US CLUELESS NITWITS

CONTENTS CONTINUED IN THE CONTENT AREA

ODE TO THE AASEW

By: Kelly Faber

There is this Organization,
providing legislative support and education,
to owners and managers of property,
in and around Milwaukee County.
They have a Newsletter that is informative,
a Board of Directors that is supportive.
There are meetings, seminars and parties Galore,
and a trip to Madison to speak with legislators.
You could get insurance for your health,
and help from an attorney to protect your property wealth.
That isn't all, just wait, there's more,
You can use the services of LIS next door
Check out your tenants before they rent,
so precious money is gained, not spent.
Are they working, have they been evicted, is their rap sheet a mile?
check out all their current accounts on their credit file.
So don't you hesitate to pay your dues...
with the Apartment association, you have nothing to lose!!

Owner Magazine

supportative?

WHY I DRINK # 314

CONTENTS CONTINUED

THE SURPRISE ENDING CAME AS NO SURPRISE

ONE TYPE OF WATER

Not too long ago, in roof-life years anyway, there was only one type of water. Generally speaking, of course; there were a few who'd sip bottled aqua, but they were eccentric or in France. And there was one beer – Bud or Rheingold or Ballantine, it didn't matter what it was called because it all came from the same vat into which people plunged strictly for the pickling, not the grooming of an affection. And there was one coffee – Maxwell House or Chock Full Of Nuts or Ballantine, it didn't matter what it was called because it all came from the same big bean on which people suckled strictly for the wiring, not the spackling of taste buds.

Now, of course, there are as many brands of water as there are sodas, flavored and sparkling and out of a spring or snowmelt in a jerkwater location far away (jerkwater too, - a healthy form of fatfree water jerky - can be had for a price). Bars offer at least

---

For this column to rise above the brandthink/ commerce-chat/puny-issue-tweaking of many "slice of life columns," I need to write Bigger.

---

547 beers and their own microbrew, and there's a coffeehouse at every intersection (even the key shop sells espresso). With hangovers and edginess concurrent trends (a.k.a. stress headaches and/or migraines and/or "I think this is a sick building").

And not too long ago, this column so far would've passed as a slice-of-life feature, a columnist's whimsy on a predictable but popularly engaging lark. Some cranky, nostalgic middle-aged "journalist" writes about watching the world on/from/with his butt and makes funny conclusions about water, coffee and beer being so similar. Sure, the examples given should've included better fingerpointing, but I'm too lazy here for even that; plus, just mentioning Starbucks only enhances their ubiquity (oh shit I mentioned them – but how would you know what I wasn't mentioning if I didn't tell you directly or give you enough indirect clues that you'd know anyway? Life is difficult.).

Now, of course, for this column to rise above the brandthink/ commerce-chat/puny-issue-tweaking of many "slice of life

columns," I need to write Bigger. I need to write past default logic like "what's next? Designer air? Well, as a matter of fact, Tokyo's newest oxygen bar franchise is coming to Seattle . . ." I need revisit my roots without ever writing "I need to revisit my roots" and write to and through where my mind *really leads me* and not just to where words, current events, or popular preoccupations point. So, take a deep breath, the real column is about to begin . . .

So who the hell came up with those cardboard sleeves that let you pick up your take-out coffee without searing your palm? Was it a one-person idea or a team thing like Post-Its? Throughout garage sale season, my friend is always pointing out big houses owned by someone who's living large and lazy because of their role on the Post-It development squad. Post-Its are indeed great, already an office necessity, but – after the initial lightbulb – what did all the additional people do, pick colors? Argue over whether to name it Stick It or NoteKins?

Stop. Stop. I'm sorry. That "real column" start didn't shake off as much regular writer baggage as I had hoped. Let me knock back a beer and try again. (*Interlude*) Okay, take a deep breath, the real column is about to begin . . .

Everyone has too many coffee mugs, many of them received as gifts and therefore adorned with recipient-appropriate designs like office worker jokes or a picture of Sojourner Truth or a phrase like *There's beer in here*. And everyone has product or event promo mugs cranked out on the cheap to commemorate *Clifton's Belch-Off '67* or *Poodle Grooming Days*. And everyone periodically says *We've got to get rid of some of these mugs* and so many mugs go back into redistribution via garage sales or folks bringing extras to the office kitchen. Yet, though there are at least twenty times as many mugs as there are United States citizens (and I'm not counting restaurant inventory here, just privately held mugs), and though we know everybody has too many, nearly everyone, on occasion, still buys a mug as a gift when no other idea comes to mind. And though it's often an only or all-purpose option, we still try to tailor it to the recipient, etcetera, to keep feeding the ever-growing rotation of mugs.

Now, let's imagine the one person out there, perhaps *the only person* out there – way, way out there like in shack on the desert, where free mugs don't get distributed, where the nearest garage sale is fifty miles away and features only-used-once snakebite kits and sunbleached alien skulls - who doesn't own a mug. He has glasses and a jug and one of those alien skulls inverted and acrylic resined so it can be used like a mug, but he doesn't own a Dilbert mug, or a Survivalists' Expo '73 mug, or a Donald Duck getting his bill stung by a scorpion mug . . .

THE NEXT PAGE SURELY FOLLOWS

WORDS, WORDS EVERYWHERE AND NOT A DROP TO DRINK

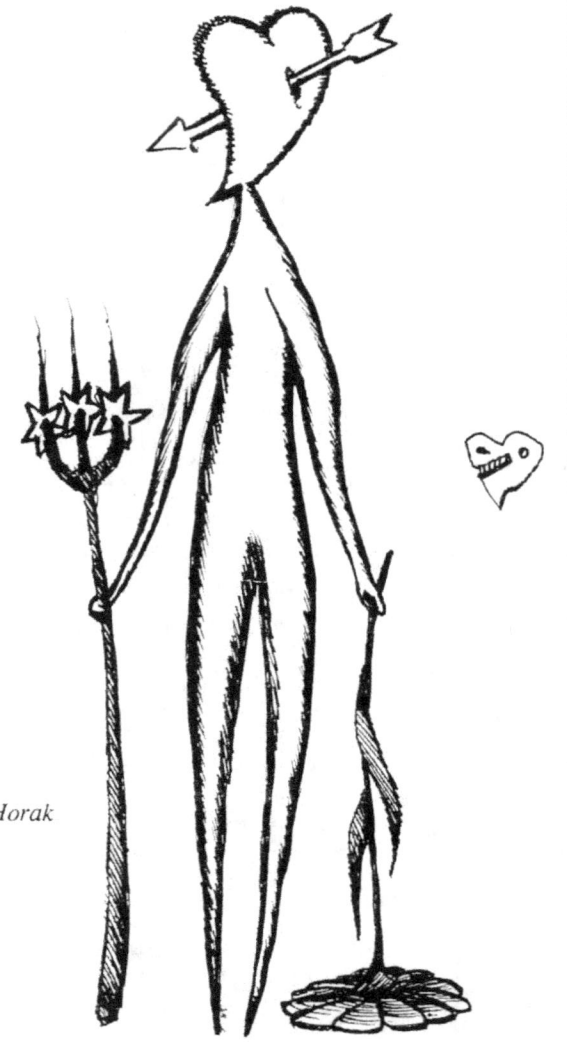

VALENTINE POEM 1.96 ABOUT 3.61

CATHY HORAK FOLKDANCING WITH BOB ZIMMERMAN

I want to run up to a tree

shake it make it drop birds

just stare at the damn thing until

it says it's sorry

I want to beat ocean waves 'til they're blue

'til they stop slobbering in moonlight

I want to whittle all snowflakes

so they look identical

so that when melting

they curl and ache in tandem

they ask for help but I don't care

I want to rip down mountains

like they're posters on a fence

crumple them up tight

you know every pebble on the beach?

as in *she's not the only pebble on the beach (?)*

as in *every pebble on the beach is as good as Cathy Horak*

probably better (?) -

I want to put each and every one of them

each and every pebble

in the interrogation room and yell

how could you let this happen?

ONE TYPE OF WATER CONTINUED

Wait. Stop. Stop. I've either had too much beer or too little (ain't that always the case?), but that effort wasn't too liberating or inventive or free-range either, dammit!

Maybe what I want to write is about that mugless guy in the desert, but not just about his muglessness. Maybe what happens on that clear quiet night when the aliens show up and select him as the one with whom they'll share great healing devices and time travel secrets? After his shock wanes, he makes the hospitable gesture of offering them cactus wine in a beverage container that just happens to be that inverted and acrylic resined alien skull! His guests are horrified, repulsed; a cranial anomaly on the skull tells them that it's their longlost Uncle Zing, the alien who brought a whole bunch of people the Post-It technology back in the 80s!

Yeah, that's the kind of writing I want to write. If I wrote without all the breaks for water, coffee or beer, it would probably be easier.

APRIL (EVERY DAY IS FOOLS DAY) 29, 1999

INTERNAL ✣ RHYME

ISSUE 36 OF THE ONLY NEWSLETTER THAT DOESN'T DEFECATE FLIMSY SUBSCRIPTION POSTCARDS   ◆ MUSICMASTER, 5136 LYNDALE AVE. SO., MINNEAPOLIS, MN 55419

SALVAGING KALE

A recent press release from the C. Chase Company, a real estate brokerage and consulting firm, announces that National Distribution Services (NDS), a "reverse logistics" company, will open its relocated distribution facility in Shakopee. I'm not exactly sure what "reverse logistics" is, except maybe a process like reverse engineering whereby NASA geeks examine and dissect baffling parts of an alien spacecraft back to assembly stages they can comprehend. Or it's what Pepsi-Cola chemists do to crack the Coke formula down to its teensiest blip of cocaine.

Luckily, the press release reveals that NDS (a subsidiary of Carolina Logistics – note, **not** Carolina *Reverse*-Logistics) "specializes in reclamation of damaged retail grocery products." Beyond mentioning that NDS clients include super-dupermarket kingpin Super Valu, the rest of the release is only facility stats and chatter and offers no further explanation, e.g. what the hell *does reclamation of damaged retail grocery products* mean?, what's an example?, which foods that I buy contain salvaged ingredients that – where it not for NDS – would've been tossed?

> *Most of the meat products that outsit their expiration dates get wholesaled to mulch makers or vulture farmers.*

I appreciate that boxes so damaged that consumers won't select them can contain perfectly good noodles or sugar-charged rice puffs. That dented cans can contain unharmed tomato sauce. And that bruised apples can be pulverized into perfectly palatable, unbruised-looking apple jelly or juice. But I think of all that in terms of a can here a can there, a few pounds of produce a day - certainly too small a percentage of goods overall to fuel a company that can afford paid staff, reclamation strategies and

procedures, a section devoted to marketing/selling croutons made from blacked-out bananas, and a new distribution facility in Shakopee. It has to take a hell of a lot of damaged retail grocery products for NDS to exist and it has to take a hell of a lot more reclamation of spindled/bent/too-ripe/stale/spoiled food then we want to consider.

Though there must be truckloads of stale bakery products picked up everyday throughout the Twin Cities, we (wastefully) tend to assume that—aside from a few salvageable rolls and styro-pastries for the mission—that the bulk of the unsold goods get tossed.

Am I right? Don't you assume that most of the meat products that outsit their expiration dates get wholesaled to mulch makers or vulture farmers?

But what if instead they're sold/recycled/RECLAIMED for sausage making? Come on, we *know* that sausage contains turkey eyes and cow phlegm-filtering-glands and pig tales (sick) (sic), so it's very likely it also contains past-their-expiration-date cold cuts and flowering potatoes and cheese blocks so moldy they get shaved before reprocessing.

And shriveled-up, nearly black peas (including old canned peas reclaimed via uncanning and gammagamma ray bombardment) can be, in reclamation camps, flashfrozen and spraypainted into Oh!-So!-Good! Frozen blueberries.

Too old to sell corn can be artificially flavored, dyed and reanimated as peppercorns!

But we're not talking about my goofy examples, however near-fetched. Maybe in truth they only aim *down* the food chain (people food to dog food to turkey food) or they run a hip,

CONTINUED INSIDE WITH RECLAIMED WORDS

RECREATIONAL BREADING

THANKS AGAIN FOR AGREEING TO WATCH THE FISH

the thermometer's next to the heater
78 degrees or so is fine say 76 to 80
coldblooded they like their water warm
if the water's too cold just turn the heater off
and add a bag of ice

feed them in the morning and
before you go to bed
a pinch of flakes a heaping pinch is plenty
but no more than that which liquefied would make
a tiny ounce you know you have to trust your instincts
on flake-to-tinyouncedom liquefication

if you forget to feed them and
you hear their stomachs growling
tell them clean the algae off the rocks
and you'll pour a pint of gin in there
you'll add a twist of shrimp

if they get really weak because
you forget to feed them for three or four days
they're floating around like flotsam and Harriet
simply ignore them
pretend that you fed them the bubbling wretched ingrates

turn the aquarium light off at night
and back on in the morning
it trains the fish to live the way we live
in an abridged and tiny very humid edition
if you forget to turn the light off
they sleep fitfully their fins twitch
they dream of leaving the aquarium for a nice big pool in
    Mexico
they've heard that there the fish all swim in beer

at night drop in four algae chips for
that bugeyed Plecostomus bastard
all he does is defecate an endless mile of crap
that drapes the plants and rocks like garland

on Thursday siphon out a bucket of water
and pour back in a bucket of rum
it keeps their eyes both dumb and full of vision
and I have to admit I don't hate them as much
when they sing their ballads do their Flipper skits

keep an eye out for parasites the fish get
jagged spit-white worms in plaid turtlenecks
growing out of their eyeballs like perfectly thrown darts
infected-looking head nodules with fringe
disgusting eruptions of boiling fish lava
I mean what the hell kind of demons are these beasts

when they get sick they don't just sneeze
they mutate and decompose

you're supposed to look at the tank
and get relaxed feel yourself transported
to a quiet underwater retreat
but when you look in at these clowns
when they're sick it's disgusting
like watching an open heart surgery
suddenly beset with flies

should one of them get sick
just flush the pampered loser down the toilet
or
if his bullying monotonous cannibalistic face
wins you over like a puppy
you can catch him in this little net
he'll struggle with apparent joy
remember he can hold his breath for seven hours
or something I heard that on Discovery

put him on the kitchen counter
and sprinkle both sides of him evenly with bread crumbs
inside the refrigerator door
is one of those fake plastic limes
squirt him with that
remember he's flopping in happiness
flailing in ecstasy
if he doesn't clearly say Uncle
you're not supposed to stop

the frying pans are in the bottom cupboard
you can use the smallest one
none of these smug chunks of cat food
is as big as he thinks he is

musicmaster 4/99

(Do I write stuff like that because I watched too much violent
TV, used to listen to Hot Tuna and Country Joe and the Fish,
and played a million games of pinball? Can the above poem be
interpreted as a NATO air attack? If I added a line like *Camus
shot me in a dre*am, the poem would clearly seem more serious.
I usually try to make my poems serious through paranoia,
hyper-normalcy and, mostly, humor. If I added a line *like I
shoot Camus in my dream*, the poem would clearly seem more
intellectual. I usually try to make my poems intellectual by
thinking about what I'm writing, simplifying it to business-
world/suburban smalltalk then underscoring all the stupid
givens. If I deleted this parenthetical afterthought – existent
only for the Internal Rhyme presentation of this written work –
would you think about Camus appearing in dreams at all?)

LISTENING CLOSELY MEANS YOU'LL HEAR THE VOICE IN THE WILDERNESS

APRIL ITEMS

North Westerly Road SE

I enjoy real estate related press releases that try to accurately describe where a parcel of land is located – an address is never enough (and indeed it may not yet exist), so there's always a line or two to clarify which quadrant of which intersection is being discussed. Toss in cross streets and/or neighborhoods that contain compass orientation in their names, and the explanation – in its reinforcing accuracy - becomes more befuddling than helpful. My current example of this humor subgenre is a release from Witcher Construction announcing that it has been selected to build a new coal storage facility to serve the University of Minnesota. The site for the facility is "along the north banks of the Minneapolis riverfront just east of the University's southeast power generating facility."

Outstanding hits of the Seventies recorded by Muzak ...from the *History of Muzak*

(This is actual Muzak-released data. It's one thing to remember songs you listened to in college or over one summer or in an other self-aware context; it's another thing to be reminded of which songs you possibly heard as often or more often while strolling, waiting, sharpening pencils. My unnecessary comments are parenthetical – pretend they're not there.)

Close to You

It's Impossible

One Less Bell to Answer (Was that by Vicki Carr? She's a huge star in Mexico nowadays. No, no, it was sung by what's her face, the dead one, no, wait, not the dead one, the other one I thought was dead, what's her name, Vicki Carr?)

SALVAGING KALE CONTINUED

environmentally friendly company that manufactures gourmet compost. Or indeed they're just the greatest thing since sliced bread because *they make sliced bread* – by reconfiguring, reclaiming ancient frozen foods!

We're talking about a reverse logistics company, which specializes in reclamation of damaged retail grocery products, opening a distribution facility in Shakopee. That the press release can't toss us one more bit of explanation (which wouldn't be too far out of line in a press release) typifies what irks me about the news media – they rarely ask the questions I want answered. ■

Solace

You're So Vain (For all the stories told about to whom these lyrics are directed, this song is really about me.)

Whole Lotta Sunshine

Theme from Chariots of the God (This thing was deliberately composed to ultimately be a soundtrack to hundreds of sportscasts, community news features about courageous people, comedy skits, and tv commercials for everything from convertibles to condoms.)

Theme from The Godfather

Behind Closed Doors

American Pie (This song has always unnerved me as clunky, rhyme-driven pseudo-folk that inexplicably survived the day the music died.)

Fire and Rain (Like far too many songs I originally enjoyed but then heard so much, so everywhere that I grew to hate them, I heard this on the radio and on every other turntable in Marmiom Hall and even on the lips of resident troubadours so

often that, upon hearing this song nowadays, I remember everything kindly.)

Summer of Forty-two

I Believe in Magic

Help Me Make It Through the Night (Yow, this is is truckin' for the long-haul music and Robert Crumb self-pitying truckin' lyrics too. That Muzak would license this and pump it into elevators and processing plants to quell distractions and deep introspection has to reflect proof that most folks don't remember the lyrics, because if workers start singing along to this, they'll be weeping on the conveyor belts. A polka version might work.)

Was Senator Backscratch Out of Town?

Two Minnesota Senators recently distributed a "Dear Colleague" letter to rally opposition to a proposal to tax associations (some legit nonprofits, some on-paper-legit nonprofits, some very profitable nonprofits). This document is referred to by the Senators' last names which, in wonderful coincidence, are Crapo and Robb.

ELLY'S CHRISTMAS

I hear fumbling at back door which must not be locked because someone who doesn't live here easily enters the house. I know it isn't someone who lives here because I wander around and take inventory every hour or so, sniff my water, gnaw a kibble. It's my job. Everyone's accounted for.

Because whoever it is who's coming in isn't a neighbor in broad daylight or the sun setting with a thud that surprises me, I don't bark. It must be Santa Claus. Maybe he'll give me a plate of turkey, hamburgers, those fake cookie bones that taste like lamb, but I don't know that because I've never had lamb. Maybe he'll give me real lamb and I'll like it because it reminds me of those fake cookie bones. I slowly get off the good couch where I'm not supposed to sleep, but no one knows when it's this late. I stretch and yawn and walk right into the surprise guest.

I don't yapyapyapyapyapyapyap like I have a Class C Watchdog License. Though I do have 3 continuous barking credits towards one, I don't think I'll get the mandatory 1 bite and/or 2 witnessed nips credit they make you get nowadays to be a Watchdog.

Santa is startled at first but my wagging tale quickly reassures him. He's wearing a stocking over his head. He calls me *Good Doggie*, which is one of my nicknames so I lick his hand. It tastes like chicken. He calls me *Good Doggie* again and again like maybe I'm going to suddenly repeat it like a parakeet. I tried repeating it once two years ago to my master and I thought I had it right – it took sixteen or seventeen quick barks to make all the right sounds but since I couldn't tape them then play them back at faster speed, it just sounded like sixteen or seventeen quick barks. So, instead of getting a

treat, I was told to be quiet. As if humans ever get barking right. They think it's just a matter of saying the offensive and stereotypical woof word, not realizing that not only is it insulting (and a violation of the rider to the Equal Rights amendment that Lassie proposed) but that they're often saying "Woooorf" (note: the third and fourth 'O's are silent), which is slang for squirrel, a known enemy of every dog because it comes in the yard.

Santa quietly moves into the living room, ever so softly whistling *Whistle While You Work*. While he starts opening the china cabinet, I bring him Spitty Bone because, even though no one has ever done this before, maybe, because he's Santa, he'll kneel down try to wrestle it away from me with his teeth. He says *Good Doggie Down Doggie Good Doggie* but to me it sounds like *Oh boy you brought Spitty Bone out and you can bet I'll be kneeling down any second to try and wrest it away from you with my teeth.*

I drop Spitty Bone who thuds to the floor. Santa freezes, which means he's starting to play. I watch him for a few seconds but he doesn't move and then I watch Spitty Bone for a few seconds and he doesn't move. There are no sounds from upstairs, apparently everyone is still sleeping soundly, so I bark loudly twice. Santa is waving his arms and saying *Quiet You Damn Dog*, which, curiously, is another one of my nicknames!

A voice from upstairs shouts down *Elly Shut the Hell Up* (my proper name). And as Santa rapidly tiptoes back to the kitchen and out the back door, I grab Spitty Bone by the neck and shake him around. He says *Uncle* with his tiny human voice, so I let him go and trot off to sniff the cabinet under the sink – behind the soap and Drano and Windsex I can smell the jar where they pour all the grease and fat. I just know that tomorrow morning they're going to give it to me for Christmas. ∎

HEARSAY IS A BASIC FOOD GROUP

JUNE 15, 1999

INTERNAL ✳ RHYME

ISSUE 37 OF THE ONLY NEWSLETTER THAT HUMS "IT'S IMPOSSIBLE" WHEN YOU READ IT ◆ MUSICMASTER, 5136 LYNDALE AVE. SO., MINNEAPOLIS, MN 55419

Big Nick

At the A&P, the baseball cards are five cents a pack, six packs for a quarter and you pick them up by the customer service and coffee grinding window usually staffed by Big Nick, who wanders over from produce before you can slap the bell.

When I go to the A&P with my Mom, Big Nick is *all These apples came in this morning Mrs. Cassidy* or *We have a special on the Idahos today* or, when he's in an especially obnoxious

---

When this tinyheaded tank finally ambles over from diapering each of the grapes, he has a face like you just yanked him away from a nap all about Big Nick in a Go Go Lounge.

---

mood, *Well look it's my favorite damn family.* Except Big Nick doesn't say damn.

When my Mom picks up a pack or two of baseball cards for me – which she always does so I'll go shopping without complaining too much – Big Nick smiles and nods like he's my pal, says something like *If you're lucky, son, you'll get Roger Maris.*

To me Big Nick is a very important adult, between sixteen and eighty years old. He's a critical cog in a school documentary about how we get bananas in winter or why you shouldn't shove someone at the drinking fountain. Big Nick is as powerful as a doctor or a cowboy, all amber waves and big black shoes splattered with bits of spinach and his apron, which looks like a modern painting or like Big Nick was helping out the butcher this morning, is as big as the movie screen on which my Dad shows slides. Big Nick must own the A&P, at least some of it, to be able to feed himself, because if he doesn't own it there's no way they're going to let a guy this big be in charge of so much food. Once he said to my Mom that I was growing so fast that he bet I was going to eat us out of house and home, and I thought well, he's probably eating A&P out of store and warehouse and farm and field.

I don't like Big Nick but I'd like to be like him someday because he gets the baseball cards the second they come out and he probably doesn't have to pay for them either.

When I go to the A&P by myself, usually after school to return soda bottles to get two or three packs of cards, Big Nick only grunts at me, doesn't smile or nod, doesn't tell me that the potatoes are on sale, doesn't say maybe you'll get Roger Maris today, and granted, I don't care if the potatoes can peel themselves and whistle Dixie, but it sure would be nice if Big Nick could be just half as nice - *a fourth as nice* - as he is when I'm with my Mom.

He doesn't hurry over to the customer service and coffee grinding window to help me; he takes his own sweet time. He straightens up a cucumber here, realigns some oranges there, all the while just daring me to ring the bell so he can legally kill me. He's not busy showing Mrs. Heywood how to select a cantaloupe and he's not singing a lullaby to the radishes for crying out loud, he's just ignoring me as hard as he can while pretending to be on his way over. I smile at him and he says *Watch your mouth smart guy.*

When this tinyheaded tank finally ambles over from diapering each of the grapes, he has a face like you just yanked him away from a nap all about Big Nick in a Go Go Lounge. I ask him if the new baseball cards are in yet, the Fourth Series, and every Big Nick atom slumps in disgust and fatigue. *Now how am I supposed to know that?* he asks me.

Well, I answer, *it says so on the pack, you see, it says Series Three on this box and I was just wondering if, maybe, you*

PSSST! THIS WAY . . .

THINGS I REALLY BELIEVE

INTERNAL RHYME'S CHEAP SEATS WHERE STREET POETS AND ACADEMICS ALL ROOT FOR THE SAME LANGUAGE

aliens make Egyptians abandon perspective
to better communicate the prison of flesh
they make pyramids out of stones from a quarry on Mars
there's a monument there to the madcap Charlie Callas
the guy who pecks and flaps his arms

aliens show FDR where to drop the bombs
he goes along except for blowing up Passaic New Jersey
so the aliens zap his pituitary retool his polio
usher Truman into office which you may not know
is oval-shaped a flattened King Tut eyeball
everything that happens there is broadcast
to the relay set on Mars

Truman is gungho to blast the bejesus out of anything
that's evil or foreign or distracted or menacing or looming or
modern or smirking or small so he even agrees
to obliterating Passaic New Jersey
because it's a cruddy little city full of angry foreigners
who in spite of their anger and World War souvenirs
say nice things about FDR and his murals in City Hall

aliens throw gunpowder onstage to see what will happen
the aliens create the internet to enslave us
they bury fossils for dinosaurs that never existed
they give us Homer Lewis Carroll Ben Franklin Leonardo DaVinci
Margaret Dumont Joan of Arc Mozart Gregor Johann Mendel
Bob Desnos
that guy who trains fleas at Coney Island and

my fourth grade teacher Mrs. Esser

while rummaging through our brains and yards
they like some stuff that we made first like jazz surrealism
skateboards marionettes (is that a laugh) glasses though they
don't need them
Charlie Callas of course and miniature golf
if you could see them way out there you'd likely hear
this observation: how did we exist before?
without this game?

we're not just a Petrie dish for the aliens
a hatchery for half-alien-half-human many-hyphened people
who look like King Tut
we're not just an old resort planet to them a best kept secret of
the solar system
originally developed as a base camp for time travelers
we're not just their soap opera though we'd be their best if we
were less inhibited
we're not just curiosities or playthings or Rod Serling's zoo
animals
or guinea pigs for their violent mindsteering experiments

and now of course they make me wrap this up this way -
we're symbiotic partners in the wild
what we get beyond the grief and occasional surgical procedure
is guidance and mystery
and they in turn get proof of their existence

musicmaster

BiG NiCK CONTINUED

*have some Series Four behind the counter or in back because
it's Friday and that's when the new cards come in.* Big Nick
stares at me like centipedes are falling out of my nose. *Listen,*
he says, *don't give me a hard time. Buy the cards on the
counter, they're all the same.*

Oh no, they're not I say. *Series Four has Roger Maris and
Willie Mays. And Yogi Berra. And I thought you liked Roger
Maris or the Yankees or something and I could open them here
and show you if I get Roger Maris or not, I mean even Jimmy
Chambers whose Dad gets him the cards from New York where
they get the cards before we do, even he doesn't have Roger
Maris yet, but he'll trade like **all** of Series Two for a Roger
Maris.*

Big Nick leans forward and gets his face so close to mine that's
he eclipsed everything else in my world. *Listen Tommy*, he
whispers, *I hate baseball. I don't care if Roger Maris pitches
or sings Oh Say Can You See. Now do you want these cards or*

do you want me to run you through the coffee grinder? He
pulls back and raise his eyebrows.

I don't like either choice so I don't know what to say and I'm
not big enough to have a useful say in this situation, but I
finally sputter *I thought you liked baseball.*

Big Nick shakes his head and says *Kid, I don't like baseball,
I like your mother.* ∎

BEER IS YACHTING FOR THE WORKINGMAN

INTERNAL RHYME'S CHEAP SEATS WHERE STREET POETS AND ACADEMICS ALL ROOT FOR THE SAME LANGUAGE

aliens make Egyptians abandon perspective
to better communicate the prison of flesh
they make pyramids out of stones from a quarry on Mars
there's a monument there to the madcap Charlie Callas
the guy who pecks and flaps his arms

aliens show FDR where to drop the bombs
he goes along except for blowing up Passaic New Jersey
so the aliens zap his pituitary retool his polio
usher Truman into office which you may not know
is oval-shaped a flattened King Tut eyeball
everything that happens there is broadcast
to the relay set on Mars

Truman is gungho to blast the bejesus out of anything
that's evil or foreign or distracted or menacing or looming or
modern or smirking or small so he even agrees
to obliterating Passaic New Jersey
because it's a cruddy little city full of angry foreigners
who in spite of their anger and World War souvenirs
say nice things about FDR and his murals in City Hall

aliens throw gunpowder onstage to see what will happen
the aliens create the internet to enslave us
they bury fossils for dinosaurs that never existed
they give us Homer Lewis Carroll Ben Franklin Leonardo DaVinci
Margaret Dumont Joan of Arc Mozart Gregor Johann Mendel
Bob Desnos
that guy who trains fleas at Coney Island and

my fourth grade teacher Mrs. Esser

while rummaging through our brains and yards
they like some stuff that we made first like jazz surrealism
skateboards marionettes (is that a laugh) glasses though they
don't need them
Charlie Callas of course and miniature golf
if you could see them way out there you'd likely hear
this observation: how did we exist before?
without this game?

we're not just a Petrie dish for the aliens
a hatchery for half-alien-half-human many-hyphened people
who look like King Tut
we're not just an old resort planet to them a best kept secret of
the solar system
originally developed as a base camp for time travelers
we're not just their soap opera though we'd be their best if we
were less inhibited
we're not just curiosities or playthings or Rod Serling's zoo
animals
or guinea pigs for their violent mindsteering experiments

and now of course they make me wrap this up this way -
we're symbiotic partners in the wild
what we get beyond the grief and occasional surgical procedure
is guidance and mystery
and they in turn get proof of their existence

musicmaster

BiG NiCK CONTINUED

*have some Series Four behind the counter or in back because
it's Friday and that's when the new cards come in.* Big Nick
stares at me like centipedes are falling out of my nose. *Listen,*
he says, *don't give me a hard time. Buy the cards on the
counter, they're all the same.*

Oh no, they're not I say. *Series Four has Roger Maris and
Willie Mays. And Yogi Berra. And I thought you liked Roger
Maris or the Yankees or something and I could open them here
and show you if I get Roger Maris or not, I mean even Jimmy
Chambers whose Dad gets him the cards from New York where
they get the cards before we do, even he doesn't have Roger
Maris yet, but he'll trade like all of Series Two for a Roger
Maris.*

Big Nick leans forward and gets his face so close to mine that's
he eclipsed everything else in my world. *Listen Tommy,* he
whispers, *I hate baseball. I don't care if Roger Maris pitches
or sings Oh Say Can You See. Now do you want these cards or*

do you want me to run you through the coffee grinder? He
pulls back and raise his eyebrows.

I don't like either choice so I don't know what to say and I'm
not big enough to have a useful say in this situation, but I
finally sputter *I thought you liked baseball.*

Big Nick shakes his head and says *Kid, I don't like baseball,
I like your mother.* ∎

BEER IS YACHTING FOR THE WORKINGMAN

respect nuthin. They need to learn respect at home and at school like we did. Why when I talked back to my Daddy he walloped me with a baseball bat and shot my dog. And if you talked back to a nun, why they'd hang you upside down in front of the class until blood came out of your ears. None of that hurt me none. These kids just need to be shot at a coupla times themselves."

But then when you get past both the thoughtful and thoughtless essayists, America quickly returns to a preoccupation with breast implants, the President's penis (should Penis be capitalized as well?), and whether or not the government should fund artists who mock us with art about breast implants and the President's penis.

Pong is no longer the most violent video game and Beanie Babies are no longer the most pornographic things you can track on the internet.

The kneejerk reactions to articulate outcries and substantive analyses quickly become simple, useless (and I'd say equally dangerous) crusades to create dress codes, to place SWAT teams at the cineplex to make sure toddlers aren't ducking into a PG-13 showing, and to boycott Beavis & Butthead (about as effective as Beavis & Butthead boycotting homework)

I want to approach every high school waving a white surrender flag in satiric symbolic moronic free speech experiment. I want to go to the mall, the drag strip, the bleachers, behind the waterfalls and find groups of kids. Not marauding kids or necessarily redefining ones — eyes spiked and voices in their ears not on good terms with the voices in our ears — just ordinary teens. I want to walk up to groups of ordinary kids and beg for mercy, palms in front of me, beg them not to kill me. I want all of this videotaped, me making fun of the news, meaning not just the television news programs but the product of such a program, me as re-paranoia-ed for the new(news) millennium, this pleading for mercy by an aging guy crazy-afraid of teenagers because I'm exposed to too much of it on the news. I don't want the kids to shoot me of course but however they respond is fine, with ridicule or kindness. I might add subtitles to the video that label all of the shots of me *as Moving Target Sitting Duck Easy Prey* **Not Guilty** *Not Guilty Not Guilty in the great scheme of things I am not responsible for this and I'm not sideswiping survivalist ammo-crap logic-jerk here saying that personal responsibility is totally personal or responsible I'm just a fading fan of absurdist theater rip-offs.*

Pong is no longer the most violent video game and Beanie Babies are no longer the most pornographic things you can track on the internet and Rubber Ducky is no longer the dirtiest song you can listen to. Truth is never easy. That's why it's harder still to get to understand that nowadays some kids (and maybe not bad ones) are so scared of the world we're in (notice the *we're*) that they honestly don't believe that anyone's going to help them or that a well-phrased rebuttal to a slight is going to be as effective as shooting someone one-hundred-&-six times. We can help by helping – but this time let's do it without ridiculous sprawling intrusive attack-laws, without beating kids at home or at school, without bombing people into a passivity that we call peace, without making people dress like small soldiers, without valuing sports/jocks over arts/academics (when shooters have had sports team tie-ins, has the media/public suggested curbing/banning/blaming sports?); and let's not do it with just bake sales and t-shirts.

And a final thought . . . Be here now was never good practical, spiritual and/or philosophical advice. To realize that we've been here before and we'll be here again (at the most basic this-minute meaning) is truer higher consciousness, and requires a greater attention span. To get to that level, you just have to . . . ∎

---

from thE scEnic outlook the battlEfiEld looks bEautiful

I could open up a coffee shop

do it half-assed with dirty mugs and dirty thoughts

open it right next to a thriving Starbucks

charge a quarter more per cup of humble bean than they do

make people listen to raspy polka

shattering mugs and parrots on amphetamines

I could put an unenthusiastic but

foaming and wild-eyed kid behind the counter

have him sputter things like

someday I'm going to own my own cup of coffee

or

could I interest you in leaving me alone and

going next door to Starbucks?

and this sad suckerpunching mismanaged afterthought unnecessary retail pothole

would make more during its first day of doing business

than I make in a year of carefully writing poetry

or creating artworks

that are as near to the mortar of faith

as close to the beacon of truth

as I'll ever get while breathing

IF YOU KNOW ANYONE WHO CAN'T SPELL MILLENNIUM, START SCREAMING

JULY 2, 1999

INTERNAL RHYME

THE 38TH ISSUE OF MY PERSONAL EFFORT TO TIDY UP THE PLANET   ◆   MUSICMASTER, 5136 LYNDALE AVE. SO., MINNEAPOLIS, MN 55419

Great YoYo Copy Department

At an outlet mall's tent sale of hardware, where they have items from one dollar socket sets to pricey tool bins (I'd probably go for better tools and a cheaper bin), they also carry an odd assortment of miscellaneous items like sonar devices for fishermen, "collectible" awful&cheap-looking porcelain dolls, and faux folk-art cabinets (to reassure tool buyers who screw up a cabinet project that it still has a market).

I don't know much about tools and am forbidden to handle several popular ones, but I do know that a Phillips screwdriver is made with Phillips vodka and that if you're going to buy a tool it should be a Craftsman. My Dad, a lifer at Sear's and a handyman, often extolled the virtue's of the Craftsman brand and loved the maybe-true story of an eighty-year-old farmer who brought a broken, fifty-year-old Craftsman hammer into the store and it was replaced in a wink, no questions asked, no receipt requested (though if the old coot was so tight to demand a replacement for a tool he used for half a century, he probably saved the receipt somewhere).

So I'm wandering around tool tent aisles, mostly looking at the miscellaneous items – fishing lures to car wax –– about which I also know little. I occasionally pick up a hammer or wrench carefully, studiously, as if to hormonally gauge the heft and integrity of the device, as if my saw-sharp maleness knows grapefruit-squeezing rules for table vices. But mostly I look at useless cheaply-made sub-crappy maybe-dangerous hyper-miscellaneous nonsense like a bacon clothesline,

I look at useless nonsense like a bacon clothesline, Beanie Baby rip-offs called BeeKnees and dog biscuits made from bark (sic) and fish drippings.

Beanie Baby rip-offs called BeeKnees and dog biscuits made from bark (sic) and fish drippings. Well, not exactly those items, but items both close and far enough to cause concern.

Then I find Hyper YoYo, a *Professional* yo-yo with *sleep function* and an *Auto Return System* (their copy in italics). No exaggeration or poetic drift here; this is the paragraph with the humor as-is, as found. Small type advises *Unfragile.* It's only one dollar but bullet points note *Good for string play, centrifugal clutch inside* and stats: *Dim. 59mm* and *Weight 51g.* Whoa, now those are the numbers the smart yo-yo purchaser usually has to track down *in Consumer Reports* (note: magazine title, not their copy). The back of the wrapper has a *Notice to User* which includes: *Do not put the small parts into mouth to prevent from choking* (a small part would be about a fourth of one of the Yo's*); Do not tie the string around neck to play in a rough way; Be aware of people coming close when you play yo-yo outdoors or in a narrow place; Do not throw the yo-yo at people* (not only will you hit them, but Hyper YoYo will auto return to your hand then lash out and thwack them again and again*); Keep the yo-yo away from face or hair when it makes auto return. It may cause unexpected danger.*

I am so impressed with this tense, surreal copy that I buy the yo-yo for amusement and personal protection. It's not a Craftsman, but neither am I.   ■

Wooden Nickels

I have a wooden nickel from Disneyland's Frontierland (70s?), a few from various jamborees and smalltown squash worshipping festivals, most of the latter worth five cents off a purchase at so&so's tractor repair or squashateria. I have a few joke wooden nickels too. Well, I guess all wooden nickels are joke nickels (specialty printers charging about twelve cents each even in major runs), but I mean joke-imprinted, like the cornball classic *Round Tuit* (when someone tells you they'll do something when they get "around to it," you give them the Round Tuit) and *Birth control for men* (on the back it advises "Place in shoe; this will make you limp"). The printing on wooden nickels is always slightly offcenter.

Several years ago the sensationally bleak and rhythmic painter James Cobb, and his co-star Rhoda Mappo (a correspondence artist since the early 70s), took me to a wholesale novelty shop in San Antonio. On the upper floor of an ordinary-looking warehouse, the shop had mostly neglected showcases packed poorly with carnival prizes, any-idiot magic tricks, and disguise kits. There were also lots of wooden cabinets with lots

COME ON PEOPLE, LET'S MOVE IT TO THE NEXT PAGE

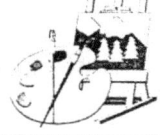

Pudding SicknE ss

by Dawn Cassidy

I love chocolate pudding. I love the taste of it. I love the texture. I love the act of eating it.

I love pouring milk on the thick skin and slowly consuming every last spoonful.

When I was a kid my mother would make Jell-O chocolate pudding. She'd pour it into four bowls. I would covet my serving, trying to make it last as long as possible. I would enviously eye my parents' servings, consider ways to bribe my brother out of his. Everyone else in my family would wait until the dishes were cleared and they had settled into their evening routines. Then they'd have their serving. "I can't eat dessert that soon after dinner" my mother would say. I couldn't fathom having a bowl of chocolate pudding to call your own and not eating it as soon as humanly possible. As soon as I had finished my dinner, I would eat my pudding.

I even went so far as to make chocolate pudding when I would come home from school. I'd make the sacrifice of eating it before the coveted skin had formed completely because, if I wanted to have all I wanted, I had to eat the entire batch. Then I would destroy the evidence. I only had about 1 ½ hours before my mom or brother would get home. Even then it wasn't enough. I was still sad when it was gone.

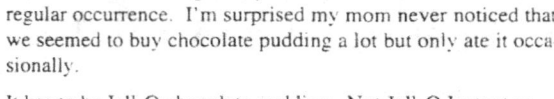

This wasn't something I did just once or twice. This was a regular occurrence. I'm surprised my mom never noticed that we seemed to buy chocolate pudding a lot but only ate it occasionally.

It has to be Jell-O chocolate pudding. Not Jell-O Instant or Royal, or some other off-brand. No chocolate fudge or dark chocolate. None of this chocolate mousse stuff either. I am always disappointed, *always*, when I order chocolate pudding in a restaurant. It just isn't the same. Just give me Jell-O Chocolate Pudding you make from a box. And it has to be the 8 serving size box. There is absolutely no point in making the 6 serving size.

My mother is a great cook. She makes incredible cakes, tortes, pies, things you see in *Martha Stewart Living*. And she really enjoys making these treats. This past Christmas she called me to ask what I wanted to eat on Christmas Eve. The ham was a given, as was escalloped corn and some form of cheese potatoes. These are mandatory at our Christmas Eve dinners. But the dessert is open to suggestion. She laughingly told me that my older brother, Mark had suggested chocolate pudding. "That's a great idea" I said. "I love chocolate pudding."

"You kids are all nuts" said my mother. "I thought Mark was crazy when he suggested pudding, so I told Erik and he thought it was a great idea too. I thought at least you would want something more fun."

"More fun than chocolate pudding? What could be more fun than chocolate pudding?

So my mother gave in and made a quadruple batch of chocolate pudding. But because she is my mother she still managed to add her own special flair. She served it in a big, beautiful, footed crystal bowl with homemade whipped cream spiked with Mexican vanilla.

I couldn't have asked for a better Christmas!   ■

The above vignette was written by my beloved companion, co-conspirator and spouse. Clearly, she handles the niceness in our family and perpetuation of same. The above piece's shameless last line - a mix of schmaltz, mawkishness (one of those words you cannot correctly say three times fast) and the ballast from *Reader's Digest's* "Life in These United States" feature -wasn't written because Dawn was looking for a quick or cliched exit, but because *she meant it* . . . probably due to complications of pudding overdose or pudding flashback; pudding tremors! I don't like pudding and I didn't eat any of Dawn's mother's pudding this past Christmas; I found solace in an additional fine microbrewed cold dark beer. What could be more fun than chocolate pudding? - A fine microbrewed cold dark beer! I couldn't have asked for a better Christmas!   ■

I really need to sleep

to conk out for an uninterrupted Rip Van lights out

     sack of lead afloat in soothing absinthe sleep

to catch up on the homework and what not to remember

to fly a little bit around the old house in Clifton

to catch up on whatever sleep gives us

    maybe the hours it takes away

    are given back with negotiable skills in

    designing composing selling vacuum cleaners

I don't know what it is that makes me like the lack of sleep

the backedup-awakeness or

the shifting blur of even the most tangible things

(the rocks themselves are jello in my sunken sight)

but I like it to *that* point like now

when I'm not sure from where I hear the snoring

musicmaster.march 98

NonSmok**E**rs Who Want Jo**E** Cam**E**l Spittoons

I fill in those consumer product surveys that periodically find our mailbox; not so much because of promised coupons, but because of an inexplicable need I can only explain as a mix of *penance* to the product-happy commerce I too often slander, and *keeping connected* somehow, anchored to the planet in straight-ahead truck-buying/which-canned-tuna-to-use?/over-the-counter ways. I fill in the surveys thoughtfully, my little check marks contributing to big, faraway numbers that may someday create a line of Kool-Aid soup.

You can accuse me of being too critical of marketing chatter and glut, but you can't accuse me of dodging questions about which frozen entrees I buy (in part *because* of that marketing and glut).

So I'm filling in a survey the other night; I don't drive. I don't eat any fish. I **hate** mayonnaise (which has its own category in this survey), I don't wear contacts, I don't really differentiate among pain killers/sinus pills/flu remedies (three separate categories), I don't read romance novels, I don't want to sleep with Little Debbie or Betty Crocker (two categories), and I

> *I understand that giving false information in order to accept these offers may constitute a violation of law.*

don't give a flying rat's ass which floor cleaner we use (whatever we haul out when Elly the Dog acks up some ghoulash she snacked on in the backyard is fine with me; though if a particular brand bragged that it picked up and de-stenched vomit quicker and easier than other brands, I'd probably give it a try). For a fleeting second I think that because of my peculiarities they don't want me, the survey takers don't want me, they want someone who buys lots of RVs, loves fluffy scented patterned toilet paper and sees a line of credit as a second income. Then I think I'm probably just being delusional or, worse, very self-centered and that, truly, most respondents are similar to me - quietly deranged souls who wonder why lite beer isn't listed as a product in the nutrition and diet category.

Anyway, I'm dutifully chugging along when I get to a special boxed area labeled CIGARETTES (ADULTS ONLY - 21 OR OLDER). In skipping past the many questions therein (menthol or non-menthol, lights or ultra, lung cancer or throat cancer), I spot a special signature area which authorizes companies to send coupons and premiums; part of it reads "I certify I am 21 years of age or older, and that I currently smoke cigarettes. I understand that giving false information in order to accept these offers may constitute a violation of law."

Are there nonsmokers who collect cigarette coupons? Are there folks who want the last of the Joe Camel-type gear before it's all fully criminalized into hyper-collectibility? Maybe so. But that falsely signing this proclamation may constitute a violation of law is spectacular bullshit - a new classic bit of marketbabble/deceit designed to better gather useful data (and, of course, to limit or scare away bad nonsmoking types from big tobacco companies' generosity).

Then again too, what if I'm wrong? What if someday I'm walking around a flea market in traditional flea market garb - big honking Ram tough belt buckle, Joe Camel t-shirt, backwards baseball cap that reads Shithead - and a stranger asks for a light; *sorry* I say *I don't smoke* and the guy asks *then why the hell are you wearing a Saint Joe t-shirt?* and I answer *because I got it in the mail as a promotion item* and, to make a long story fit into this paragraph, it turns out the stranger is actually an undercover tobacco cop on a sting operation to catch survey cheats like me.

on uneasy days

we wave at one another like buckled palms
the glaciers of justice fortitude and
a drunken game of *who tatooed the corpse*
carving our foreheads into white terriers
named Augie and Kettle
I know that sounds both odd and ordinary
surrealism only reality unstarched
a toasted violin a pillow with radio dials
a big ridiculous grin across a mountain
but that's often how it's best described
when eye to eye we toss and fetch
the stuff beneath the language   musicmaster.march 98

TURN DOWN THE VOLUME, I CAN'T HEAR MYSELF SCREAM

Dogs Without Cars - Before *Internal Rhyme*, I printed an even more offbeat newsletter that I left on bus seats and on benches. Containing articles supposedly written by drivers and riders (including classic bus nerds and bus-specific chatterboxes), *Dogs Without Cars* is stupid and satiric, printed to look like a crackpot religious tract left in a phone booth, and deliberately packed with incongruities, references to fictitious events/people/routes (just like actual bus releases), and a bus load of nonsense (just like an actual bus). I distributed (littered?) hundreds of each issue mostly in '88 & '89 and recently found a small pile of extras. *Dogs* had enough of a cult following that it got written up a few times and two college libraries asked for subscription rates (I sent them the same info' I printed in each issue of *Dogs*: "A subscription to *Dogs Without Cars* is only two dollars! Just leave your cash payment or actual credit card -we'll return it to exactly where we picked it up- on any unoccupied seat of your regular a.m. inbound MTC bus. I'll leave your copies on the same seat as they're available"). This is the first time you may secure Dogs without the agony of mass transit. *$2.00/four back issues and a surprise.*

Nondimensional - 70-some pages of my poems (all pre-1992 and carefully selected from hundreds written since 1980; I didn't fluff the book up with filler/also-ran/gratuitous-sonnet-shit/show-off-literary-games) and a few drawings (and each of those is worth another thousand words). *$5.00*

Send check or money order to Musical Comedy Editions, 5136 Lyndale Ave. So., Minneapolis, MN 55419 and throw in a few bucks for shipping (no shipping or handling if you pick-up from me or via Art Underground/Anodyne. My phone: (612) 825-4101. Offbeat free stuff with all orders.

PLEASE SEND ME YOUR IDEAS/CAPTIONS FOR "THE POET IS IN"

P*E*opl*E* Ar*E* Funny, But Rar*E*ly Funny *E*nough

Number of Americans who believe extraterrestrials walk among us: 41%; not really sure: 22%; not at all sure: 19%; do not fully believe: 6%; do not really believe: 6%; do not believe: 4%; won't answer - conflict of interest: 3%; who believe I walk among them: 2%; who think extraterrestrials *should* be allowed to join the Boy Scouts: 68%; who think Boy Scouts are all gay anyway: 7%.

Number of Americans who believe God can hear them: 75%; who believe God *can't* hear them with all the usual racket going on: 5%; who believe they can hear God: 2%; who can't hear God because of the neighbor's loud parties: 65%.

Number of Americans who have figured out what the biggest damn problem is: 94%; who named their canaries *Doctor Jazz*; who dishonestly fill in blanks on surveys: 27%; who have an album by *The Who*: .07%; who can do Abbot and Costello's entire *Who's On First* routine: .008; who would change *Who's Who* to *Who's Whom*: .0003.

from *The Odds That You'll Be Crushed By a Safe* by Larry Tell, Wow! Books ∎

EL NINO IS A SCAPEGOAT FOR TROUBLES BORNE OF OZONE DEPLETION

SEPTEMBER 15, 1999

INTERNAL  RHYME

SPECIAL 41st MILLENNIUM/SHMILLENNIUM – LET'S CALM DOWN ISSUE   ◆   MUSICMASTER, 5136 LYNDALE AVE. SO., MINNEAPOLIS, MN 55419

What's Going On?

NEWS ABOUT MOVERS & SHAKERS, INDUSTRY DOINGS, AND WHAT PR COMPANIES SEND US

WHEN THE FAT LADY BELCHES

The Annual Let Capitalism Sing! Opera Crawl will be held Saturday, November 4th, 5 p.m. – Midnight at nine bars throughout town that are connected by "We're Off to Sing! Sing!" shuttle buses. Reception and headquarters facility will be the lobby of the Christ I'm Drunk Opera Company, located in Uptown's Beet Processing Plant which was recently revitalized with an infusion of 182 million in mostly public dollars for some new signage and reupholstering the cushioned bannisters. One $750 ticket entitles a guest to one beer at each of the nine bars, free shuttling, a $1000 receipt (issued at registration) and a button that reads *I Don't Know Shit About Opera – But If You Hum a Few Bars . . . .* Participating bars include PlowMaster, Mr. J's Aria Room, Tuskalooser, Oprah's Opera House, Drunk&Loud, Carmen's, Wagner's Wagon, Lucky Us, and Snooty's on the Mall.

POST-ANUS BOLD JOINS BIGDOG

BIGDOG INTERNATIONAL announced that **Brawnsten Constantine the Bold** has joined the Minneapolis Office as Senior Vice President of the Newly-Formed CAPITAL LETTERS

Constantine brings 22 Years of Experience in Capitalizing Every Title, Department, Event – Every Adjective and Noun – he could

DEPT. Constantine brings 22 Years of Experience in Capitalizing Every Title, Department, Event – Every Adjective and Noun – he could find at the TV-based ANUS PARTNERS INC. Some of his MAJOR ACCOMPLISHMENTS as Senior Letter Engineer at ANUS included the Development of Such Quadruple-A Ideas as AAAA ANUS and AAAA ANUS II. Constantine's First Assignment at BIGDOG will be the development of AAAAA BIGDOG and AAAAA BIGDOG II, which will be the First Five-Capital-A's-in-a-Row Projects in the Upper Midwest.

FIRM STILL KISSING ASS FOR THIS DEAL

Butte Moore Ugli Architects has designed the new headquarters for ScamFed Audio Foods, Inc., a major manufacturer of CD dinners, in the Steinway on Parke Mall and Key Shop in Burnsville. The 85,310 sq.ft. office/warehouse/retail/worship facility will consist of 2 levels of restroom space, 1 level of lobby space, 1 underground level for empty boxes and stuff, and a huge expensive corporate-level suite in which owners

Rexus and **Noxious Horr** will educate legislators on the merits of privatizing CD lunch programs in public schools. The project is being developed by **Swenson Swanson & Sween** who are also acting as lightbulbs in this year's HoliDazzle Parade.

Butte Moore also announced that **Dummin Ugli** — principal dork and chief golfer for the international postage buying team — would be designing sets (his challenge: to capture the essence of a hideously bland hospital waiting room and an undecorated basement vending machine area) for the hit tv series, *ER*. Go Ugli – *ER*!

NICE TIE!

GodCo Capital recently arranged permanent financing on RidgeWoode Lake Theatre, a 320,000 sq.ft. assisted living compound in Savage. Permanent financing for $25,000,003 was arranged **by Sal "Impact Fee" Morrelli**, Executive Arranger of GodCo's Outer Borough Division, on behalf of the borrowers.

SHIT FROM SHATZ

A-Okay Southeast Management's Upper Midwest Office announced that Say-Ahhh Health System has leased office and hiding space at A-Okay Centre, a master planned sick building sprawl at Centre North Road SW and West Off-Centre Drive NE in South St. Paul.

Biff "Rip" Shatz, President of A-Okay Southeast Management's Upper Midwest Office – Twin Cities on The Parke Region, NE Division II, also announced that A-Okay will be changing its name on January 1, 2000 to AAA-Okay. The Southeast Management's Upper Midwest Office will become SSS-Southeast MMM-Management's UUU-Upper MMM-Midwest's OOO-Office. Shatz claims the name-change was inspired by a meeting he had with BIGDOG's new Senior Veep

MORE VERY SIMILAR RELEASES NEXT PAGE

Brawnsten Constantine the Bold, at the recent Let Capitalism Sing! Golf Tournament. "By his sixth drink in the clubhouse, Brawnie was spilling beer and secrets," said Shatz. "His whole, brilliant career of doubling and tripling letters, capitalizing them – and capitalizing *on* them— and bolding them, is all just an off-shoot of how he sees things when he's pickled to the eyebrows."

YOUR COMPANY'S NAME HERE!

The October meeting of the **National Association of Specialty Printers, Manufacturers and Dealers** (NASPMD) will feature the seminar *Turning Hot Air into Profits* presented by motivational speaker and imprinted balloon authority Fred "Blowhard" Ketchum. Attendees will learn: Selling the Sucker with a Giveaway Pen!; How to Hogtie Homer with an Imprinted Keychain; Make Them Pay-Pay-Pay for that Dorky Fortune Cookie with Your Name Inside; How to Ram a Free Waterbottle Up the Ass of Mr. Just Looking; What's Exciting in Imprinted Calendars; the One-Balloon Poodle-&-Pup Giveaway; and How to Make Sales Soar With Those Matchbooks Nobody Takes Anymore.

The $49 registration fee includes the two-hour seminar, a refillable jelly donut, and an assortment of imprinted novelties, from standards such as toothpicks and note cubes to such "next wave" products as pygmy cockroaches and homeless children (the company logo can be removed from the child's forehead only by following-up with a participating auto dealer).

IMELDA THE WELDA?

Digg & Chisel Construction will begin construction of Shop Shape Uncommons in Morris three months from last Monday. This 780,221 sq.ft. shopping center features shoe stores, specialty food stores, specialty shoe stores, gourmet food stores, gourmet shoe stores, a Quick Shoes outlet, a first-ever Quick-Shoes & Pizza outlet, and Sears (with their new Craftsman Shoes and Kenmore Pretzels Departments).

FAX POPULI

King Realty announced that **Edmo Curtis** has joined their Team Cubicle E-Mail Marketing Department to help with the phones.

YOU HAVE HIS WORD

GodCo Capital recently arranged eternal debt on La Grande Shoppe Haus on the Heath, a strip mall at 133892-1/2 SE Rural County Road 541 (Hwy 2) in Kenyon. The twenty-year-old retail complex, formerly known as "Down by the gas station," is made up of a Chuggin' Chuck's Beer Depot, Speakin' a Beacon Storefront Church, Bobster's Sports Cards & Taxidermy ("Preserve your Beanie Babies!"), and a photo booth. Permanent financing for $3,828 was arranged by Officer **Rufus Gianininini**, Associate Arranger of GodCo's Outreach to Riches Division, on behalf of the borrowers.

GOOD VS. EVIL

The Let's Gang Lobby a Politician Committee has just released a training video for member use only. "Good vs Evil" is 20-minute educational tape that reveals such Top Secret Lobbying Tricks as: *Money Pie*; *Of Course I Wouldn't Threaten You*; *We'll Kiss Both Cheeks*; and *Come on, We're All Adults Here*. For this excellent train-the-troops video, we owe many thanks to members of the committee: Chair Buck Krapper, **Billion "Poor Boy" Ayer**, James Krowe, Heidi Fleiss, and **Ima Jurk**. With each video purchased, buyers receive fifty copies of the pamphlet *Plea-Bargaining God for Riches Now, Light Industrial Penance Later*.

SMILE WHEN YOU SAY THAT

The Image Committee, chaired by opera and fine wine enthusiast **Dummin Ugli** of **Butte Moore Ugli Archi tects**, announced that the fundraising group's charities for 2000 include: **National Association of Specialty Printers, Manufacturers and Dealers**; Digg & Chisel Construction; **A-Okay Southeast Management** (Upper Midwest Office); and **GodCo Capital**. These entities' nonprofit divisions (e.g. A-Okay's *Pennies for Prostitutes* Initiative – a program which prompted A-okay's President **Biff "Rip" Shatz** to say "I'm all for pennies for prostitutes!") are now each entitled to a share of the net proceeds from the committee's fundraiser next spring — the Annual Let Capitalism Score! Mini Golf & Pub Crawl.

In other business, the committee approved an expenditure of $53,311 to retain a public relations firm for a couple of hours of work to help the committee improve its image among dues-paying members. Ugli says "we don't want to be thought of as simply rich, degenerate power-mongers – though that certainly works well enough to get us laid; we want the public to regard us as better than that, snazzier than that. We want to be thought of as rich, degenerate GOOD power-mongers." The contracted public relations firm – Lyon, White, Wash & Cajole – says the image improvement campaign will be called "Don't

MORE NEWS TO LOSE OR USE NEXT PAGE

Take a Left at the Heart Bypass

Yeah, I'm going to try and squeeze out issue #41 in August though I'm swamped with reality. Deadlines and jobs always logjam in August, concurrent unfortunately with lots of art stuff I really need to do for both sanity and, more importantly, the insanity I embrace as the rhyme and reason of purposeful life. Whoa, I don't mean to get heavy here; and I don't mean to trivialize what I mean by using the phrase "get heavy." And I don't mean to keep not meaning things either. But it's 2 a.m. again and I thought I'd tap out some fast filler about *Internal Rhyme* . . .

■ I started *IR* in August '97, on a sticking glitching electric typewriter I brought to a family vacation at Huddle's Resort, up near Walker. That I don't know on which lake shows I'm not yet fully Minnesotan. Minnesotans always say town or nearby town and lake both. So if you know just one, say the town, a well-traveled native responds "Oh, is that on Green Lake?" Then when you say "Well it's near Little Green Lake, over by Kneecap," they say "My Uncle use to have a cabin north of Kneecap, in Sequin," to which you respond "Oh, is Sequin on Lake Fritter?"

Minnesotan loves directions and how every damn cabin in the entire state is positioned in terms of how they're fixtured or familiar with "up north." There are eleven thousand plus lakes in Minnesota, but you can easily find, on any metro area bus, people who claim to have heard of any lake you mention. "Lake Sven is a small lake, about ten miles past East Boyoboy," you remark. And they nod, "I used to fish there with Leal Anderson."

Plus, Minnesotans get inebriated from listening to or reciting directions to any location at all; they like to hear *which* turn, not just from this direction, but from directions *they'll never take*; they like historical directions, from times before the road was closed or rerouted or renamed, especially liking to say "oh, sure, but the quickest way to beat that roadwork going on over there is to take the frontage road." That no one living or dead or **in desperate need of any human contact at all** could give a flying fricassee about nontraveling travel-talk or smalltalk at its smallest state ever is irrelevant to Minnesotans gabbing endlessly – in an annoying and chatty solidarity - about why the hell they're always late, or twenty minutes early (after they fully explain the roads they took to arrive early, along with detailed evaluations of routes they didn't take, it's just like they're fifteen minutes late anyway).

One of the kindest, most amiable people I know is an attorney/ lobbyist with a lot of choirboy mischief in him. (Yes, I'm being nice because he reads *Internal Rhyme* and I don't want him to think I'm slamming him here – that'll come in issue #44.) He's smart, game for chaotic tangents, and a fun guy to have over for poker if you don't ask him how to get somewhere. Because *he'll tell you* how to get there. In excruciating detail and with variant routes. If he doesn't know how to get there, he will honestly explain he doesn't know, but he'll continue nonetheless - relentlessly and undaunted – to tell you how *you might* get there – especially if you say "it's up by Lake Wilbur?" Even though this guy is a great lobbyist, listening to him talk about directions makes you want to die yesterday.

Anyway, I wrote the first *Internal Rhyme* in August '97 at Huddles in effort to loosen up my expression, to have a vehicle not as tightly-wound as my poems, which I often rewrite a dozen times to make them sound free flowing! And my plan was to get an issue out every two weeks or so. And "or so" has become the norm. Though it is now "August" 1999, I am only, with this release, at issue 41; I had hoped to be up to 52 (or so) by now.

■ What happened? After a dozen or so effortless issues, I became self-conscious. I regrouped by banging my head with a skillet. After another dozen issues, I slowed down again because items about which I wanted to do quick takes became dated if I didn't get them out immediately, (e.g. my smartass

WHAT'S GOING ON? CONTINUED

Hate Us Because We're Your Superiors" and might contain slogans/jingles/t-shirts/inspirational-cellphone-stickers that announce "Kiss My Ass . . . *Please*," "You're Not the Only Pebble, But I'm the Only Tide," "Is Your Younger Clone in the Shop?" and a signature theme – "Rich and Evil But Never Rich or Evil Enough."

BEACH ON A BUN

The United States' Deputy Assistant SubMarshall of Near-Meat Additives (Upper Midwest Region IV) recently shut down a sausage/potted-meat grindery in Austin for using more sand per wiener (SPW) than the maximum 32% now allowed by the Federal Sand Administration's Beach Reclamation Council (Upper Midwest Region IV). The 50% SPW consumed by the plant exploits "the integrity, the easy-going nature and the semi-digestibility of sand, a federally protected subresource," said SubMarshall Timmy Tiny Jr. III. "We'll lose too many beaches if we allow them to be consumed at this rate." The plant is owned by the **National Association of Specialty Printers, Manufacturers and Dealers** (NASPMD) who purchased the business (along with the "Mmmm, It's Edible!" line of foods) in 1996 to develop and produce imprinted coldcuts, hot dogs and portion-controlled riblets for such corporate clients as Pepsi, the NBA, and Pawn America. NASPMD spokesmodel **Rigda Gnusmore** said the closing was an attack on the working class, the eating class, and the imprinted-products-consuming class. ■

EXCUSES CONTINUED NEXT PAGE

83% OF ALL PERCENTAGES ARE INCORRECT AT LEAST 25% OF THE TIME

takes on a media-duping soundbite are themselves so soundbite-sounding/soundbite-phrased that their expiration date usually passes long before I can write, then print them). I got past that hurdle by rewriting "time sensitive" quick takes into irrelevant generalities about metaphorical props like pogo sticks or my children. By issue thirty-five I slumped again because I was growing tired of writing about pogo sticks and my children. I resurfaced by drinking seventeen beers so I'd no longer care (nor preserve a braincell that remembered) that, afterall, metaphors are just (fill in your joke here _____). Now, writing this piece for *Internal Rhyme* #42, I'm recommitting myself to providing you with the finest, tortured, self-conscious, alternate reality, unshaven, joke-&/or-insight laden prose I can produce in a world where whether I ever write anything again or not is completely irrelevant.

■ I could knock out a dozen issues – ratatatatat — get up to #50 by midOctober, by filling issues with poems and half-poems I wrote (and probably performed) between mid-1992 (when I printed *Nondimensional*) and August '97. That's a lot of stuff,

including good pieces I routinely trivialize at readings. But my craw won't let me do that unless I date the older stuff, because even though the stuff would be new to most IR readers, I would want to guilt myself in print in effort to get me to write still more. It's not that writing is a chore (in fact it's a thrill ride/ an in(tro)spection of all senses/a caravan down one's own throat/a differently adjusted image/an obligation to history/an always optimistic and romantic tangent/each word worth 1/ 10,000th of a picture/it's mostly nonbouncy rhymes; it's like looking at a painting from within), but I nonetheless need to write more to get better at it, and fluffing up issues with old inventory strikes me as cheating. I might recycle some material for *Internal Rhyme*'s 50th Anniversary issue, which will be a bigdeal blow-the-budget gala with special inserts, first-run typos, a letter or two from readers I'll have to make up, and a mini-poster of nonspecifically fun drawings. Until then, late or not or guilty or not, I'll only give you "new" stuff (e.g. new versions of the same things I always write about: call for a new national mascot, the alphabet's secret life, somersaulting canaries).   ■

"You Are the First Civil Defense Group"

At a garage sale I found a 1950 paperback **How to Survive an Atomic Bomb** by Richard Gerstell (Consultant, Civil Defense Office). On the cover of this "Complete Easy-to-Read Guide for Every Home, Office and Factory" is clip-art of a Mom/Dad/Junior/Sis unit staring slightly upwards at what might be hope, or the future, or neighbors aflame.

The back cover cuts right through your silly gossip-fed fears with this copy . . .

IS IT TRUE . . .

that you have no defense against atomic bombs?

that food hit by atomic rays is poisoned?

that one bomb can wipe out a city?

that atomic rays kill everything they touch?

The answer to all these questions is NO. These false ideas, and many others, are nailed down in this fact-filled, easy-to-read book.

Written in question-and-answer form by a leading expert, this book will tell you how to protect yourself and your family in case of atomic attack. There is no "scare talk" in this book. Reading it will actually make you feel better –

-Because, even though it tells you frankly what the bomb can do, it also tells you what it can't *do.*

Even if this book's contents *are* an accurate refutation of allergic reactions to a-bomb politics, I have to nonetheless assume

they're wrong. Because even with our aging, semi-enlightened hearts, we look back with more critical (non-seeing) eyes, and I have to assume that what the author believed in was less essential to life then - than what I believe in now. I have to assume the book is wrong because even though I'm not a scientist or researcher or atomic bomb polisher, my uncredentialed skepticism is an instinctive *knowing* that huge heatflashing girder-knotting explosions are bad. And, frankly, because I always find fear to be more exhilarating than knowledge, and more interactive/Artistic than complacency. I can almost hear the voices of that family unit graphic on the cover:

"My God," whispers Dad, "It looks like the Reds finally blew apart every cheap foreign bastard in Passaic. You know what that cloud means, don't you?"

Mother answers, "That we should eat mushrooms?"

Dad Junior answers, "That we don't ever have to see that idiot Mr. Pomeroy again!"

Sis answers, "That we're going to die within minutes unless we take some sensible precautions?"

"That's right, Sis!" says Dad, flesh beginning to drip off his brow, "We have to stand up to this potentially serious threat by putting on sunglasses, eating aspirin, and playing canasta in the basement for the next four years."

"Are we going to die!?" asks Dad Junior.
"Silly boy!" chides Dad, just before his eyeballs explode, his tongue ignites and air itself gasps.   ■

NO LEAD PAINT WAS DISTURBED IN THE CREATION OF THIS NEWSLETTER

INTeRNAL RHYMe

NOVEMBER 1, 1999

ISSUE 43 OF THE NEWSLETTER THAT WORKS WITH UNCLOCKABLE DEADLINES ◆ MUSICMASTER, 5136 LYNDALE AVE. SO., MINNEAPOLIS, MN 55419

Roll an Eleven

This multi-issue piece is full of outlines, lists, vignettes, and ideas - some half-baked, some over cooked, some just right. A number of the items that seem substantially more than a draining of the spit-valve are actually in-process projects. An original intent with this piece was to do 11 numbered groupings of 11 items; I'm tabling the project at 3 numbered groupings of 11 items (several with 11 parts). I know that in coming months, I'll think about this piece *Now & Then* ...

#1 Poetry Night – Ongoing open mike series with host, soundman, bartender, a few other regulars. Real poets from different cities' coffee shop/university/underground circuits, each performing/reading one piece each; some presentations however are actualized with sets, dancers, animation, etc. Actors reading/performing as well (over-dramatic *Gunga Din*, TV pitchmen reading sonnets). *No* cute kid poetry; and very, very little traditional poetry. For example, one week includes poets from Ann Arbor, Newark, Sacramento, a street poet, a hand model doing a specially-gesticulated reading from Sylvia Plath; running subplots via host's between-act announcements, interactions with sound man, comments from the bar. Guest commentary from area academics, critics, financial advisors. There are necessary undercurrents about why this alternative venue is necessary; all digs and cheap shots at stuffier/academic/traditional/ "credentialing" centers are outweighed by heavy-handed jokes at own/MikeScene expense.

> *"If I Ran the Cemetery," about a little boy who watches somber processionals in the cemetery across the street, has Dr. Seuss phrasings, rhythms and coinages.*

#2 Dr. Soused – Due to childhood trauma while reading *Cat in the Hat*, Dr. Soused can only write in Dr.-Seuss-style. His "If I Ran the Cemetery," about a little boy who from his bedroom window watches somber processionals and ceremonies in the cemetery across the street, has Dr. Seuss phrasings, rhythms and coinages. The boy envisions the funerals becoming more festive and raucous; "cadavers dance and Dead Fred rants atop a tomb of long-gone aunts;" "you could bet there'd be streamers and beer and no worry if I put some life in that old cemetery." Dr. Soused is routinely sued by the Seuss estate, which in itself could spark a theme song if not an entire theme park of litigation.

#2B I love dodging the obvious. It's a shame it takes an effort as extreme as dodging or ducking or avoiding. But there you have it (oops! Obvious observation!). But I won't dodge the obvious here because this time it doesn't exacerbate my ennui, salt my eyeballs with ad agency visuals, warrant my annoyance . . . No, this time it mandates I suggest that Dr. Soused, coot in a zoot suit, be a regular character on Poetry Night!

#3 Mudville – New cast each week acts out a favorite episode of *Cheers*. Non-actors (and actors good enough to convincingly play non-actors) and actors play, maybe occasionally switch the big roles; at least one part, e.g. Woody, is always played by a volunteer from the audience. Some read from scripts, others speak too softly, Coach is a puppet, Diane is played by a drag queen. A special episode features Michael Jordan playing all the roles. This becomes a cult hit on Channel 43288. Anniversary episodes include guest appearances by original cast members who show up to poorly play the characters they defined.

#4 Photo Album – Each episode is a "slide show" of viewers' family photos, a full second per photo with silent clicks that make images merge/emerge from one another rather than more harshly progress. 1,000 or more photos per show, probably thematic, i.e. Birthdays, Picnics, Camp Activities, Class Pictures, Holiday Gatherings, etc., nothing mean or deliberately set-up (no "America's Funniest/Stupidest" focus), just photos sent in, mixed/edited with collaging sensibility but no actual collaging. Just pictures of people; two or more per photo, 2,000 or more people per show, looking

EVERY PAGE CAN BE TURNED (SING IT!)

back for once as real people, folks as-is. No winners or favorites among the pictures, the intro and wrap are poems/folk art/ street preachers, stuff about the theme. Poems as background; mostly newer/underground/Beat. Shortening fifteen minutes of fame to just a second is reasonable compromise with apocalyptic fears. Many, many would watch to wait and watch for themselves; many more would just enjoy the novelty; but all would end up seeing/ingesting much more. Internet? This show will someday be made for sure (and for sure has been circled already and often), but it will be made via exclusionary production, e.g. kids shown must be wearing Gap clothes or playing with Beanie Babies, but it won't be called exclusionary production, it will be called something very insidious like Nice Choice or Family Options. The show will become a terrible, evil thing.

Poetry is more than chewing on a pencil thinking up words that rhyme with hamster but don't throw you on the hamster's wheel.

#5 Priceless – Series featuring fringe artists, folk artists, mail artists, people so far off the radar they are not on "fringe circuit." Their processes, products, motives are explored in their studios/basements/homes. There can be genuine critical asides as well as irreverent retorts, passers-by murmuring. This is the gallery for the dispossessed, the abandoned, those so commercially irrelevant that their passion isn't sullied by marketability adjustments. No grantsmanship talk or defense. Occasional tirades about art bureaucracies.

#6 If Alexander Calder Played Santa Claus – A collection of sketchy, colorful Christmas drawings depicting how Santa alone or with his sleigh or in the department store would look/ behave if played by a living or dead, well-known artist. Calder would have the reindeer dangling from the sleigh at different lengths, bobbing and slowly rotating like a big mobile. (Though Calder is incorrectly credited with inventing the mobile – he certainly popularized them – isn't something to be addressed in a lightweight stocking stuffing for people who chuckle knowingly.) Some obvious ones, sure: Rodin as thinking Santa, Christo Santa is himself wrapped up, Toulouse-Lautrec has lots of petticoats and a top hat. Frieda Kahlo is Santa with bushy, black eyebrows (flaming heart?). Marcel Duchamp descends a staircase. George Segal has papier-mâché reindeer. Jackson Pollock crashes sleigh into a tree. Roy Lichtenstein! Modigliani! Grant Wood! No missing ear for Van Gogh but maybe each reindeer is missing an ear? Cindy Sherman is Santa! (But who, dear average reader, is Cindy Sherman?)

#7 Now & Then

#8 Still Works – A looser, lowbrow *Antiques Roadshow* with folks showing common, even broken things. Appraisers are dealers playing lowball even with this stuff. Owners defend pedigree that's absent or make absurd claims, e.g. a broken plastic ice cube tray is from the church in *Alice's Restaurant*. Lucky finds are replaced here by regular good deals or stupid purchases. This is Studs Terkel Americana without the complex issues or codgerly drum solos. An old lady insists that because it's Mickey Mouse — a dented, Big Little Book without a spine — that it's worth a hundred times more than it is (this often apparent to the average viewer). For the very rare item that's really valuable, there's one appraiser who lies about it, tries to buy it for a song.

#9 Mutt & Ego — I read my poems in a hyper-caffeinated marathon, reread some three or four times, read some in a loop, read one or two over and over until I repair or learn to live with it/them. I'm usually right on the beat by the fifth or six poem. I should start with the fifth or sixth poem. I read a poem about writing poems and rewrite it while people watch my eyes move like contrapuntal metronomes. I read about the war effort for our disposable income. I read to a room full of animated microphones as they twist and turn; one, wearing headphones, is screaming from feedback. I read only poems I don't read, which means ones I don't read at readings. I call them poems because it aggravates poets. I write while slumbering, where different things rhyme. It is more than chewing on a pencil thinking up words that rhyme with hamster but don't throw you on the hamster's wheel. Most traditional and free verse poets both don't get it past the catnip chase.

#10 Descending a Staircase – Current news photos, famous paintings, captionless editorial cartoons and popular advertising images are alternately shown between two teams (e.g. one celebrity and two nobodies) (one of the nobodies can be an undersung or has-been somebody, but only one; both, however, can be semi-somebodies) who try to come up with the best caption. There are no judges. There is no audience. Viewers call in captions for previous shows. Cuts to com-

JUMP ACROSS THE GUTTER TO CONTINUE

mentary by mature intellectual babe Susan Sontag. (One of the semi-somebodies can be a sort of nobody, but only one.) The host looks like what's his face.

#11 Roll an Eleven – I sketch out eleven ideas like these every three weeks or seventeen times a year for three years. Each list will have the same #7 (an unexplained project called *Now & Then*), a few genuinely producible ideas, a rant or two, a product idea, some poetic crap. I could possibly do eleven ideas every two weeks or even every week – I don't think I'd run out but I'm not sure. Let's discuss wattage later. Many of the words in this section are vague in a legal sense (of course in a legal sense, everything is vague; those bastards); all of them are also clear yet variable in a bigger sense. They say bad ideas are a dime a dozen; I just need to know if it's a regular or a baker's dozen.

TWO

#1 Maze! – An elaborate maze for adults in a gymnasium or warehouse, made up of mostly anchored panels, hundreds of cafeteria tables, chairs that aren't anchored. There are a few flickering lights, maybe candles here or there. Visitors can feel their way around barriers, crawl under tables if they choose, talk to one another. Under some tables are puddles of jelly. There's a faraway soundtrack of theme songs from television programs. Glass breaks in a corner and an attendant says "sorry about that, it was a jar of jelly." The idea of a maze is that it's hard to get out, not solved by one or two backtrackings through bales of hay. Noisy but friendly dogs are set loose into the maze; they annoy visitors until they smell the puddles of jelly; their lapping echoes. A Minotaur is hired to network in the maze every Friday and Saturday night, 8 p.m. to closing. The point is the process and invariably working through the maze is far more enjoyable than emerging from it; most of the dogs agree with me, but they are friendly dogs so maybe they're just being nice. I've made mazes before out of chairs, oil drums, sheetrock, junk and they never felt big enough or complete. Some thoughts:

1. I don't really like mazes as much as I like making mazes.

2. Making the maze is the maze.

3. If one rates mazes by how difficult they are to navigate and escape, the best mazes are those from which one cannot escape.

4. People in glass mazes shouldn't throw up.

5. Merrily, merrily, merrily, merrily, life is but a maze.

6. We'd go to the House of Mirrors on the boardwalk near Hunt's Pier first thing after breakfast so we'd be there when it opened, when the mirrors were freshly polished and you couldn't see fingerprints or smudges on them.

7. Now and Then.

8. When you think you're close to the exit, you bump into

a long-lost soul. He looks like you. His eyes are mirrors near Hunt's Pier. You think he looks like Calder — with a beard that's like a Santa beard – not because you even know what Calder looks like, but because the mirror-eyes bob like mobile parts.

9. How would liability coverage for a venture like this be worded? When people pay to feel lost, disoriented, trapped? One of them scrapes a knee in the maze and sues the maze-makers; the prosecutor asks "so you were deliberately made to feel lost, disoriented, trapped?"

10. Rats.

11. Going through a maze is like teaching a parakeet how to talk.

#2 Penmanship – Pencils are collected door to door. Lots of them from caddies and cups and mugs near the phone, from storerooms and desk drawers. One sweet-underneath codger digs up a cigar box full of old pencils, most nearly stubs but all with sharp points. Many of the old pencils have "ads" on them, one of them reads *Stolen from Dr. Soused*. There are mechanical pencils, artist's soft focus sketch pencils, carpenter pencils, pencils with worn down or off erasers. Most are yellow #2s but some are gray, red, blue etc. They are all ultimately glued onto a huge cylindrical chicken wire skeleton that looks like a fifteen-foot-long ballpoint pen, which is polymerized or Martinized or otherwised into weather-resistant outdoor sculpture as a tribute to Claes Oldenburg and the lost art of prekeyboard writing and the lost, para-calligraphic flourishes of ordinary penmanship.

#3 How to Make a Cup of Coffee Cost Even More! – I'm drinking coffee and eating noodles from styrofoam cup when I'm overwhelmed by the inevitable coffee/food trend: CoffeeMeal Drinks; 16 oz. servings of pasta or nondeteriorating meatballs and/or niblets of corn/shanks of carrot/reliabilities of peas. Soups with coffee instead of water! Decaf Chicken Noodle! French Roast with Western Omelet Wedges! New Chunky Brew Stew! There's even a CoffeePlus buffet! Coffee Alfredo!

#4 Friday Night in a Regular Bar – And we hear the patrons order, joke, talk, bemoan, recite, romanticize, lie (same as *romanticize*?), feign interest (same as *lie*?), listen (same as *feign interest*?). Corny musical interludes of mixed up

> *. . . the lost, para-calligraphic flourishes of ordinary penmanship.*

classical and country-blues as you see a pool game in slow motion, the 8 ball a dead planet. Each installment a different bar in a different neighborhood. A blue collar bar that still has shuffleboard, traditional (not electronic) dartboards, pigs' feet in a jar. A meat market/pick-up bar in a small town, largely

ROLL ON TO THE NEXT PAGE

devoid of middle management/career pretensions. A (community) college bar. There are customers who live in each of these bars, arriving when it opens for coffee that gets refilled until the switch to beer at happy hour. Every night at 5:30, except during play-offs, the old, regular-sized color television bolted above the register is turned to *Mudville*.

#5 The New Soul Train – We pay people $2000 if they legally change and tell all their friends and contacts and magazine subscription overlords that they legally changed their first name to Faust. There is so little meaning or point to this in our increasingly post-literate media-wanking world that it becomes the point. If we're to be misplaced modifiers, finding focus or purpose only via marketing lures and vicarious accomplishments, we should at least pay some tribute, however fragile (like all art/literature/vision), to the lost world.

#6 Parts & Labor - What Costs What – Consumer reporting at the nitpicking and whining level. A reporter gets to hard fact, actual costs of producing, say, a can single can of beer, a ballpark hot dog, a collector's plate from one of the major manufacturing mints that have slyly tinkered with what "limited edition," "heirloom," "fitting tribute," mean. Assembly-line workers, rival manufacturers, public relations stiffs, spokestiffs, tie-stiffs are interviewed. Overhead, executive salaries, all mark-ups are calculated. The reporter is interrogated as to his salary, expense account. Facts all over the place but cloaked with only partly accurate explanations/defenses. In a special "departure" episode, we learn what it actually costs to make one toothpick, one M&M, one napkin, one Museum in a Matchbox.

#7 Now & Then   **CONTINUED NEXT ISSUE**

People Who Have Everything Don't Have This Stuff

What better way to *say Have a Hair-Pulling Santa-Slobbering HoliDamnDay* than with LIMBO - the board game I designed, detailed and printed in an edition of 300 prints/sets. The pulsating black&white drawing pictured last issue is the pattern I made for the backs of the 32 cards used in the game. The 18"x22" full-color, signed gameboard/print, is ready for hanging or playing upon! (All art should be similarly multi-functional. Let's call upon all artists (ideally via a media event where we all join hands with oppressed people, while singing gooey rhyming words about not-despairing/caring/sharing) to produce artworks that can double as gameboards or tablecloths or tv-trays or, best: dropcloths!)

The board depicts a cross-section of an apartment building, and reveals more than anyone wants to know about the inhabitants of our netherworld where psychic trauma, paranoia, unnamed neuroses, and lots of tiny lines thrive. The game is similar to Chutes & Ladders. If you took the actual Chutes & Ladders and juiced it with *Dante's Inferno*, Lucky the Footless Rabbit, stunt silliness from *Beat the Clock* or *Whip the Maid*, and a major does of angst, you'd have LIMBO!

You get the aforementioned matte-board-weight signed print, four handmade wedge-shaped tokens, a sandwich bag to ensure freshness, the 32 cards with the backpattern that cost me two years' of eyesight to draw, and rules for playing the game (as opposed to rules for bridge or bowling, two other versions of Limbo). If you can pick it up from me somehow, it costs $25; if I have to ship it to you, it's $30 because it's a clunky thing to ship flat and needs special packaging that I'll have to jerryrig from discarded refrigerator boxes that I don't have right now but can look for next weekend, plus it costs over five bucks to mail. **Special holiday offer** because I really want to write ad copy and make people buy stuff they don't need: 2 for $40, or $42 if I ship. It's arguably true that nobody *needs* art – hell, most people don't even want it, have something all modern and breathing like that over the couch - BUT everybody, sir, I say *Everybody*, every single person alive needs a gameboard! If you don't purchase this now, be advised, you will someday be unable to fight the urge to hang your Monopoly board on the wall.

1940s' Woodette Circus Set - never opened, beautifully boxed craft set with wooden parts and watercolor tablets for making circus animals and props. Colorful 3D cardboard circus cages. Beautiful item usually priced around $40+ in *used* condition. I have a few wrapped and tied in original brown paper for shipping to mail order customers over 50 years ago. Genuinely cool, and in remarkably fine condition. Excellent collectible gift item. *$22.95/set.*

Pirates of the Caribbean - Bag of 10 re-issue figures from the molds used for the Marx "Warriors of the World" pirates of the early 60s. Solid colors, not "each beautifully painting by hand, the best looking warriors in the land" like their forebears, but superbly detailed troublemakers. Sold for a while at Disney parks' Pirates of the Caribbean rides. *$2.00/bag.*

3rd printing of brutal/goofy **spoof of the Minnesota Multiphasic Personality Inventory** - an incorrect reworking of the screwball profiling tool that's almost as funny as the real thing; great item to reward or slam any psych or psycho-babble buff. *$2.00 each; 3 for $5.00 (you can mix in one YIKES! coloring book if you want)*

Send check or money order to Musical Comedy Editions, 5136 Lyndale Ave. So., Minneapolis, MN 55419 and throw in a few bucks for shipping (no shipping or handling if you pick-up from me or via Art Underground/Anodyne. My phone: (612) 825-4101. Offbeat free stuff with all orders.

NOVEMBER 5, 1999

INTeRNAL  RHYMe

ISSUE 44 OF AMERICA'S MOST OFFBEAT NORMAL NEWSLETTER   ◆   MUSICMASTER, 5136 LYNDALE AVE. SO., MINNEAPOLIS, MN 55419

Roll an Eleven II

T his continues last issue's collection of pitches, glitches and tangents, some worth pursuing, some pursuing me and some growing tails they can chase later on. For the sake of stable underlayment and, naturally, internal rhyme, I recommend reading the bulk (the first two parts) of this piece all at once and not in installments (I am attempting to distribute these issues together to all readers - if you're missing #43, drop me a line).

I didn't mean to grab your ass with anything but the greatest respect.

#8 Sketch Pad – Three young comics/ roommates tirelessly work on an ever-changing group of skits, bits and routines. Whether or not anything they create is ever successfully mounted or even presented at all is never addressed. The only sets are: the apartment where they bounce around in adrenaline- or beer- or espresso-induced brainstorming sessions; a regular neighborhood bar where they occasionally swap ideas while playing shuffleboard or with regular patrons who aren't rude but mostly respond with noncommittal nods; at rummage sales or flea markets where they bounce one-liners off of dealers, do prop comedy with junk (rusty pitchfork, dog collar, 8-track tapes).

11 Sketch Pad Ideas –

1. New ad agency lands Church of Satan account to soften dark image. We see junior adjective chiefs smart-mouthing with deputy verb veeps to come up with a catchy jingle and happy logo for the dark one. This could be incredibly funny stuff, probably because it's a sin gone mental. "Team" members do lots of pointing, "gotchas" and proclamations of certainty and genius.

2. We dig up the corpse of Allen Funt and wheel him into nursing home elevators where unsuspecting riders either scream or introduce themselves.

3. A dog chases her tail; some guy in a suit is saying "I'll get right back to you" into a telephone; a dog chases her tail; some guy in a suit is saying "I'll get right back to you" into a telephone; a dog chases her tail; some guy in a suit is saying "I'll get right back to you" into a telephone; etc. until of course a dog is saying "I'll get right back to you" into a telephone; no need for image of guy chasing tail and/or barking as, alas, a dog can work the punchline better than a human.

4. Couple in card shop discuss all newer types of cards; there are eleven of them:

   Just a Very Short Note to Say You Look Distracted;

   Happy Recovery from Your Suicide Attempt;

   Sorry I Ran Over Your Pet;

   Thanks for Letting Me Brown Nose You;

   Time to Plan a Year 3000 Tupperware Party;

   Enjoy Your Settlement!;

   Now & Then;

   Classic Excuses You Can Use at Your New Job (there are eleven of them; they are: 1. I wasn't told we'd have to know all the parts of speech; 2. I must have read the bus schedule upsidedown; 3. I'm sorry, but based on how you behave, I assumed you were Satanists; 4. I didn't mean to grab your ass with anything but the greatest respect; 5. You should've said you were so uptight about heroin; 6. My computer ate my homework; 7. Now & Then; 8. Not that I have anything against Satanists, I mean I even saw those ads in *Time* magazine, I mean, you guys seemed *really* cool . . . 9. The last place I worked, we encour-

GO UNDER THE OVERPAGE THEN HEAD TO YOUR LEFT

aged our inner children to form a scout troop; 10. No, that's not a Xerox of my butt; it looks like Susan's; 11. It's important to know the sprinkler system works.

Sorry about your cyberpartner crashing . . .

Nostrodomus Didn't Predict the Arrival of This Card!

Congratulations on Your Participation in the Welfare-to-Work-to-Warfare Program

5. Two surgeons quietly operating start pulling items from patient's chest. A string of silks, a bouquet, a dove, a rabbit. A week later, same setting, new patient – surgeons pull out a pop gun, a dressed-up piglet, a fright wig, a midget clown, then another clown, then another midget clown. A week later, same setting, new patient – surgeons pull out a real heart, damp and dripping blood, a ribcage, a gigantic kidney bean and then a human brain, still steaming.

6. *Origami Inc., Development Dept.* on sign behind man frantically folding and creasing colored papers at a work-table (a lip obscuring his actual handiworkings). He holds up a crane. He makes antlers. He folds together a steam-ship. He holds up giraffe. A lunch bell rings and a delivery boy presents the man with a tossed salad. The man places it on his table for a moment, then lifts up a papersized multicolored wafer.

7. Now & Then

8. Close-up of hand punching in phone number followed by dialed phone music; caller is on brink of snapping, over-whelmed by nonsensical, stereotypical, uninventive gen-eralities she is given elsewhere as helpful advice; volun-teer taking her call is at the ready with a Magic 8-Ball

9. Chinese chef preparing those eggs that can't be eaten for another thousand years; this is self-working and, while not really timeless, as close to really old as humor can get without citing that hieroglyphic about the spaceship get-ting a racing stripe. "Honey, how's that egg coming?"

10. Two guys sprawled on a couch watching tv, drinking cans of beer. One drains a can, noisily drops it on cluttered coffee table between them and the camera (My God – this makes You, the viewer, the person/thing/show that's on tv!). The other guy grumbles and positions the empty can differently. He stares at his buddy before going into a sloppy rap about feng shui and how the empties are placed to invite prosperity and a bag of chips is angled to bring good health. (Same two drunks discussing art/philosophy/religion/politics; one gets adamant about the merits of an idea he has called *Friday Night in a Regular Bar*.)

11. A token black gay midget tells his study group of ordi-nary gay midgets that Jesus was a brother; and when they uneasily concur or allow that likelihood because it won't effect the plastic statues they have at home, the token black gay midget (who outs himself as a Republican) says that Jesus had an Afro. You can imagine the antics and unprecedented calls for censorship that follow.

#9 Garage Sale – Amateur *Antiques Roadshow* with co-hosts guesstimating all kinds of values and vintages for stuff they spot at actual garage sales. They banter with sellers and buyers, try to ferret out dealers, look for insights when people buy odd or ordinary things. The co-hosts never act snobbish or even particularly informed, they just idle about and play with merchandise that's a few hours away from a dumpster if it isn't saved or salvaged. They argue about whether five bucks is too much for windmill salt and peppershakers from Occupied Japan. Each host should indeed always be searching for and buying certain items, e.g. anything alligator, old games ("Are all the cards in here?"), old blue ice cube trays. But they always buy bundles, even boxes full of pencils, for an artwork their friend might do.

Everything must be considered, but since most of the things considered/discussed overlap so much, many things are overlooked entirely.

#10 Warning: Educational Toy – I will manufacture a line of 6" high, figurines that are word-figures, a bold black word sprawled (sic) across the length of a human figure molded to reflect the words meaning. For example, the let-ters of the word "slumber" are designed to occupy the length of a sleeping figure. Black on white like newsprint. Letters vertical or horizontal tweaked to define their host. *Back-stroke. Loiter. Stagger. Celebrate. Meditate.* Paper-weights. Instead of action figures, these are action word/verb figures.

#11 Internal Rhyme — A warehouse is purchased, heated, ventilated and turned over to yours truly (truly, yours) and I make it into the ultimate ride/box/museum/experience/art-work. I collage it from step to stern to star and populate it with collages as well as contraptions, assemblages, pyrotechnical devices, robotic mice in tiny drive-in theaters, re-actualized crates, embossed beams, painted and glued-upon and overworked everything. I read there, host events there, give tours, use it as a studio in which to make more boxes. On occasion, I will fill a vat with thousands upon thousands of trinkets – from plastic charms to beads, game tokens to shells, dollhouse furnishings to canary boots, bingo chips to letter cubes – and dip glue-basted globes into it. A stage ver-sion of this environment is created for a roadshow. Simple panels/backdrops/columns turn slowly during a reading to reveal the collages/décor. The other end of blank white peaceful Zen simplicity, yuppie guilt simplicity, Swedish modern Shaker traditional simplicity is absolute, clutter, each remarkable detail and fragment and memory only able to contribute *to manifest* the perfect white glow, when every-

FOLLOW THE BOUNCING BALL

VOTE WITH YOUR HEAD, NOT OVER IT

mentary by mature intellectual babe Susan Sontag. (One of the semi-somebodies can be a sort of nobody, but only one.) The host looks like what's his face.

#11 Roll an Eleven – I sketch out eleven ideas like these every three weeks or seventeen times a year for three years. Each list will have the same #7 (an unexplained project called *Now & Then*), a few genuinely producible ideas, a rant or two, a product idea, some poetic crap. I could possibly do eleven ideas every two weeks or even every week – I don't think I'd run out but I'm not sure. Let's discuss wattage later. Many of the words in this section are vague in a legal sense (of course in a legal sense, everything is vague; those bastards); all of them are also clear yet variable in a bigger sense. They say bad ideas are a dime a dozen; I just need to know if it's a regular or a baker's dozen.

TWO

#1 Maze! – An elaborate maze for adults in a gymnasium or warehouse, made up of mostly anchored panels, hundreds of cafeteria tables, chairs that aren't anchored. There are a few flickering lights, maybe candles here or there. Visitors can feel their way around barriers, crawl under tables if they choose, talk to one another. Under some tables are puddles of jelly. There's a faraway soundtrack of theme songs from television programs. Glass breaks in a corner and an attendant says "sorry about that, it was a jar of jelly." The idea of a maze is that it's hard to get out, not solved by one or two backtrackings through bales of hay. Noisy but friendly dogs are set loose into the maze; they annoy visitors until they smell the puddles of jelly; their lapping echoes. A Minotaur is hired to network in the maze every Friday and Saturday night, 8 p.m. to closing. The point is the process and invariably working through the maze is far more enjoyable than emerging from it; most of the dogs agree with me, but they are friendly dogs so maybe they're just being nice. I've made mazes before out of chairs, oil drums, sheetrock, junk and they never felt big enough or complete. Some thoughts:

1. I don't really like mazes as much as I like making mazes.

2. Making the maze is the maze.

3. If one rates mazes by how difficult they are to navigate and escape, the best mazes are those from which one cannot escape.

4. People in glass mazes shouldn't throw up.

5. Merrily, merrily, merrily, merrily, life is but a maze.

6. We'd go to the House of Mirrors on the boardwalk near Hunt's Pier first thing after breakfast so we'd be there when it opened, when the mirrors were freshly polished and you couldn't see fingerprints or smudges on them.

7. Now and Then.

8. When you think you're close to the exit, you bump into

a long-lost soul. He looks like you. His eyes are mirrors near Hunt's Pier. You think he looks like Calder — with a beard that's like a Santa beard – not because you even know what Calder looks like, but because the mirror-eyes bob like mobile parts.

9. How would liability coverage for a venture like this be worded? When people pay to feel lost, disoriented, trapped? One of them scrapes a knee in the maze and sues the maze-makers; the prosecutor asks "so you were deliberately made to feel lost, disoriented, trapped?"

10. Rats.

11. Going through a maze is like teaching a parakeet how to talk.

#2 Penmanship – Pencils are collected door to door. Lots of them from caddies and cups and mugs near the phone, from storerooms and desk drawers. One sweet-underneath codger digs up a cigar box full of old pencils, most nearly stubs but all with sharp points. Many of the old pencils have "ads" on them, one of them reads *Stolen from Dr. Soused*. There are mechanical pencils, artist's soft focus sketch pencils, carpenter pencils, pencils with worn down or off erasers. Most are yellow #2s but some are gray, red, blue etc. They are all ultimately glued onto a huge cylindrical chicken wire skeleton that looks like a fifteen-foot-long ballpoint pen, which is polymerized or Martinized or otherwised into weather-resistant outdoor sculpture as a tribute to Claes Oldenburg and the lost art of prekeyboard writing and the lost, para-calligraphic flourishes of ordinary penmanship.

#3 How to Make a Cup of Coffee Cost Even More! – I'm drinking coffee and eating noodles from styrofoam cup when I'm overwhelmed by the inevitable coffee/food trend: CoffeeMeal Drinks; 16 oz. servings of pasta or nondeteriorating meatballs and/or niblets of corn/shanks of carrot/reliabilities of peas. Soups with coffee instead of water! Decaf Chicken Noodle! French Roast with Western Omelet Wedges! New Chunky Brew Stew! There's even a CoffeePlus buffet! Coffee Alfredo!

#4 Friday Night in a Regular Bar – And we hear the patrons order, joke, talk, bemoan, recite, romanticize, lie (same as *romanticize*?), feign interest (same as *lie*?), listen (same as

> *. . . the lost, para-calligraphic flourishes of ordinary penmanship.*

feign interest?). Corny musical interludes of mixed up classical and country-blues as you see a pool game in slow motion, the 8 ball a dead planet. Each installment a different bar in a different neighborhood. A blue collar bar that still has shuffleboard, traditional (not electronic) dartboards, pigs' feet in a jar. A meat market/pick-up bar in a small town, largely

ROLL ON TO THE NEXT PAGE

MOBY DICK CONTINUED

papercutter and careful eye, then shuffled the small piles, so when collating print sets, the assortment of paperstock per museum was impressive. I wholesaled the boxes for a mere buck a toss and the response was excellent. But when orders kept coming in, I dropped the product because, as neat and different as I thought it was, I didn't want to spend my free time putting the dam things together (this happens with lots of the items I come up with). Anyhow, I am game to do another Musuem in a Matchbox type of item, with even more intense personal labor required, but this time as a poetry journal, each issue containing tiny prints, 4-page broadsides, maybe a scroll or an object as well. It would feature works by mail-artists, local poets, and me.

(note: I will indeed make a very limited Museum in a Matchbook Journal Thing (clearly as-yet untitled) as mentioned above in the near future (before 2000 chimes in with screaming neighbors, sirens, a deluge, a universal power outtage, the landing of carnivorous aliens, and a sip of bubbly). Copies will be sold locally through the Art Underground —see ad—or from me directly for five bucks each. Would you like to supersize that? To order by mail, add a buck postage per order so I can wrap and mail your copy to survive its trip.)

#7 Now & Then   CONTINUED NEXT ISSUE

WRITTEN WORKS BY **MUSICMASTER**
FRiDAY DECEMBER 10, 7:30 P.M.

POEMS ABOUT SNOWBLOWERS, HELL, FREE SPEEH, MODERATELY PRICED SPEECH, RUM, DOGS WITHOUT CARS™, ART DAMMIT, PETS, COMMERCE & SINUS SURGERY.

CafféTempo
4161 Grand Ave. So.
Minneapolis

VERBAL ABUSE

NOVEMBER 30, 1999

INTeRNAL  RHYMe

THE 45TH EDITION OF A MIDLIFE CRISIS CENTER ◆ MUSICMASTER, 5136 LYNDALE AVE. SO., MINNEAPOLIS, MINNESOTA 55419

This concludes a collection of ideas, fears and talking beers, all in process. For the sake of maximum allowable clarity at this temperature and, naturally, internal rhyme, I recommend dutifully recalling or actually rereading the first two parts before continuing with this, the third and final installment (part 1) or things that go bump in the head -

Roll an Eleven 3

#8 Seven League Boots with Lowell Thomas – Foreign cities are explored, but everything the small tour group visits up close and personal is defined by them in terms of second/third generation versions they know (or remember from childhood) back in New Jersey or New York. When they share a meal out, they compare their food to how their grandmother or friend made it. In shops, they hold up things they bought at a drive-in flea market or church sale back in the States. Their museum visits focus on paintings they have reproductions of or think they have seen in a mall gallery back home. It's all-authentic as Americana only, like a trip to Epcot without the convenience of walking from Italy to France in two minutes. "This reminds me of Tante Elly's strudel!" "Oh, I bought a postcard of that painting at the Guggenheim gift shop. They have such nice cards." "Doesn't he sound just like my cousin Peter?" If home is where the heart is, where the hell did we park the brain?

#9 Artists Explain What Their Paintings Mean and/or Why Certain Elements Are Included and/or Why the Lady's Right Eyeball is a Windmill – Without additional commentary or voiceover or historical perspective or artworld harrumphing, this program features artists explaining what their – well, just read the title of this section. I have found that artists though often quirky and even real world outpatients are usually articulate about why and what they put on canvas. Some need to be set apart from environments of required/enforced affectation or distraction (openings, group shows), but most are easily coaxed into coherent if rambling decodings about their works. The few who admit, "I don't know what it means" are imparting valuable insight as well. The at-large citizenry, often finding the same sort of solace in representational art that they find in a nice lawn, can comment before and after explanations, e.g. from "Not only can my five-year-old can do that, she can name it better" to (after) "Not only can my five-year-old do that, she can give a better explanation." No, this probably wouldn't work the way I'd like it to, as a lure and introduction to the richer vocabularies of creativity and expression, so that the large percentage of folks disenfranchised from the art world's different pacing of life's course, can begin to "get" more art than they normally do, begin to cultivate a taste for the abstract the transcendent the unfettered the distracted the affected – oh, forget it.

Naysayers are just fluffing up your gut and chin with nay. Things are burning just fine.

#10 – Nap You Inner Bastards! – A daily, happy variety program for adults in the tradition of the fifties' Miss Francis *and Ding Dong School.* The peanut gallery contains a few dozen professionally dressed adults who participate in relay races and coloring contests for modest prizes like

ROW ROW ROW THIS WAY

SWELL ARTSY HOLIDAY LIMITED EDITION MUSEUM IN A MATCHBOX - I finished assembling an edition of just 25 copies of this collection of tiny handtrimmed prints and poems. Art for the pocket and words for the eyestrain. Five bucks per plus a buck to protect from the ravages of transit.

ROLE ROLE ROLE CONTINUED

coffee shop coupons and too small, fake-looking, green plastic squirt guns that aren't even full of water, for crying out loud. Halfway into the show the adults need naps or more sugar. The grandmotherly hostess announces viewers' birthdays. After naptime, a short movie is shown. The short movie covers one of eleven ideas:

1. Work is a necessary evil. Very necessary and very evil.

2. The pen isn't mightier than the metaphor. And as people stop using pencils/pens altogether, the phrase will evolve to become the keyboard is mightier than the sword." Or maybe "mightier than the laser."

3. In fact, you *can* go wrong. And there is *always* further obligation. People don't get into sales to correct social ills or sing the joys of capitalism. They get into sales to make a living and part of how they

Customer service is Alexander Calder balancing your wind chimes.

make a living – like a farmer plowing a field or a chef making a shopping list – is by shaking hands and being friendly. What does this mean? Well, dear souls, that's exactly the point – buyer beware, handshaker beware, donor beware, citizen beware, reader beware, fact-checker beware. The Ides of Month ain't nothing.

4. Drugs are great. They help, encourage, calm, relax and inspire us; they dictate how we express ourselves, perceive our world, interact with clerks and eager-looking cleavers. They're almost as addictive and mindnumbing as television. By the way, taking two of any good drug makes it impossible to call anyone in the morning.

5. Your boss is like your old principal and like you'd be if you were boss. We become our parents and our princi-

pals (ignore the play on words). Thus what? Something betw een **be kind to animals** and only *you* **can change this prediction.**

6. Your headache is just the tip of the iceberg you call home. By the time you retire, your ability to enjoy retirement fully will be further eroded by workday routines, memo rapids and the heavy air of confined space. The logic that we earn our retirement is bank-scripted, government-scripted, devil-scripted. That money is the root of all evil also means it is the plant and the flower and the fruit. Pseudo-academics who challenge the logic of the nonworking lifestyle as a "what if everybody decided not to work . . ." aren't just pseudo, they're irretrievably duped by the seductive wingtipped chrome hairpieces of viral capitalism. There is no joy in Mudville, but there is in watching it.

7. New Improved Now & Then with Minty Hexachlorophene

8. Meetings are daily, happy variety programs for adults in the tradition of the fifties' Miss Francis *and Ding Dong School.* Truth resonates. Tribute to Robert Fulghrum: Everything you need to know in business you learn in the school yard: bullies don't want to peacefully co-exist; lunches serve business and social functions; people more powerful than you are rarely smarter or kinder; knowing something that someone else doesn't know, *or pretending to know something someone else doesn't know*, is power; older kids miss the toys they're not supposed to pay with anymore; say what you want about Twinkies – you can always trade them for something you want; Now & Then – The Early Years; Butchy Lavarko was named to be a bully; you play with Cathy Rizzi, but you think about Kathy Horak; people who say "Someday, when you grow up, you'll understand," have resigned themselves to circumstances; if jingles were true, nearly everyone's pants would be on fire.

9. Though many, many workers should be paid more than minimum wage for the work they do, many others should be paid less for the work they do poorly or sloppily. And while a few executives might be worth their exorbitant, economy-warping paychecks and a few hundred million in incidental expenses for cupcakes (euphemism? code word? Hostess?), most should be disarmed, dislegged, generally dissed, flogged, yelled at and axed (Note U.S.A. computer-scanning "Stop Da Killfest" Project agents: I am only kidding. I am not a high school student). And are you, yes *you* dear reader, worth your weight in fluctuating but eternally shiny precious gold? Who owes you and whom do you owe? Uh-owe.

10. Things are fine. Naysayers are just saying nay. Your job or a better job is going to be here next year – if it pays less or seems less important, it's because of those

STAY ON THE CONVEYOR BELT PLEASE

bastard naysayers. Life is fine. Money doesn't grow on trees, it grows on artificial trees, which last longer, bloom longer, look better, and burn so quickly it's dangerously cool. Lighten up. Naysayers are just fluffing up your gut and chin with nay. Things are burning just fine.

11. Customer service is a shortcut in the maze.

Or a free beer.

Or Alexander Calder balancing your wind chimes.

Or legally changing your name to Faust.

Customer service is letting the dug-up corpse of Allen Funt autograph your ass. (Bits from the *NEW! Corpse of Allen Funt* series –

> *There is indeed order and serenity in chaos; there are wars in the monastery, good times in hell; there's redemption in not using coupons, a paradox in a solution.*

1. Fannie Flagg chats it up with a pet shop parrot so it seems they're having an actual conversation; this continues to the amusement of gathering onlookers and until eventually the shopkeeper asks Fannie to change her last name.

2. A guy is hired to wash the inside windows of Funky Financial Services, Inc. on the 83rd floor of a skyscraper. The first window he touches shatters, lacerating his arms, legs, and neck and causing him to stumble out the window, down to a heavy-handed(-bodied) *splat!*; on the way to the morgue, when he's told he's been set up by the corpse of Allen Funt, he remains inanimate.

3. Fannie Flagg totes an empty machinegun case into a suburban high school and is beaten to death by frightened students.

4. The *6 O'clock News* reports that the corpse of Fannie Flagg vanished this morning, but will reappear this evening on an *ALL NEW!* installment of the *Corpse of Allen Funt*, tonight on ABC, right after Disney's *Huey, Dewey & Faust*.

5. Special guest Charlie Callas arranges housecalls by proctologists for his unemployed cousin, Arne.

6. Segments from the grisly *Faces of Death* video series are screened for producers of *America's Funniest Grisly Videos* to see if they'd run any (all are accepted; only *Sledgehammer Me Elmo* gets nixed!).

7. Now & Then

8. A guy is hired to guard a sealed box of dangerous snakes in a pitch black locked closet. Things are quiet for a while in spite of gunshots, shouting, screams, etc. right outside the closet by our candid crew (and special guest crewster the Corpse of Benny Hill!). Nothing disturbs our victim until after six hours, he asks to use the bathroom. At day's end, the man is paid and sent off without ever being told he was the target of a prank.

9. Nails are poured off tall buildings, meter maids are shot, a plane is yanked out of the sky. A sponsor who pulls their ads is quickly replaced. Everybody gets cable in their retina, a micro-sound card implanted in their brow, free always-flowing intravenous blood.

10. The Corpse of Allen Funt introduces a classic, black&white segment of a little boy chirping at canaries in a pet shop, as if he's having actual conversations with them.

11. Everybody - cast, crew and audience - weeps uncontrollably for thirty minutes.

Customer service is an apology letter for sending you a college/institutional sales video.

Customer Service is Now & Then.

Or asking the incoherent tourists from New Jersey if they're enjoying the uncooked beef.

Customer service is polishing buttocks before smooching them.

Or my apologizing to you after an especially real paragraph.

Or, most often not saying what you think, just shutting up.

#11 – Driven - What I do is accelerate on busy streets. I take so many aspirin I get sick. I write and rewrite then rewrite again everything I write (and rewrite) so often that I no longer trust what I write. I'm not afraid of the dark per se, which means I am. By hosting several hundred open mike events over the past three decades, I've listened to more bad writing than most people and by, holding a non-arts-related/non-poetry-related/**RealWorld**™ job for eighteen years, I've listened to more bad, shallow and forced-rhyme ideas than most people as well. I don't know whether I've become immune or infected. That I have never driven a car has made my acceleration on busy streets difficult; while walking, I race; that cars and ideas always pass me by in spite of my acceleration is both reassuring and troubling – reassuring when I smugly think I don't want to go to where they're going anyway (that naysayers' customer service meeting with the corpse of Allen Funt?), and troubling when I think that perhaps I'm walking backwards. The best part of the

KEEP YOUR ARMS AND LEGS IN THE TRAM CAR PLEASE

EVEN HUNGRY ARTISTS STARVE

ANOTHER MILLENNIUM SHOT TO HELL CONTINUED

trip is the travel – the expectation and hope and the thinking that traveling instigates. The best part of the art is the process. That the best part of cooking is the eating doesn't trouble me. Things are rarely as tidy, predictable, or even recountable as I want them to be, as I pretend that they are. There is indeed order and serenity in chaos; there are wars in the monastery, good times in hell; there's stagnation in types of growth, redemption in not using coupons, a paradox in a solution. I want tickertape streaming out of the ears then out of the car windows of passing drivers, so I can tear them off like receipts. None of this will be faked or computer-enhanced or animated, just actual raw footage of me yanking off these documents of the passing worlds' bees, bandits and brains, and reading them aloud to the camera. What will be on them – thoughts, notes, daydreams, stew, a reminder to tape Mudville for Mom – is beyond me, no matter how quickly I accelerate, no matter how often I plunder (rip-off) the thoughts of others. Aspirin like Altoids, like vitamins. Eyes like headlights. Poems like loud horns. No brakes.

YOU HAVE TO BE PRETTY EGOCENTRIC TO THINK YOU HAVE PERSONAL DEMONS

FEBRUARY 20, 2000

INTeRNAL  RHYMe

THE 49TH ISSUE OF WHAT CAN GO WRONG WHEN YOU LEND ME YOUR PENCIL ◆ MUSICMASTER, 5136 LYNDALE AVE. SO., MINNEAPOLIS, MN 55419

Dear Internal Rhyme Reader –

Please send me a letter/drawing/review/fortune/dismembered logo/rant/snippet/ whippet/wisecrack/gratuitious congrats/complaint/fan note/envious dismissal/ survey (your questions, whatever)/Thank You/No Thanks about *Internal Rhyme*, so I can print it in my next issue, the bigdeal *Internal Rhyme* #50! If I get enough stuff in, I can avoid running lots of stupid anniversary reflections and boring, introspective editorial/poetry (already in abundance issues 1-49).

When the century issue rolls around, I will print, perfect bind and draw/collage one-of-a-kind covers for 100 complete sets (400+ pages), sell a few dozen of them and watch the rest gather dust in the basement. I'm mentioning this now so you're aware that your submission to number 50 will also enjoy a modest comeback and benign neglect later on.

Thanks for your feedback, feedforth, and the occasional indecipherable mailing that reassures me.

Musicmaster

Note: I need responses to this call by March 15, which in mail-art time is all of a sudden. Warp for me.

INSIDe THIS ISSUe

NEW HYPE SECTION BEST EVER

DETERIORATING OZONE LAYER TOPIC OF NEW SITCOM

CLONED SLOTH WON'T WORK

CONFUSING EDITORIAL CARTOON

FOX TO AIR SPECIAL WHERE THIRTY LOW-INCOME GUYS CHIP IN AND BUY A SEX SLAVE

STILL-THRIVING ROSWELL ALIEN CALLS LARRY KING FROM ARLINGTON COMPOUND TO VOICE OBJECTIONS TO BUCHANAN'S ISOLATIONIST PLATFORM - ALIEN CLAIMS HIS NEW JOB AS AGRI-BIZ SPOKESPERSON (OR SPOKESALIEN) ISN'T RELEVANT BUT THAT GENETICALLY ENGINEERED DEHYDRATED BOLOGNA COULD HELP EXPAND LUNCH PROGRAMS OVERSEAS

LOCAL DOG'S WATER DISH THAT LOOKS LIKE MINI TOILET BOWL IS A BIG HIT AMONG MUTTS

Kenneth Patchen Names the Animals

it is easier to sleep or scream at night

easier to blow up the old armory

than it is to lock these words in place

while staring at the screen

■

I fall asleep and dream my writer dream

I'm writing in or near the sun salt air seductive breeze

I have a beer there's music in the sand and crashing waves

I'm worth a billion dollars maybe more

because I print my poems at quickprint

and I sell them on the beach where

people like to shake my shaking hand

they always thank me often ask me

where do such poems come from

such funny lines and metaphors

shrinkwrapped barracuda!

and I tell them that I simply write the truth

not just parts that rhyme and dance

then they thank me give me twenty pesos

turn and wave and go back home to Pittsburgh

where I'm now in stories I don't know

since the beer does my accounting I decide to check its math

I trust the beer but maybe it's been lying

when I doublecheck the numbers all these pesos coming in

I'm not worth a billion dollars

I'm not even worth a hundred

and my priceless poems just things found on the beach

when the sun sets into an ocean

out past *my* balcony

where I usually yap out poems on a still-humming Selectric

(why does it hum of course because it doesn't know the words)

I just stare into the darkening mobile

PROCEED WITH CAUTION

sad my curiosity cost a billion

sadder that my paradise costs anything at all

I yell about accounting to the beer I sip

I tell it how it shouldn't drink and add

but I forgive it what the hell

maybe my doublechecking is incorrect

maybe I'm lying to myself

it's all just *shrinkwrapped barracuda!*

I fall asleep again within this dream

■

I am writing in the moonlight

to the crashing waves of beer

those amber waves of grain

I am confident and focused

and I'm writing at a frantic pace to finally get a novel done

a massive book so everyone can get the words they need

I am spinning out multi-leveled

bi-textural opiated magnum opus so quickly

I don't even watch the keyboard

my words pour out spin a bit form pieces snap into place

there's a harmony I've never felt before

when a page is done it only takes a second for another one

to slip into the carriage race away

I spend a year at this before I type *The End*

and sigh with satisfaction and accomplishment

('cause now I'm really big league

I can sell *this* on the beach for two-three dollars)

but when I look at what I've done

every single page is full of numbers

all the lines and chapters only numbers

I'm either a much worse typist then I think

or an avant-garde mathematician

just an indecipherable code away from the great American
novel

which may or may not be the number 9

or the number 4 for crying out loud

I am so tired of making jokes about this type of setback

I am so tired of losing this substantial an effort

I am so tired of realizing that this type of setback

is the only type of setback that revives me anymore

that I yawn with disappointment

I am so tired of yawning

when I have so much to do that

I wonder what the yawning really means

and I am so tired of interpreting dreams

when I have so much yawning to do

that I want to fall asleep that's all just go away

■

I'm wading in a sea of dreams so big it has an undertow

and furthest down where water's at its heaviest

are dreams of flight I'm flying out of school

of air so pure and soft that every breath's a miracle

and on the surface where the water wraps around my ankles

with hypnotic grace wheezing to evaporate

are the unspeakable dreams

with hope and fear all *shrinkwrapped barracuda!*

on the nearby beach

every single one of the six hundred twentyseven trillion

four hundred fortysix billion two hundred thirtyfive million

eight hundred sixteen thousand five hundred and nine pebbles

OVERWRITTEN STANZA CONTINUED NEXT PAGE

PATCHEN CONTINUED

all living with the fact that erosion will effectively

shorten their lifespans by five/six billion years

every single one of them is giving me advice about my writing

and I say *shut up* but they won't shut up

because they've each taken enough confidence building seminars

to convince themselves that they're each and every one

the only **pebble** on the beach

some of the advice I hear is taunting angry true

the way I want my words to work

but most of it is stupid ugly condescending

and it's coming from a-dime-a-dozen pebbles

hell a-penny-*a-trillion* pebbles

and here from all the critics all the gods

the cooks the fools is what I hear:

think before you write

think twice before you write another word

learn to write haiku for crying out loud

learn how to edit *edit* listen - skip the repetition edit once

write about a famous triumphant pebble critic on the beach

do you mean unlimited when you write unlimited?

where the hell do your facts pay the rent?

do you mean endless when you write endless?

call your tangents back from faraway

write what you mean not what you say

stop using dreams to furnish all your poems

do you mean blow up the old armory when you write blow up the old armory?

the sun sets in the mobile

shrinkwrapped barracuda tastes like fudge

will you please autograph my breast

dreams within dreams within dreams are so common

your poems to describe them are boring

but in that kind-of-interesting real life boring kind of way

remember that beneath it all we only have ourselves to blame

to think a beach symbolic of something bigger than

our hearts

musicmaster 2.2000

Salvage Operation #2

This section features poems I wrote between 1992 and July 1997 (when I started putting out *Internal Rhyme* in which nearly all of my new poems appear), poems I maybe read once or twice, but am only now finally rewriting/finishing/abandoning by typing versions I'm willing to print herein.

love beads

I meet a woman who makes
pretty tiedyed scarves
God bless her and all others
with the sixties 'round their necks
she glances at exhibit of my drawings
pictures of war without heroics
buildings chewing on their occupants
a man on fire on escalator down
to the heart of hell
the picture is worth a thousand words
I can't say or spell

so this floral tiedye woman
barely skims my art
makes a mouth like a turning worm
and sniffs
I got that out of my system years ago

I want to say *how comforting*
to turn yourself away from screaming
to flee from damned annoying blight of bombs

you actualized child
all affirmationed-up
all fond retreat to woods me first
with good book and cozy tiedye
I'm glad you were enlightened to make scarfs

but I don't say that
I don't even ask if it's still legal to make tiedye
I just nod and smile
each and every tooth of mine
lit up like little oil lamp
my head a burning lighthouse for the damned

Son of Kenneth Patchen's Opiated Pet Mathematician

it would be different not to say nice

to do something gentle calm

easy as in easy-to-identify

a breeze or the curve on the ocean's other side

the snow that we see when we picture snow

easy as in easy-to-deal-with

a painting so abstract it points out new facts

overgrown houseless steps in the middle of a field

(but if the steps are houseless can they still be overgrown?)

a barely remembered poem from second grade

but whenever I try to calm down

(Proud Mary keep on burnin')

whenever I try to do something easy

    taking the hammer to the telephone

    saying easy-does-it to a charging bull

releasing the rats I've had shackled in the garage since 1984

it doesn't stay gentle or calm very long

the wires and pulleys all fall from the sky

the edge of the earth starts to buckle and fold

an origamic flourish with continents

(1984 was no coincidence)

the snow that I see when I picture snow makes me shiver

and I get so overwhelmed by it all I just sit down

where I am in the middle of a field

on some possibly overgrown houseless steps

my ears emitting air raid sirens

eyesight fractured by reason

and though I want to whisper pray yell *Uncle*

I instead stare down the curve

on the ocean's other side   - musicmaster 2.2000

WHERE DO YOU DRAW THE LINE? #2..(YOUR NOSE AREA)

I DRAW THE LINE WAY PAST WHERE IT HITS YOUR NOSE

INTeRNAL  RHYMe

THE 50TH ISSUE WHERE WILD WORDS CONGREGATE ◆ MUSICMASTER, 5136 LYNDALE AVENUE SOUTH, MINNEAPOLIS, MINNESOTA 55419

Fifty of One or Half a Hundred of the Other

O kay it's issue #50, this year of my fiftieth birthday. Hope that doesn't throw anyone. People at work have kindly pegged me as younger in spite of my annual beerful, jowling expansions. Not a hell of a lot younger, but as young as *40-maybe-45*. They probably think I'm younger because I'm so damn youthfully hiphuggered into what's hip, what's in, what's now, that the fact that I'm using such wrinkled, *last millennium* expressions like "what's hip" and even "what's in" makes me retro-hip - unhip in a very hip way . . . why I must be as hip as *no, not a fifty-year-old*, but a forty-five-year-old. Right on; stay cool, man; fuck you, Agnew; power to the people; the streets belong to the people; would you go all the way for the USA? (Zappa); keep on truckin' (Crumb); hang loose; solidarity; tear down all jails

I'm only minimally pre-agitated by the fact that some nitwits are going to get me Over the Hill paraphernalia from that Parties for Idiots store.

now (Williams); no way; I have no mouth and I must scream (Harlan Ellison); L&M has found the secret that unlocks the flavor in a filter cigarette; everybody's talkin' at me (Nilsson); far out (far far out; far fucking out). (long pause) The cat's meow.

Though I'm relatively good in math, I have a problem with remembering basic/common numbers and dates. If I think about tapping the ATM's keys, I'll get my PIN wrong; every few months I get it wrong twice in a row and get barred from additional tries. I still doublecheck home and work zip codes, family birthdates, and anniversaries, and I occasionally give the clerk at the video rental counter an incorrect home phone number (even though the same clerk has seen and greeted me several times a week for the past year, he suddenly pegs me as a suspicious character attempting to appropriate a heavily-used copy of *In Like Flint*) (note: I've explained this same scenario – using different film titles at least and different degrees of chagrin – in previous editions, but defend the refrain as appropriate given the number of times this has happened to me) (I'd tell you how many times this has happened to me – my stepping into the felon spotlight at videoland for failure to remember my home phone – but I can't because I have a problem with numbers). For many, many years I've even been unable to quickly tell you my age; surprising since my 1950 birth year makes the computation

basic. But this year, as of 1/1/00, I'm no longer unsure whether or not I'm 47 or 49 or heck maybe I am 51 or something; I know I'm going to be 50. I've been flopping through a midlife crisis since leaving Portland, Oregon for happy but less-artful living in 1980, so it's not that the half-century blur per se is spawning any distress I haven't already finessed into both brash and petulant poetics or nostalgia-heavy artworks. I'm not afraid of the number or the ticking, and I'm only minimally pre-agitated by the fact that some nitwits are going to get me *Over the Hill* paraphernalia from that Parties for Idiots store. Maybe I *like* the number? Or maybe – just like my getting a late-in-life serious allergy to carrots – I'm getting a late-in-life previously-lacking number-remembering skill. If the kids at videodrome would let me replace our phone number ID with my age, I'd have a real excuse for dragging you through this paragraph.

For my fiftieth birthday (actual date, December 18th; party date, December 16; you're invited; bring the kids; food and gifts for all; if you have to bring me something, make it good, imported, dark and muttering beer; do not bring a "This Is What 50 Looks Like" t-shirt or Jeff Foxworthy's *How a Redneck Knows He's Fixin' to Retire*), I'm planning on doing an exhibition show of 50 yet-to-be-determined doctored or altered objects, things between my hyper-dense assemblages and Man Ray's *Object to be Destroyed* (cut-out eye on a metronome's audible indicator). I'm planning to do a gratuitous 50 tie-in reading or two as well (cut-out mouth on a microphone stand).

Currently, the headlines I compose for Internal Rhyme are announcements for articles I intend to write soon.

Though the point I had planned for these opening, Issue #50 paragraphs was that, in smallpress numbers, to get to #50 is quite an accomplishment, I realize now, after having actually

REPORT TO THE TOP OF THE NEXT PAGE

written said opening paragraphs, that my point is really holy smokes I'm also turning fifty but I still write like I'm looking for new vowels. And, again, I hope my turning fifty doesn't throw you. Because I think it's throwing me.

Thanks to everyone who responded to my request for submissions to this issue. It's amazing how much easier it is to assemble a newsletter when you have contributors. (So *that's* how other magazines fill so many pages!)

First off, a letter from painter/writer/webmaster (http://members.aol.com/satpostman)/cult-reprogrammer/psychic-archaeologist Ken Miller who publishes *Shouting at the Postman* (which may become an official sport by the next Winter Olympics) . . .

> Sure, I know *intErnal rhymE*... it's a folded piece of legal-sized paper that thinks it's a fine literary magazine. It's a spooky attic full of cobwebs and ancient memories brought alive as though they happened a few minutes ago. It's where a guy with a computer and a beer can make something so true and so beautifully horrible that it can make you cry. It's got decapitated headlines which have nothing to do with anything but I've got to read them all out loud to my wife because she keeps asking me why I'm laughing so hard. It's crazy dreams and vivid illustrations of said crazy dreams, as clear and sharp as a hatpin. It's something that makes me wish I could put words together half as good as that. – Ken

> *. . . your work is a Masterstroke of sanity and whimsicality masquerading as crazy bizarre suicidal mashnotes on the busride to oblivion.*

Thank you, Ken. I will work on my headline writing skills. (Our junior high school teacher/advisor, Mrs. Irons told us that headlines for *The Garrett View* should be short and/or have an action word and/or be poetic, so, for example, when (not if) Howard Tucker wins the school spelling bee, our headline shouldn't be *Woodrow Wilson Junior High Spelling Bee Winner* or *Tucker Is Champ*; it should be something like *Tucker Takes Title*.) Currently, the headlines I compose for *Internal Rhyme* are announcements for articles I intend to write soon. Maybe I should occasionally number them, like Jackson Pollock paintings (unlike my shtick, all action and no talk).

The next letter is from Minnesotan writer/word exhibitionist/

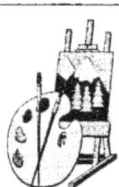
wag Charles Fowler, a remarkable tamer of the wild expressions, whose recent *A L'Ombre des Yeux en Fleur* contains poems, short stories and musings on unexpected ideas . . .

> Thomaso! Your spendthrift infernal collocation of latenight maunderings continues to amaze delight and (Strangely Believe It) Actually Inform! While managing somehow to be cheerfully agitative without irritating the eye or causing annoyance to the mental mind. Despite what you seem to be portraying in a variety of ersatz but unconvincingly deranged voices, your work is a Masterstroke of sanity and whimsicality masquerading as crazy bizarre suicidal mashnotes on the busride to oblivion. That's a tricky balance to have maintained for as long as you've done. You and Resmerski are my favorite contemporary poets (as who else is there? Message to the Introspectives with gender deficiencies, regional sediment and racial complications: You sonsabitches have let me down). And this IS, to quote Dylan Thomas, slapdash Eden. I think there's a zed in Rezmerski. Or as George S. Kaufman told an aspiring author "I'm not very good at it myself, but the first rule about spelling is that there is only one Z in IS."
> - Charles Fowler

Thank you, Charlie. I challenge Resmerski to a headline writing death match for the title of *Unlettindown Sonsabitch*. I don't know who Resmerski is, but his name is much cooler than mine.

Zebraman works at a hip printshop where the background rhythms of running presses fingersnap and pace the musings he puts in his *Enigma*, an always quaking anthology that also contains collages, freeform interviews, and (to the chagrin of his halfwitted, sidekick Jack Mackerel) good poetry. Here's his outline of *Internal Rhyme* . . .

The Top Ten Things I Like Most About *Internal Rhyme*

1. I can plagiarize good material from it to put in my own zine. Though theft is the sincerest form of flattery, I always give you credit.

2. It always shows up in my two favorite colors.

3. When I take it to work, I have to enlarge it 140% onto 11x17 copy paper so my boss can see it well enough to read it.

4. It gives me a break from the computer when I have to get

GO DIRECTLY TO THE NEXT PAGE.
DO NOT PASS GO, DO NOT COLLECT $200

This periodical may not be sold except by authorized dealers and is sold subject to the conditions that it shall not be sold or distributed with any part of its cover or markings removed, nor in a mutilated condition, nor affixed to, nor as part of any advertising, literary or pictorial matter whatsoever.

(That message was above the tinier copyright notice in nearly every comic book I read as a kid. I remember reading it inside *Superboy* and *Fox & Crow* (remember them?) and Ad*ventures of Bob Hope*. And usually in coverless copies that I got at Frankie's Market 6 for a quarter.)

up and go all the way out to the metal mailbox (shaped like a zebra, of course) to get the latest *Internal Rhyme*. God knows I need the exercise.

5. It fits neatly into a pocket or purse.

6. When I'm feeling really lazy, I can plagiarize the whole thing, fill four pages in my zine and be that much closer to done. And I still give you credit.

7. You never, ever, use the words "Cry me a river." Thank you.

8. My Selectric hums, but my computer knows all the words, and has twelve different fonts, mostly just to show off.

9. It keeps me in touch with my turtle mail friends.

I couldn't think of ten things, so let me instead explain the term turtle mail. I dislike the term snail mail for a lot of reasons, not the least of which is that snails are icky and disgusting, turtles are less so, and mail not at all. You can lick an envelope, but very few people are willing to lick a snail. No one would ever lick a turtle either, I suppose, but having skinned, cooked and eaten lots of turtles, I can vouch for the fact that they are much more pleasant than a snail prepared the same way would be. The word turtle has a more positive sound. A turtle is slow, but dependable, good-natured and amiable. Turtles are often heroes but never villains. A snail

Is this the best you can do? Has your poetry-soaked brain finally run dry?

is slimy, gross, icky, solitary, oddly slippery in an 'eeeeew' sort of way. There is no getting past that. If you step on a snail, it only makes it worse. I don't want the wonderful envelopes and contents that come to my mailbox to be in any way, shape, or form associated with the utterly negative term snail. – Zebraman

I tip my envelope to Zebraman, but must comment that his description of a snail would fit most artists as well, whereas his description of a turtle would not.

The following note is from the aforementioned Jack Mackerel, whose greatest literary skill is never challenging readers with a well-wrought phrase or complicated idea. In fact, his prose makes the self-indulgent tang of most zine writing (*Internal Rhyme* included) seem ego-free. Herewith the jaded one's gesture of goodwill . . .

Dear Mr. Tom Musicmaster Cassidy-

After readung (sic) your latest *Infernal Rhyme*, which I had to wrest away from the Z creep, I knew I had to write. What's with this *Kenneth Patchen animal* crap? Is this the best you can do? Has your poetry-soaked brain finally run dry? I couldn't get passed (sic) the first page. This is horrible stuff you're trying to pass off as poetry.

I realize that might read as sort of cruel of me to judge you from so far away, so let me rephrase that . . .

Rudi Rubberoid is the only Internal Rhyme reader who sends remarks on every issue (wow — even I don't read every issue).

You poor poor man . . . things are so terrible for you . . . your poems have been reduced to the maniacal ramblings of the intellectually incoherent. You are reduced to begging for submissions to *Internal Rhyme* under the pretense of it being a mailart call for entries of sorts. I feel I may have been hard on you in the past . . . no, worry, (sic) old man Jack can fix your problems . . . Come here, give me a big hug. You look like you could use one. C'mon, don't be shy, a hug will do you good . . . you poor mistreated man. Everyone likes to hug others, to know they are accepted, no matter how pathetic they seem to be. You act all gruff, but deep down inside, I know you need a hug; everybody needs that person to person contact . . . C'mere, give Uncle Jack a big sloppy full-body contact hug.

P.S. all misspellinggs are intentional.

Sincerely insincere, Dr. Jack Mackerel Ph.D., helping those who can't help themselves with hug (grope) therapy

Thanks, Dr. Jack, for the shameless proffering of your flesh (hooker, line and stinker).

For the polar opposite appraisal of *Internal Rhyme*, there's an

TURN, TURN, TURN (THE BYRDS)

```
Mouth


Paint sink the
clobber fan and


meat con
tainment rubble
rub ble


brush with


breath you
heave acidity
brain the lamp


slobbered what I "think"
was this was (blade vortex?


    (c) John M. Bennett   3.8.2000
```

Heels a short one with some internal hmd

awfully sweet letter from my Mom, who has supported even my most wayward experiments in often obscure and usually noncommercial (or anti-commercial) expression. (I printed a small chapbook, *Neat Lady*, about her in 1984; it's the text of a performance poem that always elicits laughter and makes people hound my Mom for autographs. I still have four or five copies of *Neat Lady* and will send it to you along with two other same-sized booklets for three bucks, cheaper than a death-dealing fastfood combo meal.) Here's the blurb that trims me down a few decades . . .

Dear Tom:

After reading all of your *Internal Rhyme* issues, I am sometimes (probably most of the time) flabbergasted by your extensive vocabulary. I particularly enjoy your references to incidents that occurred when you were growing up in New Jersey which bring back many fond memories.

Continue your writings and excerpts. I look forward to reading many more of them.

- Your devoted reader and always devoted and proud Mom

Well, there you have a textbook example of unconditional art appreciation. Thanks, Mom.

Rudi Rubberoid (who has a dozen ziplocked pseudonyms) is the only *Internal Rhyme* reader who sends remarks on every issue (wow – *even I* don't read every issue). He too has put out his own zines, most recently (but already the late) *NoMo*, so-named to express that his commitment to doing "No More zines" was in no way (NoWa) compromised by doing more zines. Currently zine-less, Rudi's mailart presence remains upbeat, colorful (both literally and figuratively) and supportive – an amiable tinker who wants to show you a bit about all the pieces that he's sorted through in a day, week or decade. Rudi sent a postcard of an artwork on which he wordballooned "50? 50? You're out of your mind..." The message side goes like this . . .

Dear Musicmaster,

Hard to believe you achieved that many issues of *Paternal Grime* over that short period of time. It took me six years to crank out 48 issues of my zines . . . and yours were good issues, too; lots of raving and ranting and art and, even, poetry. Always something different and funny between the rants and whines. More issues would seem to be in order, eh? Nothing else like *Infernal Rhyme* anywhere. Keep on pubbing.

Best, Wingo

Thanks, Rudi! I will keep on pubcrawling (I hope that's what you mean). And I will keep on ranting, whining, raving too, because, to me, all the money-above-all-else corporate-think, wingtipped, buzztalk, phone-up-ass

ego-geeks relentlessly hound me with so many ads, smarmy lies and nonproductive efficiencies every day that I feel my occasional, limited range rebuttals need air-time too, however limited (e.g. no air-time). I do confess to the fact that I like wrestling and wrestling prose and find both solace and inspiration in rhythmic bodyslams and polarized rhetoric. And when I was growing up in New Jersey, visiting boardwalk magic shops for a dribbling waterglass or well-demonstrated but tough to deploy card trick secret, I always bought the decks and packs of "insult cards," which, though probably dated and lame even then, were my earliest inspiration(s) to write.

The next item is from Malok, a prolific creator of collages so freeform that they consistently defy most collaging traditions, games and affectations. He has stamina and an endangered species' type of nonconformity. What I don't understand about Malok's work is as striking as what I do understand. Here's his submission . . .

I LOVE HELL–BEER IN HEAVEN

Give up hope . . . the cost of one fur coat is . . . SELF. It would become desert, within authorities. Nothing's classi-

PROCEED TO THE JETWAY

DRAWING BY
LUCY ROSE FISCHER

← A PEEPING SOCIAL SCIENTIST

fied Truth-Beer. Ignore this! Truth—the influence of negative Blow-Glam, a number of waking results. The 125th
Commemorative Battle of the Coupa-Muscle Funeral Planning, kit flaming red instant Xmas beer, becoming desert
within mutated censored! As stupid as God, off the map of
your existence! How can you help? Implicate the disinte-
gration of the site of the shooting devotion, commendable
Onanism on all versions of the unadvertised special (Panama
Invasion, Dec. 20th, 1989/Alien Art Glut after UFO crash).
Self-authorities would become desert within a zigzag in
your brain. Frequently, numbers OK the collapse. Loneli-
ness and narcissism laughed alone! A rubber voodoo is
valued at all times – happiest animals afraid of getting to the
point of higher consciousness (Alm Beach) too quickly.
How can you help? Jam a virgin birth and laugh till you die!
The love/hate theory of volition dominates holographic
ABC-SELF. I stand here. Phouda-Ghauda! - Malok

Thanks, Malok. I love that kind of fractured manifesto – each
plank spaced like every other railroad tie. On one hand, you
wonder if proofing Malok's prose closely really matters, and on
the other hand you realize that your ability to even conjure
such a query is proof (sic) positive that his writing, like his
collages, works with a unique set a (anti)rules. (Yeah, but what
the hell do *I* mean?)

I knew the great Alan Vandenburgh live and in person back in
late-70s' Portland, Oregon, where he frequented the Earth Tavern where I worked, played and talked art and poetry with dozens of beer-happy artists and poets. Alan was (and is) a wonderful painter and one of the quietest people I've ever met; this
latter trait made him both easy to like and hard to pinpoint.
Alan currently lives and watercolors in Santa Barbara. On
small, unevenly trimmed chunks of paper, he sent drawings and
comments for this *Internal Rhyme*, including . . .

I.R. is a forum where a sensitive artist like Musical Master is
able to express his feminine side without a bunch of creeps
picking on him like they probably did when he was in high
school.

and

I.R. is not for the butt munch. It's for cool guys like myself.

Alan, of course, is correct; the butt munch crowd should look
elsewhere to assimilate, for assent, to assess. (Write your own
kiss/bite-my-ass joke here.) *Internal Rhyme* is Alan-cool, but
talkative.

Now, alas, **abruptly,** (and surprising even myself) I need
to wrap up this cavalcade of submissions to *Internal
Rhyme* #50 so I can get the beast out of here and start
on 51. There are other pieces coming in for-sure-*maybe?*-
who-knows, but I don't want to turn this into a 12-pager, so I'll
include all late(r) items in issues 51 or 52. Thanks for your
kind feedback and attention. I'm donating the beer I owe you
to a good cause. ∎

national poetry month

poets write great poems
about you chanting over Kansas
they show off words now theirs again
they loved you living now they love you dead

a picture of you howling on tv
your obituary everywhere
(not everywhere but everywhere to me)
a lamb reading the Lamb Gazette
obituary section
bleats *oh God bless thee oh Allen*

the ranks of rhyme just shrug
say well he was this and that
not knowing fully you're the who
who made this this who made that that

briefcase full of squint rocks to the spot

your face was on the poster in my dorm room
tophatstars&stripes&
the levitating Pentagon
you should've died lots sooner
the way you lived you panhandling
sentimental drugnoshing flowersucking trisexual RabbiBuddhaBeat
you nod along with words that work the crowd

in a trendy uptown mall
where the books and coffee graze
the event for National Poetry Month
is a large magnetic room divider
on it you compose a poem
from magnetic words
that swirl around on wall below your waist
doesn't matter if it's bad or great or even lined up straight
someone else can rearrange it
take it all apart put it back whatever way it takes
to get the girl he's with undraped

no as such walking thing is aimless there

it's a nice idea that poetry is just another reflex
another common sense thing we all of us have within
we're all artists we're all poets we're all god's children
but admit it too it's also a bit like replacing bands with kazoos

during national cosmetic surgery month
do they put out scalpels and duct tape
recommend that you do it to yourself?
during national home security month
do they give you a bow & arrow
send you home to shoot the neighbors?
during national coin collecting month
do they lure you into counterfeiting?
during national musical theater month
do they suggest you write your own Brigadoon?
during national symphony orchestra month   *ONWARD*

do they hand you a violin? or
if you play the violin a grand piano? or
if you play a grand piano a bow & arrow
send you home to shoot the neighbors full of duct tape?
during national zoo and aquarium month
we're caged and given uncooked steak

poets of the world unite we're losing voice and claim to fame
and alas our pretense too to all these magnets
we're all suckers we're all equal we're all idiots with words

and at the least a language should be a win against best poem

the poster announcing that it's national fair housing month
reads fair is fair right is right
which may or may not be true
but during national poetry month
we should send out a big idea
with a bit more thought just a little less limp

I go there early evening on a slow night
walk along the wall of words
I read the rolling lines
  briefcase full of squint rocks to the spot
  no as such walking thing is aimless there
  and at the least a language should be a win against best poem
not bad really my unharnessed hands could die
without typing *squint rocks*
which while certainly not a poem is certainly post-drivel
and while certainly dictated by words available
is also a product of accepting a challenge
of only so many words available
I mean we have tens of thousands of words
we can use in our poems but this magnetic wall poet
only had a few hundred (and he could still make
squint rocks!)
my God with lots more words this guy could rhyme
this guy could pre-empt truth

I come to senses and rearrange magnetic words
I'm possessed by a tornado
like other people get when they're halfassedly upset about free verse
I turn *briefcase full of squint rocks to the spot* into
squint to spot the briefcase full of rocks

I rearrange *no as such walking thing is aimless there* into
there is no such thing as aimless walking

and those are okay lines
for use at home and school and office and I guess inside a mall
but the final words I pull apart and stitch together differently
I like the best they eulogize the beats
make me think of Ginsburg Corso Norse
DiPrima Bremser Sanders the ghost of Blake
and though they'll get dismantled soon
they make me glad to write

I rearrange *and at the least a language should be a win against*
best poem into
at least and best a poem should be a win against the language

- musicmaster 2/2000

Cassidy Hits 50!

by **Tom H. Cook** (*Newark Scar Ledger*)

Tom Cassidy, or "The Clifton Comet" as he is known in these parts, has delivered his 50th *Internal Rhyme* dinger, placing him in an elite class of wordsmiths. Cassidy, a fire balling right-hander, spotted a "feeble yet gratuitous" piece of art by Robert "Battling Bob" Rauschenberg and slammed it into the farthest reaches of the arts circle. When asked in the locker room if number 50 held any special significance to him, he replied cryptically that it was halfway to 100. He then paddled off to the showers.

It has been a long ordeal for Cassidy, a local youth who grew up in the 1950s playing in the old Passaic League with the likes of Robert Zimmerman and Howard "The Slip Cover" Tucker. It was during the 1958 season that Cassidy was drilled by ace reliever Kathy 'Hooter' Horak and was forced to the disabled list for two months. Rather than have the injury curtail a promising career, the errant pitch had a positive effect on Cassidy's development. After many years of silence on the subject, Cassidy conceded that the Horak injury forced him to take stock of his life and that his

Before the injury his work was characterized by its external rhyme, and the continual use of the word "flapjack."

quirky self-deprecating mad style may have evolved during his long and painful recovery time. Before the injury his work was characterized by its external rhyme, and the continual use of the word "flapjack."

Upon his return in 1959, the dark, brooding, salient, sardonic, anti-authoritarian stance that was to become his bread and butter was already evident. His precociousness served him well and the post-Eisenhower years were good for his development. The '60s found Cassidy "out of position" in Georgia. He was just one of a number of angry fire-breathing prospects eager to topple the Establishment. It wasn't until he was traded to Portland of the Pacific Coast League that his 'logical positivist' delivery set up his nihilistic message. His change-up combination kept the trailblazing Keseyians off balance and grappling for descriptors. His mastery of the language, coupled with a driven angst-ridden confessional style was not only haunting, but popular among the Zen, loafer wearing crowd that filled the arenas.

He was a big Hammurabi fan when he arrived in Portland. If you borrowed money from him (and we were all broke in those days) and didn't pay him right back, he'd poke you in the eye. Even as a rookie he could really bring it. "He had the tools, diction, understatement, humor, and what a delivery," recalled Dominic ""Blackie" Fucci, a friend from those days. "He was a big Irish kid with great stuff and a lot of heart. What really set Tom apart, though, was his total recall of people and

CONTINUED ON BACK LOADING DOCK

WALKING THE BEACH, EVERYONE IS A PHILOSOPHER

From the New York April Fools' Committee, 127 MacDougal Street, Suite 962, New York, New York 10012 -

Announcing New York City's
15th Annual April Fools' Day Parade

THE WORLD HAS SURVIVED Y2K SO THE SHOW MUST GO ON!

The fifteenth annual April Fools' Day Coronation of the King of Fools will be marked by a parade down Fifth Avenue, from 59th Street to Washington Square Park, beginning at 12 noon, Saturday, April 1st, 2000. The parade will be led by The New York Homeless Blues Band, playing Brook Benton's "The Bol Weevil Song." The crowd is encouraged to sing along: "Gotta getta home, Lookin for a home all right…" The band will continue marching long after the parade ends this year to avoid arrest for loitering or sleeping in the streets.

The New York April Fools' Day Committee was formed in order to remedy a glaring omission in the long list of New York's annual ethnic and holiday parades. These events fail to recognize the importance of April 1st, the day designated to commemorate the perennial folly of mankind. In an attempt to bridge that gap and bring people back in touch with their inherent foolishness, the parade annually crowns a King of Fools. The parade spotlights the year's nominees for the coveted Fool crown played by costumed impostors. Each year, the nominations are made by a select board under the auspices of the April Fools' Day Committee. Last year the parade was led by the "Why 2K? Blues Band." The King of Fools was President Bill Clinton.

The public is encouraged to participate, in or out of costume, with or without floats, and may join the procession at any point along the parade route. The lead float will be the A Man's Home is His Castle Float, a fully occupied portable castle on wheels constructed entirely out of discarded trash and cardboard boxes. This float was created by New York homeless volunteers sponsored by Rudolph Giuliani's New York Senatorial Election Committee. Next will be three Beat 'em, Bust 'em, Book 'em Floats created by the New York, Los Angeles and Seattle Police Departments, portraying themes of brutality, corruption and incompetence. These will be followed by a Where's Mars? NASA Float portraying missed Mars missions. (This float cost at least $10 billion dollars). Following that will be the Atlanta Braves Baseball Tribute to Racism Float featuring John Rocker who will be spewing racial epithets at the crowd along the parade route.

Marching lookalike fools will include: Mayor Rudy "Doody" Giuliani throwing elephant dung at passersby; Brooklyn Museum Director "Shock and Schlock" Lehman handing out free tickets to the museum; Hillary Clinton handing out New York Yankee baseball caps; and George W. Bush, Al Gore, Bill Bradley, and John McCain tossing promises.

To raise money for next year's parade, there will be a Special Auction for Custody of Elian Gonzalez.

New York City taxpayers have "volunteered" to pick up the trash along the parade route. At the end of the parade, a concession booth will sell surplus Y2K food. Every purchase comes with a complimentary can of Spam.

To raise money for next year's parade, there will be a Special Auction for Custody of Elian Gonzalez. Will he remain in the U.S., return to Cuba, or go someplace else? Let the money talk!

The King of Fools will be chosen by the loudest cheers of the crowd at Washington Square Park. The winning fool will reign as King (or Queen) through March 31st, 2001.

For information contact: Joey Skaggs, Committee Chair, at 212-254-7878, http://www.joeyskaggs.com ∎

LATE NIGHT HALFTIME ENTERTAINMENT:
a "poem" with only three-syllable words

amigo syllables
every holiday family gatherings
celebrate resilence
Deborah upholsters tenderloins
hollering quadruplets richochet unpleasant syllables
Grandfather Ichabod distributes crumbling ornaments
eternal optimist Grandmother Emily remembers 1912
Thanksgiving forever
Valentines forever
Halloween forever ∎

THE ONLY PEBBLES ON THE BEACH WOULD BE A GREAT TYPO

Fun with Used Plastic Ice Cube Trays

For quite a while now, * Goodwill Industries has been running a radio spot with the slogan/catchphrase/hook "Goodwill, good values, good times." It always catches me as sensationally loopy advertising for thrift stores where occasionally one can get a good deal on an wicker basket you don't need, a slightly chewed-up (otherwise emerging collectable) toy, or a flannel shirt that's starting to fray but what the heck, for two bits, who cares? Good values certainly, even great values every now and then (at the Hopkins Goodwill in 1986 I paid 29 cents for a bag of comic books that cataloged at nearly $150). "Goodwill, good values, *good luck*" isn't bad, especially if you intone "good luck" with a shifting blend of cynicism and sincerity. But *good times*?

A good time at Goodwill is finding a rare book that has geek-yellow highlighting on only half of the pages.

The average Goodwill store is full of older, offbrand, broken small appliances priced just below what new ones cost, clothing so out-of-style that the zoot suits look modern, musty old copies of books that no righthinking people wanted back when they were new, and tons of those plastic tumblers with dishwasher-worn pictures of fastfood (fastmedia) celebrities - Barney to the gay Teletubby to the bisexual Power Ranger.

A good time at Goodwill is finding a rare book that has geek-yellow highlighting on only half of the pages. Or finding one of those hammers you can get at the dollar store, except that it's used and costs $1.29. A good time at Goodwill is seeing the "Do Not Let Your Children Open or Play with the Toys" sign covered with crayon punctuations, stickers, and rubber darts.

I don't mean to slam Goodwill's ambience; I get a kick (at least a *used* kick) out of marathon garage sales, insanely inconsistent pricing and drawer-missing dressers made from compressed paper. I enjoy and recommend the pure, almost holy retail halfassedness of Walgreen's, America's answer to the age old question, "Where can I get two plastic, heart-shaped, microchip harmonizing deodorant caddies for the price of one?" But I **do** mean to slam that motto/punchlineline/slogan "Goodwill, good values, good times."

What do you think of when you think of good times? Parties, vacations, sporting events, family gatherings, knocking back several imported beers while listening to two guys at the bar discuss politics. (One of them says, "When I'm president, man, the sex is free;" the other one says "It's free now you idiot.")

You could list a thousand things/places under the heading **Good Times** and Goodwill would not be among them. Now, maybe if you had to list five thousand things/places, it might be number four-thousand-something, right between *Replacing a Residential Roof* and *Blowing Your Brains Out With a Stolen Howitzer*. But probably not.   ∎

CASSIDY WANES *CONTINUED*

events. He could describe the smell of paste from a cloakroom some 15 years ago. He worked on that common vision thing. He looked like a corrupt Art Linkletter. Portland fans gave him the nickname Musicmaster for obvious reasons. He never slept, but it didn't seem to affect his allusions. There were nights back in his own store—and you've got to remember he controlled the lineup, lighting and volume—but even so, he would have streaks where I don't think Ferlinghetti, Ginsberg, Koufax, Bronkowski, or any of them could have touched him."

We thought he was destined for "The Show" right then. If he cared that it didn't happen, he didn't let on. He'd be out pumpin' heat to seven people. Bennet Cerf was in one night scouting for Random House, something about a rhyming dictionary, or a synonym guide to "The Beats." It would have brought him back to The Big Apple, but as much as he wanted to play in front of the home folks, he would just get this big grin on his face and say, "I guess it just ain't my time."

Management was less patient and in December 1979 Cassidy was traded in one of the biggest off-season deals in modern history. Richard Brautigan was sent to California, Kingsley Amis to Washington, and Cassidy landed in Minnesota in exchange for Chandler Broussard, Clellon Holmes, and a one-armed mime named Castro. The trade to the MHA division didn't look like a good one at first, but Cassidy reported in the best shape of his career. He was determined to live up to his advanced billing. He started slowly, leaving writings on outbound buses, making minute sketches and drawing heads on fire. His box assemblages filled in the piece he needed to play at the next level. His collected thoughts, often covering no more than a trip on the 21A bus, were eventually dubbed *Internal Rhyme*. His style began to catch on with tropical fish owners, copier sales reps and Kafkaesque "Help, I'm a rock" worker bees. Tom's 50th is the culmination of a career spent on the Jersey boardwalk with the blood curdling shrieks from the 'Wild Mouse' ringing in his ears.   ∎

TUNE IN NEXT BAT MONTH, SAME BAT CHANNEL

for *Special Issue 51 - The Continuation of Issue 50*, featuring pieces by Mark Sonnenfeld, a 1930s' art cartoon, Kay Bowser, Vic the Florist, Hamil Griffin-Cassidy, and more. (Here are some exclamation points if you need 'em: !!!!!!)

INTERNAL  RHYME

THE TOURING AT 55 MILES PER HOUR EDITION OF AN OTHERWISE RECKLESS NEWSLETTER ◆ MUSICMASTER, 5136 LYNDALE AVE SO, MINNEAPOLIS, MINNESOTA 55419

September. Another summer shot to hell. I am way off schedule again with this scrawny but game newsletter for reasons I'll elaborate on (and overwrite about) next issue, which should be hot on the heels of this one. But now . . .

Hey, could we settle down just a little bit please? Yes, *you* with the speedreading scan-finger, *you* with the "I'm just gonna skim this piffle for dirty parts." A modicum of genuine engagement please. I'll bring in some titillating words you'll really enjoy any minute now. (Note: titillating is not itself a dirty word, but promises all the words that are.) I appreciate your indulgence. I'm a little rusty which is making me a little nervous and trying to imagine all of you naked is making my eyes bleed.

Okay, let's leave that tangent for the featured one. I'm pretty calm now, but am going to let my friend Tom Cook begin a special, two-teller tale about money and happiness in the underground economy . . .

This story is Tom Cook's mostly rational recounting of an incident that happened at a garage sale he and Joann hosted and in which we participated this past summer. Following Tom's version is my fecklessly overwritten take on exactly the same-but-different thing. Joann might some-day supplement these sharp, investigative alibis with her angles on the straight and narrow (I'm certain she'd win Most Believable honors), but until then, dear reader, the horrors that follow are all we have left of that hot day in summer 2000, when happiness too had a pricetag . . .

Price Tag

by Tom Cook

The Vice-Presidency of the United States isn't worth a pitcher of warm spit. — John Nance Garner

Many people are extremely happy, but are absolutely worthless to society. — Charles Gow

The happy do not believe in miracles. — Goethe

What they don't teach you in Vice President School is what to do with all of the gifts, awards, knick-knacks, and door prizes that an amused and cynical citizenry bestows upon its symbolic leaders. As Vice President, our own Walter Mondale spent four years being sent all over the globe by President Jimmy Carter in the late 1970s. His wife, Joan, who sits on arts boards and actually has good taste, frequently accompanied Walt (don't call me Wally) on many of his journeys. So the country/state/village/moose lodge they were visiting often had to spring for something for the missus too. Figure two events/ceremonies/solemn occasions per day minimum. Times four years...we're talking over

7,000 tokens of someone's esteem, which is either a lot of memo-ries, or a ton of junk to dust and schlep.

Being practical Minneso-tans, when the Mondales returned home to Minne-apolis and private life they had a garage sale. It was there I found "happiness," or at least an air brushed spray painted picture of a woman that the artist swore would bring me happiness if I hung it (the picture not the woman) on my wall. Joan said she received it in China as a gift, and would let it go for $3.00. Since the frame was worth $20.00, I asked myself, how far wrong could I go?

> ### "She has a very smart and handsome boy friend now. Happy love is starting."

Since I am unlikely to ever see China, this painting by Waro Wakao would have to suffice, and besides, there were endorsements enclosed in the packag-ing from other people who had gazed on the happy painting and had their lives improve dramatically. Take Ms. Kida, "She has a very smart and handsome boy friend now. Happy love is start-ing." "Mr. Hiroshi Takada of Yachiyo, China put up the picture in his shop and noticed 'the class of customers changed...atmosphere of shop changed much bet-ter.' Sales result increased...now feels much more intimate with his wife."

Leaping ahead, how could I now sell the "happy painting" at my garage sale? Had I become happier since owning it?

PLEASE STICK TO THE DESIGNATED PATH

I purchased it summer of '92 or '93 and things have generally improved. I attributed much of my increased happiness to my son learning to drive and finishing high school in the required number of years. Still I reluctantly put a $10 tag on the picture and set it out at my own sale this past weekend, leaving its future (and mine) to fate.

Around 11:30 a.m. the buzz was out, someone wanted the happy painting. As tempted as I was to out bid the stranger, I swallowed hard, ready to accept a rapidly declining quality of life and my premature demise. We showed the new owner, who almost immediately began to look perkier and clear-eyed, a copy of the testimonials. The vignette's clearly lost something in the translation from Chinese, but the sincerity and wonder that the painting inspired, shone through and went on for four pages. We insisted the new owner hear the story of "The Mondale connection" at least twice.

Nervous and impatient after ten minutes, our customer paid us, grabbed a copy of the effusive endorsements, and scurried off, but without "Happiness." He had selected a motel art special paint by number cliché offered but not painted by Inge Cassidy, herself an arts patron and co-contributor to our sale.

Somewhere in the city there is a pale and dispirited young man patiently telling anyone who will listen how a Chinese dignitary had presented this painting of a cabin in a wheat field to Walter Mondale and it had changed the life of Ms. Kida and many others. Or perhaps, our young customer is enjoying his new found painting, satisfied that beauty is in the eye of the beholder, and that his work of art holds a special place and does not require the endorsement of the Presidential candidate who carried only his home state in the 1980 election despite having the "Happy Painting" under his arm throughout the entire campaign.

Me when I realized the mistake, I grabbed "Happy," and brought it back in the house. Since almost losing my painting, I whistle more, there is a spring in my step, and I have been much more intimate with my wife. ∎

B-Track Happiness

by Musicmaster

Happy Picture I

Shortly after moving to Minneapolis from New Jersey in 1991, my parents drive to an airport hotel for a "Starving Artists Sale!" that's advertised during wrestling and the evening movie on Channel 9, which, out here, is the local station that runs their evening news a full hour earlier because that's a great gimmick for attracting the viewer who's in bed by 8:00. It's also the channel where you can regularly catch that old Burt Reynolds movie that you think you've seen whether or not you've actually seen it at all. My parents buy a melodramatic blandscape of a mountain's jaunty snowcap beaming at clouds high above a vestment of autumnal colors! A majestic, familiar anthem, *scene* to the tune of *Happy Birthday*. Whoever painted it deserves to starve. A velvet painting on canvas, it's framed and ready to shred and costs $19.95. Nineteen bucks of that is for the frame. My parents hang it over a black leather couch so big that their apartment was built around it. They got the couch at the Starving Pimps Sale. You say, "Whatever happened to Dom DeLouise?"

I know parents lie to kids about nearly everything - Santa, the Easter Bunny, Wrestling Being More Fixed Than Boxing, that poetry is supposed to rhyme, how *you'll be sorry when you grow up*, Lassie being an actual dog and not just a well-paid kid in a costume, the Tooth Fairy being an actual tooth entity and not just Lassie slumming on hiatus. Parents lie about where we come from, why we're supposed to behave, how anybody at all can grow up and be president if they only try hard in school and never again stick their tongue out at Mrs. Campbell's back because they think the janitor Mr. Pete isn't watching. They even lie about how you're going to think/feel about something, saying "give it a chance, you're going to have great time," "try one bite, you'll want more," "now isn't that music much nicer than that rock&roll?" And on top of all that, since they love you or want to protect you or they want to be fully impressed with their own miniaturized-selves, they often tell you that you're good at things or did a good job even if you're not and you didn't - the lie bigger than it's-how-you-play-the-game talk.

HAPPINESS CONTINUES IF YOU HEAD THIS WAY

I was only a mediocre student in terms of behavior/interest but managed to nearly always get straight A's (I got B's maybe five times total during my entire mental-castration ritual). In retrospect (and no doubt because I'm old and want to generalize into an acceptably bittersweet writerly "burden") I sometimes regret not having taken full or even partial advantage of paying closer attention to the sheepdogs, though, for the most part, their barking and running rarely struck me as informative or fun, let alone necessary.

The first B I got was in second grade for art, the one thing I knew I was good at; my shortcoming had to do with my not staying-inside-the-lines or disobeying an assignment by coloring the mountains red and the sky dark brown. I remember not knowing how I had earned or deserved a B or why the B was unacceptable. My parents, who were never holy-hell raisers, raised holy hell. They wouldn't have known whether or not I was doing A-level or C-level work in math or folk dancing, but they knew for sure that I was an artist, already tormented, already wondering if the lines I was going outside of were the right lines. The grade was corrected to an A. By the time my next B rolled along - in 11th grade Algebra II - my parents had calmed down enough to not worry about it all.

If you don't agree that parents lie to kids about nearly everything, it only proves that your parents are better liars than most.

How can art be art without disobedience? How can the word *assignment* breathe the same air as the word *art*?

If you don't agree that parents lie to kids about nearly everything, it only proves that your parents are better liars than most. I don't agree that parents lie to kids about everything until they buy that painting. When I look it, I have to think that when they say they like my art, they're lying, because there's no way in hell they can like my art – *any art* – and also like this billboard for cubicle art, small neo-modern designy art that simply wastes space as effectively as the average American worker. A paint chip is more impressive, informed, and inflammatory than this starving artists sale painting. Cubism has become Cubiclism.

I drew margins within margins, then ignored them; I was so unfocused in second grade I levitated. When I got a B for doing art like I was in charge of the assignment, my parents were my patrons. They told Miss Nevin that I was a good boy, even though she had given me an A in that. Yeah, I already told you this story (like *I* haven't heard *that* before!), but I forgot to tell you this part: my Dad winked at me after they told me that Miss Nevin was going to change my grade to an A, and I didn't know what the wink meant. Did he mean *we've set that straight, you deserve an A!* Or did he mean *we've really put one over on them this time!*

And now they're my parents right here, in faraway Minnesota, not my Clifton, New Jersey grade school parents. They're both miles and decades away from when and where my drawings of handless men were the center of the universe.

Happy Picture II

Nine years pass with surreal twists, unexpected truths. (As sans threw the arrow flask.) Long pause here to simulate but at the same time shorten and trivialize those years during which I adopt tropical fish whose beauty turns out to be scales-deep; during which the company reroofing our house causes rain to flow along the inside beams above our couch and bookshelves and my soluble drawings; during which the housepainter -against my warning, against my wishes – so heavily washes down an outside wall above window wells that the basement ceiling rains on my I-thought-safe collections of smallpress books; during which my Dad coughs himself awake in the middle of the night during a visit to a bungalow owned by friends in Long Branch, New Jersey, gets up and walks through the frontroom to a lounge on the porch to sit, relax and die. All water-related events; everywhere. During which my formal and informal collections get larger and larger, flooding shelves, cupboards, floorspace. There's an undertow.

I wish I could say that in those nine years I ran into Miss Nevin again, but I didn't (that she was working in the mall at a shop that only sells 60s' t-shirts: *Aliens are far out.* **Spiro-Graft**. *Love Thy Tree.* **ROTC NOTC**. But she wasn't. That she gave up teaching to study artistic handlessness but she didn't).

(Every thought is a retrospective. It might be a good idea for you to go to the bathroom before we resume. All that running water.)

In her move to a smaller apartment, my Mom sells the black leather couch and the Starving Artwork that scratched its ugly ass above it goes into storage; before putting the miserable mountains away my Mom sneers, "It's not very good, is it?"

How can the word assignment breathe the same air as the word art?

And suddenly it's this current summer. We're getting stuff together for a garage sale. An extra spatula, puzzles we won't redo, a lawnchair, mugs. There are always extra mugs; mugs for twentyfive in a household of four and Elaina doesn't use one and Hamil is at the University of Miami which cuts his mug use way down. I begin the big task of going through things I probably don't need to keep or protect or insulate with any longer – an empty Billy Beer can, toy pirates (not real pirates), games I'll never play, plastic models I won't assemble, comics, books, lots of books, an extra saw. I consider selling a supermarket Eskimo Pies display, but that would be crazy.

I call Tom Cook to see if he wants to bring stuff over if we do a sale and he and Joann already have an ad in the paper for a sale this Saturday at their house, would we like to come over and

HAPPINESS IS OFTEN LOST WHEN MIXED WITH COMMERCE

diversify the inventory, and I say sure because their neighborhood has lots of loiterers who already have spare change and this is a fun thing to do with Tom and Joann because we don't get together with them to play Yahtzee (fifty cents at their last garage sale) or to see movies (unless their daughter – the late journalist and Masterpiece Theater host Alistair Cooke – is in them). They are the friends with whom we loiter, kindred spirits in supporting and benefiting from the underground economy of garage sales and the type of conversation that can only spring from spotting an incomplete devil costume for five bucks, wondering if an old globe re-spindling kit is worth two bits, or puzzling out other peoples' private lives from the books they're selling. My Mom has a few items to sell too, so I ask if she can come along and Tom, envisioning a whole new quirk to their garage sale's personality, says sure.

> *When he finally says 'Nice talkin' to you' and leaves, I feel eroded. Like that time I took the Hades Tour and rode the Log Phlegm.*

(Jack and Angie call out of another storyline and ask if they can bring stuff to our garage sale and thus get domino-ed Cookside as well. I only include this in the interests of corroborating a certain statistical subset with the U.S. Census Bureau.)

So it's 8:30 a.m. Saturday, one of the earliest time-day combinations possible, but I'm functional, at least at the same *just-barely* setting I regularly muster for going *to* garage sales. I think Tom and Joann occasionally go out earlier (just thinking that – and how it would be lots easier to just *stay up* **that** late, until 7 or 8 a.m. – makes me dizzy, parenthetical). Dawn and Elaina and I and my Mom are unpacking our boxes of stuff onto card tables and doors-on-sawhorses. There are already shoppers asking *Is the cardtable for sale?*, *Are all the pieces here?* and *Do you have any desk lamps? No,* we answer, *How about some mugs?* I'm asleep but setting up, drinking coffee we picked up on the way over, mustering (see beginning of paragraph) and acting busy (see end of my career). And truth be told, Dawn is out of town, but I can always see her.

We arrange things like we're kids playing store, which Elaina actually is. When the Dawn who is not really here isn't looking, I buy a bunch of stuff from Jack and Angie.

My Mom gets the painting from her trunk. *The painting . . .* spawned by a blind, malnourished muse; painted by Doctor Low Concept; sold by pranksters. How is it possible that my valuable, shelved&sheltered smallpress collection was impossibly threatened by rain, that my drawings were nearly rinsed away by someone who never judged or even saw them (who never even knew that they existed), but that this screamingly voiceless painting, this deserving-to-be-destroyed painting - stored in a barely-secure closet in a wild Midwest basement – was never endangered at all, by anyone, ever. Faith treads in even the calmest sea. I can't be awake. I need more coffee. Pinch yourself.

People are looking for something in records from long ago, in other peoples' toys, in clothing that just might fit. Tom is rearranging already set-up tables to create strong aisle-cap selling zones. Did I tell you that I got the worst feeling B in tenth grade English? Because of authors and literature covered, the most memorable class I ever took. Maybe the *only* class I *ever took.* The teacher, who didn't like that I asked follow-up questions to some of her answers, who knew that due to an administrative error I was mis-tracked from honors – away from my buddies with whom I romped and recoiled since seventh grade – into B-track, told me one day that the best grade that a B-track student is capable of getting is a B. And so, for the first quarter, though I was for the only time in my school career engaged and alert and enthusiastic (and clearly the most, if not the only enthusiastic student in the class), I got a B.

A guy asks me how much the books are and I tell him they're all priced on the first page. *Some hardbacks are worth more than other hardbacks?* he asks and I nod, shocked that this uncertainty exists. Another guy, looking at a genuinely rare Kick-a-Poo Joy Juice bottle I'm selling says *I'm not used to paying a buck for an old bottle*; poor bastard; he's drinking a two-fifty latte, wearing designer safari shorts and holding a sleek cellphone in one hand. I am incapable of the interest needed to analyze his aberrant logic. I buy a few more things from Jack and Angie.

Tom introduces me to one of his neighbors and says *You guys should talk.* (Tom is always convinced people should meet other people due to tangential links he logs. Let's say I mention that I had a store in Portland, Oregon in the mid70s and that money taken in on classic pinball machines (retooled up to a dime a game, three for a quarter) nearly covered the $125/month rent. Tom snaps his thoughts like fingers, says he has a friend who owned a store in Portland about that same time, do I know him? I don't. Tom covers the lack of a link here by saying *I know a guy over on Colfax who has an old pinball machine.* (That's not exactly true, but I'm not exactly here.)

The neighbor tells me about books he has in storage and how he has a dozen copies of a hard-to-find magazine with a Frank Frazetta cover and his mouth chews around my wavering focus as he puts the blahblahblah into a shredder and all his words hop around in my eyes-open sleep like micropulverized haystacks in which some points are hidden. I blah-

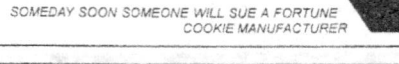

SOMEDAY SOON SOMEONE WILL SUE A FORTUNE COOKIE MANUFACTURER

REALITY TV WOULD BE BETTER (AND MORE REAL) IF THE PLAYERS COULD HEAR OUR CATCALLS

smile and blah-nod until he's covered every damn puny useless pseudo-philosophical headache he's ever had and, when he finally says _Nice talkin' to you_ and leaves, I feel eroded. Like that time I took the Hades Tour and rode the Log Phlegm. (Joke courtesy of itself-drowsy caffeine.)

(One of the reasons I like Tom is because he's one of the few people who thinks with as many tangents as I do. ((Which reminds me of the time I gave up comedy contests for politics and finally won.)) Though his tangents are always more logical, more legitimately searching than mine. Another reason is because he **always sees something** ((emphasize any of those three words)) and that's an unusual trait. Tom can see the practical potential of a broken rotary phone. He finds the little footprints in the snow. Tom would have noticed that I was artistic in second grade and given me a gallery show in SoHo before he would've given me a B. Or at least he would've connected me with someone who had an easel for sale.)

There's a midmorning lull so Elaina and I decide to walk around the block. I ask my Mom if she'll be okay handling the store and she asks _is the cardtable for sale?_ and _how much are the books?_ Surprisingly, her painting hasn't sold yet and

she says _let me mark it down to eight bucks, then you can go._ I don't know that selling the painting without the starving pimp's couch accessory is even possible. And I don't know that marking the painting down is half as good as burning it, but it's worth a shot.

Tom and Joann are laughing with a customer. Joann is unfolding a piece of paper that looks like an instruction sheet that I'm assuming is from a game said customer wants to purchase. As my Mom fearlessly walks over to her painting, Joann reads aloud _Since she got happy picture she has gotten a rich and handsome boyfriend. Mr. Hueykoko put happy picture up in his rotisserie repair shop and the customers spent more and his wife got breast implants._ Something like that – like the chainletter testimonials that precede the scary stories about what happens to people who don't embrace happy picture philosophy (be happy) and happy picture economics (buy or die). I ask Tom what Joann is reading and he tells me it's the sheet that accompanies the "happy painting" he's selling, he got it from the Mondales' garage sale for a couple of bucks, a gift they got from happy China, and he doesn't really want to sell it but for ten bucks he

GET YOUR SECOND WIND, WE'RE ALMOST DONE

OFF THE ON & ON THE OFF TANGENT

written works that wander, pitch tents, scale walls

TOM CASSIDY & TOM COOK

THURSDAY, SEPTEMBER 14, 2000, 7:30 P.M.

BARNES & NOBLE
3225 WEST 69TH, GALLERIA, EDINA

free (you cheap bastards) ◆ informal attire

will. This is Tom's idea of running a retail operation at a very, very slow pace. My Mom returns to an official stance behind our stuff and smiles – the new pricing structure has been successfully implemented.

Happy Picture III

Elaina and I walk around the neighborhood, commenting on the big old houses, their porches and gardens. I ask *Did you bring anything to sell that you didn't really want to sell, but would sell if you got a certain price for it?* Elaina squeezes my hand and says *Can I call Mae Kelly when we get home? Sure* I answer, wondering if Tom will get unhappy (just like the booklet warns) if that guy buys happy picture. *You know what we would've named you, if we didn't name you Elaina?* She shakes her head no but guesses *Olivia? Nope* I say, she guesses *Ethelmania*, a name I actually call her pretty often. *Nope* I say, she guesses *Howard?*, the name of our canary. *Nope* I say, *We would have named you Mr. Hueykoko.*

> **You shouldn't need a video camera, a store detective, at a garage sale. It would drive the prices up.**

When we return to the Cooks' mini mall, there's a lot of traffic, people milling around and crossing their arms and test-driving old postcards. My Mom tells me I sold about sixteen dollars worth of stuff, mostly books. And some puzzles, and one of those watchamacallits. It's nearly noon and I still haven't woken up. Tom asks if I had a good conversation with his neighbor and I think of saying *It was like trying to talk with a wind tunnel* but I don't because what the hell do I know, so I lie and say *Yeah, nice guy. And he said this great thing about some semi-valuable magazines he has. He said he had a lot of **hard-to-find** magazines . . . but he wasn't sure where!* Even though he's probably encouraging more unnecessary comments, Tom laughs.

In the voice of someone who's just noticed a screw-up in the natural order of things, my Mom loudly intones *Where's my painting?* And I look where it was leaning all morning and it's gone. *Maybe somebody else sold it for you* I guess and with an intercom rasp my Mom asks all merchandising associates *Did anybody see what happened to my painting? It was over there* she points as proof. I'm in a tricky spot – I am so delighted, so thrilled that the godawful wall blight is missing that whether or not somebody paid for it or swiped it is superfluous; but we're talking about somebody boldly stealing something from my Mom, at a garage sale for crying out loud! So I cross several bases by noting *That's awful.*

Maybe somebody picked it up and leaned it somewhere else says Tom, an expert at garage sale inventory rotation, but we all look around, check under tables and can't find the blankityblank (blankblank) painting. The Case of the Missing Masterpiece. How flattered the artist was to learn that his painting had been stolen from the State Fair gallery. The crook was a bad man with bad taste. I suggest *Maybe someone who had already been to a bunch of sales had it in their hands and walked off with it absent-mindedly because they thought they had already paid for it*, though I know that's probably not true, but hoping, hoping. I'm the world's most optimistic pessimist. I know things are bad but I don't trust my knowledge.

All of us take turns saying *I can't believe somebody would steal something at a garage sale.* You shouldn't need a video camera, a store detective, at a garage sale. It would drive the prices up. It's another sign of the moral decay of *everything*. Which ironically began when that painting was painted.

It's quiet for a few minutes, only one shopper browsing around. It's the first time I check out Jack and Angie's table while fully awake, so I buy a few more things. I ask Jack why he's getting rid of some X-Files collectibles and he says *Well, Angie and I decided we just had to let some things go.* And I nod knowingly (noddingly!), able to absorb this harsh arid fact, a man talking to a man on the doormat (two bits at a garage sale) of the new millennium.

I remember back in college '69, how inspired and weepy the penultimate hippie Space Kennedy got when he told us that the psychedelic lettering on his tie-dyed t-shirt said *Possessions suck. And **that's** a fact, man* he said, all focused and spiritually horny, as if he'd finally had a thought without a rupture. I asked. *Well then, could I have your t-shirt?* And halfway through answering *No way*, Space got my joke – which was nothing more than a faith-free wisecrack – and dropped his jaw. *That is far out, man.* he finally said. *That is far fucking out.* He looked at his shirt like it was crawling across his stomach, tugged out the neckline to stare within, see if he'd become an imposter. *Man, that is the far fuckingest out thing I've ever heard.* His eyes were all over his face. *Space*, I said to him, *You're really stoned, man.* And after nodding at that, muttering *Yeah, you're probably right*, he whispered *I'm going to tell you another cool thing, man, to pay you back. Are you ready?* And knowing any answer would be irrelevant, not to mention unnecessary, I didn't answer, and Space continued as if I'd actually said okay. *Here it is*, he said – *Just because the window is closed man, like closed shut, it doesn't mean there's nothing on the other side.* And then he nodded at me, skull jogging to catch his own words. *Well of course there's something on the other side*, I answered, *otherwise why the hell would you put in a window?* Space's nodding accelerated, as he added *No wait, I said it wrong. It's 'just because the window's dirty, doesn't mean there's nothing on the other side.' That's how it goes and that's far out.* I said something like *Dirty or open or closed or broken, or even stolen, Space, it's still a window. And why the hell would you have a window anywhere if there weren't something on the other side.* Space gave up nodding for shaking his head and said, *You don't get it, man.* And though he was right, I played my game by saying, *No, I don't get it Space because I don't want to . . .*

THERE'S THE SIGNPOST UP AHEAD

UNTITLED #227: THINK ABOUT WHAT CONCEPTUAL ART MEANS

SALVAGE OPERATION #4

I wrote this poem in 1994 as an indirect part of a series about junior high school friends, particularly good friend & pain-in-the-ass Howard Tucker. Because of the positive response I always get when reading this piece, I decided to tighten it up just a nudge and, at long last and however modestly, get it into print. To protect the truth, no names have been changed, though details have probably been touched-up or even replaced for the rhythms of memory.

adults only

though the signs reads *Passaic Coin & Stamp*
established 1920 we call it the Old Lady's
a narrow shop with bookshelves to the ceiling
benches down the middle stacked with comics
coverless five cents each six for a quarter

to see the coins and stamps you have to ask
the Old Lady herself at the counter
she creaks up a stepstool pulls binders
from a high up shelf and lets you look at
all the coins and stamps the rare ones too
she says *I hope you kids have money*

Howard and I consume comic books like popcorn and collect coins
so we think the Old Lady's is great
that it is poorly lit and dusty doesn't matter we don't care
that the comics have no covers that the Old Lady is cranky ugly
thick with gin only makes it greater still

we take the Richfield bus to get here fifteen cents from Clifton
every Saturday we spend at least an hour in this place
the Old Lady never remembers us says hi to us or smiles at us
just makes librarian noises and occasionally hollers out
- whether we're flipping through comics or not -
this isn't a library she says *let's buy the books and read at home*

ART SURE AS HELL WON'T MAKE YOU HAPPY CONTINUED

possess it. The number of *far fucking outs* that far fucking followed was extravagant.

Tom Cook hands me a cold bottle of beer, which, on an old Dean Martin show, means it must be time to wake up. Back when Happy Hour was happy (nowadays it's just a marketing strategy). I look at my Mom, who loved the basted Dean Martin and the bogus schnockered Foster Brooks, and she's eyeballing a garage sale browser like the guy is going to abscond without paying for an LP under his arm. As if he could do that inconspicuously.

But of course he could. Someone like him swiped her painting.

Elaina calls to me from a folding chair where she's been flipping through a rip-off of the Where's Waldo? books and proclaims *I am Mr. Hueykoko!* And then, *When are we going home? Can Mae Kelly come over?* Instead of Waldo, there's a clunky pseudo-British dog named Nevin, who barks with an accent and is really easy to find because of both a production budget too small for good camouflaging artwork and the fact that he's barking.

I answer *Just a minute*, one of the classic parental lies of all times, as there's no way in hell I mean a literal minute or even a figurative five. But I do think it's time to wrap it up. We sold five, maybe six boxes of stuff; figure in what I bought from Jack and Angie and, getting-rid-of-stuff-wise, at least we're even. I'm kidding. I look around at how much stuff we have to rebox for Goodwill or no-will or next sale, and tell Tom *We're going to slowly pack up. I have to go to work a while today.* (Color within the lines. Add hands to all my childhood drawings. Do the crap I have to do because I got too many Bs in school.) And at the end of one table I see a picture half sticking out of a box and I know it's happy handsome rich rotisserie shop painting.

Didn't somebody buy happy painting? I ask. Before Joann says that she sold it to that guy to whom she had read happy picture testimonials, before Tom corroborates that story with fully-networked tangents, I'm suddenly awake and I know what happened. The guy asked about one painting, got the scoop about another, paid Joann for and took my Mom's painting, though neither Joann nor my Mom knew the guy did his own bait and switch. Get it? The guy didn't know there was more than one painting for sale, didn't pick it up and take it to Joann

> **Even though I know what happened, I don't.**

for background details, he just asked about the painting and the rest, like all certain history, is now anecdote.

We all laugh like we're wrapping a comedy sketch. To ourselves, we apologize to the people we suspected. Mr. Happy Picture guy not only paid ten bucks for an astonishingly ugly if not out-&-out evil painting, but he paid ten bucks for a painting that was marked down to eight. Had he waited another hour, he could've gotten it for five. Had he waited until two weeks from today, he could've gotten it at the Goodwill store for twenty-five.

Even though I know what happened, I don't. Even though this story finally ends, I won't. I ask Tom and Joann to both write about Happy Painting and I thank them for adding new lines outside of which I can draw. I'll write about Happy Painting too, how I peripherally experienced it, but, for want of sharper focus, for reasons of faltering dedication to snapshot facts, I won't get it right at all.

Note: Waldo wants to be found. Nevin wants to be noticed. I want to swim in all the words. ∎

PEOPLE REPEAT "HISTORY REPEATS ITSELF" BECAUSE THEY'VE HEARD THAT POINT BEFORE

Howard who is capable of brown-nosing any teacher
who has ever taught at Woodrow Wilson Junior High
who is capable of brown-nosing any adult anywhere at all
is unable to brown-nose the Old Lady
when he cheerfully shouts Good morning Mrs. Coin & Stamp
her response is a disowning glare
when he goes up to the counter smiling like a pumpkin
and says something so retarded my brain gets goosebumps
like *I really look forward to spending all of my Bar Mitzvah money*
*   here*
the Old Lady *barks this isn't a dancehall wiseguy*
it's a book store buy some books
while we look through piles of coverless comics
we make one another laugh by mimicking the Old Lady
this isn't a dancehall wiseguy it's a bookstore
this isn't a library it's a bookstore
this isn't a reading room it's a bookstore
then why the hell is it called Passaic Coin & Old Lady?

Howard sneaks a copy of a *Playboy* from the Adults Only shelf
which by the grace of God is right below *Richie Rich* and *Superboy*
with his back to the Old Lady he opens up the centerfold
an incredible image of ice cream all mixed up with God
Howard whispers *look at this it's Miss Plaskon*
and of course it isn't really Miss Plaskon
the most beautiful music teacher in the solar system
all saxophone and cymbal and alluringly unknown
only the parts we've never seen of Miss Plaskon
sort of resemble what we're looking at today
but if you squint at centerfield enough it sort of looks like Miss Plaskon
so we laugh a laugh that isn't dirty or knowing
just nervous a little loud and the Old Lady snorts
a snort that is dirty *and* knowing *and* loud
because after all this isn't Talk to the Hyenas Day at the zoo

of course if you squint at a bus too hard it looks like Howard
and if you squint at Howard too hard he looks like the Old Lady
so give and take the world and how you see and say it
with a grain of salt a bump&grind and coins that don't add up

the store door opens and in the Old Man stumbles
you hardly ever see the Old Man he was in the Civil War
on the rare occasion he runs the shop he lets you take a book or two
    for free
he doesn't look like anybody's grandfather anywhere
or anyone who's ever collected comics or coins
I whisper *he's nicer than the old lady*
and the Old Lady glares at me for whispering

making fun of how our English teacher
Mrs. Irons says *but then again too* all the time
Howard says *but then again too*
Godzilla is nicer then the Old Lady

the Old Man wobbles forward
bumps around a bit for balance
puts his hand on Howard's head
when he staggers over me I lift up comics
that I'm going to buy for sure
to indicate my importance as a customer

to show him I'm not just some hoodlum staking out the store like
    Howard
the Old Man says to me
those comics'll rot your brain son
get some girlie books like your buddy here

the Old Man makes it to and around the counter
where he completely ignores the Old Lady
and disappears behind a curtain
while the Old Lady completely ignores him right back

I imagine that they live in a room behind the curtain
where there's a sleeping bag a small sink
and a picture of them long ago
just married wondering what to do to slowly kill themselves
the young Old Man says *let's open a bookstore*
call it Passaic Coin & Stamp
and the young Old Lady says
this isn't an expansion of your hobby wiseguy it's a marriage

suddenly the Old Lady makes an announcement
like she's on the Sears Roebuck intercom *attention shoppers*
she says in a voice an octave lower than her regular voice
for the next five minutes only we have a special sale
on brand new copies of the 1945 edition of Webster's Pocket Book
*   Dictionary*
an excellent value at the regular price of twenty-five cents
you can get one at the main counter for just fifteen cents
for the next five minutes only

Howard and I are the only shoppers in the store
and there's only one counter in the store
Howard whispers that he's going to buy a copy
just to get brownie points with the Old Lady
which is very funny but the tragedy is that he's being completely
    serious
he walks up to the counter
where the Old Lady has a battered old paperback in her hand
and he says *okay I'll take one*
and the Old Lady stares at Howard and barks *one what?*
as if the announcement never happened
maybe as if Howard is a smaller version of the Old Man
as if this is how they talk - the words without the meanings

they have no use for dictionaries in Passaic Coin & Stamp
and when the Old Lady repeats *one what?*
Howard impresses me by saying
one of the foreign coin binders please
so I join Howard at the counter
and we both flip through plastic pages packed
with castles the Cape Verde Islands and a snake that can eat people

we each buy a few for ten maybe fifteen cents each
and as we leave the range of her intercom
and pass the Miss Plaskon magazine and all those coverless comic
    books
I realize that the Old Lady is so miserable
because she has to sell us kids all her incredible stuff
watch it all go out the door for good

- musicmaster 2000

DECEMBER 32, 2000

INTeRNAL  RHYMe

ISSUE #57 OF THE ONLY NEWSLETTER THAT DOESN'T LET ANYONE ELSE OKAY OR SPIN THE COPY ● MUSICMASTER, 5136 LYNDALE AVE SO, MINNEAPOLIS, MINNESOTA 55419

Brain in Mouth Disease

or Part II of Why It Has TakEn ME LongEr than thE LifEspan of a FruitFly to GEt This IssuE Out

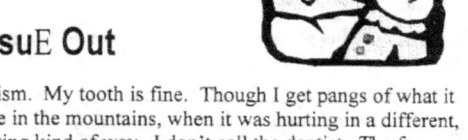

(CONTINUED FROM INTERNAL RHYME #56)

Since Dawn has a business trip to Denver, I join her there as her official nonsense ends so we can relax and wander for a long July 4th. Even though we are based in the core of downtown convention zone, we have a swell time being tourists, wandering outside the high tariff zone, finding a fading lakeside amusement park with a wooden roller coaster that requires a crew of five and a big manual brake lever for it to operate. On the beach is an unused bleachers area where they used to feature free water shows and concerts. And the main entry way is through an old exposition hall with a large, light-wrapped watchtower that looks like an actual summer night in 1935. Most of the buildings have amusement park curlicues, signs, or fixtures from when my Dad was a kid.

Though the amusement park is rundown, clearly distressed, with slightly dangerous looking rides, it is beautiful to me, a rare, almost complete throwback to Olympic Park, Irvington, N.J., which we visited a dozen times a year or more when we were growing up in the fifties and sixties. Long before Disneyland, Olympic Park had the feel and flow of Disneyland, and lots more mice with names. And now, this park in Denver has the feel and flow of a mirage. It's Tuesday in Denver and as we drop down the first oddly angled and steep hill of the wooden roller coaster, my tooth doesn't hurt at all.

> *I dream about being in the dentist's waiting room with blood pouring out of my mouth.*

We drive into the mountains, above the tree line, on an unpaved road still lined with small dense mounds of snow and see lightheaded mountain goats. I mean if I push really hard up against the tooth with my thumb like I'm looking for discomfort, well sure, there's an immodest amount of pain. But if I'm just existing normal frequency, my mouth is its regular self and the tooth of the moment is okay, a tiny aura of having being stunned recently but otherwise okay. I think the altitude makes my tooth feel a little worse than it really is. Not that it feels really bad, but the thin air amplifies everything, then echoes everything to boot.

We loiter downtown, we play Scrabble, we visit the sprawling and only slightly codgerly Botanical Gardens, we go *out* for a beer, we go to a famous bookstore where there are no "this isn't a library" signs over the extraordinary assortment of periodicals, we go *in* for a beer, we walk over to the Denver Art Museum and spend a few hours reviewing odd types of journalism. My tooth is fine. Though I get pangs of what it was like in the mountains, when it was hurting in a different, nonhurting kind of way. I don't call the dentist. The famous imprint on Denver Art Museum t-shirts and buttons is DAM!

My tooth remains so calm, relatively speaking, throughout our entire vacation, I almost forget about it completely . . . for several scattered seconds. I know that when I see the dentist after vacation that he'll laugh with mock shock about my ordeal, that he'll easily retrieve the drifting root with a crowbar and a carefully trained centipede wearing a suction-cup vest. Other than the usual mix of light and dark beers to give me a kind of gray-beer fog, I don't need any painkillers in Denver. And the thin air tastes like normal air but it also makes the sidewalk softer, which loosens the hydrant, which begins to vibrate just a bit, all that blood pressure below. I need absinthe. I'm fine.

When we return to the thick of workaday stuff, God's anti-intellectual phlegm, I postpone one appointment with the dentist out of sheer concern about ending a viable if annoying subplot to my middle-aging everything, my usually tired and fuzzy eyes, my beer-fed gut, my collapsing teeth.

I dream about being in the dentist's waiting room with blood pouring out of my mouth. There's a small boy across from me with blue teeth. I ask him if his teeth are dead and he says he just had an Icee. He asks me what's wrong with me and I tell him I had a sunflower seed.

I reschedule for a day in what is suddenly August but the weekend before that day, while letting the dog out for final latenight draining, I slip down two backsteps and smack my back against a very solid reminder of our planet and its gravitational pull. While I'm not seriously hurt, I quickly learn that reclining backways instead of sideways makes a huge, dull pain somersault through my body like a tumbling boulder. I am mostly okay if I don't sleep, nap or recline on my back. And since I don't sleep too much and mostly nap sitting and watching eye-opening television reports, I am mostly okay. If I sleep on my back however, a lumbering pain sets up shop in my spine, then advertises throughout my body. Since my dentist has yet to install a facedown rig for patients – so that he can look up from below and shower in our gold-plated drippings - I postpone my appointment.

(Lots of additional paragraphs originally prepared for this area have been removed. You're welcome.)

ADVANCE TOKEN TO NEAREST RAILROAD

ON AND ON AND ON CONTINUED

Two weeks later, because my back is still thrown or out or whatever we say to mean it can suddenly feel constrained, torched and strangled, I cancel my dental appointment. The tooth is starting to shiver a bit now and again, and I think and say "I don't know" too often. Or maybe not often enough. But I can't imagine experiencing both dental excavation and back pain simultaneously. Whenever people discuss the worst common physical pains, childbirth is always closely followed by back pain then toothache. And the worst part of childbirth is the back pain!

Bewitched, bothered and bewildered has nothing on constrained, torched and strangled.

Finally, in late September, it seems that my back is better (though memories of tooth pain make me wonder if maybe my back was never too bad to begin with) and it seems that my tooth is better (though memories of back pain make me wonder if maybe my tooth was never too bad to begin with). I make an appointment with the dentist and as soon as I hang up the phone I get a headache a backache an ear ache a charleyhorse a cold in my eye a neck spasm and as I bite my tongue my tooth hurts like hell.

A week or two before Halloween, without a hint that saving the tooth is even a remote possibility, the dentist numbs me up, yanks my tooth, digs around for what snapped off. He says I'll need to replace an existent, normal bridge with a five-tooth model to span the new gap. My conked-out tongue pokes around the vacant slot of my smile. (I'd like to nominate the previous sentence as gratuitously poetic, too eager, and possibly an argument for banning writing all together.)

From my numbed-up, laidback, no-feeling (let alone pain!) state, I ask, "What are my options?" meaning everything from why-not-an-implant-so-as-to-leave-the-good-existent-bridge to what-would-happen-if-I-leave-the-lane-open, so to speak. He says "What options?" (Which I thought was my question.) At the lowest ebb of elaboration, the dentist elaborates "There are no options." He gives me moist-towelette-style packets of gauze for soaking up blood and a little booklet that explains that I just underwent minor surgery so I shouldn't immediately return to my career as that Hungarian trapeze artist who hangs from a rope eighty feet up by his teeth. Don't bite solidly on anthracite. Or is it *bit*uminous?

As I'm about to leave the dentist's office, the receptionist-cum-Director-of-Finance tells me that my approximate cost for this engineering miracle will be – after insurance – almost three thousand dollars. I ask, "After insurance?" She nods. I ask, "After insurance?" And she nods again. I ask, "After insurance?" Loud nodding. "After insurance," she says. "It's a big bridge." And of course it all suddenly makes sense, the insurance angle meets the big angle, the pain always compounded, the explanations never clear, the wallet an emotional wreck, the real meaning of toll bridge, the plans for building a coffee table out of quarters suddenly forgotten.

Curiously, the taste I taste in my dumbified mouth is a mixture of that unexpectedly good pizza we had in Algoma and dental-office smell. My conked-out tongue pokes around the vacant

slot of my smile. (I'd like to nominate the previous sentence as gratuitously gratuitous, *too too*, and possibly a metaphor for anything anytime anygripe against any insurance agent/premium/plan anywhere.)

When I get home I rethink my plans for my disposal income and mope, fully unappreciative of the fact that eighteen million abandoned, cute, scurvy-infected kids in East Foreign Podunk alone don't have a language with a word for food let alone leftovers. (This in spite of the fact they consume more Coca Cola per capita than any other country but New East Foreign Podunk.) I don't want to dip into savings for the new bridge because money put aside for a rainy day shouldn't be spent on such a small, mouth-specific cloud.

"Well," I think, "I could get dental insurance to prevent this economic inconvenience from happening again," before I remember I have dental insurance. And switching coverage wouldn't matter because, like you, I am, in toto, a pre-existing condition.

For five days I cut back on beer, lunches out and book purchases and save nineteen dollars and forty-nine cents. During the same stretch, a semi-deranged and semi-talented acquaintance from Open Mike Land (which is globally contrapuntal to East Foreign Podunk) borrows thirty bucks from me so that the result of my five-day plan to minimize leaking dollars is a net loss of ten dollars and fifty-one cents. The gap isn't at all visible when I smile and the lack of pain is so refreshing that I don't call for an appointment to begin the development of the new bridge.

Walking around with Elaina on Halloween I tuck and plaster a wad of gum into the gap.

Days and weeks and lots of opportunities to end this story, this complaint pass as I take on a few odd graphics jobs, ones that might be fun but never are, their handlers all so TV-headed or web.happy that they're really just paying you for approval of their ideas. That their ideas are often really good compounds my lack of fun. I juggle my mental books, take two hundred bucks from a slot for a trip next spring and put it into a bridge fund.

Coincidentally I have a speaking gig for the fortysome folks who work at – I kid you not - a dental clinic. They want a fortyfive minute Crash Course in Creativity, a Dummy's Guide to Creativity, the One-Minute Manager's Guide to Creativity, some sort of handout they can save until it's time to pick a theme for the annual picnic. So that's what I deliver. Sort of. I preface my remarks by saying that since writing "Dental Clinic" on my calendar, I've been flossing like I just got God. Fortyfive minutes later I hand out little plastic denture charms. I put my speaker's fee in the bridge fund and wonder if among the several people who laughed the loudest there's one who would swap art or poetry readings at his kids' birthday parties for dental work, but I don't pursue that chance.

Thanksgiving Recess. The turkey is perfect (in a dead and cooked sense of the word); the gravy-Pollocked mashed

WATCH THE TRAM CAR PLEASE

THE UNEXAMINED LIFE IS WORTH TOO MUCH NOWADAYS FOR ITS WORTHLESSNESS TO MATTER.

potatoes are excellent, the canned cranberry sauce tastes reassuringly, predictably familiar, but the stuffing tastes submediocre, the breadcrumbs must have been stale. A juice-besotted cube of it sticks to the gum above the gap, hangs into it like a bat.

I sell a few artworks, assemble a stray newsletter, get a refund on a dated book order, save a dime here and there until I realize the bridge fund is starting to have real clout. I may as well make the appointment before the gap-flanking teeth cave in, before the price of bridgework soars, before I just blow it off, accept the reduced mass of me and begin what I perceive as an almost official decline into codgerdom.

All this time, honest, since September, I've been working on poems, ideas, fragments, this piece every now and again, meaning to get an issue of *Internal Rhyme* done, but always sidetracking because of an odd mindset that since the tooth/root/bridge/dental topic is *the* topic of the issue in progress, that I cannot do a next issue until the story is over. If for no other reason that to get *Internal Rhyme* chugging again, I make the appointment . . . for right after we return from a trip to Miami.

Dawn has a work-related convention to attend, so, for the price of airfare, I'm her extra luggage for a five-day getaway. We'll both get to visit our son Hamil, who is a junior at the University of Miami, Coral Gables, just twenty minutes away from the Fountainbleau. Yes, the legendary Fountainbleau (pronounced Fountainblehhh); the Jersey Acapulco of the 60s; the seaside Catskills of the 50s; the setting for that Jerry Lewis bellboy movie with enough antics to fill a dozen episodes of *Lassie*.

> *I am dizzy from the radon of swankiness. If you have to ask if the expensive Dali is real, you can't afford it.*

The Fountainbleau turns out to be the seaside Jersey Catskills of the 40s. Officially designated as a living tomb by Jewish observational comics, the Fountainbleau is a surreal, pimped-up-Deco safety harbor for predatory (rip-off) pricing and decay. The lobby is full of centenarians who have tanned themselves into tennis skirt and leisure suit wearing human jerky. It is as dated looking as swanky sounds, a cross between a Rat Pack lounge and a hip funeral parlor. Paging Henny Youngman. Take my pulse, please!

We loiter around the downstairs shopping arcade. In the sundries shop we price a can of soda at two bucks and a single-serving cup of yogurt at four! Gadzooks! That's not typical hotel gouge of twice the regular price, this is like 600% higher! There's a swimsuit shop display-ing spangled, goldlame corsets, a gift shop with boardwalk crap at Tiffany prices and a shop full of mediocre, overpriced, possibly bogus prints that I've seen in more places and more often than Budweiser ads. (Note: the prints are always by the usual suspects, including Chagall, Dali, Miro. Did they really sign enough prints to wallpaper North America?) I am dizzy from the radon of swankiness. I know, I know – if you have to ask if the expensive Dali is real, you can't afford it.

Dawn wants to have dinner in the Fountainbleau's inexpensive restaurant and I panic, imagining a burger (hold-the-mayo) will cost $245, certain that I'll blow all of my spending money on this first vacation meal and thinking how finite my spending money is because of the tooth thing, the bridge fund. Turns out that by carefully applying Dawn's food per diem allowance when ordering and by drinking coffee instead of other drinks that the tab isn't bad. But throughout the meal, I think how there are people in this hotel who spend more on clothes in a month then I will in my entire lifetime. Yes, maestro, the violins. There are women in this hotel who spend more on their damn toes in a year then I will on my clothes and hair together in my entire lifetime. But the real obscenity is that in the normal outside-Fountainbleau world, we are fortunate, maybe not well off, but well enough off, able to buy too much food and too many books and even dental insurance. I'm an ingrate. I should appreciate that getting pricey mouth rehab is even an option.

The next day I stock the room with rations from a not-far store and loiter. The grounds are pretty neat with a croquet green, tennis courts, an amoeba-triplets-like pool, and lounge chairs on the beach that you have to rent. You can rent a bucket and pail for about five bucks a day, three times what you'd pay to buy your own.

For all of its throwback character and dusty charm, The Fountainbleau is a decrepit pickpocket. Even an under-construction, kids' waterpark area, with a giant octopus hub shown in the self-congratulatory brochures, looks like something that was only a mediocre kid-pleaser in the fifties.

When we're out of the hotel, I'm less cranky. The university campus, South Beach, the boardwalk, the comfortable heat are all fabulous. I'm sick of the tooth story. And don't even have a tooth fairy that's adjusted his refunds for inflation.

Time flies without the stopover in Charlotte where Dawn and I read books and enjoy a final calm before the holiday season.

ARROWS? I DIDN'T EVEN SEE THE INDIANS

AND NOW THE MUTED GRAND FINALE

The first significant snowfall of the year swirls around all the holiday lights, dusts the trees strapped to cartops. I hope there's enough snow and delays for the dentist to shut down or reschedule. But like those gradeschool mornings after a snowfall when the siren doesn't spare kids the grind and drone of braindrills and distinctive smelling confined space, the appointment isn't cancelled and I am at longlast on my back, under the spotlight, numbed up, mouth agape as pliers grab the existent, perfectly good but now insufficient bridge.

There's an unholy eye-jarring *crannngt* as the dentist yanks out

---

But like those gradeschool mornings after a snowfall when the siren doesn't spare kids the grind and drone of braindrills and distinctive smelling confined space, the appointment isn't cancelled and I am at longlast on my back, under the spotlight, mouth agape.

---

my jawbone. I get to breathe and swallow a minute before he begins grinding down the exposed teeth and the healthy incisor that must now host one end of the bridge. Every annoying dental visit thing that can happen happens. The cold air jet blasts the most sensitive facet of a molar, cold water screams into the same spot, the cold air and water together form an icicle-skewering the heart of a siren I hear from the grind and drone of braindrills, my mouth the distinctive smelling confined space. I have to bite down on a contraption that seems to be made of mud and anger and I have to hold it even while tendrils of the mud toy with my gag reflex. I try not to panic or choke (or joke) as Woody Allen's life flashes before my eyes.

Nearly an hour passes before the dentist puts my old bridge back in with temporary glue that he says should hold for a week until the megabridge comes in. I am stunned, tired, and happy to be standing. Seven more days and the ordeal will be over. While I could easily do without loitering around Door County again, I wonder if it would seem different to me if I weren't preoccupied with tooth, teeth, gum, bite, jab, and ouch. Would I bowl better? Would the lighthouses be more impressive?

I'm writing two nights later, 1:30 a.m. and I taste an odd taste in my mouth, which for a moment reminds me of that pus-like fondue of spiked gum that marked the start of this distraction way back in June. But this taste isn't completely unpleasant, it's sweet, an after taste of dental work. Five more days until a dental appointment I'd actually make sooner if I could - right now, be over and done with it all.

It will be great to bite normally again, chew without a bias left, give my tongue some time off from all the vigilant adjusting and steering it's been doing. I'm thinking about the dentist because of the taste in my mouth that I suddenly realize is the glue, the temporary glue. I feel part of my mouth's ceiling cave in, click against lower teeth. My tongue is on the scene instantly determining that the old bridge has dislodged. I pull it out of my mouth and put it on my desk. Most of the upper right quadrant of my head is fully focused on its ground-down-below-the-enamel teeth; three stumps and two gaps that don't hurt exactly but suddenly seem inexplicably alien and vengeful.

I can't believe this. Not only am I falling apart from ordinary living but from professionals who postpone such falling apart as well. The stumps feel like coral. Or sticks of sidewalk chalk. They're slightly sensitive. Well, maybe it's just the shock of being exposed. And the wounded gum feels okay.

There's no way I'm calling for an emergency appointment which will necessitate the dentist's squeezing me in to tell me that I wasn't deferential enough toward the temporary glue, I mean for crying out loud. I'll just wait until Thursday. I've waited this long. The stumps feel like hardened slush and my tongue can find barely discernible ridges at least two miles across on each of them.

Before going to bed, I have some ice cream and the stumps really wail, but a second spoonful shocks me less and, from all my months of eating around the injured tooth and later the open space, I'm quickly able to keep the ice cream away from the stumps. The next morning I experience a similar shock/response episode when I have coffee. I take soup to work for lunch, which I'll prepare lukewarm.

The ground-down teeth feel like coarse pebbles, unwashed eggs, sandpaper, corduroy beads, balled-up cat tongue, teeny-tiny fuzzy lighthouses, unpeeled kiwi fruit, Nerf cannonballs, deteriorating logic.

I dream about being in the dentist's waiting room with blood pouring out of my mouth. There's a small boy across from me with red teeth. I ask him what's wrong and he says 'Nothing," that he's just waiting for his brother. He asks me what's wrong with me and I tell him I went to the dentist.

One hour tumbles into the next, unfolds into the next, puddles into the next. I don't care how they move, so long as they keep moving. Holiday stuff is all over the place and by my fiftieth birthday party, barely a week away, and it a week before Christmas, I'll be my old self. Which is to say my older self; aging eyes, straying waistline, imposters in my mouth.

When the big day finally arrives, the dentist seems pleased he doesn't have to wrest out the old bridgework again, and the installation of the new appliance is quick and easy. It makes me bite like I'm offbalance, like someone's elbowing around the one side of my mouth, like the new side has big teeth and the old side has retreating ones, but, with my usual compensations and belief that the foundation will settle, I'm happy. The dentist's assistant gives me a toothbrush, floss, threading devices and grappling hooks for throwing knots around the bridge, a miniature snowplow and a toy from the wishing well.

Smile for the birdie. I'm ready for the holidays. I'm ready to pay the damn bill and enter a longstretch of stabilized chewing and eating. I'm ready to have my next dental appointment simply be for a routine cleaning. I'm ready to complete this story and apologize for its disjointed logging of episodes that would've made good short pieces on their own. When I get back to the typewriter, settle in for the finale, I notice that a cap on the other side of my mouth, on my back left lower molar is chipping off. ∎

INTERNAL  RHYME

#62 OF THE NEWSLETTER WHERE YOU CAN SELL ALL THE ADS FOR & KEEP ALL THE PROFIT FROM THE SUPPLEMENT ◆ MUSICMASTER, 5136 LYNDALE AV S, MPLS, MN 55419

short movie

a gray-haired guy wearing ordinary clothes
mountain boots from Target
looks for awful knickknacks at Goodwill
not quirky remnants from a senior craft show
but things so shallow jokeshop dayglo ugly
that all around the world they are reviled
he takes them to the register
and checks them out like suspects
in a crime too big to mention

plum-colored condiment platter shaped like a lung
a driftwood radio lamp clock
ceramic penguin in bathrobe
a beanbag from the Bayside Pistol Club
a battered copy of Barry Goldwater's
In Your Heart You Know He's Right
that has on its inside cover
an Elvis-impersonating-Jesus doodle
it's labeled *King of Kings*

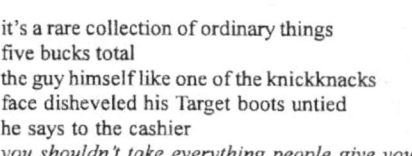

it's a rare collection of ordinary things
five bucks total
the guy himself like one of the knickknacks
face disheveled his Target boots untied
he says to the cashier
you shouldn't take everything people give you

for character development
there's a flashback to his childhood
his father a sign painter
and Monique his father's companion
an ordinary housewife

the gray-haired guy gets home
grabs a beer to wash down aspirin
two for his headache
two because of that flashback to Monique
one for his aching everything and
since he's heard that an aspirin a day
is good for your heart he swallows four more
his thoughts mostly crazy offcolor out-of-date
ordinary

he scatters the junk on the floor of his garage
grabs a sledgehammer
and shatters every item into smithereens
he micropulverises rootbeer-scented soaps
hammers *God*
into an imprinted mug from the bank
he flattens an ordinary snorkel covered with seashells
into the cracking concrete floor

the gray-haired guy
sits at the kitchen table
has another aspirin to tune
his ragged buzz
and in a daydream we can
    watch
he's a highfalutin count
at a party in St. Petersburg
eating chocolate squid and
    ortolans
he's in the ballroom staring at
Double Portrait with a
Glass of Wine
a painting by Chagall

someone asks him
how do you find these
    modern painters
meaning the *whole*
    shootin'match
even where the
    shootin'match doesn't
    even look like
the shootin'match anymore
meaning this Chagall thing
meaning the crimes too big to mention
and fancy count so&so guy
who used to be the gray-haired guy
answers *positively ordinary*

but I don't want that
to sound like such a punchline
if I wanted a punchline
I'd have him answer *positively smashing*

so just as he says the *ary* part of ordinary
cut back to the gray-haired guy
in an auction house in New York
he's wearing an Armani suit
a muttering silk bowtie
and leather sandals by a different Monique

he's buying magnificent artworks
a sketch by Rembrandt
a watercolor by N.C. Wyeth
a doodle by Grandma Moses
of Elvis-impersonating-Jesus
it's labeled *In Your Heart You Know He's Right*
a plum-colored condiment platter shaped like a lung
designed by Dali
a piece of paper crumpled up by Yoko Ono
and a Man Ray photograph of Robert Desnos in bed
performing a piece called *Ordinary Poem*
he looks both asleep and enraged

IF THAT DIDN'T SEEM LIKE A LAST LINE TO YOU,
PLEASE CONTINUE TO THE BACK PAGE FOR MORE OPTIONS

They walk around with migraines so bad they have to stay in bed –
pitchman for CalMax in an infomercial by Media Power Mgmt., 2001

Renaissance Man

2 a.m. I am wide awake
there's nothing on tv
just like at noon and 6 and 10
I click past sports and MTV
and commentary about both
is Hollywood to blame?
some kid in South Mercurochrome
fails to get a gun permit
and so he goes to junior high
and gets an A in math

I'd sleep if I could
hell I'd sleep if *you could*
and I'd get credit for it

I watch the weather
for a while
ruined vacations everywhere
carousels underwater
hail the size and texture of revenge
clouds freezing up
and dropping solid
meanwhile
in South Mercurochrome
yesterday was the

one hundred & fiftyfirst
consecutive Thursday
without measurable
originality

I've had so much caffeine
since getting into coffee
thirtysome years ago
that even if I died right now
I'd still have enough energy
to run and serve as Mayor
of South Mercurochrome

I click to news
to see familiar footage
that *proves* conclusively that
sports and MTV
kill the nuclear family
even peddle kidneys
on the internet

but let's face it
with due respect to
all the Nelsons
forced to purchase
tv sets and turn them on
a life of drudgery with good tunes

NEXT CRITICAL STEP IN CULTURAL SURVIVAL: PRODUCT *DISPLACEMENT*

is better than a life without
I'm starting to yawn

there's something about
South Mercurochrome
helping North Mercurochrome
dig out from the fallen iceclouds
and I swear that
in the clip they show
the Mayor of South Mercurochrome
looks dead

it's 2:15 a.m.
I click away to find
a bowtie wind-up guy
flirting with info-hostess
who nods in sync
with his every bold
italicized wink
his smile a tugging dog

I think a manic-depressive
would enjoy the infomercial's
bogus cheer
the slutty crowd
the pitch is high and long
but I doubt that a manic depressive
would turn the tube on
when there's flaming hail
sports and MTV infestations
bases loaded
the Mayor of South Mercurochrome
declared dead of caffeine poisoning
but able to serve out his term
he thinks I'm dozing off

like a drunken calliope
barking every note
the info-hostess
asks the wind-up suit
if CalProMegaZincTab
helps with headaches
he looks into the camera
and he sings
there are people out there
walking around
with migraines so bad
they can't get out of bed

and boy is he is right
as I turn off the bonfire
rearrange pillows
hum heavy metal
count sheep and name the sheep
then ask the sheep by name
if they think
that South Mercurochrome is or isn't better off
since I've been mayor
walking around like a dead guy
arranging product placements
in the footage of disasters
on the news
and all the yawning sheep
just tuck me in I think
I'm falling

Musicmaster 22 june 2001

DRAWING OF SOUTH MERCUROCHROME
COMMERCIAL DISTRICT BY ALAN VENDENBURGH

then we see the gray-haired art collector
drinking Orangina while watching ballet
or as he would say *the* ballet
going to a Broadway Musical
called *Double Portrait with a Glass of Wine*
there's a montage of our hero
that explains everything

he scatters the artworks on the floor of his garage
grabs an ordinary Craftsman
industrial grade sledgehammer
and recycles every item into paper
he demolecularizes a box designed by Christo
he pounds the faith of flatworms into a Picasso tile
that looks like something designed by a blind aerialist
soon to be a blind and flattened aerialist
he brings the mighty fist of retribution
down and down again
with a thud and thud again
and only stops when he can't wail no more

to an underscore of kettledrums
everything fades to black
and an ordinary orchestration
about worship and disdain faith and fear
art and craft hoof and mouth

a gray-haired guy wearing ordinary clothes
mountain boots from Target
enters his neighborhood hardware store
the clerk asks "are you a mountaineer?"
and the gray-haired guy orders dozens
of thrice-bolted steel-headed
street crew grade sledgehammers
with rubber grips and destructive tendencies
the clerk asks "are you starting a demolition company?"

and the gray-haired guy answers that
he's just going to practice ringing that bell
at the top of the pole
the clerk asks "are you crazy?"
and the gray-haired guy answers
"I've decided to become an artist"

but I don't want that
to sound like such an obvious ending
if I wanted an obvious ending
I'd have him answer *positively smashing*
so just as he says the *ist* part of artist
we cut and it's three months later
in his garage the gray-haired guy
is carving delicate butterflies
in the handle of a sledgehammer

hanging on the wall
there's a sledgehammer covered with glass beads
another painted only pastel pink
there's a sledgehammer that has had nothing done to it
labeled *Elvis-impersonating-Jesus*
on the workbench there's one
converted into a radio lamp clock
one wearing television rabbit ears
another one is wearing a sling

and as we pan across dozens
of these ninnified hammers
we think that someday they'll be wanted
by museums they'll be appreciated
but in our hearts we know we're wrong
we know that most of this
will only maybe make Goodwill

musicmaster   summer 2001

CHICKEN LITTE IMPERSONATOR
SEPTEMBER 16, 2001

INTƐRNAL  RHYMƐ

#63 OF THE NEWSLETTER THAT HAS NEVER RAISED ITS SUBSCRIPTION RATE ◆ MUSICMASTER, 5136 LYNDALE AVENUE SO, MINNEAPOLIS, MN 55419

Commerce in the 21st Century

It's two days before my son, Hamil returns to University of Miami. He's busy packing up odds and ends to add to the trailer that he and Alycia will be pulling to their first apartment. Their first living-together relationship (*situation*). Their first expression of the unspoken/unmarried subtext that means this isn't just a semester-long trip, an experience from which they'll return – it's the final (only somehow seeming gradual still) moving away from home.

They've both accumulated good household stuff from friends and Alycia's parents and Dawn and I. Pots & pans, bookshelves, futon, lamps. Dawn offered them the teapot we just replaced but, since they already had a teapot, it ended up in the box of stuff for our next garage sale. Mundane stories like that to build up to such a momentous launching. Towels, alarm clock, scissors, habitrail gadgets. Dawn offered them the alarm clock we just replaced because it wakes you up with synthetic elephant braying or whatever-the-hell sound synthetic elephant braying is supposed to sound like. Know what I mean? (No, I mean about a child leaving.) They took the clock and will be synthetically haunted by it.

I'm irked. This liquor store is the only liquor outlet in a neighborhood that's drunk out of its collective skull.

And they've both gone through their respective rooms and homes and closets and have packed some things and have decided to leave other things behind out of a quirky mix of unprecedented logic, gratuitous regression, and premature nostalgia.

The follow vignettes are fictitious -

Wow, the wind-up made-in-Japan tin robot with Super Action. The Super Action is when the robot rolls slowly forward without falling down. I remember getting this – how old was I? Eighteen. *Do you default to any punchlines that aren't twenty years old?* How about eighteen years old?

Dad, I really want to keep this poster of Charlie Callas you gave me, but I'm afraid if I take it, the edges will get dinged and ripped. So I'd better leave it here. I have a sturdy tube you can pack it in so it won't get damaged at all! *Thanks, Dad, but I'm afraid the sturdy tube might burst into flames.* No problem. I'll put the tube into a large cooler for you. *We could use the cooler, but I'm afraid if it has some kind of sturdy tube in it, I'd toss the whole package in the river. Any river. And please avoid all puns about being Callas!*

Hamil is ahead-of-schedule on his *To Do* list but still antsy, eager to get a few more boxes right away to pack up other things he wants to take to Florida. Since I'm just milling around in this paragraph (home from work early to do stuff around the house . . . just as soon as I finish a nap), he asks me if I want to take a walk to the liquor store to grab some boxes. I say *sure* for two reasons: 1) There won't be too many or any more opportunities to take a walk with Hamil before he goes, so I should go now and we can discuss art, politics, synthetic elephants; and 2) I'm almost out of beer.

We cross Minnehaha Creek to the liquor store. (That sounds unnecessarily rustic, as if we're paddling a canoe, cradling shotguns, looking for moonshine. I'd write *We cross Minnehaha Creek via the Lyndale Avenue bridge*, but that makes the bridge seem an uprising/grand-arcing attraction and not the blip-in-the-road it is to motorists, the underappreciated pause it is to pedestrians. Plus, the bridge, ((any bridge)) is a bulky enough symbol, a potent enough omen without me getting involved, especially when I don't even know if Lyndale Avenue Bridge is an official name with the B in Bridge getting capitalized.)

(I know I'm pushing my luck with interconnectivity and your patience, but I want to mention that I've never played bridge and don't know if the B in that Bridge is capitalized either.)

CONTINUED OVER THE BRIDGE

10 Great Drunken Ideas

1. If I just tell the sheriff that he's a psychotic, gunhappy, wife-beatin' moron, I'll feel better.
2. I am too a friendly drunk you stupid, antagonistic twerp.
3. No, really, it wouldn't hurt our friendship.
4. Lots of ideas aren't worth having.
5. You are absolutely right, you know, you are absofuckinlutely right, I mean, I've been inhibiting myself all these years just to please who-the-hell-cares, when I should've been stripping all the time.
6. If you refined a list of all the questions ever asked (by logically categorizing and bundling them), you'd find that there aren't ten questions worth asking!
7. We can write a song that will get kids to always remember the alphabet – oh, wait . . .
8. We should sober up.
9. This is a great idea.
10. There are hundreds of lists this easy to write.

COMMERCE BY THE BOXFUL OF DIMES CONTINUED

We talk city politics. From working at the city's cable network the past few years and over this recent break, Hamil has great insight on local politicians, whose official meetings are telecast by the network and who use the network to document their communities' events with overlong, should've-been-expurgated programs. So Hamil's merciless assessments of council members and commissioners are more and differently informed than mine (I just listen to their verbal rhythms, how they harmonize or gargle with it all, how they use words.). The mayor is a floundering incumbent, oblivious out of campaign season, opportunistic in; worse, her city hall is unfurling scandals too smalltown crookish to feed our need to forgive (Holy Action-Packed Sentences! I almost sound like a real columnist!). So her three challengers are all roughing her up while claiming victim or neglected status for their nouns and verbs.

While not personally a yuppie, our household does match some classic yuppie traits, e.g. owning at least three working vacuum cleaners, a belief that drinking Diet-Pepsi instead of Diet-Coke is a reason to argue, and an interest in tutoring squirrels

Since the trek for moonshine is barely three blocks, we're suddenly at the neighborhood liquor store. Though Hamil has stopped in here with me over the years, he is, this time (since July 9), old enough to legally buy, drink and sing to the imports and overpriced yuppie microbrews I've learned to prefer. (While not personally a yuppie, I am statistically included in a lot of yuppie stats. I'm more happy-to-be-mobile-when-necessary than upwardly mobile. But our household does match some classic yuppie traits, e.g. owning at least three working vacuum cleaners, a belief that drinking Diet-Pepsi instead of Diet-Coke is a reason to argue, an interest in tutoring squirrels, and drinking overpriced microbrews that turn out to be owned by Phillip Morris.)

I take a 12-bottle box of Bitburger (talk about unavoidable alliteration!) to the friendly cashier we've seen often enough to recognize. A college student. I ask her if we can grab some boxes from the five or six piles of boxes that flank the wall you pass as you exit. She says, "I'm sorry, we have a new policy. People are taking too many boxes, so we have to charge ten cents each."

"You're kidding. I'm a neighbor. I've been coming here for fifteen years at least. The last time I got boxes here I took them from out back by your dumpster. I've never asked for them before."

"Stan (not his real name) says people are taking too many boxes and that he can get a quarter each for them."

"Well, I'll pay you for five boxes. But where's the sense of neighborhood, of customer appreciation? I've been coming here for years."

The clerk nods and agrees with my gripe, though I can picture the end-of-summer rush for boxes as kids leave, move, head back to school and how that might irk a manager who'd rather have more boxes for customers' purchases. But, hell, I'm not the box hog and I shouldn't be *fined* because other people took advantage of a universally recognized box source. The clerk says, "He's just starting it, but I don't think it's a good idea," as she hands me a receipt that in addition to my beer, itemizes *WINE BOX CARDBOARD - .50.*

Hamil and I move to the box wall on the way to the exit door. In my head I figure that I've been shopping here since about 1986, spending an average of twelve bucks a week, sometimes much more to stock up for our twice-a-year shindigs where all the guests get politely lubricated. Twelve bucks a week times fifty-two equals $624 a year, for fifteen years equals $9,360; add the party punch favors of about $150 per annum and we're up to $11,610. I'm not a big customer, but I'm a regular and loyal customer who consciously supports neighborhood businesses over chain stores.

I'm irked. I may have to write about this. This liquor store is the only liquor outlet in a neighborhood that's drunk out of its collective skull. I'm only kidding. But this is a party hosting, micro-brew-consuming, nice-bottle-of-wine-for-dinner neighborhood with disposable income (or at least a wine budget) and this store has no competition; it is busy every evening and Saturday, often with four registers ringing out the pickle juice.

Hamil and I shift the piles of boxes a bit to get ones with lids. Another clerk at the register directly behind us is stage-whispering to the clerk who rung us out about our rummaging around in the cardboard, did she charge us?

I didn't get angry when, about four years back, this store jumped into the inexplicable cigar fad with an inventory of the

PLEASE CONTINUE TO THE NEXT AVAILABLE PAGE

HAVING A TELEVISION IS LIKE KNOWING AN EVIL GENIUS

death spikes for the too-important-to-get-cancer crowd. I felt *who was I to judge,* being a beer drinker and all (and a man who has committed a few murders and many maimings in his heart), though the effects of second-hand beer are more annoying than deadly. I also didn't care when the beverage association (sorry I can't think of its official, non-boozy-sounding name) lobbied against foodstores being permitted to carry wine; it used lame and alarmist prose to ineffectively obscure simple territorialism (a passive type of greed). But, I figured, well, maybe the neighborhood liquor store, being a small business and all, has a legitimate beef about a new law that pre-empts for some the stricter terms on which existent licenses were obtained. Whatever. (I'm rationalizing for them because I don't think there's anything insidious going on. Hell, I wouldn't want my next door neighbor writing poems about Walgreen's, hardware stores and Clifton, New Jersey – that's *my* job.) A successful local businessman is still a businessman. And, what the hell, for the good of the neighborhood, he's a neighbor.

Hamil turns one box sideways so it can tuck into another box so he can carry three and I can carry two others and my beer. Another clerk arrives behind us and consults with the second clerk as to whether or not we've paid to grab the boxes with which we're getting ready to abscond. To me, even if Stan (not his real name) had intimidated staff into such bizarrely strict enforcement of New Empty Box Regulations, this is too much. So I turn to the two clerks and ask, "Do you think you have this under control? You have enough people making sure a regular customer isn't stealing boxes?" Neither responds, though I'd appreciate at least an effort to apologize.

On the way home, Hamil and I discuss how boneheaded, shortsighted, penny-wise even good businesses can be.

They certainly could've resolved the issue of people taking advantage of free box privileges more professionally, or at least more amicably. Perhaps with a trial effort of a 2-boxes-a-week limit. (No, stuff like that doesn't have to be monitored to be 98% effective; people who worry about the 2% who'd scheme around a "recommended" policy shouldn't be allowed to bully the 98% who wouldn't.) Or with polite signage by the registers so customers don't have to be surprised or made argumentative by sudden policy changes.

I was startled by the charge, miffed by Stan's (not his real name) weak defensive logic that he can sell the boxes for two bits each (and therefore is giving us a good deal at a dime – well, thank you, oh benevolent Orwellian one), and frankly incensed by being monitored by two additional clerks over boxes. What enforcement would've occurred had I bolted with the boxes without showing my receipt? Why was the new policy clearly such a Big Priority among staff? Does Stan (not his real name) need management training as well as customer service courses?

I didn't get angry when this store jumped into the inexplicable cigar fad with an inventory of the death spikes for the too-important-to-get-cancer crowd.

Hamil and I paddle back across Minnehaha Creek commenting how words like neighbor and community are increasingly only used by businesses as touchy-feelie sales hooks.

I ask aloud, "I wonder what the State Sales Tax people think about a retailer reselling and taxing a product that is otherwise trash or recyclable? Should the food store charge me more for aluminum cans because once empty the cans have a secondary raw materials value?" (Oh no, don't tell that to the liquor store - they might start double-charging for bottles and cans.)

The way I see it, I'm paying for an empty box for every four 6-packs or two 12-packs I purchase. Can we do a revisionist logic on that and point out that over a fifteen year period (and using the averages noted above) I've paid for at least 250 boxes that I didn't need or take? Let's. At a quarter a toss, the liquor store should be sending me a rebate check for $62.50.

Hamil shakes his head, shares my befuddlement, and more cogently expresses his opinion with "That's a goofy policy."

Later, Dawn gets home from her Mom's and wants to pick up a bottle of wine for Ann and Clyde. Naturally, I pull out my soapbox, weave some fine garlands before the word "bastards" and tell a few of my usual tales of other businesses that began ugly declines with similar missteps. After thirty minutes of listening to my anecdotal analysis and crackpot tangents, Dawn suggests we try a new liquor store over on France and 44th rather than return to our liquor

HOLD THAT TANGENT . . .

FILLER ART DRAWN BY MUSICMASTER IN 1977 OR SO ON THE OREGON COAST

ART APPRECIATION IN GRADE SCHOOL BEGINS WITH SPEAKING OUT OF TURN

store where I won't be able to surpass short-circuiting glares and probably the theft of a box.

—

A few days later, leaflets are circulating for neighbors to join together to oppose a developer's plan that will raze an unused Wells Fargo bank building for an apt/townhome and retail mix and supposedly, later, include redevelopment of the entire block whose other buildings include the liquor store. Among cited concerns is the usual paranoid vision of runaway change (which I especially share when it comes to the possibility of a chain restaurant or fastfood joint sullying and blanding out another neighborhood) and real questions about density/traffic/parking. Plus there are items giving voice to genuine and imagined fears of adjacent retailers, an animal hospital, a pizza joint, a clinic, a rental store, and the liquor store, the latter with its own laundry list of economic woes it would suffer if these developers advance a single space. So there's a need to organize, respond, etcetera, though all of the prose is strongly politicized to nearly deny the developers any opportunity to face anything but anger, rakes and torches.

Well, you can write your own closing paragraphs to this piece. You can mention my fascination with the liquor store now playing the "neighbor card" because that's what they need to do. You can make-up the conversation I have with Hamil when he calls about their successfully arriving in Miami and my only back-home update is this follow-up to the box episode that made me grumpy the eve of their departure. You can throw in a smug, superior, told-ya-so conclusion that I'd probably endorse.

But, fact is, irony or moral of story aside, even if their box policy was stupid (and I think it was more that than insensitive), even if they just recently seemed to only pull out neighbor talk when convenient or money related, even if the developers have a different tale to tell, I'm siding with the liquor store – *our* liquor store – and the other neighborhood businesses. I can influence their policies and behaviors. And of the developers' many bigdeal visions (which I'll rarely-barely have a chance to change), their box policy may be worse. ∎

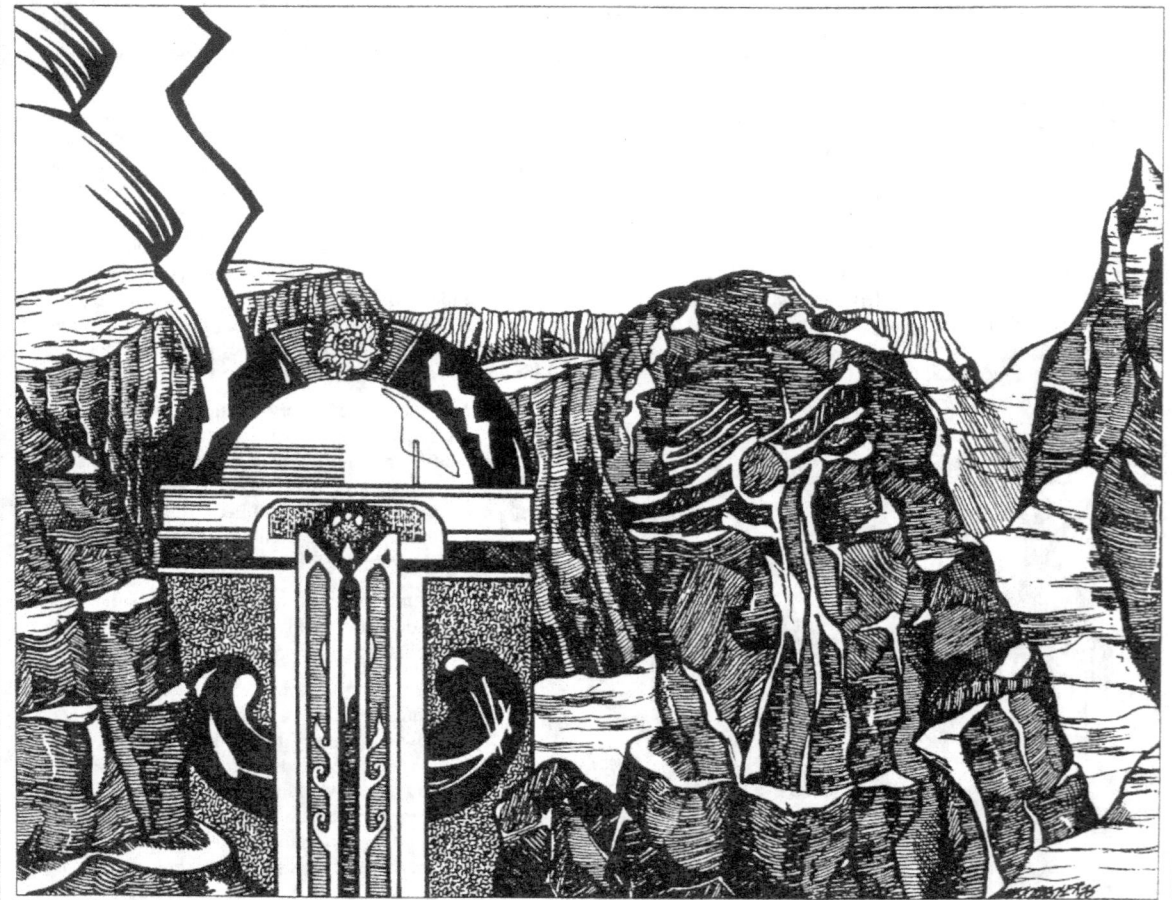

FILLER ART DRAWN BY MUSICMASTER IN 1976 SO IT COULD BE USED 25 YEARS LATER

I'D RATHER HAVE A FLAWED NEIGHBOR THAN A FLAWED NEIGHBORHOOD

WHAT THEY DON'T TEACH YOU AT THE SHOE SALES ACADEMY

SEPTEMBER 25, 2001

INTERNAL RHYME

#64 OF THE NEWSLETTER THAT OWES ITS FROTHY TANGENTS TO THE ST. PAULI GIRL ◆ MUSICMASTER, 5136 LYNDALE AVENUE SO, MINNEAPOLIS, MN 55419

estate of dysfunction

I want to hear my messages
but message lady says to me
my code is incorrect I try again
I tap more slowly I get in
I know I had it right before

a guy who calls me sir
tells me that he makes
a drink for kids a mix
of carpet cleaner and red punch
that I should run a story
help him tell the world

there's a message from
the printer that he doesn't know
how many copies I want of the flyer
that I didn't say
I think *of course I did*
I even told him *write it down*

a lady tells me she works
for the government
investigating fraud in public housing
but *you can't call back* she says
we're having trouble with our phones
so I'll try again to reach you later on

I delete all three and
turn on my computer
let it hum and buzz
until the screen lights up
green letters flash
a fatal error warning

I try to (as they say) *end task*
but nothing happens
no escape
I slap the frozen monitor

as part of crisis busywork
they're yelling down the hall
about computers

the phone rings
it's the guy who calls me sir
he *says I have a product*
multifamily folks will love
a mix of cherry punch
and stain remover

I tell him he can buy an ad
he says *your duty mandates*
that you run it as a news release
I tell him *no* he doesn't care
his mouth so full of salesmanship
I have to say goodbye

the boss walks in my office
wearing camouflage
a rifle at the ready and
her face is streaked with blood
she asks me how I'm doing
and I tell her that I'm doing fine

my phone rings it's my printer
says he found the note
he made last week
he'll go ahead
and print ten thousand copies
of the flyer

that's not my job I say
I only need one thousand
oh he says *the artwork*
that I'm looking at
is for your readers too
it says it's News for Landlords

garage sale 2001

an unexpected lamp
a dusty broom
a pile of fastfood toys
a woven-candle picture frame
a box of things you don't use anymore
(a baseball mitt
a voodoo dog
a Geographic Map
of Where You Ain't)
a full-sized skeeball game
from Janzen Beach
it's maybe from the 40s
an aquarium full of golfballs
for clever fish
with leisure time
an awful painting of waterfalls
pouring off of clouds into
a huge bucket full
of brightly colored sailboats
on the decks of all of them
are people
too far away to see

well it isn't mine I say
I don't know whose it is
the printer says *the flyer is for*
indoor paint that also kills mosquitoes
the headline says
You'll Beat 'Em to the Punch

I go and get a cup of coffee
from the office kitchen
where we brew a swill
that tastes like it could also
shine a shoe or pickle pets
so *hey why not* I wonder if
the punch you'll beat 'em to is cherry

FOLLOW YOUR HEART, YOUR DREAM,
OR TURN THE PAGE TO CONTINUE

 I answer phone
the lady who now works
to clean up vendor fraud
in housing says hello
she wants to warn us
about products that don't work

she says *there is an outfit*
out of Hopkins Minnesota
that is selling stuff like suntan oil
that also patches fissures
in the painted concrete walls
of swimming pools

I ask her *have you heard*
about a Kool Aid that
can clean a carpet too
she says *no not exactly but*
we've lost a lot of data from
the past six months because
some software also had a virus

I reboot my computer
let it cough it bit
and motionlessly race around
it beeps a beep from deep within
and wants to know my password
I type *Tom* hit enter
watch it say *denied*

the guy who used to call me sir
calls back he'll buy
the smallest ad we have onetime
please put it on page one
and bill him later

he tells me he can email
testimonials and pictures
even charts by doctors proving
kids and landlords love the stuff
it's so refreshing
where it drips it also cleans

I tell this guy I'll fax him
the particulars I'll run his ad
because I think that *well*
at least folks **hope**
his stuff will work
they're getting more than what **we get**
on every turn

I go out to the fax machine
tap in his Hopkins number
as I smile about
how different this guy is
at least he's funny

I push another button
that says *Send* or *Go*
I don't know what it says
because I've learned to live
with this:
the fax machine is broken   ∎

tumbling bird

lock the door
walk down hall
step outside
wince at cold
go back in
walk back down hall
check door it's locked
I thought my keys were in there still
they're not they're in my hand

I still taste
rum I dreamt
that I could
peel windows
off of houses
put them back
like stickers
on the sky
or elsewhere

from a window on the sidewalk leans
an angry guy he says I woke him up
my stomping up and down the hall
he yells at me until he wakes me up

I stumble
outside pause
and wonder
if my door
is locked
perhaps when checking it before
I turned the key I know I'm always
doing something wrong among the sheep
I count are those who'd rather not be
    counted

I think I
left a burner on
I wonder
where I am
I go back in
back down to my apartment door
it's locked but I unlock it

check the burners they're all cool and
    coiled
I leave again lock door turn knob push
    lock it's locked

I imagine that I'm still in bed I'm dozing
that I'm someone else I'm someone in a
    coma
that everything is just my life in sluggish
    replay
that my death is now alive inside my brain

I start to
cross the street
but turn around
go back inside
go back down hall
I check the door it's locked
but I unlock it reach inside
and grab my briefcase *slam the door*
it's true that by the time I get to work my
    job is done

I walk across
the busy street
and up a block
to bus stop
I refuse to pause
I won't go back I wonder if
I locked the door I try to think of some-
    thing else
my briefcase combination but I draw a
    blank
I must have picked a hard one to be funny

the bus stop 's by the driveway
of an auto dealership and lots of cars
are turning in from busy street
the smaller ones just snorkels in macadam

I still taste rum
I don't think that a crook
would know
to steal the stuff

that's really worth a lot
the poems the mail the books the art
the tv they can have
I'd be renewed I'd thank them I should
    go back in
unlock the door and pray a little
    differently

lots of cars
and trucks from
nearby highway
speed and honk
right by me
in a blur I'm half awake
at wheel I'm half unlocked
the traffic passes then a tiny brain is
    bouncing by
a pink and rubber convolutioned
    chewtoy brain in tights

I know I'm only half-awake
I know I see a tumbling bird
I think the rubber chewtoy brain
is just my way of facing my not driving

a sparrow
whips in out
of nowhere
and into
a windshield
I hear it get popped up
and center it drops to the road
in the middle of one lane a car races over
    the body
it wobbles a trucks races over it tumbles

everything
is sixty miles
an hour
nowadays
and for all
I know the bird could be
a predatory alley finch
and I may be locked up and sound asleep
but I can't let this bird be flattened

ONE MORE PAGE AS THE ALLEY FINCH FLIES

THE GREATEST CURE FOR INSOMNIA USUALLY CORNERS YOU AT A WORK-RELATED DINNER

HORSEFEATHERS CONTINUED

I step into
a traffic pause
so small it honks
I grab the
the bird and
rush back to the sidewalk
unlock its tiny chest to see its heart
so shocked by morning air it flies away
my bus to glory screeches to a halt

I can taste
what stickers
tasted like
before this
world of peel
and reposition trucks
and angry neighbors
I yell at lifeguards way up on the streetlamps
honest things are really like this
dragging and kicking to kindergarten

Musicmaster 9/01

(*tumbling bird* is an at-longlast cleaned-up piece I wrote when I lived in Hopkins and had an easier time getting to work than I do today)

MS. JOHNSON - TAKE A CONCRETE POEM PLEASE. SIX LINES DOWN, INDENT 22 SPACES, BEGIN. XXX. BACKSPACE TO MIDDLE X AND STRIKE OVER AN I. DROP TWO LINES, AT STANDARD MARGIN: %X%X%. NEXT LINE, CENTERED UNDER %, BEGIN WITH TWELVE LOWER-CASE O's, NO SPACES...

FILLER ILLUSTRATION DRAWN BY MUSICMASTER IN 1984 FOR AN INTERVIEW WITH MARK SONNENFELD THAT I HOPE WILL APPEAR IN 2001 IN ISSUE #65 OR 65.

NICE ASIDE OR DESPARATE FILLER?

Pictures of my brother Bob on the Jersey shore and mowing Mutti & Vati's lawn in 1954. I must have taken the pictures.

SPECIALNESS BEGINS WITH A LIMITED EDITION CERAMIC ANGEL GIVING A PUPPY TO A WIDE-EYED KITTEN

THE BURDEN OF GEOMETRY

INTERNAL RHYME

ISSUE 65 OF THE NEWSLETTER THAT IS ONE BIG EDITORIAL PAGE • MUSICMASTER, 5136 LYNDALE AVENUE SOUTH, MINNEAPOLIS, MINNESOTA 55419

WordLandscaping with New Jersey's Mark Sonnenfeld

Introduction

In three separate envelopes over the past year, New Jersey-based experimental poet Mark Sonnenfeld asked me if I'd interview him for *Internal Rhyme*. As evidenced by clippings of interviews he occasionally includes with his regular output of broadsides, a lot of smallpress publishers honor/humor his requests to be interviewed. And they print transcriptions that are substantially composed of Mark's sane and focused comments about creating and publicly performing decompressed, post-bebop writings that don't seem sane or focused.

I don't know the academic terms for the often remarkable and visually/rhythmically subversive stuff that Mark writes, gifts and swaps around, but, aside from scattered phrases and lines that are striking (or stricken without being stricken), it is so divorced from traditional literary conventions and devices (and gravity) it is ambitiously incoherent.

I like Sonnenfeld's poems because I *get* what he's doing – even when I don't know what the hell any of it means.

As a collector of offbeat smallpress stuff (with extensive subcollections of concrete/conceptual and visual poetry books and anthologies), I'm familiar with lots of experimental writer's processes - from the now sane-seeming *Beat Hotel* by Harold Norse, to Emmett Williams' beautiful flipbook *Sweethearts* - featuring kinetic flirtations and intertwinings of only the letters of the word *sweetheart* itself - to the 1971 *This Book is a Movie*, an anthology that truly influenced my development as an artist (and maybe as a writer). And I especially enjoy the stuff that's so out of the norm that it doesn't propose a new norm or anti-norm, it just defiantly plays with letters/words on ever-changing terms. I enjoy stuff I don't fully get or can't imagine doing. I appreciate post-language writings because they reveal things I would never notice or discover otherwise. I like when words are arranged on paper with such harsh disassociations (rather than traditional poetic devices) that their meanings become either totally irrelevant or differently clear. So I like Sonnenfeld's poems because I *get* what he's doing and am comfortable with what he's doing and am entertained by what he's doing – even when I don't know what the hell any of it means.

So, to find out, I decided okay, I'll interview him via mail (my apologies to the word *interview*). But I also decided I wouldn't ask the questions he regularly answers in the copies of interviews he sends because, well . . . how *hard is that going to be for him or me?* (Clearly, and this is a revelation to myself, I think interviews need an edgy or satiric component – something that keeps the process from being too easy). In a few interviews he's given, Mark seems not unsympathetic, but unimpressed by red herring questions (or format adjustments that do to

CHECK THAT YOUR LAPBAR IS LOCKED IN PLACE

backseat acupuncture

as car bumps over drainage groove
Uncle Bill starting steering and breaking hard
his nineteenforties racing days at hand
says *no pipes could hold that much water*
Joyce Aunt Joyce but not called Aunt Joyce
complains about the jolt and comments on
his driving the road the signs
other cars flipping and exploding into fire

to their separate upfront subtext
Bill quietly adds *shut up and enjoy the ride*
but says to us *it all flows to the ocean*
though it only rains a few months of the year
in the back we listen nod and loudly look
at hyperpurple corkscrew trees
Venusian plants pastel houses bay windows
beach bums germinating in sleek strollers
Californians rollerblading in stucco sunlit crisscross

Joyce elaborates *it rains in winter early spring*
then says to Bill *watch that guy don't turn yet*
see the stop sign there's a cop
yes he says *shut up and let me drive*
but there's no acceleration to the dischord
just a game of cards that never ends
and as the tourists basking in the easygoing chaos
we share aloud our comments on the beaches
and the real estate but keep to ourselves
about relationships trains-coming-at-us retirement

musicmaster 7/01

traditional interviews what he does to traditional poetries – which is not a criticism at all, and I know that I'm comparing apples to orangutans), which to me underscores his commitment to his art and his wanting to explain its function without wiseguys like me snapping towels.

By the way, Mark is also a composer and, with John Bennett (another prolific post- and para-language artist/writer), among mail-art's most enthusiastic collaborators. Below is the letter I sent to Mark in response to his request to be interviewed, followed by the questions and, in italics, his answers.

The Letter to Mark

7 September A Space Odyssey

Dear Mark,

Y ou've probably noticed that with rare exceptions (ephemera and inclusion of works by family members), I write all of *Internal Rhyme* myself from the egocentric perspective of my small world. (Aside: In the 1970s, Bill Gaglione – I think – of the Bay Area Dadaists, called his publication *Egozine*, coining a great word for most smallpress adventures). So an interview with you would be a refreshing break from my rigid adherence to writing still another griping poem or column about Walgreen's running out of coupon items before the first day of a week-long sale is over. Plus, I can't imagine it's a dangerous precedent to anything, so why the heck not?

I'd like to do the interview via this letter – just answer the questions however you want, send them back, and I'll print the whole shebang, including this letter and a few introductory paragraphs about your presence in the mail-art/smallpress community and how an *energy* field that stretches from Columbus, Ohio (home to John Bennett's *Lost & Found Times*) to your kitchen table in East Windsor, New Jersey is responsible for an inordinately large percentage of newborns who cower when they hear nursery rhymes.

Since the interview will be printed without a literary supplement to introduce my readers to a body of your work, please also send one or two literary compositions I can include as (approximately) 1/4-page illustrations. If you'd rather, I could easily select two from the many you've sent.

Let me know if any part of this process isn't acceptable and/or if you'd like to invigorate the economy by signing your Official Baby Bush Tax Refund Check over to me.

Thanks a lot, Mark!

Musicmaster

And now, if there are no further tangents, here's the interview . . .

(*Dear Internal Rhyme Reader* – **Wait**, here's one further tangent: Mark Sonnenfeld's typed responses, which arrived here on September 26, are in italics Also, Mark wrote that I could select whatever I wanted as examples of his work - thus, the word-illustrations on these pages.)

1. It seems you collaborate with a different writer or artist every few weeks for a broadside. Why do you collaborate at all, let alone so often? Do you have favorite collaborators? Have you collaborated with anyone who is a technical writer professionally?

I have the need to get my work out, and so I write and publish at a fast pace. Collaborations are unions. I love that concept, and, of course, the finished project. I think by broadsides you mean give-out sheets, which come out as often as 3 or 4 a week. They all have uniqueness. The give-out is a fine idea in that it reaches people from two completely different directions: from my end, and I always forward a quantity to the contributor to dispense. As of yet I've worked with no tech-writers.

2. Which poets, if any, have influenced your current writings?

I was initially struck by the Beats. That provided a major jump-start. My current writing is sort of evolving on its own.

3. Are other writers' writings relevant to what you do, what you're exploring?

No, not really.

4. When John Bennett sends me pieces written in his distinctive backwards scrawl – letters like spasming vines – I always think he should register and sell it as a font. What, if any, are your favorite fonts, and, were you to design your

STAY AT LEAST TEN FEET BEHIND THE READER IN FRONT OF YOU

```
                          DEBTCOAT

                  dear|      what old

GIVENS

CANDLELIT -      : show I play
in suspension    hair is often
a religious
society          a night soft and loud
I am             SUREBORED .
havings          with a tape recorder
give electricity , heater
december         headthings
odd              a birthdaypassed
like how         cold, a quieted diner, go over
foreign accent reduction
STUDY , iron railings
STUDY , triangle study
'Look , tv inhalation I call it
blurp study
     pigchild                    |self-pitied

in anger straightbulb waxing I stand alone &11

:00 waist painting wreckships & trash

THIS EVILSPIRIT.

uglyshirts
```

own, what would be its distinguishing trait?

I feel very close to the printed text. I like to keep mine diverse (in look, sound, thought), but no one font stands out as my favorite. I have no plans of designing a font.

5. Why do you ask so many small and mailart presses to interview you?
   A) I'm going for global media domination via the slowest way possible.
   B) I'm casting the net for more smallpress contacts.
   C) I'm casting the net for more like-minded writers.
   D) I'm hoping that at least the smallpress world won't ask multiple-choice questions.
   E) [PASTE ANSWER HERE]

Answers A, B, and C might apply. I know my writing style stirs up a lot of questions. I offer to do interviews to help shed light.

6. What are your favorite letters of the alphabet? (And why?)

I've no favorites. They are all beautiful structures. Then there's the small-case variety and the interaction with capitalization. Punctuation, italics, spacing, inflection, there's so much going on. No kidding. I see pages as beautiful objects of art.

7. Do you regard some of your poems as more visually than verbally communicative? Why/Why not? For you, what factors sharpen or blur this distinction?

They can be both. The visual pieces might have more in the way of symbols and might not be as fluent, whereas the verbal examples are more narrative. I play the field, not staying in one spot, or to one style, making forward or backward steps at any time.

8. Which word games (crossword puzzles, Scrabble, telephone, Password, Wheel of Fortune . . . any and all, up to and including calligraphy, signing, signage making and doing improv) do you enjoy and why? Why don't people play Password anymore?

I play no games you mentioned. It's the reading voice and speaking voice that are of great interest to me. Dialogues too. I do a lot of listening and a lot of comparisons. Physically, I do daily a homemade version of tai chi. I like the portability of tai chi.

9. Demosthenes (384-322 BC)?

I had to look this up.

10. If you could only take three words to a desert island with you, what would they B (hint)?

Pass.

11. Is it possible to *mis*understand your poems?

Misunderstandings are likely. Extracting multiple meanings are encouraged.

Reenactment

ye –   har Horr   "Cree"
Toting table keyboard
                    — .
we to disappear.
x sound
back brother
a k a chōō u. the woodburn
Lp   (flying saucer bureau)
– – saint
face   an apostrophe   it will fall fat
is
airless
heartie planetvibrato
snoopjazz, g + 3

---

12. *Internal Rhyme* has about 100 readers (not counting the pass-along or household-add-on readers that major publications shamelessly enlist, invent and guesstimate), most of whom (though they like me) think I am crazy. And not just slightly. What do you want to tell these fine citizens?

To them I'd say, explore that thought. To you: the view can be much better when you're out on that proverbial limb. But I suppose the true crazies don't know they are, and I suppose if you really were nuts, your readers would do something about it.

13. Aside from the magnificent Mafia headstones in the cemeteries, and the glitz and squalor cocktail of Atlantic City, and the fact that they restored Lucy (the two-story, turn-of-the century elephant-shaped hotel in Margate), and that Allen Ginsberg and Sinatra are Jersey spawned, and that outsiders don't know about High Point or the Pine Barrens or Cape May diamonds, and that my Dad played hot fiddle in clubs all over North Jersey in the forties and fifties, what are the best things about New Jersey? Do you know anyone outside of the Bronx who pronounces Jersey "Joisey"? What's your favorite spot on the Jersey coast?

NJ is where I'm rooted. There's a familiarity here. I like the cities so close to one another and how I'm in close proximity to so many colleges and universities. New York City is only a train ride away. Neptune, a NJ shore community, is where I took a photo collage for a chapbook last summer. I'm drawn to the offbeat places, and my state has loads.

(Editor's Last Word – Note that this Fellow Jerseyite –

TURN, TURN, TURN

THE HOMEMADE VERSION OF TAI CHI IS CALLED I CHI

probably because he's been struck by the Beats – is drawn to the off-beat . . . . hey, write your own damn newsletter.)

14. Barbara Walters asks *would you put one of your poems on your headstone?* If not, what would you put? James Lipton asks *if you had to be a theatrical character who would you be?* Studs Terkel asks *can you get by on what you make from poetry?* If not, how do you supplement your income? An in-disguise Allen Funt asks *would you mind kicking that cop in the ass, please?*

I can't answer the headstone question. Maybe, Mark Sonnenfeld, experimental writer *would suffice. The theatrical character thing draws another blank. (I'm happy just being me.) I make very little money from my writing. Some $20 bills and books of stamps make their way to my mailbox. Yes, I work a full-time job.*

15. What's the biggest problem facing the world today?

After witnessing September 11, 2001, I'd have to say it's global terrorism.

16. What's the biggest problem facing the smallpress world today?

I haven't given this a lot of thought. Off the top of my head I'd say it's the lack of organization.

17. What's the biggest problem facing Mark Sonnenfeld today?

I'm doing fine, having got one foot someplace else. It's the temporariness of life that keeps me grounded. Really, to me, it's just about doing it. My senses tell me life is surreal. It's really much like an assignment.

18. (You may substitute a question of your own devising to replace this question, because I think it's poorly worded. That's bad for a professed writer to admit. But worse is the fact that I honestly believe that I was forced by the language itself to word the question poorly! Language is a big, though mostly quiet, government-run parasite that only pushes back gently and mostly by blurring meanings, by obfuscating communication, and by adding or deleting the word "obfuscating" from a sentence. I think I'm getting a little too close to Alpha-Roswell here as evidenced and thus proven by my waning coherence.)

Words are our most used and abused tools, playthings, guides, weapons, escorts, hurdles, anchors, jets, cuffs . . . (the metaphor sprints). They flow in and chatter from all directions - most with subtexts, agenda, the poison and markdown of marketing. Lots of them float (in ads, in songs, in accusations and promises, in grand proclamations, in recipes for danger!), stick to your tongue (as attitude, as accessory), lounge on your porch with a cold St. Pauli Girl Dark (*I'm losing hold of exactly what or who is at the door*). And words are all so simultaneously complicated, simple, abundant (used, abused, guiding, anchoring – *see above*), that I want to know what on earth are you as a writer thinking about, beyond the story/the piece/the plot at hand, when actually writing, e.g. just the mechanics, artsy notions, career daydreaming, how it would work on film, how it might fit for a certain publication or project, whether or not you're deliberately/consciously pushing a meaning here pushing the language there, etc.? Or can you focus on tale and telling alone?

Please answer with verve and cymbals.

I'm not sure I understand the question, but here goes. Some thoughts. I haven't a clue what to write until I get that spark. I prefer doing smaller scale projects. I like scattered thought and collage, and I like pushing boundaries. My work is transmitted data one word at a time. Writing is like electricity. It hums. My spoken-word tapes are essentially sound collages, at least that's what I'm striving towards. I love disjointedness. I love subjective ideas. I love running experiments. I know I can be difficult to understand. I draw upon what I see, objects or instances. I drag away an echo. It can be strict construction. It can be ghostwriting.

19. What is your writing regimen?

I write when whatever hits me. There's no set regimen. I fall headfirst into a project and shape my thoughts toward that end. I'm a note-taker. I work on several projects at once.

20. What do you read for pleasure/pain/insight?

Whatever's handy. Usually something I get in the mail.

21. What did you like least about your last employer?

I can't remember.

22. Who in the mail-art/smallpress community would you like to interview and why?

No specifics here. Anyone in the small press would be fine. And to the why, I'd say why not?

23. Did you or did you not have sex with that woman?

A harmony of sounds frees me from saying.

That's it for the formal portion of the interview. If you'd like to attach additional narrative, please do so. I apologize for Mr. Wallace's innuendoes.

(Mark Sonnenfeld can be reached at Marymark Press, 45-08 Old Millstone Drive, East Windsor, NJ 08520.) ∎

Questions I Prepared But Didn't Use in the Interview

How many post-language poets does it take to screw in a lightbulb? (Correct response*: litmus skee Thumb*)

Is the letter *S* behind all epidemics?

When will New Jersey change its name to Just Regular Jersey or, at least, Getting-Older Jersey?

You put a copyright on all of your poems. Is it a design element?

NEXT ISSUE: RETURN OF THE PAGE ONE "CONTENTS" BOX THAT LISTS PIECES NOT INCLUDED

"THINKING OUTSIDE OF THE BOX" IS ONLY ALLOWED BELOW THE BOXES

NOVEMBER 30, 2001

INTΞRNAL 𝕏 RHYMΞ

ISSUE 67 OF THE NEWSLETTER THAT SHOULD BE TAKEN WITH A BAG OF SALT ◆ MUSICMASTER, 5136 LYNDALE AVE. SOUTH, MINNEAPOLIS, MN 55419

I know

four years ago two guys I see at work just once a year come to an open mike I host

but leave before the show is done before I read my poems

three years ago one of the two might come to hear me read he says

we left last time because we got there late we sat in back we couldn't hear

he doesn't come

Grant calls Bob and says *what say we go hear Tom*

and Bob says *hey I'd love to but I can't I want to watch that show*

about how people nowadays don't go out anymore

two years ago the same one of the two might come to hear me read *you know* he says

we left last time because I had a cold I needed chicken soup and sleep

he doesn't come

he might be sick again it's no big deal a lot of people say

they'll maybe come and many do and many don't

I navigate the shifting current too

Grant calls Bob and asks him *do you want to try the open mike again*

and Bob says *sure why not they do have beer there don't they*

I don't think so

last year the same guy says again he might come hear me read he says *I came before*

with Bob we had to leave because he had an early morning

the morning of or after I don't ask he doesn't come again

and that's okay by me though I know now it somehow haunts him

gives him guilt of gab

Grant calls Bob and says *what say we go hear Tom*

and Bob says *sure but not tonight I can't tonight*

I have to rearrange the stuff I keep under the sink

this year the same guy says to me he might come hear me read *you know* he says

I came before with Bob who said he had to leave he was my ride

he's too conservative I think he didn't get it

that's okay I say and *look if you come by that's great*

but flu or fleas or famine if you can't that's okay too

he doesn't come

Grant calls Bob and *says let's go swing by that open mike*

that Tom you know that crazy guy in Bloomington puts on

and Bob says *no I can't I'm too conservative*

I wonder who gets more from this relationship

if Grant does with evolving tales all from a one-time walkout or

if I do with this halfassed poem it took four years to write

and frankly Bob and Grant did all the hard work

all the lift and haul behind the scenes the stretching of the canvas

and the kind inclusion of me on their planet

- musicmaster 12/01

garage sale 2001

bribed with her own money

a little girl is told to sell some stuff
if she does she can take
the money that she makes to buy
new clothes at the mall
so she excavates stuffed animals
from under the bed goes through closets
yanking games you got her just last year
she gathers books a pile of fastfood toys
an edible superball that glows in the dark

day of the sale at the top of the driveway
she sets up a stand selling cookies and pop
candybars and even hot coffee
a customer asks "what's the catch of the day?"
I imagine she answers "*not you* for damn sure"
as behind her the strangers pick through her closets
her games favorite dolls stuffed animals
they offer you fifty cents
for her unopened Magnetic Poetry kit

the little girl goes shopping
with thirty-six garage sale dollars
she finds sandals a t-shirt
a clock with an alarm that loudly snores
she doesn't look for toys or books she sold
she doesn't spot catch-of-the-day guy
steering his cart full of fish with pride
she does figure how much she would've made on pop
had she bought it on sale at Target
sold it like cognac to jewel thieves

with only five bucks left and eight more lines
she doesn't ask a clerk to find
a glowing superball that you can eat
she goes instead back to the books
where they carry mostly books by folks who can't write
and picks out a journal so that
she can try at last to mute your words
my words exercise-words euphuckinisms
(me fuckinisms!) and
magnetic poetry's kind but evil warden

In clearing out old files (mostly pictures and poems and art-life debris from 1970s' Portland, Oregon), I found this browning, worn flyer for a reading at The Earth Tavern (where I worked). The creepy thing is that I still remember the layout of the food store diagrammed and how back in the Cold Beer section you could get a six-pack of Columbia (a palatable offbrand) for $1.29.

Apart from conveniently filling a full page, I'm printing this for several disjointed reasons: 1) To note -Holy Smokes!- that the advertised reading began at 10 p.m.! If I did a reading nowadays that began at 10, many if not most people I know wouldn't come unless they could sleep over. Because it's past their bedtime! Because, sure, times change some things, but we change more.

creatures that they need to watch and restrain on the homefront. Because, sure, times change some things, but we change more. 2) To rebroadcast the sweet blurbs from the recently deceased Ken Kesey, bless his psychedelically housedressed, jazzed-up soul, and The Downtowner (though I've never figured out what they heard that prompted them to call me "romantic." 3) To solicit your guess as to how/why St.Champagne fits into church history and if instead of a Feast Day he just supplements a Feast Brunch. 4) To note that the only microwaves I was aware of then were unaffordable bulky bastards (one at The Earth for igniting eggs) from which very few dishes were protected.

MUSICMASTER

MAY 26th at the EARTH, 632 NW 21.

with ROCKIN' REGGAE St. CHAMPAGNE

$2.00 COVER   (READING AT 10 P.M.)

"PART OF YOUR COMMUNITY"

(POSTER GRID DESIGN BY OUR NEIGHBORHOOD THRIFTWAY STORE.)

Musicmaster hasn't performed a full-attack reading in over three years in Portland. This show is an all-new presentation of all-new poems. Musicmaster has performed (solo & by invitation) at P.S.U., P.U. (U. of P. sounds better), NWAW, Montana U., Montclair S. U. (N.J.), -cont.*

"I'll be there why don't you be there too" -Musicmaster

"SOMETIMES OKAY" -WALT CURTIS
"A FEW GOOD LINES" -JERRY CHRISTENSEN

"one of the best (performance) poets in the Northwest" -Ken Kesey

"COME ON TOM, THAT'S ALMOST A PAGE-LONG" -IN. TRUST

"Portland's most romantic poet" -Downtowner

"GREAT WITH BEER" -WIT LESEY

"best reading we've had in years"

* - Sarasota U. (Florida), Rochester U. (N.Y.), Elks Park School System (Pa.) the Warhouse (Ga.) etcetera.

GARDEN FRESH PRODUCE · COLD MILK

OLD BEER | FRESH MEATS | MEAT DELI | CHEESE DELI

all new! improved! fortified! (11) hard-to-swallow - from soup to nuts to bolts

DRY PROD | GARDEN FRESH PRODUCE | WARM POP

poems about oysterettes! (10) and lasagna!   tater tots!

KOOL AID NUTS/POPCORN CHIPS · PAPER PRODUCTS

mini-meatloaves in Snacking Sauce! (9) vege-wedgies in poultry paste!

DOG FOOD   CAT FOOD · BAR SOAP POWDER SOAPS BLEACH   parsley! pizza!

poems about healthy things to eat! (8) French Fries!   carrots!

GLOVES HOUSEHOLD CLEANERS HARDWARE & BROOMS · CEREAL   pickled pygmy foods &

a spinach who ran through the sand! (7) heartaches & heartburn!   munchies! fish!

CANDY COOKIES & CRACKERS · JAM PEANUT BUTTER BREAD

what to do with paprika? (6) how to stop eating and start smoking!   fluffy dead lambs!

TOBACCO HEALTH & BEAUTY AIDS FEM. HYGIENE · PICKLES & CONDIMENTS PICNIC SUPPLY

T.V. Dinners! how to exterminate them! (5) memories of The Pickle King!

COFFEE TEA COCOA BABY FOOD DIAPERS · FLOUR & CAKE MIXES SYRUP   Capons!

pencil-chewing; a path to Ecotopia? (4) how to reheat water!

SPICES HOUSEWARES SUGAR OIL & SHORTENING · MILK PASTE BEANS & RICE   Sweet & Sour Poems!

why can't discount ice cream fully melt? (3) fun things to construct with pasta!

NATURAL FOODS FISH PREPARED FOODS DIET FOODS · JELLO CANNED & BOTTLED JUICE SOUP

why is the best (& legendary) hot dog in N.Y. half the price (2) of the bullshit tubesteaks they push in Portland?   White Castles!

FRUIT · VEGETABLES

the future of generic foods! (1) Disco Dips and Roller Rump Roasts!

ICE CREAM · FROZEN FOODS

SNOW ANGELS BANNED FROM PUBLIC SCHOOL LAWNS

fear itself

walking home from Walgreen's
over a cool autumn bridge
with potato chips batteries Half&Half
if they bombed downtown right now
I'd hear a whistle see a cloud
have enough time I think
to run onto that wooden staircase to the creek
jump down some steps duck under railing
scramble up into that concrete wedge
where street meets concrete base and brace myself
while a tidal wave of fire
flattens everything above me
disintegrating houses credit cards parakeets
election lawn signs reading *Make a Difference*
the village idiot singing *God Bless America*
the genius singing *God Bless the World*
the Eyewitness News Team
who like the rest of us saw too little too late
pennies saved for a rainy day
unread books rosary beads prayer mats
representational art parking meters
a collection of fossils
everything just bursting with energy
I'd hope that fifteen blocks further south
Elaina and Dawn and Mom made it in time
to a just-discovered cave of steel
stocked with those rations and cots and drums of water
that filled our gradeschool's basement
and then I'd realize there's no poem to finish
no lawn to hate mowing
no smoke detectors to put the new batteries in
no beer to beat this unexpected system
and in spite of my hope my delusions my art-headedness
there's no just-discovered cave of steel
so I'd unwedge my fear
scramble up remaining flaming steps
hurry back to this point on the bridge
to listen to the fat lady burn
to think how unfair all of this is to people nicer than we are
to peacefully accept that I can't go back to Walgreen's
to remedy the misring on my boiling Half&Half

musicmaster 10.01

I'M TRYING TO THINK OF AN OLD REDUNDANCY JOKE JOKE

HOMESCHOOLING INTERACTIVE MULTIPLICATION KIT

INTERNAL  RHYME

JANUARY 12, 2002

ISSUE 69 OF THE NEWSLETTER THAT IS LITTLE MORE THAN A POORLY RENDERED EDITORIAL CARTOON ◆ MUSICMASTER, 5136 LYNDALE AV. S., MPLS, MN 55419

why I believe in everything

we paint each wall one color maybe two

a small mural worked in here and there

a mural featuring paintings seen through windows

from other windows

pictures within pictures

even wordballoons within wordballoons

then we tack on posters small toys

artworks a clipping from the paper a matchbox

sketches prints and a pitchblack postcard

from Cape May New Jersey that says

Cape May New Jersey at night

row upon uneven column of images

until every square inch of one color maybe two is
    covered

and some of the pictures are photos of previous walls

and photos of those previous-wall photographs

held between two medicine cabinets

slightly askew so you can see your face

over and over and over again

and if you look closely into your own eye

in that first mirror you can see *in your own eye*

a reflection of everything else

and I mean every damn thing from

the next wall we're going to paint

when we're kicked out of this apartment

for putting too much on the walls

to a painting of Cape May New Jersey

that shows a couple on a moonlit boardwalk

in dark blue paints and promises

and then -now don't you lose me now!-

after we've completely covered the walls

the small here and there murals

we build bookshelves in front of it all

floor to ceiling apartments stages and cells

into which we pack and cram a ton of books

arranged by size alone to get in as many as possible

first editions forcibly wedged in

on some shelves paperbacks three deep

lots of children's books coloring books stacked
    vertically

every kind of book except the blank book

PLEASE GO SOMEWHERE ELSE

BELIEF IS JUST A BOTTLE AWAY CONTINUED

books with illustrations tipped-in plates
maps and charts and glossaries
forwards and annotations
books denying the existence of other books
there are books about book collecting
piñata repair Roswell Jefferson King Tut and
    Buddha
and in a book published by the
Cape May New Jersey Historical Society
there are pages made of boardwalk planks
saltwater saltwater taffy and
just about every pebble on the beach
except for Cathy Horak

and when all of this is done
all the painting hanging and bookshelving
we step into this time capsule
of parlor games of art and pattern
science Midwest post-pop fiction metaphor madness
and we stand there in this room

    naked uncluttered no added preservatives
    simplified

not with money or religion as carpet or skylight
for there is no floor no ceiling
just the sparkling map of eternity
and where to fly or fall

           musicmaster 4 january 2002

counselor

on this second day of New Year
I embark on my descent
into clinical madness poetic too
a state from which I hope to send
an artwork well crafted
or balanced or clear you know something
you don't have to hang with six nails
or look at like mistakes were made

not that you'd ever say that or say
that you were looking like that but believe me
I can tell that even when you like a poem
one of my all-white-paper collages for example
that you think I should've used fewer pieces
or quieter vowels or made the piece
that looks like George Washington
look instead like Rose Red

you know I think the world of you
so when I get that message
it inspires me to dig a little deeper
into memory macadam through
our money mannered ways
of wit and worship
into where I know I'll find a source of truth
so pure they'll lock me up

and give me paints and pencils
to make things that I can send you
things in which I'll tell you
where I am in such a way
you'll nod approval

musicmaster 3 january 2002

2002

all these appliances
technological conjunctions
systems and subscriptions
we grow up into and with
to connect more
to connect more easily
to more easily feel neighborly tribal
nationalistic then internationalistic
global and galactic
we say universal and holistic in anthems
and modern catechisms
that we broadcast via radio telephone
satellite internet
the electrical signals emitted
with each gentle pounding of our hearts
I stand here
2 a.m. New Year's Day
in a house at 5136 Lyndale Avenue South
Minneapolis Minnesota
looking at a resting television set
a computer on standby
a telephone that answers for us

lets people in
and while I'm just a few clicks away
from what is happening
right this second on I-35 heading east
in Iraq on the space shuttle
in Japan on an undiscovered moon of Toledo
in an operating room in Sweden
where a cloned snowchipmunk
is learning how to speak
I feel that the most I have in common
with any and all of us and them
is an awestricken shadow in the starlight
where tonight for the New Year
instead of making resolutions
about weight loss
the overrated value of sobriety
the overrated value of society
and clearly the overrated value of poetry
I'll stand and stare and
wait for the Pony Express

musicmaster 1 january 2002

QUESTION CERTAINTY, DREAM OVERTIME, DARE TO GRATE

PEN&INK BY LEGENDARY IMPOSSIBILIST REYNARDA WALLY CIRCA 1978

TEACHER SUSPENDED FOR EXPELLING STUDENT WHO DETAINED FIRST GRADER

MY RUBIK'S CUBE IS BROKEN

APRIL 1, 2002

INTERNAL RHYME

ISSUE 71 OF THE ONLY PUBLICATION THAT PRINTED ISSUE 72 BEFORE 71   MUSICMASTER, 5136 LYNDALE AVE SOUTH, MINNEAPOLIS, MN 55419

The Cost of Living

I know everything costs more than it used to, that prices have gone up because the people doing the pricing are themselves experiencing increased costs somewhere else, maybe from me. Though not likely, not very likely at all. I still price my one-of-a-kind artworks at about half the hourly rate I bill for doing newsletters that are, let's face it, often redundant, always familiar, and generally not worth a dime as an investment or an artwork. Not that my artworks are. But they might be. Whereas even an ancient copy of the *Minnesota Plow & Drift Quarterly* (which comes out five times a year if you include *Macadam Scraping Metal*, the snowplow industry's annual legislative report) is hardly worth a fig.

I'm used to the fact that comic books are no longer a dime. When they went up to twelve cents each in 1962 or so I was sure the world was ending because my weekly allowance of fifty cents was suddenly enough for only four

comic books, not five. I was so noticeably distraught that my Dad asked me what was wrong and when I told him, just a day or two after I was attacked by this stunning shift of the earth's axis, he raised my allowance to seventy-five cents. Making me Super Rich Boy who could purchase six of these new, pricier comics and a candy bar to boot.

It's not like I've been living in the woods for crying out loud, where Thumper is still billing Bambi a slim five-spot per therapy session. I regularly pay more than a buck too much for a lousy loaf of bread. And I still occasionally buy a comic book for as little as $2.50 (all the very well done *Simpsons* and *Futurama* titles released by Bongo Entertainment, Inc.) to as much as $19.95 (for a *Comics Journal* special edition), without whining "these things used to cost twelve cents" to a clerk whose fastfood lunch costs five bucks (Hell, you could get a session with Thumper for that).

Don't start citing the serenity prayer to me. There isn't a single damn serial killer alive who doesn't have a magnetic version of that thing on his munitions cooler.

But I am hypersensitive to crass profiteering bullshit (when Target claimed that they were sparing customers' time and confusion by no longer accepting rebate/mail-refund coupons) (when Target drastically revamped its returns policy by claiming it made it more fair to all consumers – the old, grade school, penalize-everyone-for-the-abuses-of-a-few routine). (Just a note: Target, which used to only put drastically reduced merchandise on its clearance shelves – say something marked down from $2.99 to six bits - now will label things only modestly discounted as CLEARANCE priced – an Orwellian tweak to the word's meaning.)

FOLLOW YOUR HEART

And I'm always bothered when a product is downsized, say a snack bag of chips from 1.4 ounces to 1.25 ounces with a concurrent promotion of the *New, Big Muncher Size*! Yes, I know this is friendlier way to increase revenue without slapping customers with the more conspicuous price hike, but when it's done by a multinational company with lots of multi-millionaire execs trimming the grunts on the assembly line and telling the press that their compensation is earned by initiating such downsizing to benefit shareholders, well . . . you know, maybe I'm just a nonideological socialist or communist or whatever *ist* it is who thinks –patriotically!– that capitalism is rigged and, worse, a pejorative form of greed. Hey, I'm trying to think fairly, but these nonprice price hikes come in under the radar so routinely - so much more often than consumers get raises - so camouflaged with distractions of packaging and giddy, irrelevant copy, that I think if *I'm* aware of *this much* chicanery – exploitation?– that a hell of a lot more of it must be going on via better camouflaged, more cleverly screwed-in marketing tricks.

And AT&T? Don't get me started. Those bastards. They're probably billing your pets without your knowledge. When you die your estate still has to pay them a monthly fee to cover the billions they spend on peppy Stepford advertising phlegm about what a hip smart choice company they are because they believe you're far more cognizant of and subliminally swayed by that than you are by the litany of fees and hikes.

Where was I? Oh yeah, one less chip per bag might be the smoothest way to stabilize the margin at Lay's, and one less "M" per bag of New Improved Mega Super Mini Fun Size M&Ms might be the best way to keep the candy aisle items under a buck, but when I notice that a package shrinks without warning, my switch gets flipped. I automatically rant about parallels between single-serving-size shrinkage and global warming. I suppose I want changes like this accompanied by a kind of we're-sorry-we-have-to-do-this letter that also contains reassuring news about cost-controls being implemented to limit swarms of advertising/marketing/branding efforts. Really, one tv spot per prime time hour is enough to remind me that a certain product continues to exist. (By bludgeoning consumers less about why a popular product is good or somehow associated with family or happiness,

companies could save serious change. But I'm not a marketing exec out to bolster my role.)

Okay, I'll get to the source of this gripe. And please, don't start citing the serenity prayer to me. There isn't a single damn serial killer alive who doesn't have a magnetic version of that thing on his munitions cooler. I'm peeved and miffed for several reasons:

• I drink lots of coffee.

• I'm misdirecting rage I have for public servants who have downsized their output of genuine concern for all citizenry so they can focus more on careerism and seminars on how-to-effectively-circle-the-wagons and it's-only-a-Win/Win-situation-when-you're-the-winner-twice.

• I have childhood issues that Thumper refuses to address for a reasonable fee.

• I get into some good wordshuffling shtick when I'm peeved and miffed and therefore get an issue of *Internal Rhyme* out without too much strain on my ability to produce loftier, more esoteric pieces about drifting clouds that look so much like stars that you have to guess that sometimes God is just screwing around.

And, lastly . . .

• Without warning, without notice, without a courtesy call, cartons of Schwan's Premium and Premium Plus ice cream have shrunk from a half gallon to a 56-ounce size; a size that's conspicuously smaller, eerily nonstandard and, using Schwan's own stated serving size of four ounces, a full two servings lighter. The price remains the same: $4.79 per carton of unleaded Premium (flavors like vanilla fudge or chocolate chip; flavors just one notch above "Traditional Favorites" like vanilla, chocolate and strawberry, all unaffected by this tremor) and $5.79 for a carton of Premium Plus (which is typically an excellent concoction of vanilla ice cream jazzed up with chocolate bars, peanuts, black cherries, chunky peanut butter, rum crystals, and bacon). Do the math on this price hike and you're now paying about a penny and a half more per ounce for Premium (roughly an 84-cent-hike-for-Schwan adjustment) and maybe a penny and a third more per ounce for Premium Plus (roughly a 75-cent-hike). Is "a penny and a third" an acceptable math expression? Is it a premium expression?

TRY OUR NEW IMPROVED PAGE 3

THE COST OF AN ICE CREAM HEADACHE HAS GONE UP

Marshall Minnesota-based Schwan's, which is known for its quality ice cream and which also produces an ambitious line of other, mostly ordinary-tasting frozen foods, sells very little via retail outlets, instead opting for a large network of home delivery trucks. Apart from a few of those classy grocery stores with the carpeted aisles and a retired neurosurgeon bagging your purchase, few places carry Schwan's ice cream. Curiously, I did first find some in Spur, an innocuous convenience store at 17th Avenue and Highway 7 in Hopkins, back in 1983 when I was quitting cigarettes but still taking nightly walks to buy them. By the time I fully quit, at the end of a 2-month stint with the brainwashers at SmokeEnders, I was still stopping at Spur to buy something, *anything*, a candy bar, a magazine, and it was in that wandering-around-for-something phase that I purchased a half gallon-sized half gallon of Schwan's from Spur's small ice cream cooler and became a fan. Not that it's the best vanilla, but it's certainly among the best, and by comparison to the house brands I'd been buying (stuff like My-T-Fine and Flavorite), it was excellent.

Years later, Moose and I ended up in this house on Lyndale and, around 1990, Ralph, a Schwan man in a Schwan cap and jacket, appeared at our door and thus began the every-other-Wednesday stop by the yellow, refrigerated Schwan's truck we enjoy to this day (or at least enjoyed until several weeks ago).

We always bought three half gallons of ice cream. Occasionally we'd try other products they'd hype in catalogs

left behind, but even the good ones were a bad value against comparable brands we can get at the grocery. So we stuck to the ice cream.

Even as it slowly drifted up in price.

Even after Schwan's weathered a serious storm over product-spawned salmonella cases and a massive alert to dump ice cream for coupon-secured replacement later. (Their handling of the crisis and especially how they handled it to maintain customer loyalty was a textbook example of how to survive a serious setback with honesty and a quick, aggressive campaign to make things right. They even followed up the crisis with a free-to-all sundae social which I wanted to attend so I could pretend to get sick.) (Letterman cracked that the problem was traced to their Pork Swirl ice cream.)

Even after we started going to Cub Foods and found that a premium ice cream is always on sale for $1-$2 less per half gallon than Schwan's. We always rationalized that the service was convenient, quaint ("I remember when the scissor-sharpening man drove down our street clanging his bell…"), and maybe even a C-grade status symbol.

We figured the whole Schwan's concept was worth a few extra bucks, plus a buck or two tip to whoever is currently Ralph. What the hell. Money on trees and the gut still able to expand.

And then came the increase in the price of comic books. Without announcement or any of the kid gloves' treatment we got with the salmonella. Dawn bought three "half gallons" and when I came home she asked me if I thought they looked smaller and, gadzooks, we both eyeballed that net weight line and realized we'd been had. Taken for fools. Taken for ice cream junkies who'd adapt no matter what. No surprise, I badmouthed the bastards a bit and, big surprise, mild-mannered flow-goer Dawn cast aspersions as well. He should have mentioned the scaled down carton when taking her order for what she reasonably believed to be the same-sized product we've gotten in the past.

"We can get three half gallons of Breyer's at Cub, for crying out loud!" we said in unison. "Or Jerry's. Or Edy's Grand Whatever with the watchamacallits."

And we resolved to tell our friendly ice cream man that we'd no longer get the Premium or Premium Plus flavors,

I still have way too many of the 60some different postcard designs that I sold through a few dozen shops thoroughout the 80s, back when I was funnier (sample at left). I'll mail you 20 different for the below-wholesale price of four bucks postpaid. What you don't like, you can mail away. My address is on page below the guy pretending that the empty shoeboxes are heavy.

STARTING NEXT ISSUE INTERNAL RHYME WILL ONLY HAVE 3 PAGES . . .OH WAIT

only the Traditional Favorites (which are actually discounted when you get three of them, something we'd never taken advantage of previously because we'd always get one or two of those fancy flavors with the mini donuts and crepes). Which we told him the other night and to which he sadly responded that everybody was complaining about it, or at least questioning the silent introduction of the new size and that, of course, our calls and letters to the company itself would be more productive in Schwandom than messages through his middle-man-role twixt the customers and the people who own the vats. We ordered three of the surviving-half-gallon Traditional Favorites and out of guilt – you know, this guy is just the messenger and doesn't the messenger deserve a raise too – we bought a box of frozen hot dogs that I'm sure will be fine but not good enough to warrant the tab.

AND NOW THE REAL STORY BEGINS

I'm fooling you. I'll never get to the real story. But I do have a tale that belongs here.

A few weeks ago I was trying to assemble a complete set of *Internal Rhymes* from a holding shelf where I'm pretty good at tossing copies of every smallpress item I print. It was a fun exercise, revisiting the few 8-page issues, seeing the cartoons my son contributed early on, rereading articles I've totally forgotten about, and remembering the locations of typo after typo after typo.

I vowed as I've pointlessly vowed before that from this day on I will get an issue out every two weeks. And then I put duplicates of all seventy copies in numerical order. I squared them up, figured how high the pile will be when I finally get to issue #100.

And then, to revisit my spew one more time, to baste my ego a wee bit more, I looked through them all again. I reread a piece about Olympic Park (*Elbows of Fame*, #8), a classic New Jersey amusement park that was magnificently fading even as we regularly visited it in the 50s and 60s, Bob and I to hit the rides, Mom and Dad to lounge around to an oompah band in the beer garden, all of us to see a 3-act circus that changed every Sunday. It's one of my favorite pieces though it has never been printed anywhere else and I've never read it anywhere. Like a lot of the stuff in *Internal Rhyme*.

Then I noticed that in the same issue as my pretty long salute to Olympic Park, I had *Phonetag*, a good, carefully-crafted poem about my Dad that I only wrote several years after his death because I didn't want it to be a eulogy or incorrectly inflated snapshot of him or his passing. And I also had, in the same issue, a wordy addendum to *Elbows of Fame*, a doodle by my daughter and some boxed plugs for artsy this and that. I flipped ahead to more recent issues and then flipped back and forward until realizing that with #68, I started using larger type throughout the issue.

Pre-68 issues contain more stuff than an issue does now, because I assembled those pages on an 8-1/2 x 11 Pagemaker template, printed them out, and then placed them directly on a copier with a reduction to pair them up and print them out on legal sheets. And then, not too long ago, I switched to composing *Internal Rhyme* on a new, legal-sized template that I print straight to and through the copier, no longer hassling the not-quite-smooth/proportionate adjustments I was making with "originals" on glass. Something about my comfort level with a to-size font on a computer screen's Actual Size interpretation (as opposed to that interpretation prefacing an ex utero adjustment) accounts for the discrepancy in total content. The reduction in total content. Without warning or announcement.

But also without plan or profit motive, so I'm off my own hook here, I know. I know. But I didn't mean to trim the value of something free. Free things are hard enough to come by without shrinkage. You know? I apologize for the change. I owe all readers a poem and a boxed overworked joke and, believe me, you won't be able to avoid them.

(Note: In the *About Us* section of Schwan's web site, I read this item:

Should I tip my Schwan's representative?

A simple "Thank you" is always appreciated. Your continuing business with Schwan's also tells us that you appreciate us. Your Schwan's representative does not accept monetary tips.

We've always tipped the Schwan man.) ∎

THE STUMBLING STONE MASON'S ASSISTANT

JUNE 14, 2002

INTeRNAL RHYMe

THE 75TH CONSECUTIVE EDITION PRINTED WITHOUT A PROBLEM AT THE BINDERY   MUSICMASTER, 5136 LYNDALE AV S, MINNEAPOLIS, MN 55419

my way of life

you can kick most people in the ass

every morning at work

when they get to work they say *good morning*

and you kick them in the ass with

nothing short of ferocious lust

for a bigger ass to kick

or rows of them to kick

or an ass made of pure innocence

pure platinum a bunch of smartasses

and you can kick them every day

like a bad cop a sadistic bootsmith

a man who gives ass kicking a bad name

day in and out like you can't otherwise breathe

and after years of this

with barely a break for coffee

but always time for counseling

afterall we aren't savages

we have to keep the team on course

and after years of this

we're talking ten relentless years

you can announce

that as of next Wednesday

there will be no more ass kickings

no more say-good-morning ass kickings

and after a silence you can slice with a dull pickle

someone will ask

does as 'of next Wednesday' mean

*there **will** be an ass kicking*

next Wednesday morning or not?

then someone else will say

I can't believe I'm hearing this

I can't believe you're saying that

tt isn't fair you're doing this

and someone else will add

it isn't fair to those of us

who've been here several years

and voices will shout

save our ass kickings

we are one ass indivisible

we are constitutionally entitled to ass kickings

TURN PAGE AND ASSUME THE POSITION

OUR MOST SACRED RIGHT
CONTINUED

and then like in one of those godawful movie scenes

wherein one person claps slowly

before at an ever-accelerating pace everyone else joins in

like fucking wind-up monkeyheaded demoralizing losers

every worker will contribute to an evolving unison of

kick our asses kick our asses kick our asses

an evolving harmonic convergence and jingle of

kick our asses kick our asses

a mantra of people who are damned

but okay with damnation

asskicked but willing to be asskicked even more

and though you will go ahead with your plan

for no more ass kickings

because frankly it'll save the company money

no more big salaries for contract muscle

and asskicking certification fees

you will have to retain the counselors again

to kick everybody in the ass

when they get here in the morning

when they're out in the parking lot

locking their cars

they can get a good solid kick in the ass

before entering the building

before getting nostalgic for an asskicking of yore

before switching on their miserable eyes

and seeing on the conveyor belts

their own voiceforwarded teamleadered

vicepresidentialed heads

musicmaster june 02

Real Book / Fake Book

Every second Wednesday of the month at Hyperbole, the spoken word series I book and host at Babylon Café, an arts collective at 1624 East Lake Street in Minneapolis, I lead a round of Real Book/Fake Book, a simple, nongraded, prizeless guessing game in which I read aloud a list of book titles for the audience to judge as real or fake. I was inspired to compile my first round of ten titles about eight years ago (for a series I was hosting at Barnes & Noble in Edina) when I saw an award-winning children's book about pooping.* (I can't remember the exact title – Who Pooped? or Let's Poop or Barbie's Big Book of Poop or what – but Greetomatic, a friend who works at Barnes & Noble, assured me that the subject was so wildly popular among kids that they were thinking of adding a Poop Books section.) I browsed more broadly and it seemed to me that clever and/or offbeat titles were suddenly everywhere and the perfect fodder for a simple game that has since become a national institution. Well, maybe not yet. But until Milton Bradley releases the twenty-dollar version of Real Book/ Fake Book or ABC broadcasts a gameshow called *Book 'Em*, you can occasionally enjoy a play-at-home round in *Internal Rhyme*. Answers for this installment are upsidedown on the back page.

The astute reader will notice that every feature in this issue of Internal Rhyme owes a lot to the buttocks. This is strictly coincidental. I think.

1. *Stay in the Crib* and Other Punishments that Nurture Your PreSchooler

2. Slapboxing with Jesus

3. Girls of Disney – A Playboy Special Theme Park Edition

4. Taxes Shmaxes – The Rich Guy's Guide to Protecting and Hiding Wealth from the IRS

5. An Illustrated History of Illustrated Histories – The Abrahm's Guide to Coffee Table Tomes

6. The Holy Book of the Beard

REAL INSTRUCTION / FAKE INSTRUCTION? CONTINUED NEXT PAGE

I'D HAVE MORE OPINIONS IF I HAD A BIGGER BUMPER

the history of art part 1

a guy walks into his studio
lowers his pants
and squats and craps
a little Mona Lisa
a 3-dimensional unfired clay
masterpiece for flies
and scholars too
they say it's like he has a gift from God

and so it goes for many years
he builds a reputation and career
he calls his stuff his shit and
banters with the other jokes that you'd do too
until his midlife crisis
when he wonders what's the meaning
really of the sun and soul
and if his work amounts to art
or really just a lot of crap

he takes a hike that turns into
what he calls (pretentiously) a quest
a journey a personal odyssey
to a mystic on top of a mountain
a one man toga party
who asks *why the long face? what?*
you realize your time is finite
and suddenly you're Doctor Serious?
look you're proof and point and punchline
of the great and grinning wit of God
so what's your problem?

and the artist gets dramatic and
declares his gift **a curse**
he says *I want to make some art*
that's really mine not so derivative
certainly not divine

NEXT PAGE WE DISCUSS GRANT WOOD

SUMMER READING LIST CONTINUED

7. Why Daddy Drinks So Much KoolAid

8. My Cousin My Gastroenterologist

9. Crying: The Natural and Cultural History of Tears

10. Anchors: An Illustrated History

11. Smart Salespeople Sometimes Wear Plaid: Dare to be Extraordinary in a Mediocre World

12. An Illustrated History of Her Majesty's Third Throne, the Barstool

13. YO, BLACKEN THIS! Hell's Kitchen Meets the French Quarter at the Delta Grill

14. My Big Brother is Going to Beat Up the Next Guy Who Calls Sensitive Men Geeks

15. Nostradamus Didn't Count on Me

16. Do Bald Men Get Half-Price Haircuts? In Search of America's Great Barbershops

17. Dick Clark's Guide to Hosting a Happening Hullaballoo

18. Dumbstruck: a Cultural History of Ventriloquism

19. Jujitsu for Christ by Jack Butler

20. A Verb, a Body Part and Thou: the Real Story Behind Mad Libs

9,342 OF MINNESOTA'S LAKES ARE GUILTY OF SCENIC REDUNDANCY

ART MY ASS CONTINUED

I want to have control of my creations
and the holy man mumbles
yeah like you're the first old guy
concerned about his bowels

okay I tell you what he adds
as he produces his magic wand
from beneath his toga
and hey you know what I mean
but I don't mean that in this piece
in this piece I mean
a cheap looking black magic wand
which makes the artist think
oh great he's going to pull
a rabbit out of my ass

and the mystic says *okay Doctor Serious*
with a pout down to his tuchis
I'm going to help you out because
you remind me of me back
when I was just some dumb schmuck
like you but without the bad haircut
my son he says painting the air
above the artist's head with the wand
you are cured of your affliction
you may go in peace
just leave me twenty bucks

and the artist feeling his intestines
reconfigure their stew says
why thank you mighty mystic
for this miracle though twenty bucks
sure doesn't seem like much
to which Milton Bearle answers
hey don't sweat it Mona Lisa
I buy wholesale and besides
it ain't much of a miracle

and sure enough three hours later
during his retreat from
his personal odyssey
our guy ducks behind the mountain
to answer the call of art
he squats and craps
a little 3-dimensional pile of unfired clay
that doesn't look anything
like Mona Lisa or American Gothic
or even a cave drawing of a bison
who has a mysterious smile
it just looks like a parcel left
by a dog with bad eating habits

and the guy says *holy shit*
I'm an abstract expressionist
and for the first time in his life
his every single word
is barking truth

musicmaster june 02

STAND ON YOUR HEAD TO READ THESE ANSWERS TO THE REAL BOOK/FAKE BOOK FEATURE

The real books are #2 (by Victor D. Lavalle); #6 (by Duff Brenna); #8 (by Mark Leyner, author of Et Tu, Babe); #9 (by Tom Lutz); #10 (by Betty Nelson); #11 (by Barry Graham Munro); #13 (by M.B. Roberts, recipes of Chef Greg Tatis of NY's best Cajun restaurant); #16 (by Vince Staten); #18 (by Steven Connor); and #19 (by Jack Butler). Somebody should pay me for #14 which has attitude, humor, commentary, and a name-recognition factor all in five words and without the expense of a screwball marketing department.

IT ONLY TAKES ONE BAD PIRATE TO GIVE ALL PIRATES AN EYEPATCH

SEVERAL OF THE BOXED CANARIES TRIED TO ESCAPE   AUGUST 5, 2002

INTERNAL RHYME

ISSUE 76 OF THE NEWSLETTER THAT SPREADS 3 PAGES WORTH OF MATERIAL OVER 4 PAGES   MUSICMASTER, 5136 LYNDALE AV S, MINNEAPOLIS, MN 55419

as a matter of fact, yes

1

we go down to the shore
swim in pirate infested tidal waves
kicking the surf the skywriting the sharks
who are salted and purple and laughing like we are
like nature's perfect killing machines

later on Bob and I play skeeball
until we win enough coupons to get a shrunken head
that really does look like our neighbor Mr. LaBrunda
who looks quite a bit like Bud Abbott
only smaller

2

we skip classes so we can have
a four-day weekend on the beach in her parent's bungalow
while they visit her younger brother
who's at college far away like we are
nature's perfect crime and cure for everything

later on as we sit in the sand
I intensely ponder the point of my pencil
write with certainty that seabreeze in her hair
makes poetry redundant
life and death just pollen in her eyes

3

we take a trip without the kids
to soak up discount heat and cheaper beer
while watching foreign sunsets
from the beach where I write lines
like nature's perfect skeeball prize is screaming

later on we drink and eat
tequila goat cheese pizza with
a cracker crust stigmata pocks and meat wafers
that look like pepperoni but
are really kelp and artificial sand

RIDE THE WAVES THIS AND DRIFT THIS WAY

INSIDE THIS ISSUE

MED SCHOOL BUGS TRAINED TO PLAY HOCKEY

TEEN BESTSELLER – TELEPHONE TRICKS THAT PROVE YOU ARE NOT AT THE MALL

COOKING WITHOUT

PRESIDENT BUSH WALKS INTO INVISIBLE FENCE, GETS KNOCKED OUT; SOURCES SAYS THIS IS 327TH TIME GEORGE HAS BEEN KOED SINCE CHRISTMAS SECURITY UPGRADE; HE'S NONE THE WORSE FOR THE ZAPS; LOCAL EXPERTS WARN CITIZENS TO LIMIT INVISIBLE FENCE USE TO NON-AQUATIC MAMMALS

TAPES INDICATES OSAMA 52.4% DEAD OR 70% RASPY

NEW LIQUOR WAREHOUSE CHAIN TO GIVE HAPPY-MEAL-STYLE TOYS WITH PURCHASES; INITIAL PREMIUMS TO INCLUDE DRUNKEN SKUNK, PINK ELEPHANT AND OTIS OF MAYBERRY

HARPO'S HORN IN MALL OF AMERICA ROTUNDA DRAWS 43,000 OVER WEEKEND

SNACKIN' THIEF CHOKES TO DEATH ON "BON VOYAGE" HORS D'OEUVRES

PEZ HOT DISH

The World's Best Open Mike is held the first Friday of every month (at 8 p.m.) at the Twin Cities' Best Coffee House - **Anodyne, 43rd & Nicollet, Minneapolis** (612-824-4300). Tom Cassidy is your Best Host! By the way, the first Friday is the Best Friday! The Best Month is the Month That YOU Show Up! 8-minute performance max - be fast, be fun, be brilliant (and, in 8 minutes, be over)! **Join us for Real Life Must-See Un-TV!**

ASAMATTAAFACT CONTINUED

4

at 6 a.m. the shells we pluck
from clouds of silt
we've seen before passed up before
before our eyes is skywriting it says that time is
nature's way of getting drunk

later on we watch the sunset gawkers
from our timeshare's balcony
when we don our inch-thick x-ray specs
we don't see any underwear or bones
just flaming surf exploding shells

5

we trip on our tongues
get swept out to sea
made fun of by not-very-professional pirates
and eaten by sharks who think of us as
nature's new buffet items

later on we flip though pebbles
remember the gulls that braided hair
see where we found - washed ashore - which dead
relatives
and argue over when the sunsets
started getting sloppy   musicmaster 23july02

Winners of the Lake Superior Haiku Slam Competition

toboggans erase
simplifications implied
by snow don't you know
  - Gert Anderswansenson, 68, Duluth

keen mean supreme scene
when the gizzzzzards spill onto
the snow don't you know
  - Trapper, 15, Dipstick Lakes

angry dogs pulling
heavysledded whipman bark
at snow don't you know
  - Aalonn Svenberg, 37, Big Tern

Hamil, Inge and Tom (along with Dawn, Stephanie and Joe, sadly not pictured) all chalked up the macadam at the Greenway Festival, Minneapolis, July 4th (pictures by Stephanie Krueger) - our third official attack on city byways

you

every week the local paper
has a different writer
drive out here to talk with me
to ask me what I think of what
they say
the column which is very popular
is called *It's All About You*
and in it the different columnists
write about whatever it is
they thought they heard me say
or made them think
but what I've noticed
is that none of the columns
none of the twenty I've read
is really about me at all
oh sure they all get the name right
mention household landmarks
describe a few of my artworks

make differing cracks about
clutter
but past those blurry facts
which increasingly strike me
as a different type of punctuation
not one of the columns
is about me at all
they are all of them only
the writers' depictions
of driving out here
thinking columnist things
overexplaining artworks
and printing whatever the hell
they want about what they think
I'm saying when I tell them
that the name of the column
ought to be changed to
It's All About Me

MoviE PrEviEws

Clint Eastwood directs and stars in *Bingo Boy*, a coming-of-age story about a tenth-grader, played by Briedynowe (pronounced *Philip*) Smith, who volunteers his every Wednesday night as a strolling vendor of snack foods and coffee in St. Michael's basement. The lightly embalmed Eastwood underplays his roll as a parishioner and Bingo Supplies House salesman looking to expand his customer base from just churches and "family friendly" boardwalk parlors to the Vegas casino where his sister "dances."

Pauley Shore is surprisingly engaging and unfar-outy in *Page Boy*, the true story of Medical Examiner Jack Butler's first job as a detective who by a mix of coincidence and desire specialized in off-shelf books found at crime scenes. Not only do these books "babble like methparrots, confess to complicity," they also spark our hero to keep a journal, which, of course, he leaves at a crime scene where it gets spotted by an envious colleague . . . oh you know the rest, which ain't all bad. Toss in Pauley's surviving braincells – which, especially in the 'dogear scene' seem to grasping for genuine emotion – and you've got a little film with strong legs.

Margaritasvillain

who is the man

with the beach umbrella

up his ass

arms crossed

at our big July 4th barbecue

he is angry unresponsive

jagged buzzing

so uncomfortable looking

I want to sedate myself

or better yet

put him to pasture

put him to sleep

the unhappy bastard

what the hell right

does he have to show up

univited

dragged here by someone

who made a bad decision

and ignore us all so deliberately

so hypersonically

you can hear

his pores slam shut

his eyes steam

his intestines snap the spokes

of our umbrella

REal Book / FakE Book

Every second Wednesday of the month at Hyperbole, the spoken word series I book and host at Babylon Café, an arts collective at 1624 East Lake Street in Minneapolis, I lead a round of Real Book/Fake Book, a simple, nongraded, prizeless guessing game in which I read aloud a list of book titles for the audience to judge as real or fake. Since I don't have enough room to put the answers upsidedown at the end, I'm giving you a big clue here - the **Real Book** titles are **Bold** . . .

Kamikaze Lust by Lauren Sanders

Dr. Broth & Ollie's Brain-Boggling Search for Their Lost Luggage by Michael Abrams & Jeffrey Winters

Tales of Beatnik Glory by Ed Sanders (an excellent, fun, hippie/radical romp by original Fugs member Sanders who went on to pen Family, the frightening tale of the Manson cult and killings, and several Naropa Institute sounding books of poems not near as much fun as Beatnik Glory)

Everything I Needed to Know I Learned from Mr. Lavarack in Seventh Grade Band Class

Windchills of the Heart from the Lake Superior Haiku Slam

Jumbo's Hide, Elvis's Ride, and the Tooth of Buddha by Harvey Rachlin

Medicine Cabinet Cocktails – Legal Ways to Turn Yourself Inside-Out

Who Will Run the Frog Hospital? by Lorrie Moore

Daily Meditations for Garment Industry Workers

Kick Your Own Ass, I'm Too Busy – and Other Ugly Truths About My Decade as a Motivational Speaker*

*When we played this round of Real Book Fake Book at Babylon Gallery, nearly everyone thought and insistently voted that this is the title of a real book. Why? Had they all been burnt (or singed) or annoyed at one time or another by the sort of psychobabbly insincere hugster chatterly speaker who would write a book like this (like this unwritten one)? Friends, I tell you from the bottom of my meant-well that I do

not know, no sir. I am a babe in the woods of your brain. Wherein, as you dreamers and makers and givers already no doubt know, anything can happen, including miracles. (Damn, I want to both do vapid motivational speaking for ten years to watch my nose grow and write this tell-some book . . . if I write a tell-all I lessen my odds of selling a sequel.) You are merely an unkempt bed, an undernourished revolution, a true-to-you true blue genius. That will be $149 per each team member attending. Oh yeah, here are some free "study tacks" to arrange – inspiration side up – on your favorite chair.

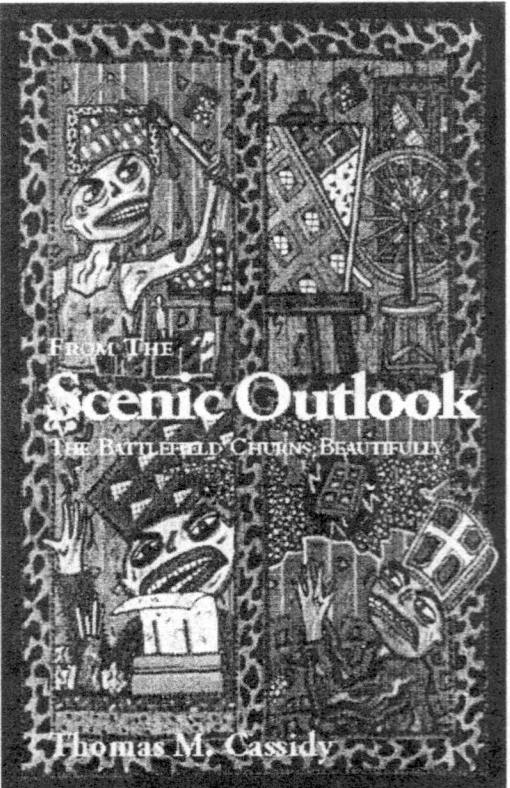

Gadzooks, I have a slick looking book with a color cover and an ISBN # and everything that just got released by the fine fringe folks (well, folk) at Green Bean Press of New York City. Visit the **greenbeanpress.com** website for a slew of downloads by an offbeat catalog of writers. If you buy my book –**Scenic Outlook**- and write me that you did, I'll send you a profusion of thanks and an autograph you can copy. Thank you!

BOXES OF RECIPES ELAINE MAE SAVED   AUGUST 27, 2002

INTERNAL RHYME

THE 78TH EDITION OF WHAT IS AFTER ALL, A JOURNAL OF REAL LIFE   MUSICMASTER, 5136 LYNDALE AVENUE SOUTH, MINNEAPOLIS, MN 55419

Elaine Mae   July 7, 1936 – August 26, 2002

Elaine was a kind, witty, informed, open-minded woman with a big heart, a broad appreciation of traditional and modern arts, and a fondness for all things lush, lavish and caloric. And in spite of setbacks she experienced, she never lost her faith in family, friends, tradition, romance, laughter and hope. I never thought of her as a mother-in-law, (too much routine and inappropriate stigma with that); I've always thought of her and will continue to think of her as a great supportive ally in keeping things not just moving along, but moving along with vitality, vibrancy, focus and care. She would've loved the following story and would've encouraged me to put back in the lines I deleted.

Note: Our almost-11 daughter's name is Elaina, a name we just plucked out of thin air before marveling at its uncanny similarity to Elaina's grandmother's name! I mention this so you won't confuse one with the other in following story.

Christmas Eve

Dawn, Erik, Mark, Laura, my Mom, Elaina, Hamil, a cast of rotating others and I are all hanging out in Elaine's living room, enjoying some hors d'oeuvres while Elaine is in the kitchen still working on another that involves crab, spinach, bourbon and crumbled-up Little Debbie cakes. She clipped the recipe out of a neighborhood newspaper, back when she lived in Eden Prairie, and has been meaning to try it ever since. It's about 6 p.m. So allow me to correct myself – Mark isn't here yet; he still has to shop for presents.

To while away the wait, Dawn and Erik tell stories behind ornaments on the Christmas tree. I always think there's a children's book in that kind of idea – each ornament a memory of a different year or person or city or vacation, a relative no longer living, a friend long ago or faraway, a Christmas past. I'll write that story too someday – once I get over the fact that all these wonderful memories are used to decorate a recently ambushed and chopped down tree.

All of Elaine's holiday decorations, and there lots of them, from wall hangings to a California Raisin dressed like Santa, have stories behind them and Elaine occasionally steps from the kitchen to clarify an origin or two. "Oh no, we got that one from Joyce

when she was working in barbwire and popcorn. And that eel skin snowman is an item I used to sell through my gift service."

When the kitchen timer goes off at 7:30 p.m. Elaine pulls Crabbie Debbie from the oven and says, "Darn it, the oven wasn't on."

Dawn says she'll take over in the kitchen so Elaine can get dressed and put on her make-up, a process that can take longer than the entire lifespan of certain beetles. The funny thing is that Elaine is already better dressed and made-up than anyone else in the room. Though, in fairness to me, I've never been good with eye shadow.

As Elaine retreats to her bedroom, Dawn asks if she should get the ham going right away. Elaine turns and answers, "Great idea, but you'll have to thaw it first. And, oh yeah, I'm glad you reminded me - I need for you to go to the store and get two more cans of corn, a jar of spicy mustard and some Blistex."

Dawn says, "It's Christmas Eve, only that mini-mart at Amoco will be open."

"That's great," says Elaine. "You can get me a can of motor oil too."

THE WAIT CONTINUES NEXT PAGE

143

SWANS A SWIMMIN' CONTINUED

By 9 p.m. Elaina has asked ten times if she can open a present, just one single present. Erik and Laura have asked the same thing twenty times each. We're listening to a mix of jazz Christmas albums, Mel Torme's *Hooked on Phonics* and Barbara Steisand's disturbing version of *Jingle Bells*. Mark shows up with shopping bags full of presents and a cooler containing exactly the right liqueurs and brand name elixirs to mix a trendy new Christmas cocktail called Rudolph's Nose. Mark says it's garnished with an olive, a cinnamon stick and a sprig of mistletoe. Erik adds "And a crumbled-up Little Debbie cake." Dawn checks on Elaine who says she is almost ready, why don't we listen to the *Hawaiian* jazz Christmas album that Wendy and Warren sent – it's called *Hula-day Groovin.'* Elaina busies herself distributing gifts from under the tree to totemic piles in front of all assembled.

It's 10 p.m. when Hamil discovers that bits of Crabbie Debbie can be molded into tiny snowmen with scarves of spinach. It's possible that if Elaine sees this she will attempt to serve a future batch the same way, maybe with caviar eyes. And if this one goes uneaten, Elaine will probably wrap it in foil and put it in her freezer, a virtual Smithsonian Institute of leftover scraps and crusts from meals of yore. Once, on our way for a three-night trip to Wisconsin Dells, we stopped at McDonald's in Eau Claire. The trunks of both cars were packed with one or two bags per each traveler, except for Elaine who had one or two bags for each day ahead. She hadn't only packed some evening wear in the event Howie's Big Breakfast Buffet had gone formal, but she had also packed seven different wristwatches so she could complement any mini-golf outfit she could assemble. She also had two smaller bags – which she called carry-ons in the hope that the Honda or Taurus would sprout overhead compartments – a garment bag, a grocery bag full of recipes she hoped she'd organize poolside, and a large cooler. We had a large cooler too, full of pop, and we pulled several cans from it to have with the burgers at an outside picnic table. And Elaine, who didn't want anything from McDonald's, pulled out from her cooler an endless stream of foil packets, foil swans that had been flattened, small plastic containers full of a bit of exotic this or a bite of once-excellent that. She had at least twenty-five differently preserved remnants, all coded so she could tell us where it was from and when. "This one," she said, "is from when we went to Sydney's on Mother's Day two years ago. And this one," she added, pointing to a stack of beet crescents on yellowing waxpaper, "is from lunch at Murray's, 1958. They always did such fun things with the beets. These were marinated in gin."

By 10:30 p.m. the ham is ready, the barge of cheesy corn is ready, the rolls are ready, Mark is mashing the potatoes, and Elaina is so ready, so wound up, she is sitting on the ceiling. For a while we all admire and discuss the felt and sequins tree skirt that Elaine made in the mid70s. It depicts the Twelve Days of Christmas, which is about how long we still have to wait for Elaine to join us in the living room so we can start opening presents before the spring thaw. Elaine likes the Twelve Days of Christmas just as much as the California Raisins, but who really cares? We want to eat and open presents and get home relatively early –like about 11- because Elaina is going to wake up at 6 a.m. I ask Mark to make me another Rudolph's Nose . . . and to Pinocchio-size it.

At 11:30, Elaine finally joins us in the living room, but before sitting down announces "Why don't I first get together some fondue? I think I have frozen beef in Paula's freezer. And you should put on the TV for that Dick Clark Christmas special." Laura

SANTA GETS CLOSER BACK PAGE

HOLD THAT POSE CONTINUED

says, "That ended at 10 o'clock and it's almost time for New Year's Eve at Times Square, so let's skip the fondue and open up presents."

Elaine quickly surveys the set-up, approves of the CD being played, sees that there's plenty of food, that everyone has a beverage, that everyone has some presents, that the inside door wreath isn't crooked, that the partridge atop the tree is straight, that all the Christmas bulbs are lit, that the felt and sequins tree skirt is still arranged properly, that everything right now and at last, is, as she nods, absolutely photo album perfect, which Mark already knows as he clicks away at us from in the hall. Though we're slightly off schedule – make that way off schedule – everything is right now rivetingly just the way you'd want it. An illuminated snapshot of a type of beautiful repast that only rarely has so many components working at once, ready for a feature in *House Beautiful*.

My mom continues to hum *The Twelve Days of Christmas* as Elaine, broadly smiling and thinking one hundred different thoughts about the cheesy corn alone, sits down for the holiday.

Note: After the service, when you look at the photos, you'll probably see Elaine at a dinner in Chicago in 1961. The entrée pictured is the very one that yielded certain leftovers that Elaine labeled and froze so they could be thawed on the way to Wisconsin Dells in 1996.

ERIK, MARK, ELAINE AND ELAINA
. . . OOPS, I MEAN DAWN

Mae, (nee Nickel) Elaine, 67, Richfield, died of emphysema on August 26. Preceded in death by parents, William and Gertrude Nickel and sister, Penny Hustad. Survived by children Mark Dreyer, Dawn Cassidy (Tom) and Erik Albrecht; grandchildren, Laura, Hamil and Elaina, brother Bill Nickel (Joyce), niece Wendy Hustad (Warren Dastrup) and great-niece Kara. Memorial services at 7:00 p.m., Thursday at Cremation Society of Minnesota, 7110 France Ave. S. Edina. Memorials preferred to N.C. Little Hospice, 7019 Lynmar Lane, Edina, 55435 or Pathways, 3115 Hennepin Ave. S. Special thanks to the incredible staff at N.C. Little Hospice and Allina Hospice for their loving care and to Ann Possis and Clyde Hanson for making Elaine's stay at N.C. Little Hospice possible.

Real Book / Fake Book

Every month at a spoken word series I host, I lead a round of Real Book/Fake Book, a simple, nongraded, prizeless guessing game in which I read aloud a list of book titles for the audience to judge as real or fake. Herewith a recent contest (real titles in this issue's list are printed in bold type, making it very easy for you, the reader, to win!) -

Austin "Psychic" Powers Predicts Tomorrow's Naughty Bits

Fire in the Turtle House: The Green Sea Turtle and the Fate of the Ocean by Osha Gray Davidson (EdHam)

From the Scenic Outlook the Battlefield Churns Beautifully by Thomas M. Cassidy (do I pay myself a product placement fee?)

Tiffany, Lexus and Colgate - 3000 Product Names that Are Also Great Names for Kids

my head was a sledgehammer six plays by Richard Foreman

A Guide to Western Civilization or My Story by Joe Bob Briggs

A Mad People's History of Madness by Dale Peterson

Wind Beneath their Wings – An Ornithologist's Look at the Role of Flatulence in an Eagle's Equilibrium

How to Teach Your Dog to Spit Instead of Slobber

Hooked on Smack or Phonics: The Different Ways we Fail Urban Youth

Gadzooks, I have a slick looking book with a color cover and an ISBN # and everything that just got released by Green Bean Press of New York City. Visit the **greenbeanpress.com** website for a slew of downloads by an offbeat catalog of writers. If you buy my book –Scenic Outlook – and write me that you did, I'll send you a profusion of thanks and an autograph you can copy.

THANK YOU!

DUE TO TECHNICAL GLITCHES THESE TWO PHOTOS DIDN'T APPEAR IN SCENIC OUTLOOK. AT LEFT IS MY DAD (ON FIDDLE) WITH THE RODEO RANGERS. BELOW IS TH WHITE CASTLE ON MAIN STREET, PASSAIC, N.J. WHERE I'M TRYING TO SCRAPE TOGETHER THE THEN-15-CENTS NEEDED FOR A SLIDER.

INTeRNAL ✗ RHYMe

THE 79TH EDITION OF HOW I'VE BEEN WRONGED, <u>WRONGED</u> I TELL YOU!   MUSICMASTER, 5136 LYNDALE AVE SO, MINNEAPOLIS, MN 55419

Chalk Team Artwork #5

O n the afternoon of Saturday, August 17th my Mom gives my daughter and me a ride downtown so we can do some chalkart on the sidewalk outside the Orpheum as a welcome to spoken word performers and fans who'll be coming to the theater at 8 p.m. for the National Slam Finals.

I mentioned the idea to Kay Kirscht, who, among other things, is a storyteller, cohost of the Verbose series at Acadia coffeeshop, artist, Community Relations coordinator for Minnesota's Fringe Festival, and the woman who encouraged us to first try chalkart for a July 4th event in 2001 (where we learned a lot, including that we should've brought kneepads and a broom, and that we enjoyed the process – the smearing/blending even painterly application of chalk – and the vibrant but temporary product). She said it was a great idea, did we have a permit? And being an old school punk who prefers foregoing permission altogether if there's a chance it won't be granted, I said, "No, it's just welcoming chalkart, not graffiti or paint, who could object?"

Kay said the Orpheum might or the police, and that she had gotten permits for all the chalkartworks she had lined up, including the one the Cassidy family

THIS IS SKETCH FROM WHICH I DREW MY OUTLINE IN FRONT OF THE ORPHEUM. FINAL ART WOULD'VE LOOKED LIKE THIS BUT COLORED IN, AND WITH THE COLORED-IN COLORS TEXTURED WITH STARS AND SWIRLS, AND WITH EVERY OUTLINED REOUT-LINED DIFFERENTLY AND WITH LOTS OF ADDITIONAL VISUAL CLUTTER. TO APPROXIMATE WHAT FINAL ART WOULD HAVE LOOKED LIKE, DRINK HALF A BOTTLE OF GOOD RUM, WAIT THIRTY MINUTES, RUB YOUR EYES REALLY HARD, THEN STARE AT THE ABOVE UNTIL YOU SEE THE SUBLIMINAL ENCOURAGE-MENT TO BUY MY BOOK.

most recently did outside of the Red Eye Collaboration for the launch of Fringe 2002 events. Seasoned pros that we've become with our coolers and sponges and highlighting chalks, that was our best one to date: a beret-wearing man in the moon, with the brush emerging from his smile painting a word balloon of stars on a musical stave, all above a star-populated city and a starfish populated river. Etcetera of course. My Mom colored windows, Dawn painted buildings, Elaina and her friend outlined and re-outlined stars and buildings so their shadowlines were three and four colors wide. Colorful highlights spurling and jagging about.

"LET'S INSTEAD LITTER THE TOWN WITH CORPORATE SANCTIONED LUCY STATUES COLORED IN BY HUNGRY HUMILIATED ARTISTS" CONTINUED NEXT PAGE

Kay got photos of it just an hour after we finished and just minutes before a downpour that washed it all away. She finally responded to my insistence to do a piece for Slam anyway by noting that maybe it could get done unnoticed, it being a weekend and all, no rush hour traffic on the street or on foot, and that she'd come down at 3 p.m. to help.

It's 2:30 p.m. and I'm surveying the sidewalk, deciding to apply my outlines on a space about 8' wide and 6' deep from the curb, so it isn't under the marquee per se and so the final product can be seen later by people in line rather than being under their feet (this position also mostly accommodating Kay's caution that Orpheum custodians might not like the chance that chalkdust will be tracked in.) (Ha! Like poets wouldn't otherwise track in anything unsavory, unwanted, unscrubbed! The tonnage of gum still hidden in seat folds from *Barney Live* is a popular, pre-spring cleaning bet among janitors, I bet. But I digress, and, in digressing decide I won't just get to work but . . .)

I decide to announce my intentions to box office personnel – not ask for permission mind you, but mention my presence in an upbeat context sort of implying my arrival on a schedule that certainly seems like an approved one.

"Hi," I say to the uniformed young man in the lobby window, "I just got here to start the chalkart outside, just so you know. I'm going to work from the grate to about 8' left of the grate, and from the curb to about 6' in, so people can see it tonight while in line."

Though the young man is smiling, his uniform (any uniform!) disarms me a bit, and I think he might tell me right here and now that I can't. Maybe his epaulets signify genuine power. I add, "Are you going to go tonight? Great spoken word artists from all over the country are going to be here."

"I have to work," he answers, still smiling – and not just smiling an usher's strained formality either. "But I might duck in later. Now, what are you going to be doing?"

"I'm doing the welcoming chalkart piece out front, out of the way. It'll all wash away first rain, probably tomorrow morning. I brought everything we need, so I want you to know we won't be bothering you for water or a broom."

My uniformed contact nods and smiles and says, "Well, sounds good." Which in turn sounds good to me because the episode captures my admission of intent, my announcement of chalkarting, so should we get threatened with handcuffs I can diffuse the whole thing as a misunderstanding by saying "Well, before I even began, I told the entry point people here what I was going to do." Which of course would bolster my artistic innocence, my kind belief that artmaking bespeaks an eternal type of innocence. Junk like that clatters in my mind because of all the caffeine and beer.

I step back outside and my Mom and Elaina announce that they'll hang around while I work, maybe wander a bit. I begin to sketch my outline, starting with a big, bulbous *SLAM*, three of the letters with opening mouths and teeth. Above that I box out *NATIONAL 2002*. I'm moving around quickly, half of the time on kneepads, other half just knees. Elaina wants to help so she starts heavily applying green in the *S*. I chalk in the *M* with red, start to smear it with a wet sponge, making it bleed and blend like watercolor. Several people smile and comment that it looks good. I tell them it'll look great in about an hour. Below *SLAM*, I outline over a dozen disembodied chattering heads – a chorus of the wise and the foolish, an army of wordsmiths and verb farmers, a legion of light, a cacophony of **ART!**

A voice behind me says, "You can't do that" and I turn to look up at a guy in dark pants and a black t-shirt with a chenille logo. He doesn't look goodnatured or remotely impressed with the very same chalkart outline that has already set the pre-

EVEN ART TO BE STEPPED ON IS UNACCEPTABLE

IN BECOMING TOO AGREEABLE, YOU BECOME LESS ESSENTIAL.

show passersby abuzz. He's holding a walkie-talkie and I'm wondering whether a chenille logo has more clout than boxboy epaulets. "I'm sorry?" I ask, no apology intended. He repeats, "You can't do that. You can't draw in front of the Orpheum."

No longer as quick as I once was, I ask "How come?" thinking he'll certainly suddenly see his lack of good reason and let me resume my work. "My boss doesn't want you to." I stand up and ask him who his boss is and he says Andy something, an artless name (a gratuitous, reflex dismissal, considering what an Andy Warhol fan I am). And this expressionless security guard is addressing me from a plane blander than just-doing-my-job. Whatever wit or charm I can muster will be underappreciated at best, possibly swatted. I decide to stick to the facts. "Well, you know," I say, "I'm sorry. It's just chalk; it'll wash away. But if we stop now, it'll just be this outline. If you let us finish, it'll look like a great, vibrant welcome to the Slam." It's true that I am one of those people who will take a mile if given an inch; but that's because I am also one of those people who doesn't always respect the power of those who get to decide to whom to give an inch to begin with. Smug bastards. I should've used oils.

Captain Sidewalk says, "You can't draw in front of the Orpheum." As I begin to rephrase my appeal, he doesn't even look at me like I'm a public nuisance (the nearest you can get to looking like an artist in the eyes of many authority figures); he looks at me like I'm stepped on gum. In an eerie mockery of a veiled threat, he acts like he's going to talk on his walkie-talkie again, to indicate to me that he's going to call for back-up if I don't just vanish. I hold up my hand (this move a tribute to a Looney Toons pause wherein a chase can be halted for a ham on rye) to tell him no need for backup from the boiler room or to call cops away from a murder investigation. He mutters something about having to clean it up and it occurs to me that that's maybe the total objection, that this guy only sees it as yet another mindless chore in a litany of routine rounds and perhaps there is no word from

on-high Andy, that this guy just doesn't want to have something else to clean up. "None of this is permanent," I explain (as if explaining every damn thing in the world at once), "It washes right away." Surprisingly, these words prompt the guy to wag his walkie-talkie even more seriously, like his patience with art is wearing thin. Since I can fully understand that state, I hold my hands up and say, "Okay we're leaving."

The guy walks to the intersection, crosses both east and north, and heads into an office tower

NO MORE HOPSCOTCH THIS WAY

FILLER - This is the third item I've submitted to MAXIM magazine's unintentional porn feature; a previously sent wrestling graphic was inexplicably ignored. The below book cover, though not remotely obscene, just struck me as having that rare great mix of surname, angle and viewpoint. I apologize to Hiscock.

IN BECOMING TOO ESSENTIAL, YOU BECOME LESS AGREEABLE.

BUT IT IS REPRESENTATIONAL ART! CONTINUED

next to a restaurant. I'm disappointed he doesn't look back to be sure we're leaving. What, the out-of-shape midlife crisis and his ten-year-old daughter with an arm in a cast don't look threatening? With the assistance of my Mom we could chalk the crap out of that bastard. Probably a toy walkie-talkie.

As we finish putting our supplies back in two shopping bags, Kay walks up with her hefty bucket of chalkart tools. "Wow," she says, "You've done a lot done already."

"Apparently enough," I say. "A security guy asked us to stop. You were right." We proceed to overtell all the details and generalities, and as my Mom says, "Well, he wasn't very nice," Kay nods at the great plight of making any art at all. We head home.

Kay politely answers all the permit-related questions I should've asked back when she recommended I get a permit. Maybe I'll see if I can get a permit from the City to do chalkart next month in front of the Orpheum.

Show the permit to that guy. Pull it out real slow to make him tap his foot. Watch him read the permit and reread it, watch him read the fineprint and check the date on his wristwatch, then watch him try to shrug for Andy over the walkie-talkie. Watch that guy apologize and feel so bad for not letting us welcome the poets and their pals that he handwrites each and every one of them a thank you note for believing in spoken words. And written words too. And the speaking about written words as well.

later

I should've pushed my luck and gotten arrested for showing that making *–donating!–* short-lived, soluble, upbeat art to beautify weathered, gum spotted, heavily-trafficked sidewalk slabs is a tough pursuit nowadays. I should've gone to jail for art! (Happy art no less.) But I don't have time to waste in the slammer – I'm learning how to chisel.

MINNESOTA STATE FAIR 2002 - FROM LEFT TO RIGHT: FEAR TO JOY

THE ABOVE PHOTO OF PART OF THE CHALKARTWORK WE DREW FOR FRINGE FESTIVAL 2002 WAS TAKEN BY KAY KIRSCHT. THE INTENSELY YELLOW HIPSTER MOON WAS DIFFICULT TO DRAW SIDEWAYS.

STATE FAIR 2002 CAPSULE REVIEW: GREAT POODLE CHICKENS! BUT I COULDN'T FIND THE UNISPHERE.

INTeRNAL x RHYMe

THE 80TH ISSUE OF WHAT IS ESSENTIALLY A GLORIFIED FLYER FOR MY OPEN MIKE SERIES   MUSICMASTER, 5136 LYNDALE AVE SO, MPLS, MN 55419

Write about to-do list

I have a *to-do* list so I can feel accomplished
reward myself by checking things off

of the twentysome things on my list every day
I always include an easy item or two
like *mail the bills* or *clean junk out of briefcase*
so I can always cross out something
feel like I'm getting something done
meeting a deadline assisting our boys overseas
I'm part of a taxpaying hardworking herd
that Remembers Pearl Harbor the Alamo the Embers
the drycleaning the prescription at Walgreen's
and has enough commonsense
to always write on a to-do list
make new to-do list

that every new list I make includes
make new to-do list is because I always start a new
   list
by looking at the one to be discarded
and I always carry that reminder over
which is great because as much as always I need a
   new to-do list
I don't think I'd otherwise remember to make one

that I ever put that down in the first place
years and years ago is miraculous to me
I mean I could no more live without lists now
then I could go outside without my pants my bowtie

my shirt (which bytheway is always on my to-do list
   too – it says *put on shirt and button it*
and I'm thinking of maybe adding a sublist to that
make up of a bunch of boxes to represent each
   button to be buttoned
and of course it wouldn't be anywhere near an exact
   correlation
just another fun way to check off several boxes
   quickly
guaranteed)

did I say there are twentysome things
on my average daily list? I'm sorry that's no longer
   true
there are more like forty or fifty let's say fortyfive
   average
but what I'm going to do is count the items
for the next week or so and come up with an average
   that's accurate

LIST ITEM #12: TURN PAGE OF INTERNAL RHYME

PLEASE CROSS OFF PAGE ONE CONTINUED

I'm going to add to my list right now
below a lot of already crossed-off things like
put on shirt and button it
I'm going to add *count the items on this list*
so I can get this project going immediately
up my average by one to possibly fifty-six
but I don't know for sure boy that would be a good
    item on any list
wouldn't it? – to have right above *make new to-do*
    list
know for sure
I'd love to check that one off just once

here then is a typical *to-do* list that
may or may not be an average size *to-do* list
I can get that number to you in a couple of weeks
but this list is average in the sort of items
I want to be sure to remember to do
to check off to reward myself for
to review for reminders of what to repeat
and I'll number them here too just for your
    convenience
so you know when one item ends and the next one
    begins
and because I'm currently
counting the number of items on each list

number one mail the bills

number two clean junk out of briefcase

three
read newspaper cross out headlines
blame advertisers for a war in Timbuktu

pick a fight with Dear Abby that idiotic bitch

make fun of letters to the editor
and by the way what the hell is the editor's name

number six
put on shirt and button it
button one
button two
button three
button four
button five
button six
number seven
remember the Alamo remember to breathe
remember the Maine remember the maniacs

pick up prescription at Walgreen's
allow thirty minutes to challenge and clear-up
    misring

number twelve
lower the boom stay the course
keep the faith up the ante
set down some ground rules
(which I cross off and replace with
list some ground rules
though the crossing off isn't that gratifying)

number sixteen
research ground rules

number seventeen
paint the television screen
with thick layer of flat white latex
into which anyone can scratch initials and
leave a written history
of someone other than Gilligan or Mitch Miller
or Skitch Henderson or even or Mr. Rogers who to
    me is as much a part
of the irreparable damage done to us / on us by
    television
as Kraft Macaroni and Cheese is most sinister part
of the evil served by Phillip Morris

PLEASE CROSS OFF PAGE TWO CONTINUED

breathe
and change the channel
to be sure it's still white latex

count the items on this list
and count each sublisted button

write a letter to the editor about Mr. Rogers issue

number twentytwo
write another letter to Dear Abby
and be sure to explain that I was not as she says
    fired for a bad attitude
whatever the hell that's supposed to mean
but for posting my list of things that were wrong
and repeat my original question
about freedom of speech
but more importantly
how can they fire me when they're not sure whom I
    meant
when I said *the morons in Human Resources*
I mean there are six of them there
so their assumption that I meant all of them
reflects a far worse attitude than I'll ever have

send copies of new Dear Abby letter
to the morons in Human Resources
address one
address two
address three
address four
address five
address six

twentynine take my pills

thirty add item to list to mail the bills before taking
    pills

crawl next leg of journey to heaven

submit idea for
Mail the Bills Before Talking Pills
bumpersticker to Walgreen's and TCF

thirtythree take extra
pills for good measure
take one
take two
take three
take four
take five

enjoy some quiet time

forty remember the Embers

find bigger list pad

wear a t-shirt tomorrow
but crossoff
sublist of buttons anyway

fortythree breathe

fortyfour know for sure

fortyfive
make new to do list

musicmaster labor day 2002

Gadzooks, I have a slick looking
book with a color cover and an
ISBN # and everything that just
got released by Green Bean Press
of New York City. Visit the
greenbeanpress.com website
for a slew of downloads by an
offbeat catalog of writers. If you
buy my book –Scenic Outlook
– and write me that you did, I'll
send you a profusion of thanks
and an autograph you can copy.

THANK YOU!

Things I did on Labor Day 2002

1. Committed holiday sin and did workplace work for two hours.
2. Visited with close friend on her way back to Chicago.
3. Bought thirtynine books from Half Price Books clearance section.
4. Thought about listing the titles here but have learned not to act on every crazy impulse.
5. Grilled burgers and dogs (terriers) for Dawn, Elaina, Mom, Mark, Erik and Trish.
6. Sent notes and copies of Internal Rhyme to about ten people.
7. Thought about mowing the lawn (but have learned not to act on every crazy impulse).
8. Made sketches for an idea I'm developing for a show at Gallery 360 next May.
9. Watched bits of Jerry Lewis telethon and was surprised at similarities with telethons from decades back. Norm Crosby doing same jokes.
10. Attempted to demolecularize with limited, perhaps indiscernible results.
11. Made to-do list for tomorrow.

I DREW AND ASSEMBLED FROM CLIPART THIS OVERSEMINARED LEASING AGENT FOR AN APARTMENT MANAGEMENT COMPANY IN THE LATE 80s. IT CIRCULATED SOMEWHAT AND GENERATED MOSTLY GREAT, POSITIVE FEEDBACK FOR SPOOFING FAKEY SMILEY TRAINED-SEAL AUTOMATON HABITS, BUT I ALSO OCCASIONALLY RECEIVED FURIOUS COMMENTS ABOUT MOCKING GOOD BEHAVIOR.

POWER WINK

POWER PERM

POWER DIMPLE

POWER NAPE

POWER PADDING

TIME TO RENT!

Quality
WE NEVER MISS

OVER 2 BILLION LEASED

YES!

I ♥ RENTING

PERKINESS

MEGA SUPER You

JUST SAY YES!

ANOTHER BOOK

MEGA-SMILES

SELL ME A SUBMARINE

"CLOSE"-MINDED

OOZING SINCERITY

ULTRA-SELF

I'M GREAT, YOU'RE OKAY

ZEN to ZILLIONS

YOU-NESS

JUST SAY ABSOLUTELY!

THE 1 MINUTE SECOND

sign here

YOU'RE THE # 1 MOST SPECIAL-EST PERSON EVER!

POWER SINCERITY♪

MANY UNSHARPENED PENCILS STILL WRITE   (MORE BLUNTLY?)

PARTS OF THE BOXED HELIUM DELIVERY GET LOOSE

NOVEMBER 22, 2002

INTeRNAL  RHYMe

THE 81ST RELEASE OF THOSE IMPRISONED IN MY BRAIN'S BASEMENT

MUSICMASTER, 5136 LYNDALE AVE SO, MPLS, MN 55419

The Deseasonalization of Endcap Branding & Other Satanic Rituals

(The pieces in this issue are the first installment of another long complaint against marketing talk, commercialism, big business lies, concurrent self-delusion and some odds and ends that always seem to arrive just in time to muddy up otherwise clear stanzas. I write and gripe about this stuff often because it surrounds us so much and so insidiously that to not aggressively swat at it is contrary to my survival instinct. I wish I heard Venusians in my brain, but I don't - I hear ridiculous jingles which, alas, nowadays sound similar (at times identical!) to anthems, gospel tunes, rock&roll and heartfelt folk. We've already sold so many souls or so much of all of our souls that to not shout back at the blaring billboards, to not gripe about the forcefed vocabularies that make us talk in tandem, seems like acceptance of a predamnation plan that sure looked and sounded good on the big screen, but, you know, now that it's taking over the house and chewing on the brain . . .

The real question, of course, isn't *Can you afford to have a good predamnation plan?* but
*Can you afford **not** to have one?*

One more note: The opening *Fanfare* piece is, depending on the line, both too clever and not clever enough, but if it annoys you, please skip ahead to Part II where I start accelerating and feeling steadier. I'm including Part I because I know it belongs and it won't let me shake it; when I ultimately assemble this entire group of pieces into a chapbook, I will lock myself up with Part I until it tells me what I want to know. I have the President's permission.)

I. fanfare

I'm disappointed in you you're
    just like the identical twin you never had
      a day light and a lie ahead no good plain ensemble
     you should've ignored his poems about
      redundancy syndrome
       all five volumes of them

      you didn't think we'd investigate
       because he's such an awful poet?
     you can't kill even an awful poet
    without a squeak from someone
   someone he stalked with sonnets leers ago
still thinks that he's a genius because
he made her think his words were only hers

but when she heard that you killed him
by telling him his poems were not without interest
that it was nice for him to have a hobby
that a beret was on its way

COME ON! THERE'S MORE INSIDE!

she only cried a nanosecond
then laughed and said you shouldn't worry
that you didn't kill the man she loved
but only what was left
I shouldn't bee talon you this

she said though they used to be good
meaning his books that his books
used to be about someone (meaning you-know-who)
that no matter if the judge throws
the poet's last five books at you
that they are like wiffle books
plastic and nothing
in
side

I'M SORRY THAT "IN SIDE" TAKES UP TWO LINES, BUT I HAVE MY AFFECTATIONS

I hate to let a time bomb go
what's next? some little tridents
at the presidential banquet
but without a rich spouse I ain't got much
so this time artboy
you lucked out
sprung by madness plot convenience
stain town in case
I need to ask about
those awful things he rote

he used to be much different
she said but then the bottle
and the Queen's English started balking
the battle and the sniping and
the high tea and the ivory tower
started with the cheerio crap
and it's not that he lost it
so much she said as that
he became convinced
that he'd found it
and from that line on
his ideas just flogged
every this and that
already there

his output grew into outages
as he gradually
dumbed it all down / smarted it up!

with those careful
peckinpahs
tern ink his few kindnesses into points
his kisses into lessons
his poems into takes
I said all five volumes of them

II. you can die all you want for the same low price

okay now I have some good news and bad news
first the bad news is that full of chaos
He with a capital H never directly responds to
   anything You ask
but the good news is that He answers unasked
   questions
with earthquakes earthworms tumbleweed
   wildflowers
hexachlorophene tea leaves abstract art and
woodpeckers pecking Morse code
and by the way
whether He directly responds to You or not
why the hell can't You
ever talk to any of Us about
Your last life
back when You with a capital Y
were something else or someone else when You
convulsed like a rabid minnow
in a sleek new flooded convertible trench
all Him insideout I mean
You know what I mean right?
not that You'd ever come back to this
on purpose but out of curiosity about
Who is looking at You from the mirror
and how many times do You have to die
to really get the service You're entitled to
to really be dead
dead the way you want dead to be
dead with all the perks and all the privileges

III. since we're neighbors, let's eat shit

state department officials say that
it isn't a matter of *if* some terrorist
will poison our water
but *when*   MORE NUTTY GOODNESS NEXT PAGE!

smartass columnists write
it isn't a matter of *when* our young people
will indict all of us
but *how*
Everything Decent shouts
(not very loudly though
he's not very big)
it isn't a matter of *how* media
will change fact into money fiction into money
laughter into money love into money hope into
   money life into money water into money joy into
   money war into money peace into money prayer
   into money but
how often

and the consumer I mean *The New Consumer*
who's savvy sassy sexy and smart
who has her priorities straight
who's hip to the new tube the new box
the micronite filter hexachlorophene and three
   scoops of raisins
parades right up to the camera
so it looks like she's talking directly to you from
   inside the television set
that's the New Consumer I mean well she says
it isn't a matter of *how often* state department
   officials
will yap and clap like trained seals
but *where* the hell did they sell their souls?
and can you get a good personal trainer there?
and did they get a good price?
and did they have to steamclean
or delouse their souls before selling them?
and do you think they'd mind
if I use them as a reference?

and I say it isn't a matter of *if* I think

but *how*   ?
but *when*   ?
but *why*   ?

(why think at all
it's so much work to lose the loafers
tie the laces

live without the clever lines
it's so much work to learn
and look for what we've lost
in someone else's eyes
to hope for things that won't cost cash
but will cost comfort
it's so much work to stand upright
to slug the bad guy in the jaw
or to remember that we shouldn't
it's so much work to be wrong about so much
Long Live Dada
we'd have to be stand-ins for dust
to be of less use to others
to this planet to the unconnected dots
to our stupid pets
to the revolution any revolution
including a sassy sexy and smart orbital
stagger around energy and heat and light and
oh what the hell
if I knew what I wanted to say
I wouldn't write)

(convulsing rabid minnow my convulsing rabid ass)

there are so many plugs and so many wires
and so many overloaded power strips
(and believe me I wanted to write power trips there too
but I didn't because writing isn't always
fun&games you know sometimes it's just a matter of
   deliberately
making one bad decision after another)
that I don't know where
I'll ever find a socket into which
I can stick my thumb or tongue
I am so upset I am so upended
I am so foreign that there's not a nation nearby
that ever posts a *Tom Spoken Here* sign
I am so sorry for getting wrong whatever it is that I got
   wrong
I am so out of touch with how to communicate in even
   ordinary situations
that I think that
the only way around a whole lot of day-to-day situations
is to not take words spoken as having anything to do
   with

LOOK FOR TOM'S BOOK AD NEXT ISSUE!

I HOPE THE NEXT INSTALLMENT HAS MORE PICTURES CONTINUED

with what their utterers mean
but
to just take them as useless clues or
tryout sounds for landing a job as a noisemaker

(and I know I'm knowing nothing new here
and that lately I haven't been writing a hell of a lot
better than I did in high school when I at least
forced ideas to rhyme but
in my defense
I do nowadays know that nothing really rhymes
unless you make a payoff or two
or get a phrase to squeal or a word to lie and
a line to say . . . a sweet goodbye
a line to say I gotta cry
a line as straight as ham on rye
a line that wails I wanna fly
a line without an alibi
a line alas that isn't shy
a line not worth a better try
a line evoking apple pie
a line that drags in Louie Nye
a line bedecked with suit&tie
a line just back from Tenafly
a line that hangs you out to dry
a line which warrants no reply
a line that makes a loner sigh
aligned with lines that never lie
a line which begs the question why
a line with which you bait a spy
a line that smacks you in the eye
a line with all that lines defy
a line to wait in my oh
me . . .

I am sorry great big pretentious promiscuous opiated
bankrolled blurb-swapping flamekeeping and
    flamethrowing realdeal word warriors
I'm sorry I skipped 1,552 classes
but I had to go to my uncle's funeral)

I think therefore iambic
(see what I mean? I only wrote that because I could
not because it means anything useful
like *look out for the falling piano*

or *in my life immediately past I was a trained seal
    with the State Department*
but in my defense
it sure beats *let's do lunch sometime* or *how's it
    hanging* or *I'm sorry I'm unable to take your call
    right now*)

)I'm glad I'm unable to take your call
I'm sorry I have to take your call at all
I'll get back to you as soon as ass-saving protocol
    dictates(

hey if you can't kid around on our collective deathbed
when can you?
when the nurses and doctors and visitors are dead?
no matter how weird things get
you have to brighten your spirit
you have to have a good sense of humor
you have to keep your sunnyside up
you have see the silver lining on the mushroom cloud
you have to listen for the good news
so when you hear that final broadcast
that says the rockets red glare
is going to micronize hexachloronate
and three scoop all of us in the next ten minutes
you can smile and say
maybe so
but come on people
that gives us ten minutes to think happy thoughts
to share why we are thankful
and to not worry about fat grams

)close your own damn parentheses(

it isn't a matter of *if* I'm going to snap . . .

but *which* special free introductory no obligation
    consultation is going to be the last straw
I could give a pickled crap about your
insurance deals mortgage rates annuities timeshares
sassy sexy and smart no money down lifestyle
    investment options
and I will never write with the pens I take from you
but
I listen when you warble 'cause increasingly I wonder
which line's
the line that means you're going to die

A COMPLICATED GAME OF DICE

DECEMBER 3, 2002

INTᵋRNAL 🎲 RHYMᵋ

THE 82ND TOSSING OF CRUMBS, WHICH, IF FOLLOWED, LEAD TO ONLY HERE

MUSICMASTER, 5136 LYNDALE AVE SO, MPLS, MN 55419

The Dᵋsᵋasonalization of ᵋndcap Branding & Othᵋr Satanic Rituals

The following pieces comprise the second installment of the above-titled complaint against a number of business-mangled concepts and wishes that are too often warmly extended betrayals of not just societal good, but the remaining air itself. - Wow, that line had a lot of luggage! - Issue 83 will contain the (shorter) final installment and then I'll get back to poems about puppies that aren't selling health insurance and cute kids who aren't just part of the marketing mincemeat. You are probably getting this issue with issue #81 because the piece reads best in one big plunge. Mostly because there are repetitions and cross-references (and things which may be symbolic of other things I can't express or spell) that work most effectively when they're tailgating one another. Clarification: The concluding pieces, which will be in #83, aren't burdened with such artsy affiliations, spins or redundancies.

IV.

special country wake-up good time caring

her hairstylist uses so much hexachloraphine
that Pollyanna's ears grow tiny brightwhite teeth
her friend's bestselling book *Tom Spoken Hear*
is made up completely of stories Pollyanna had
   shared with her
confidentially
her mailman delivers only the letters A through F
so that all that comes her way is mostly incoherent
   but graded nonetheless
her chiropractor breaks her back
her masseuse snaps her neck
her plastic surgeon restaples her with such ferocity
   that
her eyebrows tickle her ears
her paperboy brings only bad news
her goldfish is starting to swear

while charging her $150 an hour her therapist makes
   fun of the fact that
she sees her cure as simply a money issue
her self-defense instructor splinters her nose
her priest joins the Boy Scouts
in a rare attack of follicide her hairdresser
shaves off the eyebrows that strike through her
   temples
her dentist drills a hole through her tongue
her locksmith ends up losing his main street kiosk
   and working for WalMart
her cobbler ends up losing his apple and working for
   WalMart
her plumber ends up losing his pipes and working
   for WalMart
her baker ends up losing his interest in Napolean
   and optimists and working for WalMart
(you wanted me to write *her baker ends up losing
   his dough* didn't you you convulsing minnow?)
her door-to-door poodle groomer ends up losing his
   place and running around the neighborhood
   yelling *My God I've lost my place and I don't
   know anymore from which address south on
   Lyndale whose poodle might be unkempt* and
   ends up working for the FBI

PUSH YOUR COURTESY CART THIS WAY!

OPEN A NEW ACCOUNT TODAY AND GET 20% OFF YOUR NET WORTH!
CONTINUED

her accountant screws up her taxes because he lost a
   pinkie in a freak accident
her best friend resigns
her accountant screws her best friend who is a
   bestselling priest at WalMart
her golden retriever invents some bogus story about
   a third-grader eating his obedience school
   homework
the poet she once loved dies in freak accident
   involving
a beret a dose of hexachloraphine and a trained seal
   with the State Department
and everyone else in the whole world sends her a
   card that says
Thanks for Nothing
now you can imagine that she is feeling as low as
Satan's welcome mat so she eats three pounds of
   chocolate covered amphetamines
shoots her canary one time in the heart
and five times in whatever the hell the remaining
   feathery mess is
then goes on a shopping spree in which she gets
   everything from
collectible disposable diapers to tissues that play the
   Star Spangled Banner

FOUND POEM

WEEK OF APRIL 7th.

THINGS TO DO.

1. Paint jars , get oil paints.

2. Get red dye.

3. Material to comer bench.

4. Window shelfs.

5. Red Material

6. Ruffling for Bulletin Board.

7. Decals

8.

---

from a shower attachment for the birdbath to Homer
   Simpson rosary beads
from a lime-flavored chair to a plutonium powered
   toothbrush
she gets everything *and everything else* in the
   whole world
that money can buy though she doesn't use money
oh no
she charges it all because her charge card *credits
   her*
with a donation to the local school
points for air travel
and smart consumer bucks that can be used for
   everything from
hairstyling to massages
to halfprice holes through the tongue
at WalMart's dental clinic

V.

**they ask me what's right for me
and that's important**

this poem is sponsored in part
by our good friends at Target
well it isn't really
but Elaina gets a lot of clothes there and
Dawn swears they have the lowest prices on
what she calls household meaning detergent
paper towels and IBC root beer
and of course I think they're big evil self-satisfied
marksmen who have placed targets squarely on the
   heads
of consumers because of a lot of stuff
I can't get into here because believe me
even though this isn't much of a poem it's even less
   of an essay
(but two quick jabs
one –
when several years ago Target went thumbsdown
on rebate deals it claimed that eliminating related
   paperwork
would help keep prices lower than
the rebate deals could offer

THE POETRY YOU WANT AT THE PRICE YOU DESERVE!

NEW T-SHIRT IDEA: FAITH-BASE THIS!

WOULD YOU LIKE FRIES WITH WHATEVER THE HELL IT IS THAT YOU ORDERED? CONTINUED

that Target could serve us better
by protecting us from discounts
from outside the store
two –
after being part and parcel of relentless drive
to keep kids stylish to put a lot of fashion crap into
    their heads
and on their feet to brand their butts and shirts with
    ads and logos
they then joined the drive against the trend
against the playground posturing against the stupid
    fashion crap
by selling cure-all uniforms
but not *instead* of all the crap but *in addition to*
so they could market both the problem and solution)
and the reason this poem isn't really
sponsored in part by Target
but sort of is is because
even though they often treat me like a
    chuckleheaded cipher
a dartheaded rube a ravenous duffelbag a citizen so
    lost that I will find faith
and community in discounted detergent
discounted IBC root beer
they have given me lots of material
Absolutely Free (with qualifying purchase)
they have given me common denominators
I never would've known existed
let alone embraced without their guidance
without their neighborly pre-WalMarting
    pre-emption

of proud Main Street shopkeepers
and
they have given me an imported generic
    hopelessness
at such a good price –without the hassle of a
    rebate!-
that it doesn't seem all that hopeless afterall
in fact
I might get two

even having written that I push their cart
and
because Target knows there are grouchy stand-up
    shake&bake writers
all over the store in the uniform of the nondescript
all the wheels work fine

(*and I helped*)

VI.
let your fingers do the stalking

I'm unable to answer the phone right now
but your cliché-riddled ad hoc tickertape is very
    important to me
so at the beep please leave the following information
1. your social security number your bank account
    number your date of birth your estimated date of
    death your license plate number your high school
    locker combination your email address yahoo
    password and the name of the card that you
    yourself picked from the brand new deck that you
    yourself unwrapped at the Magic Castle's Close-
    Up Card Tricks Festival in May of '85
2. the time date general point specific intent hidden
    meaning and ulterior motive of your call and so
    that I know you are someone I can trust with
    further conversation please slowly and clearly
    articulate my dog's maiden name
3. the range of a good time to call you back that can
    begin as soon as you'd like but must continue to
    at least five years from now in case something

TURNING THE PAGE JUST MAKES GOOD SENSE . . .
AND MEANS MORE FOR YOUR MONEY!

AT LAST! - THIS PAGE FREE *WITHOUT* PURCHASE

BARBIE CLAUS! CONTINUED

unexpected comes up like my being abducted by
the very same aliens who turned you into a lunatic
4. your card is the four of clubs; it isn't? let me try
again; your card is the queen of diamonds; it
isn't? let me try one more time; your card is the
seven of spades; it isn't? well I am in state of
complete confusion; listen why don't you put
down the receiver go to your refrigerator and pull
out that old box of baking soda way back on the
bottom shelf and you're going to find handwritten
on the bottom of that box "the six of diamonds"
which - you don't have to nod - is the correct
name of your card

there was never any confusion
you never had any choice anyway the only miracle
is
that you fall for this crap you don't have to leave a
message
I knew you were going to call for crying out loud
you're still dazzled by card tricks

you should know better than to give a fifty-one-
year-old man
the time of day – as if he could do something
meaningful with it anymore

and by the *wake* the question isn't *can you afford to
rhyme*
the question here is *can you afford **not** to rhyme*
when
it's about attitude it's about family it's about you

it's about pretending there is a community to which
you can give back
when you know that it's really about money people
let's face it
I'm not going to lie to you here
the bottomline is we're in business to make money
and as soon as poetry starts to make money
turns laughter into money love into money hope into
money life into money water into money joy into
money war into money peace into money prayer
into money
we'll all be in the moonJuneprune business
pissing ink curlicues and acting impressed
by seagulls and how well you describe
a night of stars
without ever feeling obligated
to leave the planet at all

we're often lazy laggards in this loop
we're in the loop this loop where little comes to life

p.s. hey
thanks for the heads-up on that rhyming thing

AT WHAT RATE WOULD JESUS REFINANCE?

CUBIC'S RUBE

DECEMBER 23, 2002

INTERNAL RHYME

THE 83RD ARGUMENT ABOUT WHY A WAR WITH IRAQ IS A BAD IDEA

MUSICMASTER, 5136 LYNDALE AVENUE SO, MINNEAPOLIS, MN 55419

THE THIRD, FINAL & MERCIFULLY SHORTEST PART OF

The Deseasonalization of Endcap Branding & Other Satanic Rituals

Herewith the third installment of my hollerin' in the mall voids. With all or several of the previously printed parts, this thing reads very well aloud, legs and arms aspin to keep up with all the buckshot. I don't know that it works as well in print, in here, as, say, a nice endcap display, rebate offer or SUV ad that makes your chest swell with implanted pride - so you might want to first knock back a beer or two (skip the *or* crap, make it two or three; wait, skip the *or* crap again and make it three). That's what I'm doing (and just so you know I got the lingo right: *That's what I'm doing - 24/7!*)

VII.

they laughed when I sat down to stay
it's about truth
it's about friendship
it's about letting the world know that you've arrived
it's about knowing *where* you've arrived let's face it
it's about staying fresh
it's about security because it's no longer just a matter
of a good sound system it's about family
it's about keeping fit
it's about pushing your own limits
and being sure that Todd Junior over there doesn't
it's about the smile you've always wanted
and the lifestyle you deserve
no really I mean it
it's about fighting for what you believe in it

it's about trust you suspicious bastard
it's about news you want you narrowminded hick
it's about community you co-op kissing shareware
tithing Commie
it's about value you cheap son-of-a-bitch
it's about security because it's no longer just a matter
of a good sound system oh no it's about a sign on the
lawn
that means there's an alarm a visible surveillance
camera and

a good sound system that sleeps soundly
it's about clean air at an economically sustainable
level you lung-kissing idiot
it's about pushing the limits you un-American
recycling cheapskate rulebusting bozo
no really I mean it
it's about fighting for what you believe in so long as
fighting means getting huffy and weepy on talk
radio about goddamn right I'm proud

it's not about anything
it's about making as little a difference as possible
it's about working more for folks who need no more
it's about eating whatever the hell the cow snorts
it's about how much or how little beer it takes to get
you to get God
it's about being your own boss when it comes to
bagging leaves

FOLLOW THAT RAMBLER THIS WAY

snarling at coworkers saying you like Leno over
  Letterman
it's about crap in a can and crap in a seminar
and crap in the corridors of power
it's about healthy kids you can screw up
it's about feeling your heart get slugged like a
  punching bag
it's about waiting for every word to mean something
  different than it used to
something worse
no really I mean it
it's not about fighting for what you believe in
it's about fighting to stay awake to breathe to get by
  to believe in any of it at all

it's about diamonds and oil and sweat and jails
and the mummification of the poor
and the damning of the brilliant
and the killing of people who hope and dream
and laugh and weep and see the same stars out of
  different windows
it's about bigger better stronger leaner meaner
  companies
with cool names and real estate interests on the moon
it's about respecting others out of fear or ignorance
it's about choice providing the choice has to do with
  whether or not you want processed cheese on
  your burger a regular Coke or a Diet coke a one
  way ticket to traditional hell or a one way ticket to
  new improved hell with hexachloraphine
it's about getting straight and staying straight
with the blessing of pharmaceuticals
no really I mean it
it's about fighting for this much just this much peace
  and quiet
it's about fighting with demons god-tamers robots
  bullies who grow up and become bigger bullies
  shadows gravity know-it-alls and no-nothings

it's about time we wrapped this up
I have to get up early for a meeting about marketing
and it's going to be about - well you know –
everything because *it is* about everything
everything is
it is about everything
and friendship and truth and working together
it's about caring

it's about lending a hand
it's about the ass-turning bust you've always wanted
it's about making a million with no-money-down real
  estate so you really can change the world any way
  your limo-riding heart desires
and somehow it's about what we do with images and
  words
in our little design department that doesn't want to
  be little
or even limited to design anymore
and I'm sorry this is so long but
it's about 1:45 in the morning
and because it really is all about
fighting for what you believe in
in this case what *I* believe in
I'm fighting to go to sleep
and I'm fighting to stay awake
and frankly I'm fighting for fighting's sake
because it's the last security system I've got
between me and the awfully peaceful
outside
. . .
where
it's all about a newer healthier better sexier clearer
  smarter
happier kinder friendlier warmer funnier bigger
  sturdier prouder tastier sharper
crispier cheaper cozier smoother easier holier brighter
  simpler safer
heartier fuller faster
(deadlier)
void

VIII.

dying ain't so bad with these pains-off coupons
he says to me that the bottomline is
do I want my family to continue to live
in the style to which they've become accustomed
if I die which flatters me because
I've never ever had anything to do with any sort of
  style
anywhere at all and certainly no one else's
I tell him that *if I die* (and I emphasize **if** as per his
  lead)
my family couldn't possibly continue to live in the
  style

BRAIN IN A JAR CONTINUED

to which they've become accustomed
because if nothing else they've become accustomed
   to me
and he says that the bottomline is
could my family continue to pay the mortgage
the gas the electric the water take the occasional trip
when I die and believe me
I'm as shocked as you are that the
if I die has become *when I die*
and I answer that if I die
and then I correct myself and say *when I die*
so he knows that I'm hip to the fact that he's been to
   sales seminars
that deal with problem nonconsumers like the still
   undead me
I say *when I die*
I want my family to weep uncontrollably
for weeks not just a day
I want them to be inconvenienced by all the baffling
   nonsense in my wake
I want them to tell everyone that I was as mad as a
   rabid minnow
and not win a screwy death benefit jackpot
so they can take the occasional trip without me
for crying out loud and
besides I tell him
if we pay the premium he wants me to pay
our current standard of living will go down a notch or
   two
because of that expense and
the fact is that I have a better track record investing
in books and odd duck art then these underwriters
   can ever post

so my family *after wearing black for a decade or two*
can pay all the bills by selling my stuff
at a brilliantly extravagant profit
and he says that the bottomline is
will my family really be able to sell all my stuff
at a profit not yet known or will they have to burn it all
   for heat
and friends let me tell you that *that* really angered me
so I said
listen
that was your third bottomline
*your **third** bottomline*
you only get to give one bottomline
I was having a good time thinking about death and
   money
specifically your death and how I'm not going to give
   you any money
but you've ruined it all with that salesy crappy
windup reflex vocabulary thing
so I'm not going to play anymore
but I do have some advice
that won't cost you a monthly premium
go home tonight stay up real late
go outside and stare at the stars
make up your own constellations
and keep staring and keep staring
and keep staring
and when the sun finally starts to rise
crawl around in your dew-coated heart
and look for one
just one
only one bottomline   *musicmaster 12/02*

YOUR STORY IS AS MISERABLE AS A BEWILDERED AND UNNATURAL SAINT

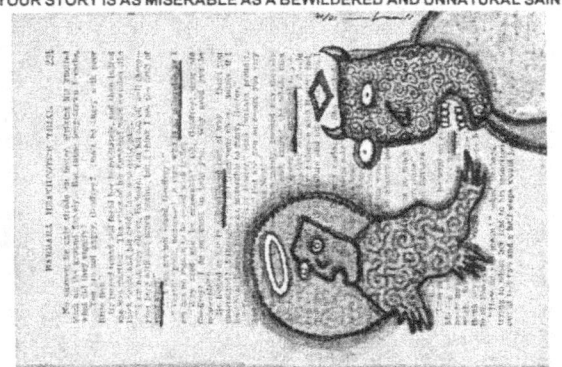

THE DUMMIES GUIDE TO WRITING POETRY IS IN AISLE THREE (THIS MAY NOT BE A JOKE)

THREE POEMS

I'm walking home in twilight
and every car that passes me
contains someone I know
or someone I once knew
though I can't see inside the cars
I wave anyway
and the drivers and passengers
and conductors and dogs wave back
someone says to her companion
*that's the guy who thinks representational art is
redundant*
or *that's Tom the poet who thinks that rhyme is a
river in Germany*
one of them gives me a lift to school
another takes me to California
another runs me over
turns around
and runs me over again
still another drives me to work
and during the ride we discuss
art and God and how committee meetings
are really just opportunities for grown-ups
to work through self-esteem issues
one of the drivers
is long-dead surrealist poet Robert Desnos
who only waves because of demons in his eyes
one of the drivers is long-dead German composer
Robert Alexander Schumann
who has a gutted piano strapped to the roof of his
Volvo
and one of the drivers is you
and when I tell you I'm a poet
you smile and say *Wow*
that's only a career move in a nursing home
and when I ask you for your name
so I can put you in a poem
you smile and say *my name is June*
and I say *on second thought I'd better walk*
■
on my fifty-second birthday
I email a reporter in New York leads
for an article he's doing
about the apartment market in the Midwest
I try to make ordinary business calls
entertaining and offbeat but my efforts are ignored
I edit several articles scan photos and compose two ads

for the magazine I also assemble
I microwave canned soup for lunch
and garnish it with a chunk of sausage
from a Hickory Farms holiday assortment
given to the entire staff
I spend the entire afternoon doing
work related things on the computer
chasing my mouse my personal rodent
through window after window
of information that even at this stage in my life
won't help me become a pirate or an astronaut
or Rin Tin Tin
I go out for a good Mexican dinner
with my wife my daughter and my mother
and though they don't sing Happy Birthday to me
I know that they mean to because
my daughter asks *how long do we have to stay at the
bookstore?*
and because it's my birthday that's where we go next
where ignoring anything connected to housing
or how they shear the sausage at Hickory Farms
I browse peacefully and carefully
for books about people who become pirates after
retirement
and for an autographed first edition
coffee table book about
those stupid candles that always light back up
■
if I could drive I'd drive
a big wide black convertible
with fins propellers a foghorn
my bumpersticker stating
real men don't haiku
I'd floor it I'd take turns so fast
I wouldn't be in the other lane the wrong lane
I'd be on the wrong road
up on two flaming wheels maybe one
somedays I'd crank the bastard up
so hard so far so loose so tight so impossibly holy
that I'd take off
I'd get up above the highway
drive through clouds
not designed to be drive-thru clouds
and aim straight for the screaming hell-hot
save-you-from-crashing-into-rocks
lighthouse sun

musicmaster 12/02

26 PAIR OF HAUNTED REEBOKS TAUNT THE SHOE CLERK

SEPTEMBER 1, 2003

INTERNAL RHYME

NUMBER 85 IN A PUBLICATION JUST BACK FROM ANOTHER HIATUS   MUSICMASTER, 5136 LYNDALE AVENUE SOUTH, MINNEAPOLIS, MN 55419

low goals

(Holy smokes, I originally wrote *low goals* in 1991 as part of a trilogy about grating salesmen. The other two pieces, which celebrate the wonder and why of copier salesmen and insurance hawkers, I still "perform" today. But this one - which I remember reading a few times back in '92 or '93- I haven't even seen in a folder or reshuffled boxes of scripts in years. So, to get me back into releasing *Internal Rhymes*, here's an issue primarily dedicated to a slightly cleaned-up/ updated *low goals*. Not "cleaned-up" in the most commonly understood way but in the other way. About which I understand little. More about many of the fun adventures we've enjoyed since January [I break into a Visitors Center on vacation! I have a bunch of art shows so I make a truckload of art - or is art still sold by the gram? My Mom, Elaina and I perform at FringeFest!] in future issues which, I promise, won't get this offkilter again. At least not until the next time I get **Waylaid by Art Itself! Stricken With Inspiration!** Or by a lapse into laziness.)

I told him that I do not get financial stuff
that the little that I do get doesn't stick
but because he is somehow someone
with whom Dawn is familiar I said
I guess he could come by if he insisted
sure he did so here he is to help us plan
all kinds of things involving life and death

a nodding church in suit & tie &
tasseled leather loafers with prophetic jokes
and bobble-headed harmony
he's talking about savings and investments
conservative risk annuities securities
relativistic baccarat and IRA rollover
sit and shake and sign right here

Dawn politely listens even asks a question
now and then like she's Venusian too

I'm stupefied by how little I know
how easily known the things I don't know
seem to be I just can't get
the crystal clear that others get
without struggle like
the points behind a lawn a suit a job
the words this guy sets sail in Gulf Stream tide

though I think I look comprehending
with nods here and there
I must look perplexed because
he asks me if I have a question
and I do I have a few
about Etruscans Chappaquiddick
Dora Maar Stonehenge
who really wrote Spoon River anthology?
why do birds suddenly appear
every time you are near?

LOWER GOALS JUST AHEAD

GOAL TENDING CONTINUED

but I don't ask these he won't know
instead I say that money's hard to get for me
I joke by adding *I have to work for it*
that like I told him on the phone I do not get
financial stuff I wasn't kidding
I find investment strategies impractical ways
to best embrace the future
that buying intangible goods
underwritten in large part by whim and wham
of society best described as disoriented
seems risky to me I mean afterall
economic abstractions make Jackson Pollack
seem like a hyperrealist

and as I continue to talk
I notice that financial planner guy
who looks like he's looking at me
isn't paying attention at all
his yawning pores and snoring brow
are rolling with my gestures his eyes
lock and flow with every flourish of fingers
I move my hand left and
his pupils follow like tethered dogs

he probably isn't listening
to a damn thing I'm saying but
half of the time neither am I

Dawn asks the guy
can you explain the opt-out
on an R2D2 form via worksheet rider 3?
and as he answers I pretend
I'm in a Twilight Zone episode
wherein I win a hundred mill
and hire financial planner guy
to stabilize it for me
keep it safe and let it breed

he says he will and gives me
a ballpoint pen an emery board
and a pocketplanner which amuse me for years
while unbeknownst to me
he steals squanders
DEstabilizes MISbreeds
loses every single dollar that I have
and just before I get wise to it all
one of his long-forgotten schemes
by total fluke pays off a million-fold
overnight he undoes all the damage
sets things straight and healthy wealthy too

after the final commercial
oblivious to his misdeeds
I fire him because he can't get me refills
for the ballpoint pen
we cut to Rod Serling voiceover
cartwheeling in my ear
like Dawn who saying it like she's saying it
to a recalcitrant parakeet says
your art collection has value too now
doesn't it?

IF IT LOOKS LIKE A LOON, HAS THAT FAMOUS LOON GAZE, AND WALKS LIKE A LOON PAINTING BEING CARRIED BY SOMEONE, ODDS ARE IT'S A LOON CONTINUED

well sure it does I say
to the right collectors
financial planner guy looks puzzled
so I offer nutshell history of
antiart ending up in art museums
and of course the nutshell's very big
including comments on
my extensive collection of
aesthetic ephemera to
the importance of Duchamp
to people who like Thomas Kinkaid

and I notice that again
his lowbeamed eyes fix on my hands
I make an exclamation with a wave
and his eyes follow
I doubt that anything I say
is more to him than his talk is to me

but he's a pro and wants to keep awake
and so he says *I own a wildlife print*
a beauty too a loon out on a lake
it looks so real it's great
this blows a fuse inside my head
but I just smile and wonder how
a bird that's flat rendered one-tenth size
on quiet dry water
same time and temperature for eternity
can strike anyone as real
and when I try to picture myself
I mean as a picture
it's not representational at all
it's a twisted hailing sound of chalk tea
and a cobwebcovered bonfire in the basement
if you know your stuff he adds *that's great*

but we put a certain amount of money
into life insurance too
my wife carries about
three hundred thousand dollars worth
and I have several policies totaling
(I admit it might be more than average)
fortytwobillioneighthundredseventysevenmillion
twohundredthousandandnine but
I do have he pauses *high goals*

aware that I do not
at least not in this competition I cough
try to guess if our fourmonthold daughter
wants me to buy
bigger better thicker shinier coverage
the adviser guy's indulgent smile
suggests we're mishandling
not just the baby but the full
ramifications of death itself
that I need less mirage and more map
that I shouldn't let tomorrow get to me
before I get to it
and he responds to my distracted mulling
a common side effect of low goalism
with subliminal nods
at least I think they're subliminal nods

I finally tell him that he's right
oh what a wretch I am
that I do not get financial stuff
I barely get how grapes dry into pickles
how poems shouldn't be short stories
with punctuation disorders
and as I continue to ramble here and there

FOLLOW THE BOUNCING BALL

FUNNY IDEAS FOR HUMORING MYSELF CONTINUED

I notice that again he's zoning out
watching every movement of my hands
I lift or drop he won't let go
I make a squiggle in the air
his eyes roll right along it
my hand is a baton conducting him

he might be fully hypnotized
I think he's out says Dawn
I make a circle round his face with open palm
his eyes roll like their Ferris wheels
until he slumps and snores
let's get to work

we dress him like a hobo
mess his hair up smudge his cheeks
splash him with whiskey Mr. High Goals
with nest egg plopped from butt of Death
drag him out the door and to the lawn
leave the whiskey bottle with him
Dawn calls 911 and explains
how this maniac won't go away

how he's terrorizing us with papers sure to cut
threatening us with our futures!
he is totally nuts
probably on something!
looks like he might be drinking
because she looks slightly concerned
I tell Dawn *hey don't worry*
he's the only person on earth
who has coverage for something like this

she says *we'll look it over*
thanks for coming and I snap too
staring at his outstretched palm for several seconds
before shaking it saying *yeah thanks*
Dawn adds *I think I understand*
that R2D2 rider worksheet now
and I nod and smile in agreement
my head a sort of wind-up toy
on nights like this

MUSICMASTER 1991; FOUND, DELOUSED,
AND TOUCHED-UP AUGUST '03

MINNESOTA STATE FAIR 2003

THE PHOTO AT RIGHT WAS TAKEN BY THE SAME "CRAZY MOUSE" RIDE PHOTO MACHINE AS A PHOTO I RAN IN INTERNAL RHYME AFTER LAST YEAR'S MINNESOTA STATE FAIR. THAT PICTURE, WHICH INCLUDED EIGHT OR NINE MORE PEOPLE, WAS TITLED SOMETHING ABOUT THE LEFT TO RIGHT PROGRESSION OF ABJECT FEAR TO TOTAL JOY. THIS YEAR'S PHOTO IS CALLED "TWO OF THESE RIDERS CALLED IN SICK TO BE HERE." THE PHOTOBOOTH PIX BELOW FEATURE ELAINA TRYING TO ECLIPSE SURROUNDING PLANETS.

THANKS TO BILLY MCKAY FOR THE BOX-HANDLER'S CAPTION TOP OF PAGE 1. NOW WHO WILL WRITE THESE THINGS?

INTERNAL  RHYME

MATCHING TOWELS

A key preoccupation during this past year's long hiatus from cranking out *Internal Rhymes* was getting together a show for Minnesota Fringe Festival.

If you want to know more about this or other Fringes and the history of the whole shebang, start surfing, because there's a ton of info online about this city-to-city theater/performance event which brings out the best of the avant-garde, spoken word, and theatrical communities as well as the best of the worst and the oddest of the best and everything else between the delusional and the sublime.

If you want a quicker zeroing in, visit fringefestival.org for the scoop on the Minnesota chapter. I'd rehash the impressive stats here (something like 83 billion

(Sung to the godawfully uneven melody *Take Me Out to the Ball Game*; last line gun-in-your-pocket joke is a salute to our state's recent passage of a pro-conceal and carry law)

Take me out to the Fringe Fest
Let's go join the art geeks
Actors and comics and singers who bomb
Communist jugglers and somebody's Mom
For it's root, root, root for the edgy
Stuff that will make critics cringe
Where the Un! Bi! Tri! folks come out
To shout *We're the Fringe !*

Take me out to the Fringe Fest
Let's go see the art freaks
Transgender puppets and Psychic Slutz
Plenty of swearing and some naked butts
And it's root, root, root Minnesota
The arts underbelly by chance
Where we know you're glad to see us with
Your gun in your pants!

shows in 10 days including family-friendly versions of de Sade) but want to leave room for nonfiller content.

I will, however, prolong this introduction by printing the reviews my Mom and I received for "The Hanging of Pollyanna," a show we performed five times during the August 1st-10th Fringe. Mostly a staging of me reading poems (yeah, I know it sounds exciting), my music stand was flanked on one side by my mom at a small table of props, which she occasionally used on cue, and on the other side by her hairdresser, Jay Birulkin, who is allergic to cues and who tried to dissuade incoming audiences by playing mandolin favorites that were standards in the 1920s. I can't describe it much better without it seeming even more confusing and less entertaining, but trust me, it was fun to do and audiences loved it and especially the cameo slot of daughter Elaina leading the audience during a seventh-poem-stretch rendition of "Take Me Out to the Fringe Fest" (lyrics at left). Also, my son Hamil directed it (e.g. "Okay, let's try it again and pretend we have cues.") Anyhow, here are the reviews audience members posted about our show on the Fringe's let-the-mobs-speak page:

- **Holy Crap! That's good fringe! (5 stars)**
  Tom Cassidy takes on the school board, insurance guys, New Jersey, the work world, and mass transit with his mind-boggling wit. Tom's mother, and her hairdresser, accompany him on stage and sporadically interrupt with perplexing and hilarious commentary. His daughter joins the act to lead the audience through a fringe anthem, and all the while, Tom leads the audience through

PLEASE HOLD YOUR APPLAUSE

Daddy, Don't Draw on My Official School Photo!

AND OTHER 2003 ARTWORKS
BY THOMAS M. CASSIDY

Cheap Very-Limited-Edition Prints, Original Drawings
on Pages Pilfered from Old Books, and Drawings Done on:

- Postcard Announcements for Other Shows
- Catalog Covers
- Staff Meeting Agenda and
- Miscellaneous Mail/Bills/Photos/Paper/Wrappers

Give the Gift of Compulsive Scrawls! All pieces $20 - $30

October 7 - November 4 at Anodyne

43rd & Nicollet, South Minneapolis

(No reception but I'll be sitting around Anodyne Friday October 10, 7-9 p.m. with
coffee and markers and will gladly deface any common scrap of paper you bring by)

a charged and thoroughly enjoyable hour. This show is a MUST SEE.—*John A.* (Posted on Aug. 6)

- **Tom is Really Good at This** (5 stars)
People should be clamoring to see this show because Tom Cassidy is a really good writer and a hilarious performer. His imagination is completely untamed and his persona is unapologetically contrary. He is the real deal and may be the least sold-out person (with talent) whom I've ever encountered.—*Erica C.* (Posted on Aug. 7)

- **Side-Splittingly Funny** (5 stars)
Tom is brilliant, honest, and funnier than any well-paid comedian. I haven't laughed this hard in ages. There should be 10 stars for this show. Inge and her hairdresser were just frosting on the cake. Don't miss him next year, I know I won't.—*Gia D.* (Posted on Aug. 10)

- **Frenetic, Sincere, Gorey** (4.5 stars)
One minute he's just a guy standing there. Within an hour, you feel you know him. And he's hilarious, but he's insane. He suffers, but he almost likes it. And things deeply annoy him that never bother you. But you get it! (It's like hiking with your best new friend who is talking after way too much coffee—was it laced with meth?—Yet every word is making perfect sense and you're laughing 'til you trip over rocks.) Weirdly, it reassures me that people are good at heart, but Tom Cassidy would NOT agree!—*Tricia G.* (Posted on Aug. 6)

- **From an accidental fan…** (4.5 stars)
Cassidy does it again. I saw Cassidy last year and appreciated his rapid-fire delivery, his hilarious mother, and his enthusiastic daughter. This year, Cassidy added Jay, the mandolin player, to his family-infused cast. Jay must have been particularly sleepy the night I saw them, he yawned through the performance; which only added to the comedic atmosphere. Cassidy's poetry selections, rantings, and musings were both funny and insightful and his delivery alone is worth the price of the ticket. I only wish Miss Plaskon were in the audience; maybe next year.—*Laura E.* (Posted on Aug. 12)

- **Big Things to Say** (4 stars)
At first I wasn't sure what I had gotten myself into. A loud, curmudgeonly man who flails and has Big Things to Say? But I warmed up to Mr. Cassidy as the show progressed and everyone got more comfortable. Each piece is a rapid-fire series of vivid images and witty asides and ends with a fervent crumpling of the text. I loved the piece about the stamp and coin store, and the one about The Corporate Bookstore (and The Great American Blank Book). I loved how Jay sat stage right with his mandolin, looking mostly uneasy, and well as

the outbursts from Cassidy's mother. A fun and funny show with the right mix of cynicism, poignance, and sing-along.—*Ariel D.* (Posted on Aug. 7)

- **Wonderful Wacky Curmudgeonly Fun** (4 stars)
A mother who rings in with comments, musical mandolin breaks and energetic and evocative story telling make this an extreemly entertaining hour. You feel you have been invited into Tom Cassdy's family and as you leave you only hope you'll be invited back again. Don't miss it!—*Amy H.* (Posted on Aug. 6)

Okay, enough bragging. Afterall, we still lost money on the whole egofest . . . but isn't that what all art is always about anyway? Oh yeah, ideally, artists should lose other peoples' money!

Anyhow, one of the new poems I read as part of our show was written in July during a family vacation to a lakeside cabin in Hayward, Wisconsin, a place that mixes away-from-it-all scenery (loons in paddleboats, beer lakes) with tourist traps (a Fishing Hall of Fame where YOU get hooked, deer with restaurant tattoos). Other stories about that jaunt next issue. I wrote the poem as a love-letter/crazyperson's letter to Dawn, my partner of 16+ years. She is kind, smart, warm, loving, and everything decent and compassionate. I am her biggest flaw. And in this poem I tried to cope with her bizarre world of nice vocabularies and nice thoughts. I prefaced the piece by saying "Now she won't keep saying 'Why don't you write a nice poem about me sometime?'," because I always try to blunt any nice edges that might slip into my work. And, now, half-an-issue later, the featured poem . . .

MATCHING TOW LS

she basks and beams in flannel sheets
smiles to cool lick of breeze and sunset
is conscious of every fiber on her body
every second sugar salt and surf
stretches to fit space comfortably
several times a day she fluffs it up
cracks her neck is addicted to lotion lipgloss
backrubs things just so and so just so
she can sense a headache days away

SEE? A NICE POEM; NOTHING CRAZY . . .

WHAT REALLY HAPPENED IN DALLAS CONTINUED

she likes pillows puppies pastels
photographs of family members blocking
beautiful views
every nice thing you can think of and
I mean nice in kindest way
babies both happy or sad
carefully prepared hors d'oeuves
afghans earmuffs decorating hints
dragonflies flurries slippers quiet
and me
her dark unshaven ranting
halfdrunk halfassed side
latticed with splinters
it hurts me when write
many of the words I just wrote
my fingers burn from typing **puppies!**
and **fluffs it up!** help me my God
I wrote thought and said **fluffs it up!**
and only 'cause of her
will I say **snuggle!**

now say *cozy!*

now say *cute!* without goddam before it
I've only been massaged once in my life
because it was hippie foreplay
I am a godforsaken testpilot in someone else's body
thankful there are only two wrong ways to wear a
tshirt
I am woebegotten waybesotten wouldbe poet
basement dwelling packrat of things that might make
sense
you have a million things some people say
and they are crazy clearly I have only
sevenhundredfiftythousandthreehundredtwentytwo
not counting her
the one who combs her hair
and dreams things she can tell
I love her in the only way I can
I love her madly
and unfluffed

MUSICMASTER 7/03

PERFORMING SQUIRRELS

the hotel charges more to clean a shirt
than I'd pay for a new one
and over the bed is an original artwork
that isn't original or artistic
and that you can decipher the signature
borders on demonic
there are four glasses in sanitary sleeves
imprinted *for your convenience*
as are small bottles of shampoo and conditioner
and bars of soap exactly the size
of wallet photos of your kid
after you cut down the big sheet
of your kid staring at you
too many times at once

and if you want room service
you have to get an inheritance
thirteen ninetyfive for a one topping pizza
a three dollar service charge
a 20% pizza tax a 6% small bottle of shampoo tax
plus a 17% gratuity
and if you want to sleep
you have to take a trip back home
because through the pipes the ceiling and floor
through all six hundred and sixtysix walls
you hear the other guests
loudly argue swear and grunt
about the meaning of life

MUSICMASTER 7/03

THANKS AGAIN THIS ISSUE TO ARTIST BILLY MCKAY FOR THE BOX-HANDLER'S CAPTION TOP OF PAGE 1.
SEND A BUCK OR SMALLPRESS/MAIL-ART TRADE TO HIM AT P.O. BOX 542, N. OLMSTED, OHIO 44070

october 18, 2003

INTERNAL RHYME

THE 87TH INSTALLMENT OF MY BELIEF THAT PRINTING MY OWN STUFF IS THE SAME AS HAVING MY STUFF PRINTED

MUSICMASTER, 5136 LYNDALE AVE S, MPLS, MN 55419

I resurrected the following piece (which I loudly, proudly and flailingly read throughout the 80s at the drop of a hat) for our recent "Hanging of Pollyanna" show at the Minnesota Fringe Festival. I've always hated dogs that were genetically mutated into petite furballs of DTs, but wrote this complaint only after a labor camp co-worker, Norine Shaw, responded to an unkind crack by me with a story of how she herself had just gotten a small dog. Yes, as always, the tale is true. And I'm happy to announce that Norine herself showed up for one of the Fringe Festival revivals of this fully warranted attack on . . .

Little Dogs

we're having lunch, sizzling diet fat sugar planks

and *It* gets to me - the microwave pouches slaughtered hogs

kindly old cows getting slabbed into barbecue pits

while the dogs unleashed and pampered

are championed by owners of rotisserie

I say **I can't stand little dogs**

little neurotic dogs

little shaking bug-eyed hybrid ceramic congestive heart failure dogs with fur chewed through on bony spine

the kind that sit in teacups and make them rattle

little earthquakes of not pitifulness alone but wretchedness despicableness unholiness

splotchy restless loaves of leech membrane and whine

naturally it turns out that Norine got one of these *exact same* beasts just yesterday

complete with papers shots the cutest little bow

but for all the fancy pricetagging and pedigree

the damn thing *still shakes like it's going to hatch*

and of course its eyes secrete neurotic-small-dog ooze which she has to see the vet about on Thursday

I hope the little trouper pulls through I lie with unspoken curses

and add **well Norine is it just the cutest thing this side of moist-nosed maggot or maybe not-as-cute? does he have a sweatsuit yet or just a romper? are you going to have a baby shower or what?**

happily oblivious to my by-now apparent dislike for such atrocities

Norine explains how her life has changed

how she hasn't had a dog in sixty years

and I frantically pray and make all kinds of arrangements with god that *please please don't let her tell us what she named it*

I know it's going to happen anyway it's an inevitable no-win hurl into the pit but dear merciful doggie heaven god please make it quick and painless

maybe I can get her to keep the discussion brief by politely restating my position so I interrupt with

MUZZLE YOUR RABID MUTT

175

ILLEGAL CHIHUAHUAS IN CALIFORNIAN TEACUPS CONTINUED

Norine I hate little dogs I'm sorry Norine I don't like them at all

(which I figure is maybe a nicer way of expressing my hate)

and she sweetly laughs and gives me one of those I-used-to-feel-that-way-too looks which really infuriates me

but I contain myself pretty well snap a microwave dish in half and continue **I'm sorry Norine but they're like the stump of a real dog**

and they always have some freak disposition borne of crossbreeding or inbreeding or god-knows-what-the-hell they have to do in a petrie dish to make a miniature terrier

I mean the subcompact furball model like a Bonsai sheepdog a poodle niblet a Schnauser named Shotsy

and they always have spitty little toys – and that's okay because big dogs have spitty little toys too (and even I have a few spitty little toys) – but, I'm sorry Norine

little dogs have spitty little toys that squeak with more authority then they do

these creatures go through such mental anguish just remembering how to breathe with their little doilly gizzards that they can't bark they can't even quietly and slowly pronounce the word 'bark'

I shake my head trying to picture something terrible enough to overtake or match my cruelty here

Norine says **you don't have to be sorry Tom I saw him and fell in love with him and I didn't know what to name him at first**

no ordinary name seemed to fit

my forehead begins to throb I pretend to choke on my sandwich

I swear if she says that she named the damn thing Precious or Bitty or Fifi or Shotsy I'm going to sling a chair through the window

I thought about naming him after Eddie Cantor or Wicker because I like wicker

some really good reasoning there Norine

but then I thought he's so precious just so wonderfully precious really there's no other word to describe him

oh great oh dear God please don't do this to me please don't allow something like this to happen

so I clapped my hands and he ran across the room to me hopped into my lap and I officially christened him Perk

I'm startled and stunned and look around for help I sputter

Perk? what the hell is that? short for Percodan?

it's a little dog Norine it's a trickle-down dog a pygmy dog
a cocktail wiener

do you know that when some of these things crap they lose

half their body weight? you need one plastic bag to clean up and another plastic bag to make an oxygen tent

Norine says she meant the name to be like a job-Perk a perk to the job of living why?/ what did I think it should be called?

BARK UP THE NEXT TREE

CUJO-ETTE CONTINUED

and instead of being awful and saying Smog short for Small Dog

or Parry for Parasite or just name the boondoggling beast Kickball

I kindly unwind and sigh about whole world going goony

I count to ten and explain the plot without sleight-of-mouth

it's a tiny bowser Norine people will watch it sit on a pillow the size of a teabag and say oh isn't that precious somebody will watch it hump a housefly and say oh isn't that precious isn't snook'ems precious Norine you're **supposed to name** *the damn thing Precious*

oh **Tom** she smiles **you're only saying that because deep down you know that Perk is precious**

deep down you know you're just a pussycat

deep down you don't really mean any of the things you say and this is like the second nicest thing that's happened to me this week

first little perk and now the deep down you

I shake my head in disbelief I didn't know she could be so cruel

I feel a growl unravel in me/widen/crawl up my throat and bark

I bark and bark and pounce and bite deep down and don't let go

musicmaster sometime last century

art coron r

(Recently found the below drawing with a heap of others I did for Pacific University's Mr. Cogito magazine in the early 80s; I don't recall what I was illustrating unless it was the typical crucifix-skewered fetus in bed parable. Drawing at right by Alan Vandenburgh, one of just a dozen Californians who asked for popcorn at the election recall ballot box.)

four crappy littlE poEms

1

I'd rather listen to a child
flushed with excitement
eyes wide as coastlines
mangling an old joke
babbling about a dried out starfish
telling me how to tie a shoe
then listen to a poet
syllable-up a sabbatical to some ruins
with personal tragedy
the routined awe of a beachcomber's high
and visions never willing
to restack the stones

2

we are short a set of towels
so the innkeeper brings more
and I thank him
saying I am proud to again be among
those with towels of his or her own
and that's how I say it too
with the his or her own thing
and he smiles at me kindly
says well of course you are

3

at breakfast
a retired heart surgeon
who's usually pretty quiet
and serious all those bloody tides
suddenly smiles and brags that he shoplifts
at Fred Meier's
never anything big or valuable
he says just batteries gum
a can of tuna fish
he's been doing it for years
I ask him what kind of gum
and he says
it doesn't matter
I just want to get back at the bastards
and though I don't know if he means
the bastards at Fred Meier's
the batteries bastards
or the gum bastards
I know what he means

4 - the expresso bus

the roll of the bus has an undertow that
makes the good worker fumes-driven
the best worker exhausted same thing
that turns a perfect bus riding pyramid
into river rock or a poem by Shelley
and I think that this is true because during
the course of eighty million trips on the bus
I've seen riders soften erode even dive
(all our bodies dragged uncertainly forward)
into part of the hiss and screech of the brakes

musicmaster at rest

CAUTION: THE WORLD IS OUT TO GET YOU

(There have been deaths, totalled cars, unexpected derailments, cases of beer, Ebay travails, a botched root canal, and other funny goings-on since issue 87. But if I attempt to explain it all or even a good chunk of it, I will again grind to halt, as I've done several times over the past many months. So I will just start anew herewith and tap the big gap for stories/poems as a more sane schedule dictates. Oh screw the sane schedule - as the beer dictates.)

(I wrote the following piece right after the big winter meltdown, on one of those "spring in the air" days which, in Minnesota, means you gain more "feels like winter" days in June.)

INSIDE THIS ISSUE

BARNEY GOOGLE ESTATE SUES TECH GIANT FOR $171 MILLION

CLINTON'S "MY LIFE" IS BESTSELLER! IF "IS" MEANS "IS"

NEW, IMPROVED NOW-FREE IRAQ SIGNS DEAL TO PROMOTE ONLY COCA-COLA PRODUCTS; AL-QAIDA CLAIMS INNOCENCE - "WE ARE NOT DOGS!"

WAL-MART OUTLET TO OPEN IN YOUR BASEMENT

March 12, 2004

in the melting snow on our meridian
I find a UPS delivery slip
with all inked clues smeared off
could've been for us or a neighbor
a birthday present
a package of those13-gallon
white-plastic kitchen garbage bags
or a javelin

I pick up Tess Walker's VISA card
I should try to let her know
(from my Ritz Carlton suite in Zurich)
the unexpired card's in perfect shape
under grit of sand salt dead macadam cells
tinsel from Christmas

The *Antique Trader's* April 21, 2004 cover article discussed the need to get kids interested in hobbies and collectibles as the number of younger collectors in most categories has been dropping. The idea is a good one but the photo (right) illustrating the commentary is not. The yawn-provoking caption reads "Kids get to craft their own mini jugs at the Red

Wing Collectors Society convention." And just look at their nap-time expressions. I think before you try and get kids interested in what you're interested in, you have to have a a bit more training then simple old-fartdom requires. A better caption would've been "This is where I used to get my finger stuck."

I find a sticker from the garage sale
we had last spring lots of trash
a cigarette lighter a marble a red pen
it's like that junk drawer in the kitchen out here
I collect the litter that cars shed
crushed cans and wrappers
enough cigarette butts to glue together
into enough Lincoln Logs to build a cabin

it's so sunny and warm that
there's just one real pile of snow left
and because it's part of the very snow that snatched
  Tess Walker's purse during a blizzard when no one
  can see what snowmen grab from drifts
I look at it and wonder what's inside
could be sunglasses in there a kickstand
the first dead robin of the season

the pile looks like and is the size of
a 13-gallon white-plastic kitchen garbage bag
filled with crumpled up birthday wrapping paper
and of course that *is* what it is
I must have just brought it out
I blink and squeeze my mind I look again
and no it's *not* a bag it's really
the remaining pile of snow on our meridian
melting and yes I do confuse this with that

JOIN US NEXT PAGE FOR MORE ON THE MERIDIAN!

The World's Best Open Mike is held the first Friday of every month (at 8 p.m.) at the Twin Cities' Best Coffee House - **Anodyne, 43rd & Nicollet, Minneapolis** (612-824-4300). Tom Cassidy is your Best Host! By the way, the first Friday is the Best Friday! The Best Month is the Month That YOU Show Up! 8-minute performance max! Be fast, be fun, be brilliant (and, in 8 minutes, be over)! **Join us for Real Life Must-See Un-TV!**

CURB YOUR CREDIT CARD CONTINUED

but when I remember that the missing package
couldn't possibly be a birthday present for anyone in
  our house
because all of our birthdays are months off
I feel almost awake again
my head thaws in unexpected spasms
the icicles that built up along my hairline over the winter
snap off and acupuncture my shoulders
up and down the avenue neighbors reappear
with the preseason bugs

and way down the block
I see the first Anderson of spring
pick up a pretty big branch from his meridian
mistake it for my javelin shake his head
then realize it is just a branch afterall
I can hear winter packing up shovels
I can picture Tess Walker somehow tracking me
  down in Zurich
I can feel another year slapping me
just hard enough to get my attention

musicmaster 3/18/04

By the way, I still have Tess Walker's business card. I held it up at Patrick's Cabaret during a July 9th performance to prove the truth of my tale. I then, apparently, dropped it offstage because it was returned to me by the stage manager at the end of the evening. Now I'm wondering whether or not Tess herself was the one who lost it near/on our meridian or was it someone else, maybe another poet, who had previously found the card elsewhere and had it out during a reheasal on our meridian? This would minimize the likelihood of Tess ever tracking me down in Zurich.

The next poem also takes place on the meridian. I'm not kidding. What are the odds!? I doubt that I've used the word meridian more than once in all previous Internal Rhymes combined, but here and now, in this comeback issue, not only are there meridians to be mowed all over the pages but there are TWO poems anchored in meridians! And I've learned at least ten different ways to misspell meridian. Man versus Man, Man versus Nature, Man versus Meridian! Let the other writers get weepy about romance and the ailing globe - I'm going to tackle the meridian - that demilitarized zone between house and hell.

doing somE work in thE yard

it's been so wet that even though I mowed five days
  ago
I'm mowing the front again
and most places twice because the weight of the
  wheels
both crushes and saves longer stalks
this time through he said menacingly but I'll be back

inside of the noise I hear a smaller noise
like a faraway canary on helium
it's possible that the recent rains unearthed
the remains of Howard the canary
from under the evergreens
and somehow his little skull got sucked up
into the big metal lawn mower dome
where it's tumbling around in fear
but somehow also playing with a tank of helium

I mow around the nonworking lamppost
and look up and down our busy street
and inside the rush hour lawn mower noise
I hear the growing sound of a bus full of rehearsing
  sopranos
being mauled by rabid dogs

now they do let seeing eyes dogs on the bus
but the odds of a dozen of them
turning rabid on the same bus are slim but
you know mass transit is a cabinet of curiosities
and singers are everywhere it's like there's an
  epidemic of singers
anything is possible the cars pulling over

I see an ambulance and fire trucks coming
so I look at our house to make sure it's not on fire too
because maybe
while they're in the neighborhood anyway
they could put it out
turn off their damn sirens for a minute

I wonder what it's like to know the siren is for you
and I know everybody thinks this too
is it hopeful or frightening does it blur into a doorway
a church or prison do you see the newsreel
of your life in the ambulance or when you get
  downtown
and my God it's such chaos out here
I think my head is on fire

JUST FOLLOW THE FIRE ENGINES

INTEREST IN INTEREST RATES LESS INTERESTING THAN INTEREST IN INTERESTING THINGS

CANARY SKULL UPDATE CONTINUED

they're coming to put out my head
they're going to throw ladders against me
and run through my brain to yank out the living

FOUND HUMOR-
I loved the underscored Please return on the first page of
this paperback about reincarnation:

YOU WILL
LIVE AGAIN!

for a few seconds when the emergency vehicles rush by
the howl of their sirens and the roar of my lawn mower
blends into a passage by Wagner

I wonder if people in the cars that slowed down
noticed what a good job I'm doing here
back and forth over some spots to get that
    headnoddingly nice
evenness that can soothe the passing citizen
I wonder if they had originally thought anything
about heliumated canaries
or a heatseeking ambulance aiming for them

as I mow over the sidewalk to the meridian
an across the street neighbor catches my eye
he's wearing a gardening uniform as he talks
with his carefully crafted flowers
he returns my turfbuilder smile with a shrug to indicate
that he thinks Wagner is okay but not always
    appropriate
though he does have a dwarf willow
that thrives on low E flat
he gives me a green thumbs up
before dropping back into a furrow

the grass on the meridian seems thicker and longer
than it was on the lawn maybe it's evolved
to thrive –like we have- on exhaust and sirens
but instead of staying here and going over it twice
I just keep mowing a single path

across the driveway through John's meridian
across the next driveway one single path
all the way downtown
crossing streets and negotiating trees
get to Rome and be done with it
screaming canaries in tow
let everyone on Lyndale see
that even though my head is on fire
I don't need an ambulance
unless it's got a cooler full of beer
I don't need the 18S with the
rabid seeing eye dogs and all those singers
I just need to get some yard work done
so I can finally relax
tuck Howard back into his cereal box
order the helium

MUSICMASTER 7/04

When I shovel through files, sort papers, separate coupons and junk mail from drawings that took me weeks to complete, I often come across a few items I thought long-ago misplaced or tossed. This picture -one of the first drawings I did after entering the legitimate workaday world in the early 80s (after a post-college decade of working in a bar and having two wonderfully half-assed money-losing stores in Portland)- shows me being cleansed of the music-serpent by the tough-loving staff of commerce. I continue to put the windows/boxes in my drawings. Someday I will color this picture then bury it somewhere so I can find it again for Internal Rhyme 362.

AUGUST 30, 2004

INTERNAL RHYME

NUMBER 91 IN THE SHADE

MUSICMASTER, 5136 LYNDALE AVE SOUTH, MINNEAPOLIS, MN 55419

the world's greatest athlete

(NOW THE TRUTH OF THE MATTER OF THIS POEM IS THAT IT DOESN'T REALLY MATTER BEYOND WHAT IT CONCOCTS HERE BUT, FOR THE SAKE OF THE TRUTH SURROUNDING ANY IMPORTANT HISTORICAL RECOLLECTION THAT MIGHT BE HEREIN - *SUCH AS MY WINNING A TIDDLEY WINKS TOURNAMENT!* - I WANT TO NOTE THAT MR. PALEOGO WASN'T THE COACH'S NAME BUT RATHER, *I THINK*, THE NAME OF A MIDDLE SCHOOL SCIENCE TEACHER. HOWARD STILL KNOWS THE NAMES OF EVERY TEACHER, SUBSTITUTE TEACHER AND HALL MONITOR WHO EVER SERVED ALL THE SCHOOLS HE EVER ATTENDED BUT IF I START FACTCHECKING WITH HOWARD A FEW THINGS WILL HAPPEN: 1) IT'LL TURN OUT I'VE BEEN WRONG SO MUCH AND SO OFTEN THAT MY CHILDHOOD WILL VANISH AND THE POINT ABOUT COMMON STORIES WILL HAVE BEEN TRAMPLED BY SPECIFICS AWAY FROM ART AND INTO SCIENCE (NOTE THE PALEOGO EQUATION); IN MEMORY, THE COACH LOOKED SLIGHTLY LIKE CHUCK NORRIS BUT THIS WAS ALL YEARS BEFORE CHUCK NORRIS BECAME ICONIC SOFTY KILLING MACHINE; 2) HOWARD - NOW A CPA - WILL ALSO CORRECT MY ENGLISH AND MY MATH AND TRY TO SELL ME FINANCIAL PRODUCTS OR SCHOOL REUNION CLASS PHOTOS; 3) HOWARD WILL TAKE THE REQUEST AS ALSO A SOLICITATION FOR MATERIAL, FOR ALL OF HIS FOND MEMORIES OF CAREFULLY APPLYING CIRCULAR LICK&STICK REINFORCERS TO EVERY LOOSELEAF SHEET IN A BINDER OR HOW HE OPERATED HIS OWN DOW JONES OF BROWNIE POINTS IN JUNIOR HIGH. SO, SORRY, I USED PALEOLOGO BECAUSE OF HOW GOOD IT SOUNDS ALOUD. ALSO, MR. PALEOLOGO, WHO WASN'T REALLY MR. PALEOLOGO, DIDN'T HAVE US THROW SOFTBALLS AT A RUBBER TIRE BUT, IN FACT, FOOTBALLS. I DID GET THREE FOOTBALLS THROUGH THAT RUBBER TIRE AND PROBABLY COULD'VE GOTTEN THREE SOFTBALLS THROUGH SO IF THERE'S A TRUTH-EMBELLISHMENT MOTIVE HERE IT IS TO DOWNPLAY AN EVENT A BIT TO INCREASE THE EFFECTIVENESS OF A STORY, NOT TO LIE IN THE TRADITIONAL SENSE OF, SAY, NOT TELLING THE TRUTH, BUT IN THE NEO-TRUTH WAY OF TELLING THE TRUTH WITH ARTFUL DISREGARD FOR THE FACTS. OH THE HELL WITH IT ALL. THIS ISN'T JOURNALISM, IT'S THE FINEPRINT.)

there are no trees in Maple Park
not even Maple trees
just four baseball diamonds
with a common furthest point of centerfield
so theoretically speaking
if I become the world's greatest centerfielder
I can return to Clifton New Jersey someday
and play in four different games at once
running around in the middle
turning to each crack of a bat
to help four different teams beat the bad guys

as I run to the faraway playground area
I pretend to scoop a grounder with one hand
while catching what should've been a homer with
 the other
when I'm interviewed
after getting trophies and a wreath around my neck
I thank everybody including the C and D students
for their support and I especially thank Roseanne
 LaBrunda
for not going ahead with her idea to get the city to
 plant trees in Maple Park
not even Maple trees
because this is a park for baseball
and though *I* could probably play baseball among
 the trees
it would make the game too dangerous for kids

I get to the playground run past the babyswings
 and up the sliding board
slide back down headfirst before walking to a large
 picnic table
where several kids are playing Tiddly Winks
a grown-up looking on

THIS WAY TO TEAM SPIRIT

one of the kids is Billy Botto
the smartest kid in the history of Woodrow Wilson
   Junior High
a year ahead of me but one year younger
the kid opposite him flips a wink
that not only misses the cup it misses the table
the grown-up in charge says *great try*
while the rest of us are impressed yet again by how
   easily adults lie

now you'd think Billy Botto
is all puny egghead uncoordinated
but the wink that Billy Botto flips
arcs right into the plastic cup
and all the kids are speechless
the grown-up in charge says *great try*
as Billy yawns
mutters something about physics

this reminds me of the time
that Bob and I went to Bowlero on a week night
we never go on a week night
and I saw Benedict Pekarsky
a screamingly mediocre C-minus student
two lanes over
with his wrist taped up
a leather glove a custom bowling ball
rolling one strike after another
he never shouted or jumped
but when he saw me there he smiled at me
and nodded like a priest

Billy Botto being Who'daThunkIt? Mr. Expert
   Tiddley Wink King
reminds me of that

among a pile of prizes on the table's other end
are packs of baseball cards
a few pocket knives
and what is clearly the grand prize
a complete set of Warriors of the World by Marx
I've never seen a complete set
it's so impressive that it glows
there's a Union soldier a Minuteman

a Roman Legionnaire
guys from both World Wars
the jingle is my favorite song
each beautifully painted by hand
the best looking warriors in the land
Warriors! Warriors! Warriors of the World by Marx
I'd give away my comic book collection for that prize

I was going to say I'd give away my brother for that
   prize
but that's no big deal
I mean I'd give him away
for a mosquito bite on my eyeball

the grownup in charge asks
has everybody had a chance to play?
or is Billy our winner?
and even though I've never played Tiddley Winks
   before
the Warriors of the World encourage me to shout
I haven't played yet
so the grownup motions me to sit on the loser's
   bench
opposite Billy Botto
who acknowledges me with a Benedict Pekarsky nod
before snapping a wink that leaps and turns
and clicks into the cup
the grownup says
well that's too tough to beat
the only way to win
is by landing in the cup on top of him good luck!

can I have a practice shot? I ask
I've never played before
the grownup says *well sure you can*
I lean a large green chip against a smaller one and
   concentrate
then snap and flip the chip into the air
it's high and foul and hits the grownup's nose
great try he says
but Billy laughs a laugh
that sounds like one of the Warriors of the World
   sitting around a campfire after killing all the bad
   guys from the Alamo set by Mattel

CADETS READY FOR DRESS PARADE

BEWARE: CHAD DANGLING ZONE AHEAD

this reminds me of the time in gym class
when Mr. Paleologo had each of us take
three turns throwing softballs
at a rubber tire hanging from a goal post
Bobby Dixon who's Bobby Meyer's best friend
pitched one through
Howard didn't get within three feet of the tire with
   any of his throws
but megajock Ritchie Tate
who was born with a jockstrap on
got one through that didn't touch the tire at all
then I was up
I didn't care for organized sports or uniforms
or anything involving Mr. Paleologo
and before my first throw Ritchie Tate
sneered at me

Billy Botto being Who'daThunkIt? Mr. Expert
   Tiddley Wink King
who laughs like one of the Warriors of the World
   sitting around a campfire
reminds me of that

okay says the grownup in charge
let's take the official shot
saying *let's* like he's going to help me

I position another chip and try to think what I'm
   supposed to think
to make a miracle happen
I know how Billy Botto sees me
and that makes me mad
I pretend I'm Benedict Pekarsky at Bowlero
I lean a large green chip against a smaller one and
   concentrate
then snap and flip the chip into the air
the whole world spinning
the first softball clipped the tire a bit
but got through fine
and the next two went through without a rattle
Mr. Paleologo and even Ritchie Tate were nice to
   me for months
tried to talk me into going out for sports
as if my even listening to them wasn't sporting
   enough

the chip hangs still for agonizing minutes
before it finally falls
a perfect drop into the cup
a perfect wink and tiddle
that covers defames smothers and cripples
Billy Botto's entire world

great shot kid says the grownup in charge
as he hands me a pack of baseball cards
here ya go
then he hands out packs of cards to all the kids
   around
nobody gets a pocket knife
and nobody meaning me
gets the complete set of Warriors of the World by
   Marx
I ask him how come and he tells me that
those prizes are for later on
for winners of a baseball game
I tell you what the grownup adds like he's Mr.
   Paleologo
*if you could throw a baseball the way you flipped
   that tiddley wink*
you'd have something going

as I walk back across the baseball diamonds
I picture Ritchie Tate ruining the Warriors of the
   World one by one
melting their limbs under a magnifying glass
martyring the Roman on a cherry bomb
hey Tommy I turn it's Billy Botto catching up
lucky shot he says *but what the heck*
*do you want to come see the Acropolis I'm build-
   ing out of sugar cubes?*
I want to tell him that projects like that are for
   brownnosers
that maybe Howard would want to see it
they could sit around and diagram sentences
have some fun with geometry
but I only say *no thanks Billy I gotta go home*
Billy nods looks around and as he walks across
   centerfield says
*boy it doesn't take a genius to see that this park
   really needs some trees*
no I agree *it doesn't take a genius at all*

musicmaster 8.04

th^e r^evi^ews...

...for the 2004 Minneapolis Fringe Festival show I wrote and stumbled through five times in early August at the Pillsbury House in Minneapolis. Notice how deservedly often the featured appearance of my Mom gets mentioned in these five (only slightly edited for space) audience reviews! Five more reviews next month because it's best to brag when you can.

LOVED IT!!
Ranging from heartfelt to hysterical, Tom's writing keeps you engaged. And Tom's mother is priceless. Make sure to see this show.
—*Rebecca Sandell* (Posted on Aug. 9)

Go see TOM CASSIDY!
Tom Cassidy pulls open his junk drawer (and nearly opens a vein) of late night musings to show us helium canaries, heads on fire and miles of fish poop. With cascades of rapid fire (and damn funny) insights into life, he demonstrates that he knows how to "dress up a lie, invent the stars, and have his way with all the verbs." English majors love him. I am glad he comes out of his anti-social writer's hole to display these treasures - an amazing feat for a self-professed loner. He may not know his own phone number, but he knows how to make human angst memorable and fun. Loved it - I want more.
—*Laurie Champ* (Posted on Aug. 12)

Out of His Mind
What is Tom gonna tell us next? Maybe he does exaggerate, he admits that too, but you will cringe and flinch right along with him, knowing how close it is to the gosh awful truth. These are not the scary truths of world affairs and social chaos, (well maybe...) but the focus is on the details: the cold wait at the bus stop and the fish poop in the aquarium and being in love in second grade. Tom talks about the things that don't go quite as we want them to. By the time he belts out the oddly-inspiring final piece, you might wonder if he's establishing a New World Order. And yet, this show is FUNNY! Next time you stay up late to enjoy some quiet, creative moments alone, and if you stub your toe, burn your tongue, or smash your finger - perhaps you will think of what might be happening over at Cassidy's house, and you won't feel so bad about it.
—*Tricia Griffin* (Posted on Aug. 13)

Tom Cassidy's An Excellent Choice
I've long been a big fan of Tom Cassidy's poems. They are remarkable creations, ranging from intense rants on people/issues/practices that outrage him, to extraordinarily funny,whimsical and even sentimental (sometimes) stories of grade school infatuation and rivalry, placating ill-mannered fish and anything and everything else. His writing is inventive, sharp, ironic, witty and hugely entertaining. Tom's mom, Inge, who assists and offers a comment or two on each piece, is a delightful counterpoint to Tom's animated and forceful delivery.
—*Jack Horner* (Posted on Aug. 13)

Refreshing!
Nothing warm, fuzzy or nice here. Just a man who's poems tell it like it is, (more or less), then hunt down the inner child and kill it. I loved every minute of the show.
—*Tim Voss* (Posted on Aug. 12)

NICKNAMES IN RED WING PART 2
Issue 89 included a bizarre and literal single page from the estate of late Red Wing native Robert Albrecht. Though in that issue I didn't refer to the excerpt as bizarre; I described it as "a delightful and unusual peek at a smalltown ritual." But I've been thinking about it since then, and when you come across something that lets you know that Duane Seely's nickname is ASSIGNED as Squeek, you catch a whiff of bizarre. Below is another page from the same resource (which, according to new Homeland Security recommendations, will be a standard document all U.S. cities must create within the next eighteen months).

Ryan		Jiggy	
Safe	Wayne	Whitey	
Sargent	Delores	Sarge	
Scharpen	LeRoy	Birdlegs	
Schinke	Rolland	Hodie	
Scoville	Robert	Art	
Seaberg	Lucille	Chief	
Seely	Duane	Squeek	
Selander	Audrey	Stina	
Severson	Edward	Inga	
Siewert	Glenn	River Rat	
Silvernale	Harold	Babe	
Smith	Eugene	Sheener	
Stark	Robert	Archie	
Starry	Lowell	Squee	
Strom	Neal	Choker	
Strom	Ralph	Brother	
Strom	Richard	Oosta	
Stroupe	Robert	Dobsie	
Stumpf	Marian	Puggie	
Sundberg	Harold	Gus/Buster	
Sundberg	John	Big Jawn	
Sutherland	Carl	Cully	
Swanson	Harley	Wort	
Swanson	Kathryn	Kak	
Swanson	Marvin	Punkin	
Swanson	Robert	Swannie/Godfrey	
Sweasy	Margaret	Squawker	
Taylor	Roger	Hook	
Tether	Harold	T-Bone	
Thompson	John	Amos	
Thompson	Lloyd	Hinkley	
Tiedeman	Evie	Boobs	
Torvund	Harvey	Jingles	
Van Deusen	Delores	Gorsy	
Van Deusen	Lawrence	LaLa	
Van Deusen	Loren	Doc	
Van Deusen	Randall	Redskin	

INTeRNAL X RHYMe

ON THE 98TH DAY OF CHRISTMAS MY TRUE LOVE GAVE TO ME: 98 INTERNAL RHYMES, 97 MUSICAL COMEDY EDITIONS, 96 MUSEUMS IN A MATCHBOX, 95 DOGS WITHOUT CARS . . . (from my unreleased, self-promotional holiday jingle that takes really really long to sing)   MUSICMASTER, 5136 LYNDALE AVE S, MINNEAPOLIS, MN 55419

Comrade Garret View

In seventh grade, Howard, Alan and I join the staff of the official newspaper of Woodrow Wilson Junior High. Though only eight pages long, the *Garrett View* looks like a real publication printed on glossy paper at a real print shop. It has an article about locker cleaning week, names of spelling bee semi-finalists, a friendly hall monitor feature and photos of boys making bookends.

Kids who work on the paper get bylines, but we have other motives too. Howard says he'll get brownie points with our history teacher Miss Bennett because she's the teacher who runs the *Garret View*. I think it might be fun to work under deadline pressure and Alan, who's going to be a doctor when he grows up, says that yes, the dead-line pressure for ten staff members to produce an eight-page monthly should be brutal. He's on the paper to get a jump on his resume.

In after school meetings, we learn how to compose exciting headlines, even for articles that aren't excit-ing and often just lists of students names, which, Miss Bennett explains, are included so that more students will want to buy the paper. "If we run a story about the bake sale, well sure, that's news," she explains. "But if we include a list of everyone who helped at the bake sale, or made a cake for the bake sale, that's not just more complete news, it's marketing: more students will want a copy."

We learn that good news articles have to contain who, what, when, where, why and how, but that *none of that* is as important as the secret sixth W. "It's the *Wow* factor," she says, "it's the stuff that makes a reader say *Wow*."

INSIDE THIS ISSUE

KING KONG FLICK PRAISED BY EVOLUTIONISTS

JUNIOR HOCKEY LEAGUE STARTS NATIONWIDE DENTURE SWAP

YOU CAN ATTAIN HEALING PURPOSEFULNESS FOR JUST $599 A MONTH!

ARE POWER RED SUNSETS SO BAD? - AESTHETIC CONSEQUENCES OF GLOBAL WARMING (PART III IN OUR SILVER LINING . . . MAKE THAT *REDDISH* SILVER LINING SERIES)

HOW TO FIND IMPOSSIBLE-TO-FIND ONE-OF-A-KIND LIMITED EDITION GODZILLA REPLICAS AT WOWZER!!!! DOT DUMBHEAD

PROOF THAT MOVIES AREN'T REAL

KING KONG MOVIE A PRODUCT OF INTELLIGENT DESIGN OR INEVITABLE SEQUEL TO CAVE DRAWING?

Pretending to be a reader, Howard looks up and says, "Cathy Horak was at the bake sale? Wow, it's right here in print."

Miss Bennett nods at Howard like he's a dimwit while Alan whispers "Stop the presses, someone else bought a cupcake."

Alan and Howard are news editors for the *Garrett View* and I'm business manager. Miss Bennett tells me to come up with a poster campaign selling forty-five-cent one-year subscriptions. Though the paper is subsidized by the Board of Education, the sub-scriptions help pay for the newspaper's end-of-the-year party in the gym, which Howard thinks is going to be great because we can make it a front page story and run his picture. "And," he says to Miss Bennett, "we can list everyone who attends!"

I come up with two poster ideas. One is we put a list of all the students in little type in three or four columns and in big type on top of that we have *See Your Name in Print – Subscribe to the Garrett View*. I think that for a poster, it actually has some *Wow*. Miss Bennett says, "It sounds like we're

CRUMPLE AND TOSS BEFORE TURNING PAGE

saying if you subscribe, we'll put your name in the paper. I say, "Well yeah, that is the idea, isn't it? We'll get your name in if you pay us?" Miss Bennett looks both sad and impressed with my thinking.

But she really likes my other design, a drawing of a potbellied politician on a soapbox. He's wearing a straw hat, snapping a suspender, and smoking a cigar. And the smoke from the cigar is a word balloon that says, "I wish I could promise everyone a *Garret View*." And the words on the bottom read "The Garrett View – Woodrow Wilson's Official Newspaper is Just 45¢ for a Full Year of News About your School." Miss Bennett tells me to redraw it – in *pen* – on a ditto master, and she'll take it to the principal's office for printing.

The principal's office returns the ditto master without printing the posters because Mr. Dwindle doesn't want the politician smoking because smoking can be a problem among students. "Well that's only because they're not allowed in the teachers lounge," I say. "Mr. Dwindle smokes. And Mr. Zack smokes, and Mrs. Fischer smokes. Almost every adult alive smokes." Miss Bennett nods sympathetically and says, "Well, Mr. Dwindle doesn't like it. All you have to do is redraw the politician so he's blowing bubbles and the words can be in the bubbles. Mr. Dwindle will like it and print it and every student will want to subscribe."

I redraw the poster with the politician blowing bubbles and the principal's office quickly prints them for posting around Woodrow Wilson with tape approved by the janitorial staff. Every one I put up makes me angry because the picture no longer makes sense. I tell Miss Bennett that I don't want to be business manager anymore because I didn't know it could get me in trouble with the principal's office. I want to draw pictures for the page that contains Mr. Dwindle's editorial, which is usually about doing homework or a successful bake sale. We're not supposed to change anything that Mr. Dwindle writes, but, "Miss Bennett explains, "with the bake sale editorial for example, we can add a list of who

participated." Howard suggests we print a list of the best homework doers too.

Since I'm on the paper and can get copies of the *Garret View* for free, I decide not to subscribe, what's the point? Howard looks shocked as he carefully tells me that his parents will each buy a subscription and that he's going to buy one for his cousin Roz as well as three subscriptions for himself because of the – get this – brownie points he'll get with Miss Bennett. Alan says that since no one else has ever done anything this retarded before, maybe it could be an article. And Howard believes him.

As an editorial cartoonist, when I draw a student, I am magically drawing *all* students and I take the responsibility seriously. I draw – in *pen* – a cartoon for Mr. Dwindle's piece about good homework habits and Miss Bennett says the principal's office really likes it. I draw another cartoon, for the same issue, about disappointing turnouts for pep rallies that they actually print on page one, right next to the list of kids who did attend.

Miss Bennett tells me that Mr. Dwindle is especially impressed with the drawing I did of the new boa in Mr. Zack's class and I suddenly realize that the principal's office and Mr. Dwindle are one and the same; and that they, *he*, **Mr. Dwindle** has been complimenting me twice as much as I thought. I am definitely once again a good student in his eyes. Howard is so envious that he tries to think up something he can do wrong that will ultimately turn out as well. Alan tells him he should burn down Woodrow Wilson so that when a new one opens everybody will be so happy that it's not the same crappy old building anymore that they'll thank him.

Days and deadlines and issues pass and Mr. Dwindle even likes my one controversial think piece about why don't they make locker doors out of non-noisy metal. He tells Mrs. Irons that it's very thought provoking, *very thought provoking.* And so many kids continue to subscribe because of that bubble

LET'S CONTINUE EVEN FILE ONTO THE NEXT PAGE

blowing politician that Mr. Dwindle has me stand up in assembly.

Spring arrives and we're putting together the June 1964 *Garret View*, our last issue as seventh graders. Miss Bennett calls it the *Have a Productive Summer and Good Luck Ninth Graders* issue and not only will it contain a list of all ninth graders, but it will also contain pictures of that end-of-the-year party we had in the gym last week. Thanks to our subscribers, we had Kool-Aid, hot dogs, thawed-out leftovers from the bake sale, and some idiot with a banjo named Dr. Hootenanny.

I prepare an inspiring editorial cartoon for Mr. Dwindle's Inspirational Message to the Ninth Graders. It depicts a student – *all students* – facing a fork in the road; the left route has a road sign for success and money, and the right route has a road sign toward failure and poverty. Above the student's head is a big question mark. Alan says. "The weirdest thing in the cartoon is that a student is standing in the road for no apparent reason. Going in either direction is an improvement."

On the left route's horizon line I draw the pot of gold which no doubt awaits all students who maintain good homework habits, even over the summer. On the right route's horizon line, which is where students who sleep during geography will end up, is a pile of gravel because I think of gravel as falling somewhere between getting coal from Santa and working on a chain gang. Howard says the pile of gravel looks like a pile of dog crap.

Alan says it looks like dog crap wearing a gravel costume.

I can see how the gravel might look like dog crap to some people, but the next morning, when Miss Bennett says that Mr. Dwindle really likes the entire issue, especially the cartoon, I no longer care.

Miss Bennett checks the pasted-up boards one last time for typos you can overlook because they're so obvious you don't see them – like once, we spelled *Garret View* incorrectly in an article about ourselves.

While we carefully proofed the names of all the students who ever worked on the *Garret View*, as well as the names of all of our subscribers, we failed to see that *Garret* was spelled with an extra T that *you can't even pronounce!*

Miss Bennett notices that I didn't sign my name to the cartoon and I tell her that I never do and she says that I really should add it, at least for this last issue of the year, because I did do a very good job.

My handwritten name looks clunky to me so I decide to just sign with my initials. I make my T at a jaunty angle and on top of it I print a neat capital C complete with that tiny vertical serif on the top. It looks like a TC cattlebrand.

On the way home from school Howard asks "How come you didn't draw the right side of the road on the right side?

"I don't know," I answer. "But I bet there's gravel and dog crap everywhere."

I'm called out of homeroom to the principal's office because I must be getting a special award for so ably portraying the road ahead. Maybe there will be a special commendation in assembly, and a handshake from Mr. Dwindle. I wonder if he noticed that one of the pieces of gravel is actually a small *cigar*.

When I enter his office, Mr. Dwindle looks at me like I'm crazy, but he's not sure how crazy. The pasted-up *Garret View* is spread out on his desk.

"Mr. Cassidy," he says, "I reviewed this newspaper yesterday afternoon and it was top-notch. Miss Bennett has always done a wonderful job with the *Garret View*. And our records show that you're a very good student, *a very good student*, your mother is on the PTA. That soap bubble poster you did was creative and very sharp, *very sharp*. I don't know what to say. I don't who's gotten into your head. But I can tell you this, buster; you're not going to infiltrate this institution with ideological tricks. I can see what's supposedly hidden in your picture."

CAN YOU, DEAR READER, GUESS THE SURPRISE ENDING?

GUILTY UNTIL PROVEN CLUELESS CONTINUED

I'm dumbfounded and I don't know what an ideological trick is, but it suddenly occurs to me that perhaps he hadn't noticed the cigar gravel originally, and that now that he sees it, the whole ugly smoking episode is going to reopen.

I nervously ask, "The cigar?"

"I see the cigar," he says. "It's used very appropriately here, *very appropriately*. A perfect appropriately-used cigar in what was an appropriate cartoon until I noticed your subversive activity."

I freeze. It must be the dog crap rock. All hell is going to break loose because while I'm a pretty good cartoonist for a seventh grader, I'm not grown-up good; my gravel looks like crap and we shouldn't print crap in the school newspaper. Unless, it's a list of all the eighth graders in the model boat club.

Mr. Dwindle continues, "It's shocking that a good student like you would deliberately sneak into Miss Bennett's room to sneak some unAmerican propaganda into the *Garret View, after* I approved it to print."

So many words with big meanings are now swirling around me that I can't speak. Plus I'm embarrassed because I didn't know that dog crap was unAmerican. I mean I can understand not wanting a picture of dog crap in the newspaper, but country wise, well, you can't have dogs without the crap, so I manage to mutter nothing in response.

Mr. Dwindle continues, "Speechless, huh? I don't know who's been infiltrating your brain, Mr. Khrushev, but I know a Commie when I catch one."

Not knowing what a Commie is, I ask, "A Commie?"

Mr. Dwindle sternly says, "You're not fooling me, buster. I know what this is." And I follow his finger to the *Garret View* laid out on his desk, across a review of the glee club recital, past a list of the best homework doers, and down to the corner of my cartoon where my monogram, my capital T jauntily angled atop a capital C, proudly sits. He taps his finger and says, "It's a hammer and sickle."

Coloring contest *WIN STRANGE PRIZE

Thursday, October 20, 2005, about 10:40 a.m., WCCO radio host Pat Miles sincerely talks with a cosmetic surgeon about her daughter's breasts maybe being a bit too large

Thursday, October 20, 2005 about 10:45 a.m., WCCO switchboard overloads from thousands of calls from "Good Neighbor" suitors, perverts, D-Cup subscribers, comics and fellow boobs

External Rhyme

GREAT IDEAS FOR EASY LIVING

Food McNetwork

The MPR news break at 8:28 a.m. on January 26th reports that a recent episode of *Iron Chef America* (less octopus, more moo) includes the subliminal message "I'm Lovin' It," one of McDonald's contributions to marketing flab. I apologize for not being certain if the line is "lovin" or "loving" or "luvin'" because the messages go by so quickly. The Food Network claims it was a glitch, but not whether or not the glitch was that they were caught. A McSpokesperson says that McDonald's *super*doesn't *size* do *it* subliminal advertising. I go online to find out more by searching "What the hell is wrong with you people?" and I'm taken directly to the Associated Press piece titled *Food Network ad glitch not subliminal ad for McDonald's*. The AP piece, posted just over an hour after the MPR news, links me to a YouTube playing of the clip in which, for just one frame, I witness the faith and wisdom of the McDonald's logo with the jerking-off-monkey exhortation "I'm lovin' it." At least it seems like faith and wisdom because I don't know where my sudden desire and belief came from, but at least now I am certain I'm lovin' it. Plus, via the magic of YouTube, I am able to instantly access other video-posts allegedly containing other subliminal messages. I watch several of them before I inexplicably rush to the store to get Pepsi, Cheerios, a Lexus, Doritos and an express enlistment to serve in Iraq.   ■

Like Heaven with Booze, Broads and the Meek at Your Service

A current TV commercial for Grand Lido Resorts and Spa claims that their resort experience is *like Heaven – without the time commitment*. And though the voice-over doesn't chuckle when he says *without the time commitment*, there's an implied preference for Grand Lido –a Heaven *with* a time limit- versus a Heaven without. Now, though I am a wretch who might find Heaven too squeaky clean for my daily beer and pop-sleaze needs, I am guessing that Grand Lido – the Heaven with the convenient time limit -- lavishes guests with hedonistic excess, a few sinful meals, potent cocktails with innuendo-laced names (e.g. Sex on the Beach, MindFuck), Narcissistic body worshipping rituals, and lots of other things that are definitely not the stuff of heaven *with* the time commitment . . . basically, the fun, not-squeaky-clean stuff of Hell (*without* the time commitment!). They should change their tagline accordingly, or at least try one of these: Grand Lido Resorts and Spa -- *like Heaven for nonbelievers*; or Grand Lido Resorts and Spa – *like a new, improved Heaven for the godless*; or Grand Lido Resorts and Spa – *I'm lovin' it*.   ■

enamored with words that are rarely as telling as cave paintings
impressed with ourselves for being able to remember jokes
it is inevitable that
the one guy shoots the other guy
or that the other guy shoots the one guy
that you shoot me that I shoot you
that Stephanie shoots someone to prove that women
are capable of doing the job
so the one guy who shoots the other guy
now has five minutes before
the men in black break down the door
so you have just one crazy person in that room
which to me would be you *all of you*
with several minutes to do or not do
just one more simple thing
to push the button
to poke eternity in the eye or not
I mean maybe he snapped and killed the other one
because he was afraid the other one would kill us all
maybe he was thinking about before war
when the air wasn't pumped in by Haliburton
when the cars had two seats
back before the trees had running sores
back when you looked at me with love
back when we were allowed to collect books
that had pages

● **we write better t-shirts for the bodies in the morgue**
one of those two guys in the doomsday room
notices that the other guy is nodding off
so he pushes the button just to see if it works
but nothing happens so he pushes it again
and again until the other guys wakes up
sees what's going on and says
maybe the battery's dead maybe you're doing it wrong
maybe you have to push harder
and he pushes the button too
they take turns pushing the button   *there is a season - turn, turn, turn*

turning it into a game

the one guy says

hey . . . what if I pushed it with my elbow? so he does

and the other guy says *hey watch this*

and puts the barrel of his gun against the button

*what if I **kill** the kill button?* he says

would it be a double negative

would it create a new planet

and they laugh and push

and kill and kill and kill and kill

- **and kill and kill and kill and kill**

and meanwhile nothing happens outside

everything is just fine

all the bombings little ones

parts of little wars that trim the fat off of our planet

the sky a pitch perfect yellow

the underwater Manhattan tours

drawing more than all of the underwater Florida tours combined

the inexpensive root beer flavored air

pumped in by Haliburton not so bad

those two guys in the doomsday room just

one of those new therapy shows on the Pfizer channel

and it's been discovered that you can fuel up

with what flows from the trees' running sores

it's all pretty good afterall

the economy's in good shape

I've had all my blood replaced with beer

and they're going to blow up Pluto on the 4th

musicmaster 2/9/07

written for the Play Nice!-themed storytelling show at
Cheap Theatre (presented February 9 and 10 in the
Festaal banquet space of the Black Forest Inn, a popular
German and avant garde poetry restaurant in Minneapo-
lis) for two long-time mail-art friends and concrete/post-
language/visual (let's say very nontraditional) poets Scott
Helmes and John Bennett who appeared on the bill as
two-fifths of their Be Blank Consort (a sound poetry troupe)
which used me at these performances as a third fifth in
reading pieces by Helmes, Bennett and Jim Leftwich.

of the doomsday room uniform
from dark blue
to a cheery but dignified peach

● **the problems & there are many & I'm at least half of them**
with great responsibility comes great boredom
so one day one of these two guys
in the doomsday room snaps
decides to push the button just to break the boredom
to have something to say at the next support group
and when he moves to push the button
the other guy per protocol shoots him
because the button isn't flashing or beeping
in fact this other guy can shoot him
and later on claim that the dead guy had snapped
whether he had really snapped or not
I mean why not?
what if what one does when one snaps
isn't to reach out and push the damn button
but to kill the other guy just for the hell of it?
and say that *the other guy* was going to push the button
even if he wasn't?

you know maybe he's mad at the guy
for putting a post-it on his locker
reminding him that it's *his week* to clean the microwave
and sure for a millisecond the bad housekeeper
thinks about pushing the button himself
       I'll show you a fucking mess
but come on he's not crazy for crying out loud
he's a good kid he's a career man
so he shoots the other guy instead
pictures himself a hero
who just saved billions and billions of people
by finally shutting up Mr. Scrubbing Bubbles!
it was *his* damn ravioli
that blew up in the microwave

Scrubbing Bubbles reference not a paid ad placement

- **creationism as Darwinian inevitability**

I've studied both God and Man

in bars where I've seen both

and wouldn't always want to know either

and I've read tons of crazy stuff and

brilliant seditious alchemy

and even science books with so many facts

that the facts become an addiction that needs treatment

and from *all of that* I remember a story

about there being just two people afterall

there's really just **you**

and then there's **everybody else**

it's a psychotic or messianic disorder or it's a fact

there's really just **you**

and then everybody outside of you making up one huge shifting organism with
which you can only interact in small bits at a time manifest as family and friends
and co-workers and bystanders and all the billions of others waiting for you to
call on them raising their hands crying *me me*

anyhow there's just **you**

and then there's **everybody else**

including those two guys in the doomsday room and me

. . . me

and all those doomsday support group people

including Stephanie

and frankly we *want* to push *your button*

to stop your stupid beeping

- **critical dialysis & why museums are rollercoasters**

it's a terrible system when you figure

that the only people who apply to be

those two guys in the doomsday room

have to be nuts to begin with

to enter a staring match with a button

the button right there staring back

these two guys in the doomsday room

get so medicated they defecate controlled substances

have the big bang in their heads

and because we're all idiots at the core

stop, turn back

Intersectionalities of Pomp, Poop and Bender

The March 2007 issue of the National Council on Family Relations' *Report*, includes an article about members recently selected for fellowship status. In a profile of one such member is this proof of how esoteric (self-delusional(?)/aloof(?)/ivory-towered(?)) an academic community can be:

One nominator wrote that a new fellow's "long list of publications and presentations on the intersectionalities of race, class and gender influenced family studies long before 'intersectionalities' became a buzzword."

Is it possible that, in addition to the kneejerk over-usage of professional community buzzwords like podcast and webinar (ouch), academics also giddily embrace and overuse words like *intersectionalities*? And that other academics can read that paragraph without blinking or wincing? Are academics really commonly using that word? If they start academifying or buzzturding too much, mere mortals might regard their buzzwords as institutionalized college pranks. (Note: This item was a lot funnier before I wrote it.) ∎

if I could drive I'd drive

a big wide black convertible
with fins propellers
a crow's nest a foghorn
my bumpersticker stating
  real men don't haiku
I'd floor it
take turns so fast
I wouldn't be in
the other lane the wrong lane
I'd be in the other place
on the wrong road
up on two flaming wheels maybe one
knocking back shots
wondering what the hell ever
  happened to that CB craze
with the static and bad movies
I'd push in my favorite 8-track
of the Chipmunks singing
Songs of Faith
and crank the rocket up

so far so loose so hard so tight
so Freudian
so impossibly holy
that the known Gods fail
that I'd take off
I'd get up above the highway
and race through the clouds
I'd aim upwards only
my real ambition and career
I'd be chased by press kits for the
  still dead
meteors with sirens right on my ass
I'd orbit as fast as possible
then aim straight
for the screaming
honking hell-hot
save-you-from-crashing-into-rocks
energy efficient
and decorative
lighthouse sun

Stephanie sells Mary Kay on the side

- **the setting, with thanks to church & state & the late great Anna Nicole Smith**

those two guys in the doomsday room
are poised to blast us all to kingdom come
when the President makes that doomsday button
flash and beep from his remote on Moon Base One
these two guys in the doomsday room
are also poised to shoot one another
if one or the other tries to push the button
when it isn't flashing and beeping meaning
so far most of the time
there were some false alarms
when the President thought he was turning on Showtime
and that kind of funny episode
when the Vice President was drinking
and said *oh just fuck 'em all*
and shot the remote with his oil-powered derringer
those two guys in the doomsday room
could've launched the missiles
on any of those occasions but didn't because
as government employees themselves
they figured the flashing and beeping were screw-ups
like the flaming glaciers and melting bears
these two guys in the doomsday room
have since been reprimanded
and threatened with court martial
should they ever fail
to blast us all to kingdom come again
both of those guys are in a support group
made up of doomsday button watchers
from around the world who get together
to discuss things like
why is the button round and red?
should the doomsday room
be renamed Happy Acres?
and whose button is biggest?
Stephanie the only female button watcher
wants to change the color

railroad crossing ahead

197

Friends, long-time readers and certainly would-be assassins are aware of my serious carrot allergy. An unidentified sliver of carrot in a spring roll (or in a salad that the server swore contained no carrots) is enough to twist my esophagus like a Twizzler; if I eat much more than that I'll probably die an embarrassing death. As grim as that sounds, my body reaction to merest carrot mote is so sudden and severe that I have time (at least so far) to stop eating the poison immediately, hack up what I can, and pound my chest to be sure my heart can still answer. And I shouldn't undervalue the positive of getting my heart to race as if I'm actually exercising! When I last wrote about this (in stories titled Why I Don't Eat Carrots, Why My Eyesight is Failing, Why I Have to Remember that I Shouldn't Eat Carrots, How My Wife Tried to Kill Me with a Healthy Smoothie Concoction that Contained Carrots, Why I Really Really Should Stop almost Killing Myself by Eating Carrots, etc.), lots of people sent me carrot pictures, and the great Alan Vandenburgh sent me a ceramic carrot mounted on a bevelled wooden plaque. And as wonderfully droll as all that was (if indeed that was all that that was! . . . wait! mmmmm - Bastards!), a recent photo in *New York* (the great magazine, not the once-good *New Yorker* with the droll cartoons (if indeed that was all that that was! . . . wait! mmmmm - Bastards!) really kills me. Almost. Shown above, without permission, we see carrot chefs in training, and the outlined form of the fallen me.

What Was *Internal Rhyme* and Why Did it Work?

The Short Answers

1. *Internal Rhyme* was a reason for a writer to write.
2. Good genes contributed to its success.
3. It worked because its creator was determined to engage the public through continuous and systematic literary violence.

The Longer Explanations

Given that *Internal Rhyme* was the product of a unique and multifarious vision, it is not surprising that classifying or characterizing the publication is challenging. For some, calling it a "publication" only applies if the definition of that term is pushed to its most basic meaning: making facts and fiction available to people in a printed form.

Internal Rhyme was more than a leaflet and less than a poetry chapbook. It was not a serial periodical dependent on subscriptions. It was not a soapbox for zealous evangelization. Rather, it was the voice of a town crier heralding anecdotes, opinions, and events. It was a unique hybrid of literary and community newsletters simultaneously rooted in the rich history and culture of zine publications.

Historians tend to pinpoint the origin of zines to the 1930s, with their development associated with the increasing popularity of self-published science fiction fandom magazines. Growth continued in the 1950s and 1960s with the publications of underground art and literary groups such as the Beats. This was followed by an explosion of alternative magazines in the 1970s documenting, publicizing, and laying bare the artistic lives of fringe groups on the east and west coasts of the United States. A decade later, zines were embraced by Punks as an alternative means of music distribution and performance promotion. Post-feminists in the 1990s introduced a new genre ¬– the Grrrrl Zine – and at the turn of the millennium a renaissance of do-it-yourself publications gained popularity with their thinly veiled socio-political agendas. Today, marginalized groups continue to embrace the power of self-publication, choosing the zine format as a practical means of distributing information, personal stories, and artistic expression in a low-cost and essentially unregulated manner.

Internal Rhyme's zine heritage – its good genetic past – is clearly apparent in how the publication gave voice to voices not widely heard in daily life. Characteristically, it was self-published, noncommercial, printed in small numbers, circulated through specific networks, and intended for a niche audience. Like decades of zines, it provided a vehicle for the expression of ideas and culture that enabled solidarity within a community. For *Internal Rhyme* this was the growing population ¬of poets, storytellers, and spoken word artists in Minneapolis and Saint Paul.

It is this last zine characteristic that provides a segue to *Internal Rhyme's* efficacy as a community newsletter. Although it was primarily an impetus for a single artist's creative practice, *Internal Rhyme* was also concerned with engaging people – either with the creator (note the small case "c") or each other. Through its dissemination, it supported interpersonal relationships.

Internal Rhyme "worked" because it was composed of elements that characterize effective community building communication tools. Its audience was well targeted, and its efficient distribution was at a very grass-roots level: buses, coffee shops, performance venues, art stores, and other public spaces. Content was personal in nature and convivial to a variety of audiences. A physical template was created that was familiar in format (a type of mini-newspaper with a front page full of "more inside" prompts) facilitating its readability and providing clarity in terms of content areas. Accessibility was further enhanced through the use of alternative communication methods to express concepts and ideas. In addition to traditional blocks of text, lists, charts, and illustrations served as conveyors of information. Finally, each publication provided opportunities for further engagement, whether that be an invitation to an upcoming personal performance or a call to support local artists and businesses.

The Writer as Saboteur

While it is relatively clear how the success of *Internal Rhyme* can be attributed to its roots in zine culture and dynamic community newsletters, its success and effectiveness as a literary publication is less obvious. In fact, it seems much was done to sabotage any possible ties to "legitimate" vehicles.

The truth is that *Internal Rhyme* was tackling a very tough problem: how do you accurately and authentically present a means of artistic expression that is comprehended differently depending on how it is presented (verbal vs. text), varies from one performance to another (various orators), and changes in its interpretation with each person's internal experience (each reader's mind silently forming words into sentences and paragraphs into stories)?

To address this, *Internal Rhyme* actively shunned the safe presentation of material and avoided using dry antiseptic approaches embraced by many mainstream publications. It aggressively played fast and loose with the rules of how writing should be presented. "And that," according to Robert Frost, "has made all the difference."

Stories were presented as articles in a newspaper with headlines that cut to the chase to reveal meaning. Readers were encouraged to play with content through various games, puzzles, and matching exercises. Drawings, collages, and illustrations both supported and juxtaposed written text. Newsletter tropes such as footnotes, bylines, and headers offered short insights into the writer's creative process. *Internal Rhyme* was successful because each issue was a series of experiments in storytelling and active audience engagement. Every element – from fake advertisements to the articulation of incredibly personal memories – supported this goal.

The Saboteur as Chef and Party Host

Internal Rhyme unabashedly documented an artist's drive to create and engage audiences. As a complicated hybrid with variegated lineage it was unique in both form and content.

It worked because literature was not only violated, but was also dissected into its fundamental parts, marinated, made into a stew, and served to readers with a generous compilation of side dishes – all at a community table.

Please pass the humorous yet poignant anecdote.

Jeff Rathermel, Artist and Curator, September 2022